This collection is dedicated to a patch of red shag carpet, a heavy wooden console television, a bright yellow, plastic Fisher Price chair, and the handful of broadcast television channels reaching the D.C. suburbs on weekend afternoons before cable. To Buford Pusser, Matt Helm, Kelly's Heroes, Hooper and Charley Varrick. Vanishing Point, Greased Lightning and Two-Lane Blacktop, Thunderbolt and Lightfoot, the Wanderers and Warriors, Cooley High and every western. M.A.S.H., Steve McQueen versus the Blob and the Mouse That Roared. Blondie and Dagwood, Harry and Walter, Arkin's Clouseau and Lazenby's Bond. To the Five & Dime, Jimmy Dean and Alice, who doesn't live here. All these and so many more, Saturday matinees.

I would also like to thank Technical Sergeant Garp.

More importantly, I am grateful for my many friends in film. High Desert was born over beers and bourbon at Cinematographer Dean Mitchell's house, from his memories about a bar in the middle of nowhere with money stapled to the ceiling. Audio mixing legend Sergio Reyes heard about Paganini during his time with the most infamous bands (and greatest movies) of all time. He continues to be one of Yardley's greatest champions. Dragonhead first appeared on Producer Sam Levine's bookshelf on a cloudy afternoon, inside a history of his hometown. And without the constant confidence and support of Producer Christian Monzon, The Quiet Ones would still be eight pages and by now long forgotten. He is Valley Football.

And all I know is, I'm very, very lucky.

PEOPLE MAKING DANGER
by Adam Fike

THE QUIET ONES
Neighbors grow together with the help of a friendly, local serial killer

The mid-sized town of Clearfield Falls is carefully carved into thick forest running along granite cliffs. A handful of cars shuffle past offices and sit-down restaurants near a sleepy courthouse. Tidy, aging neighborhoods crisscross into the distance, church steeples anchoring block after block.

Solemn grave markers spread down the long, rolling hills of a sprawling local cemetery. A row of gleaming power mowers roars to life. Straddling each one, ball-capped teens in a tight, green company work shirts, *Power Mower Incorporated* printed large across their backs. The small fleet fans out among the stones.

In the distance, down a narrow asphalt path, beside an idling hearse, six aging, former frat-boy Pallbearers in tailored black suits impatiently grumble in a circle.

Look, I have to be on a call at eight-thirty, so can we please get this moving . . . No one cares about your phone calls . . . Don't start with me . . . How bad does this look, half the town council burying their Chairman on a Tuesday? No service. No people. It's weird . . . Heard they had to pry a ball gag out of his throat. The freak . . . Hey. Come on. Rudy Morgan would've been Mayor Morgan someday. People liked him, what do you say we keep it that way . . . Why? We didn't make him do that to himself . . . No, but that little freak bailed every one of us out at some point. And, evidently, we are very much his only friends, so, there's that . . . And also, there's Ruth . . . Who's Ruth? I don't know a Ruth . . . His twin . . . Twin? Never had one in school . . . What? Yeah, he did . . . Doesn't say much, but sort of that hot-nerd category . . . Huh . . . Think she's into the ball-gag thing?

Together they chuckle and, on cue, together find Ruth Morgan standing among them. They jump a foot.

Ruth, plain to the point of near invisibility, painfully eyes the hearse. She hides behind large glasses, long bangs and shapeless clothes.

A wheezing Undertaker stomps toward them.

Sorry to keep you all, he says, throwing open the hearse door. Damn lawn service couldn't wait to get paid. Let's get started, shall we? Yes. It's going to be a warm one.

How long was she standing there, one Pallbearer whispers to another.

Just grab the box, somebody coughs.

A few miles away, on a wide, blue-collar street, happy birds chirp outside Junior Mazurski's house. His overgrown yard crowds a wide brick porch. High wooden fences and huge hedges help form a sleepy and inconspicuously secure bunker.

Inside, fading family artifacts stretching back decades line the walls. Mostly family photos and vacation landscapes. A jumble of yard-sale-ready furniture and art. Shelves and shelves of crime and adventure paperbacks. A handful of classic, carefully positioned plastic action figures along the mantel. A high-school diploma. Unused in the corner sits a tiny, ancient television with big rabbit ears.

Junior, an enormous, hairy, harmless, gentle giant, greying at the temples, coughs and smacks his lips as he wakes on an oversized couch. Cats scatter. An equally enormous dog at his feet stretches, part wolf, nearly always happy.

Morning, Rusty, Junior says, scratching his ears. How you doing, buddy?

The big dog yawns back at him.

Stumbling down a dark, dusty hallway, he pulls a tattered, blue bathrobe over his t-shirt and boxers. The kitchen is cluttered but clean. On a counter near the phone, a first-generation answering machine blinks. Putting an old copper kettle on to boil, Junior punches the button.

THE QUIET ONES

Hi, uhm, my name is Cathy Stubbs, a fuzzy speaker warbles. Sorry to call so early. I got your number from the phone book. We moved and need somebody to do our lawn. There are some hedges and a tree that may be dead . . . Or dying, maybe. It just seems unhappy. Anyway. Sorry. It's not too much. Only a couple things, and our neighbor loves you. My number is . . .

While the message plays, Junior digs through a junk drawer for a short, dull pencil. Finding no paper, he tears the back off a box of kids' cereal and scribbles.

Junior's backyard is an impressive, high-walled, carefully manicured and sculpted garden full of color and quiet spaces. At the center, a patch of lawn as precise as a pool table. A big, industrial shed stands locked beside the house, along with a handful of other equipment. This is an isolated oasis, hidden from all but the sun.

Barefoot in his robe, he tends to a patch of flowering bushes with long clippers. Satisfied, he sets the clippers down and picks up his mug. Sipping, Junior gazes at his creation as he begins to pee.

An hour later, Junior throws open his front door, ready for work. A ball-capped, teenage guy in a Power Mower Incorporated shirt was just about to knock. He looks barely old enough to drive the truck. The Teen launches into a speech from a clipboard.

Hello, sir, the kid mutters. I am pleased to represent Power Mower Incorporated in your area, and I'm thrilled to let you know that you are chosen for one week of our free front-yard mowing and hedge-trimming service, because we, I mean I, are, I mean am, sure that you will find for yourself that Power Mower Incorporated is far superior to our local competitors, who frankly can't beat our prices or . . .

The Teen glances up from his clipboard to see that Junior wears a faded work shirt with the *Mazurski & Son Gardening Service* logo, along with the name *Junior* stitched below it.

Rusty bounces past their feet. The Teen turns to the driveway and spots a broken-down pickup with an aging mower perched in the back. The faded letters of *Mazurski & Son* are stenciled on the truck door. Rusty pants at them from the passenger seat.

Oh, I'm sorry, the Teen says. I didn't . . .

He backs away from the enormous man looming in the doorway. Junior smiles down at him.

Not so fast there, pal, Junior says. Don't forget to trim the walk. And don't be afraid to get up there and square off the tops of those hedges while you're at it. I mean flat as a board, got it? Thanks, champ!

Junior climbs into his truck and drives away, leaving him alone and puzzled in the overgrown front yard.

In the cemetery parking lot, a police cruiser cools next to Rudy Morgan's hearse. In the distance, Ruth and the Pallbearers stand over his grave. Behind the wheel, Officer Carroll is lost in thought, cell phone to his ear.

No, he says. No, of course I didn't mean that. I want her back home safe, same as you. I'm just saying, she's going to learn one way or the other, and, sorry to say, if I can't break her, I'm afraid of what the hell will.

A loud squawk from the phone cuts him off as he pops open the glove box. Inside, a pint of vodka rests on its side. He opens and pours it into a cold cup of coffee, swallows hard and sets it back, softly clicking the latch.

You're right, he says. Sorry. Another bad choice of words. No, she's not a horse. I know that. I only mean . . . You know what I mean. I'm here now. Got to go. Yeah. Love you too.

At Rudy's grave, Ruth and the Pallbearers bow their heads.

Well, the Undertaker says. I don't usually do this part, I mean, normally, so I guess if anybody has something to say . . .

To their collective surprise, Ruth steps forward. She takes

another step. Then another. Then all at once she lifts the edge of the casket lid with both hands. They leap to grab her, but freeze as the lid opens.

Inside, Rudy is the male mirror image of Ruth. He seems happy. Lip quivering, Ruth digs into her bra and finds a small figurine of a little girl, smiling with bows in her hair. The men collect themselves and move again towards her.

Leave her be, Carroll says, now only a few feet away. The Pallbearers are halted by the timber of his voice.

Ruth reaches into Rudy's suit coat pocket and finds a matching figurine of a smiling boy holding a bucket. A chip is missing from the boy's ear. She holds them side by side and tears flow to her eyes. Ruth tucks the girl figurine into Rudy's suit coat pocket. She tucks the boy figurine into her bra and closes the lid.

My apologies, the Undertaker says, flustered. That is supposed to be locked.

Carroll takes Ruth by the shoulders.

Alright, he says. Let's get going now.

Ruth nods and they walk away together.

The Undertaker quickly works the mechanism that lowers the casket. The Pallbearers look to each other in dismay and gratefully scatter back to their lives.

In the kitchen of their cottage-style house, Bob and Cathy Stubbs kiss, lingering for a long time. In her arms is their potty-training Daughter.

Say goodbye to Daddy, honey, she says. Have a good day at work.

You too, he smiles.

Their Daughter squirms in her arms.

Thanks, I'll need it, she says. Alright, you, time to eat.

Bob is halfway to his car with a travel mug when his cell phone rings.

This is Bob, he says. Oh. Hi . . .

Cathy waves from the window. Bob waves sheepishly

toward his house, covers the phone receiver with his hand and hustles toward his car.

Hey, can't really talk, he says. Wait, are you calling from my desk number? Me? Um, the brown suit with . . . Oh you are, are you? Well, by the time I get to the office, I expect to find that report under my desk. That's right. That's what I said. Oh, you do, do you . . .

Fumbling to get into his car, Bob drops his keys and is startled to spot Junior at the end of his driveway, staring at him, holding the address written on cardboard from a cereal box.

Their eyes meet. Bob forgets about the phone.

Can I help you, he asks.

Cathy is at the front door with a smile.

Are you the person from the yard service, she asks.

Yes, ma'am, Junior nods to her.

Terrific, she says. Please come on in. I just put on some water for tea. Bob, honey, you better get going.

Bob is stunned for a moment as gigantic Junior strides toward his front door. He collects himself and finds his keys.

Yes, Bob continues loudly into the phone. As I was saying, Harold, please make sure that file is on my desk by the time I get there or else . . .

Junior and Cathy shake hands.

Harold is Bob's assistant, she says. They're on that phone all day. Blah, blah, blah.

Junior follows her into the house and Cathy closes the door.

Concerned, Bob lingers indecisively, then drives away.

In the kitchen, Cathy pours steaming water into cups and gets out a box of tea. Her Daughter squirms in a high chair, throwing peaches to the floor.

You see, Bob and I both grew up apartment people, she says. We don't know one end of a lawnmower from the other.

Junior is fixated on a mall studio portrait pinned to the

fridge with a big ladybug magnet.

You have a lovely family, he says.

Cathy hands Junior his mug.

Thank you, she says and turns to scoop up her Daughter. Alright then, what do you say we take this nice man outside and show him around our tiny little yard. What do you say? Hmmmm? What do you say?

The toddler smiles. Cathy balances her squirming Daughter expertly on her hip. Junior follows them out the door.

The photograph from the fridge is gone.

Next to his car at the cemetery, Carroll comforts Ruth, silently sobbing with a look of pure woe.

There there, now, he says. Rudy always asked us to look after you, and that is just what the missus and I will do. Remember, we are always right next door.

Ruth looks up at him, face smeared with tears and snot. Carroll looks around.

Ruth, he says. Where's your car?

She shrugs.

Did you walk all the way here, he asks.

She sniffles and nods.

Well, get in, he says. I'll drive you.

Ruth suddenly looks past him, eyes wide, in a general panic.

Officer Carroll, shouts Stan Reynolds, hurrying toward them in a rumpled suit, dodging tombstones, waving a notebook. Officer Carroll!

It's that jerk from the paper, Carroll says. Don't worry, I'll take care of him.

Morning, Stan says.

Yeah, Carroll says. What can I do for you?

About Councilman Morgan, Stan says. I know you were friends. Neighbors, correct?

Carroll yanks open his car door, not interested in talking.

Ruth is already inside. Stan never saw her with Carroll.

Wait, Stan says, moving slowly forward. Please. I was talking to someone at the coroner's office this morning. They used the term accidental suicide but wouldn't elaborate. There's still no official report. I have just a few questions concerning Mr. Morgan and how he was found. Whether it seemed suspicious at all. Whether there's any kind of ongoing investigation about if this was the action of an otherwise stable, sober and even cheerful person, frankly. I mean, I don't know how else to say it. Did he have enemies?

No, Carroll glares. Do you?

Rudy Morgan was an important part of this community, Stan says, trying to stay on his toes with Carroll. I mean, how would you like to find your name in the paper associated with covering up an important story?

How would you like to find that pen sticking out your ass, Carroll asks.

Carroll means it.

Right, Stan says. Duly noted.

Junior's truck creaks to a stops in front of a large, ornate but tasteful house. Rusty pants from the passenger seat and obediently stays as he climbs out. On the mailbox, a bright yellow advertising card from Power Mower Incorporated, including coupons. Junior sighs and gathers his tools.

In the backyard, he wrestles a rusted wheelbarrow piled with soil down a steep row of flowing hedges. A long wood-handled shovel rests with one end on his shoulder, the other in the dirt.

Junior smiles, content. Treetops sway. Birds sing. He plants the wheelbarrow beside a neat patch of tulips. The shovel head drips careful piles of soil, until a back door slams in the distance and persnickety Mr. Henderson, the owner, runs at him like a dart.

I told you, Henderson says. How many times do I have to tell you? Seriously.

8

Junior sighs and leans on the shovel.

Henderson, uptight in trendy eye glasses and khaki pants, clutches a flower by the stalk. Healthy and in bloom at one end, thick dirty roots dangle in the air.

These roots are bone dry, Henderson says. See? I pulled this one to show you what happens when you don't follow my watering schedule. Do you think I post you such detailed memos in the shed for my health?

Junior stares mournfully at the damaged plant.

When Senior died, I pitied you enough to let you continue tending my yard, Henderson says. But now I just don't know.

Junior's mind is on the dying petals.

You know, it's polite to answer people when they're talking to you, Henderson says to no reply. You know, when you take a job, it's only right to warn people you're retarded.

The shovel head swings, catching Henderson above the jaw with a painful crack. His glasses fly. Henderson goes down hard, limp before he hits the ground.

Junior picks up the plant and straightens the stock.

Now then, he says. Let's get you back in the ground before it's too late.

Across town, Ruth's office is a windowless former storage closet buried deep in the basement of an already stuffy office building. She's perched on an oversized, outdated swivel chair, behind a desk covered in neat stacks of paper. Tubes buzz bright above her.

Combining pages from each stack, she carefully collates them into matching green binders. Perched between two stacks, the tiny figurine. She finishes a binder, winks at the boy and picks up another.

Appearing at the door, Gretchen from upstairs is much younger, heavily manicured and poured into a pricey sweater. She holds out an open cardboard box stacked with paper. Gretchen speaks with a lot of question marks.

9

Uhm, Gretchen says. Where do you want these?

Ruth stares back at her, concerned at what she means, chewing her lip.

Uhm, Gretchen says. These are for you? Hello? Marketing pages for the green binders? Did you not hear? Our binders were misrouted again, so, like, now you're putting all of our pages into yours before the deadline.

Gretchen particularly enjoys that last part. Ruth can't manage a whisper in defense.

Alright already, Gretchen says. Got it? Great.

Ruth can do nothing but nod. She grimaces at the figurine. He smiles up and they share a private joke. Gretchen sees this flash of contentment in Ruth as she drops the box with a thud.

You know, they really don't like personal items on our desks, Gretchen says with a smirk.

But he's, it's, just, uhm, Ruth says in a sudden panic.

Nobody cares, Gretchen says. Just put it in a drawer or something?

The door slams behind her.

Ruth finds a safe home for the figurine in her top drawer.

Outside the local hardware store, Junior carries bags of topsoil out to the bed of his truck, two on each shoulder.

The Hardware Store Owner leans back in a chair beside the door, watching him, smoking a shaky cigarette. In the back of the truck, the ancient lawnmower, metal camping cooler, various burlap sacks, garden tools, and the growing pile of soil bags.

Nearby, two overly muscled Power Mower Incorporated Teens in their matching shirts try to intimidate a soda machine.

Take the frigging dollar, one yells.

Bang on it, says the other. Bang on it!

The first one hits the machine hard with both palms. Then his shoulder. It rocks back and spits out a soda.

Fuck yeah, they cheer and head for a brand-new Power Mower Incorporated pickup with a shiny, new mower in the back. They pass Junior's crumbling truck, cackling as he drops another set of bags into the bed.

Dude, one barks to the other. It's even got his name on it!

Well, the Hardware Store Owner says. Know what they say when you can't beat them?

Yeah, Junior says.

Make a good living working for those people, the Hardware Store Owner says. You know a lawn a ton better than those dumb kids. That's for sure. Probably'd make you a manager. You'd end up running the place. That's what Senior'd tell you to do, I'd betcha.

Junior lifts the green cooler out of the truck bed.

Thanks, Junior says. But I doubt they got a shirt my size.

Deep in the truck bed, the crumpled body of Mr. Henderson is now only half covered by a nylon tarp.

I got you a new cooler, Junior says, setting it by the door. Dad wore yours out, fishing over the years.

You didn't need to do that, the Hardware Store Owner says. He was welcome to it.

Out of view of the Hardware Store Owner, Mr. Henderson stares dead-eyed into the blue sky. Junior throws a bag of soil over him and drives away.

Around noon, Ruth steps slowly through a tiny and crowded lunch room, kneading the edges of her brown paper sack. Employees happily huddle around oddly spaced tables, leaving no real place for her to sit. Ruth looks over her options, dreading this time of day. When each tight clutch of Coworkers see her heading their way, the cheerful talking stops.

Actually, we're saving this one, says one after another.

Everybody's already here, Ruth says, too low to be heard, and once again she and her figurine eat a sandwich at her desk.

11

In a grubby newsroom behind a grimy office park, Stan takes a gulp of coffee, shuffles some notes and types furiously. Another reporter strides by holding a fax from the printer. Stan keeps typing, eyes on the screen.

What's that, he asks.

Crime log for today, she says. Nothing much. Another missing persons on that Julie Carroll, though.

Stan stops.

I just saw her Dad this morning, he says. He really likes me. Anyway, she'll show back up in a couple days. Always does. One time, I think she went the whole way to Canada. I'd like to go to Canada. Think she did any fishing? Here, let me hold onto it.

Suit yourself, she says and hands it over.

The sun sets as Carroll's cruiser rolls through a stop sign near his house. An approaching car honks. Carroll is startled and blurps the siren as an awkward cover. When the other car is gone, he pulls to the side of the road and cuts off the engine.

Hands shaking, he fights to catch his breath. Carroll pops open the glove compartment and reaches for the bottle. It's already empty.

On her front porch, Ruth fights to transplant an oversized house plant into a larger pot. She sets it down, takes a breath and struggles with it some more. It doesn't want to let go.

Carroll's car pulls into the driveway next door. He climbs out and just stands there looking at his keys, lost in thought. Ruth waves at him from her porch with no sign of stopping. Carroll doesn't notice at first.

Sorry, Ruth, he says after a while. I've been wandering around like that all day. Like I can't remember what I forgot. How are you?

Ruth smiles.

Have a good night, he says. If you need anything, you

12

know, call.

Carroll goes into his house. Ruth goes back to her flowerpot.

Junior's truck pulls to a halt across the street with squealing brakes. His yard is now neatly mowed and trimmed. There is a bright yellow Power Mower Incorporated flyer on the door. Junior sees the flyer as he pulls a sharp metal garden trowel from the truck bed. He shakes his head, stomping toward Ruth.

Startled, she looks up at him. Junior smiles.

Need some help there, he asks.

Ruth smiles. Together, they wrestle the plant free of its pot.

In her kitchen, Ruth gathers glasses and a pitcher from the fridge and pours. The little boy figurine smiles up at her from the window sill over the sink. She smiles back. The house is filled with photos of Ruth and Rudy, their knickknacks and remembrances. They are always side by side.

Outside, Junior stands and peels off his sweaty overshirt. He reaches for the sharp trowel. It flashes in the porch light.

Stepping out the front door, Ruth screams. Glasses shatter at her feet. A thick streak of blood stands out on the shoulder of Junior's t-shirt.

I, uhm, I hit a deer, he says. Had to drag it off the road . . .

Ruth nods warily, grabs a broom and sweeps up as he repots the plant.

Sorry to hear about Rudy, he says. He was a real good guy. Dad and I voted for him every time. How are you holding up?

Ruth takes a deep breath.

I spend all day feeling trampled by the most possible people in the smallest possible space, she says.

I wouldn't like that, Junior says.

Ruth's voice grows as she gains momentum.

I don't mind the office, really, she says. A little stuffy. It's just that dealing with people in general is not my strength. You know, I have this dream sometimes. There's this bright spotlight that doesn't come from anywhere. Just follows me wherever I go so that they all can't look right through me.

Well, you know, one thing my Dad always used to tell me, Junior says, standing. They always underestimate us quiet ones. Then he'd say, so don't let the bastards get you down. I've always found the second one useful. Anyway, you have a good night now.

Next door, Officer Carroll now paces as Mrs. Carroll looks through a box of family photos at their kitchen table.

I think she looks prettier in the other one, she says. But this's the one she'd pick.

Which one looks most like her right now, he asks as patiently as he can manage.

She begins to cry and picks a photo.

This one, she says. But she's frowning.

Come on, he says. We're not gonna do that now. She's just off doing her thing. Like always. We're not going to need these.

But she didn't bring any of her medicine, she says. Her needles. Not even that awful jacket. I found fifty dollars in her room. It's like nothing was touched.

She probably wanted us to not realize she was gone for as long as possible, he says, lying. To get a better jump on us this time. Probably been planning this one for a while. With a whole backup supply of her prescription squirreled away. Clothes packed. Organized, the way she can be sometimes. Honey, she just doesn't want to be fussed over anymore. Too much of that for her growing up, with all the doctors and the tests and everything. It'll be fine. Her friends are up at that lake. So, she is too, that's all there is to it.

But if she goes more than a couple days without an injection, Mrs. Carroll says, trailing off.

I know, he says. She knows.

She hands him the photo, all cried out.

14

Julie Carroll, she says. Woman of the world.

Later that night, at her own kitchen table, Ruth and her figurine enjoy hot sleepy tea and read the local newspaper. She's staring at a photo of Stan Reynolds at the top of his weekly column.

A low hum from outside catches her attention. She goes to the front window and meekly looks out, turning to a portrait photo of Rudy for reassurance.

Ruth opens the front door. The road is quiet. No one in sight. She walks to the center of her yard and looks around.

Ruth clears her throat.

Hello, she asks.

Ruth looks down. All at once, a large, round spotlight circles her feet with a hum. The big dot of light has no discernible source. Ruth steps left. It follows her. She steps right. It follows her. She runs in a circle. Same thing.

Well, I'll be, she says.

Ruth runs. It follows. She throws her hands into the air.

Well, I'll be, Ruth shouts happily. Well! I'll! Be!

The porch light goes on at the Carroll house. Mrs. Carroll emerges with curlers in her hair.

Ruth, honey, she says. What's wrong?

Ruth looks down. Her spotlight is gone.

Nothing, I guess, she shouts. Go on back to sleep, please. Nothing at all to see here!

Mrs. Carroll goes back inside, a little concerned. From Ruth, that was a world-record-level outburst.

Ruth looks down. Her spotlight returns, following her closely as she skips merrily across the yard.

Meanwhile, Junior's truck is cooling in his garage and the door is closed. Sharp garden tools hang neatly on hooks above the workbench and around the room. Poking out of a fifty-gallon drum is Henderson's torso. Grinning from the workbench, his dismembered head.

So, what I learned was pretty simple, he says. Done right,

parts of the human body make an almost perfect fertilizer. But more about that tomorrow. Trust me. Your begonias are going to love you.

Junior perches Mr. Henderson's dripping head at the top of a metal coatrack in the corner with a pan underneath it and turns out the light.

Thudding room to room, he shuts off lights throughout the house. Almost as an afterthought, he opens the basement door.

Night, Julie, he yells. Sleep tight!

From the basement: a muffled and panicked scream.

Junior shuts the door, yawns and trods off to bed, his dog close behind. He hits a last switch and all goes dark.

On a sunny afternoon a few days earlier, Julie and her friend Anna press their faces into the Carroll's bathroom mirror, ringing their eyes with heavy makeup.

No, look at the magazine, Julie says. You got it all wrong.

I see it, Anna says. I got it fine.

They ignore a knock at the door, followed by Mrs. Carroll's voice.

Julie, honey, she says.

Their eyes roll in unison.

What do you want, you stupid twat, Julie grins.

Julie, Anna says. Don't . . .

Don't worry, Julie says. She knows she's a dumb twat.

Julie throws open the door and barges down the hall, towing Anna by her sleeve.

Honey, Mrs. Carroll hesitates.

What, Julie yells. What could possibly be so crazy important to bother me when I have a friend over?

Honey, your medicine, Mrs. Carroll says. It's past time.

Julie plants her feet and screams.

Look, stupid, Julie says. Want to see? Look.

Julie rolls up her sleeve and points to a fresh needle mark.

There, she says. Satisfied? First stab of the day. Two to go. Maybe three. Right?

Anna is mortified by the scene.

Julie, she says. Come on . . .

So now you're on her side, Julie says. Let's none of us forget, it was this woman's weak genetics that put so many marks on my body that every school nurse thinks I'm a fucking heroin addict. Right? So when it comes to when I do or don't want the damn medicine, I'll decide. Everybody got it?

Mrs. Carroll bites her lip and meekly stares at the floor. Julie again has Anna by the arm, dragging her embarrassed friend out the front door.

In the yard, Anna shakes herself loose and stomps away.

Not cool, Julie, she says.

Julie is genuinely confused.

What's wrong, she asks. What'd I say?

That afternoon, Junior carefully tends to his backyard as Julie scales a tree branch just above his fence. She's trying to be sneaky.

Hello, Julie, he says. May I help you with something?

Julie smirks.

No, just bored, she says. What's in your shed?

For the thousandth time, he says. Fertilizer and lawn chemicals.

Junior keeps working, never looking up at her.

Then why the lock, she asks.

It's full of fertilizer and lawn chemicals, he says.

Lemme see, she says.

No, he says.

You grow pot, she says. Don't you?

No, I really don't, he says.

Then let me see, she says.

Junior looks up her.

Julie, he says. I remember one time you were just a little

girl, six or seven, pigtails even. You had this cat.

Mr. Bones, she says.

Sure, he says. Mr. Bones. And Mr. Bones was way up in our tree. Remember? And my Dad and I, we're on our way out to work. But you stood there and you looked so sad. We spent all day chasing that cat around that tree. We'd go higher and it'd go higher. Remember that?

Duh, she says. Yeah.

When we finally handed Mr. Bones to you, know what you said, he asks.

No, she says.

You said, you guys are my best friends in the whole wide world, he says. That was a nice day, Julie. You were a good kid, then.

Yeah, well, next day that cat scratched me and I got a rash, she says. Dad put him in the trunk of his cruiser and that was that. So, uh . . .

Still, he says. Julie, you have to trust me. I have no reason to lie to you.

I'll call the cops, she says.

Fine, he says. Let's call your Dad.

No, she says. I mean the real cops.

Want to use my phone, he asks.

Julie caterwauls and drops herself down out of the tree.

Adults are so fucking stupid, she yells from the other side of the fence. Stupid! Stupid! Stupid!

A little after midnight, a beer bottle lands and shatters on a dead-end street. Then another. A handful of cars are crawling with kids drinking beer. Music booms throughs the trees. Every time they finish a bottle, they throw it as far as they can. Two more crash side by side.

Julie sits on a station wagon tailgate, smoking a nub of a joint. She burns her fingers and drops it, intoxicated to the point of collapse.

Damn, she says. Somebody roll another one.

That's it, kid, an Older Guy laughs.

Hey, pal, don't call me kid, she says. What's it?

That's it, he says. No more grass.

Bullshit, she says. Call Ernesto. He owes me. Go on.
We're not getting any younger here.

Her eyes are barely open.

Ernie got busted, the Older Guy says. Sorry. Have a beer.

Yeah, she says. Good idea. Hand me a beer. I've got
something to say.

She stands up on the tailgate and nearly falls.

Watch it, sugar, the Older Guy says.

He props her up, all hands.

You watch it, asshole, Julie says.

We should go to my house, he says. You and me. I live in
the basement. My parents are asleep.

She forces her eyes to focus.

How old are you, anyway, she asks.

Don't worry about it, he says.

Yeah, she says. I got a better idea. You jerks want some
free pot?

Now she has their attention.

I'm driving, she says. Who's got a car?

Julie tumbles from the tailgate with a thud.

When they arrive, loud and stumbling, Junior's secluded
backyard is pitch black.

Alright, Julie says in the darkness. Everybody. Over the
fence.

The fence creaks and branches snap. An army of tiny
flashlights, open cell phones and glowsticks, flood the yard.

Quiet, Julies hisses. Follow me. Over here.

The lights group around Julie at the shed door.

Open it, she says. You'll see.

It's locked, the Older Guy says.

Break it or something, you asshole, she says.

Fuck this, he says.

When floodlights illuminate the yard, the kids yell and

19

scatter, leaving Julie alone among the trampled flowers, laughing.

Hey, Junior, she calls out blindly. Can you believe these fucking jerks tried to break into your shed? I chased them off, though, because you and me, we're pretty much best friends in the whole wide . . .

One giant hand lands on the back of her neck, the other covers her mouth. Junior drags flailing and terrified Julie Carroll into his house.

Bright and early, Bob brushes his teeth in their kitchen sink, tie thrown over his shoulder. Cathy is at the door laughing at him.

What in the world are you doing, she asks.

She wanted her privacy, he says. I figured, why fight progress? And this is the only other sink we got.

On your way home from work, pick us up a second bathroom, she says.

All in good time, sweetness, he grins. All in good time.

She kisses him. Their Daughter crawls onto a chair at the table.

Hello, he says. Everything work out alright?

She giggles and shakes her head.

Gee, Daddy's late for work, Bob says.

Thanks, Cathy says. Come on, let's get you cleaned up, young lady.

She scoops up their Daughter. Bob straightens his tie. Something at the window catches his attention.

That guy is outside, he says.

Cathy looks. It's Junior clipping a hedge.

That's the lawn guy I hired, she says. He's unbelievably cheap. But I didn't expect him to start so early.

Bob sips from his travel mug as he heads from his front door to his car. Junior stands beside his truck with his big shovel perched on his shoulder.

Morning, Bob says.

THE QUIET ONES

Morning, Junior says.

Well, have a good day, Bob says.

You too, Junior says.

Bob climbs into his car and drives away, Junior eying him the entire time.

Cathy appears at the door.

Like to come in for some coffee before you get started, she asks.

Junior smiles and drops his shovel.

Again, Ruth makes her way through the tiny, crowded lunch room with her brown-sack lunch, still hiding behind her gigantic glasses.

There's nowhere to sit. Employees happily huddle in clusters around tiny tables. Ruth spots a chair. She goes for it. A tight huddle of workers sees her heading their way and stops talking.

Actually, we're saving this one, they all agree.

Great, Ruth says. I'll keep it warm.

Ruth plants herself and unwraps her lunch.

So, she smiles. What's new?

Bob wrestles his Secretary on the bed of a cheap motel, the remnants of fast-food lunches piled on the end table. His phone rings and he fumbles for it. She thinks this is awfully funny.

Hi, honey, listen, Bob says. Listen, I'm in a meeting. Can I call you back? Great. You too. No problem. I will. Bye.

He hangs up. Again, she's all over him.

Let's have a late meeting at my place tonight, she says.

I'm leaving early today, Bob says. It's my Daughter's birthday.

That's sweet, she says, kissing him.

On a middle floor of the dingy office building, Ruth drops a heavy box of green binders on Gretchen's desk.

21

Good news, dear, Ruth says. The warehouse found your lost binders and sent them right over. They said the routing information came directly from you, but I told them your department isn't in the habit of making mistakes.

Steam is coming out of Gretchen's ears.

Thanks, she says coldly.

Don't mention it, dear, Ruth says.

At a little town drugstore around the corner from the motel, Bob stands in line with a box of diapers under his arm. Junior steps into line behind him.

They exchange an awkward nod.

In the office building's dingy bathroom, Gretchen and another Coworker stand one sink apart, washing their hands and fixing their makeup.

I don't know who she thinks she is all of the sudden, Gretchen says. I mean, seriously, she's nobody to start telling people what to do, am I right?

Fifteen years in the same clerk job, her Coworker agrees with a smirk. What does that tell you?

A toilet flushes. A door opens. Ruth takes the sink between them.

You know, ladies, you're right, Ruth says. My years here don't add up to a whole lot. Except that I'm the only one they trust enough to both set the petty cash budget and do the audit at the end of the year. Also, expense account totals. Inappropriate charges. That sort of thing. Ooh, I understand the marketing conference is in Manhattan this year. Wow. Exciting. Sounds pricey, though. I'm sure those New Jersey hotels are fun too. Have a nice time, girls!

They exchange silent looks of fire, leaving Ruth alone at the sinks.

Ruth studies her reflection, dries her hands, then walks over and flips the light switch off. Darkness, except the sourceless circle of light at Ruth's feet.

I don't care if they can see you or not, Ruth says. I'm sure glad you're here.

At a sleepy filling station along a winding road, Bob pumps gas, watching the numbers turn. He glances at his reflection in the car window. At the pump directly behind him is Junior. Rusty pants at Bob from the passenger window of their truck.

Oh, hey there, Bob says. Again. Small town, huh?

Junior grins and nods sincerely.

Sure is, he says.

Bob's phone rings in his pocket. It startles him. He answers, grateful for the distraction.

Hi, he says. Yeah, I got them. Yeah. The large ones. I don't think they make them any bigger, so she better start figuring this out quick. Oh. That's fine. No, I'm at a gas station. They have a little store. Just milk? Alright. Love you.

Bob hangs up and heads for the mini-market. He emerges minutes later with a gallon of milk. By then, Junior and his truck are gone. Bob starts his car, pulls out of the station and gets up to speed. A tire blows.

Shit, Bob says, wrestling the car off the road.

Bob groans and reaches again for his phone. There's a tap at his window. It's Junior.

Oh, hi, Bob says. Thanks, I've got this covered. I'll just call the auto club.

Junior taps the window again. Now he's using the barrel of a mean-looking revolver.

Holy shit, Bob yelps.

His only thought is to reach over and lock the car door.

With the flat of his palm, Junior presses a photograph against the window. It's the studio portrait of Bob's family from their refrigerator. He swings the pistol. The glass shatters.

In the police station file room, Officer Carroll is agitated,

rifling through drawers. He spreads folders across a desk.
Each file shows a different teenager, same age as Julie.

Alright, dirtbags, Carroll mutters. Where's my little girl?

The door flies open. The Police Captain charges in.

Carroll, what are you doing in here with that door closed,
he growls.

Oh, uhm, Carroll can't help but sputter, shuffling the
pages. Yeah. Somebody needed these.

The Captain is way ahead of him.

Really, he says. So you're telling me we're putting
together a report on the kids that drink up at the lake?

No, Carroll says. I, uhm . . .

When was the last time you slept, the Police Captain asks.

Julie's gone again, Carroll says.

I'm sorry to hear that, the Captain says. But she always
comes back.

It's different this time, Carroll says.

As I said, the Captain says. I'm sorry to hear that. But
we've got a budget review coming up and that means
everybody pulling their weight.

Officer Carroll yells in a flash of frustration, much like
Julie does, punching a phone off the desk and across the
room. It lands in the corner with a crash. Conversations
outside the door fall quiet.

Like I said, it's different this time, Carroll says, now icy
calm.

The Captain has a hand on his gun.

Let's get us a nice breath of fresh air, he says.

Big front doors swing into a bright and sunny day
outside the station. Officer Carroll and the Captain step out
together. Another Officer is on his way in.

Hey, Wayne, the Captain says. Mind giving this old boy a
lift over to his house? They need him there.

That's alright, I have my car, Carroll says.

Better just leave that here with us for the time being, the
Captain says. Go home. Get some rest.

The Captain holds out his hands. Carroll studies them for a long moment, then hands over his badge and gun.

For how long, Carroll asks.

The time being, the Captain says. And don't worry, she'll call. She always does.

Bob jolts awake in Junior's dark garage, choking and coughing. He's shackled to a folding chair, bleeding from the temple. His eyes fight open to find Junior forcing Henderson's severed arm through an industrial meat grinder. A little frustrated, Junior seems to be caught on a hunk of bone. A heavy, satisfying shove sends it through.

Henderson's decaying skull watches from the workbench. Junior's dog snores in the corner. Beside him, Julie droops, bound to a kitchen chair.

Junior sees Bob's awake and wipes his hands.

Well, hey, there you are, he says. You really went out hard. Sorry about that. Don't know my own strength sometimes. You're a fighter. That's good!

Bob has to spit blood to talk.

Who are you, he coughs.

I'm the guy who cuts your lawn, Junior says.

Bob is fixated on the bloody workbench.

What do you want, he asks.

Good question, Junior says. I need your help with something, Bob.

Julie doesn't even twitch, but Bob realizes her eyes are open, locked on him with terror.

Me, Bob says. Why me?

I like your family, Junior says, wiping very bloody hands. They're nice.

So you attack me and tie me up, Bob says.

Yeah, Junior says. Sorry I walloped you. Needed to get your attention. I have to be able to trust you. So we have to understand each other.

Junior scoots over to free Bob, then opens a heavy door at

the back of the garage. On the other side is the dark, huge, lush backyard amid a chorus of crickets. He returns to his workbench.

Here's the deal, Junior says. There's about ten miles of wilderness between this old farmhouse and anything resembling a phone. You run out that door, it's me and you in a little race to your family. I get there first, I'll kill them both, then come find you. You get there first, I'll kill all three of you together. But stay in that chair, it's just you. Only you. Truck's all tuned up. You make your own choices.

Cleaning tools at his workbench with an old rag, Junior turns his back to them.

What about her, Bob asks.

She's not your business, Junior says.

Julie fights to make eye contact with Bob. She nods toward the door. She wants him to run. Junior happily works at his bench. Sharp tools dangle around the room.

I know this all seems really gruesome, Junior says. But trust me. It all makes perfect sense.

Julie glares at Bob.

I'll come back for you, Bob says and jabs a pair of hedge clippers into the truck's front tire. It explodes. He rushes out the door.

Junior takes a long, sad breath.

Well, Rusty, Junior says. Guess I owe you a dollar. Go on. Go get him.

Rusty stretches a moment, then charges, growling after Bob.

Bob sprints directly from Junior's back door to the garden fence. He scrambles over, disappearing into the dense woods, completely unaware of the neighborhood all around him.

Rusty sniffs his way to a rabbit hole beneath the fence, shimmies under and gives chase.

Junior strolls out his front door, whistling a little. In the driveway, he pulls a tarp off a gigantic late-model Cadillac.

THE QUIET ONES

The headlights flair as the big car lunges into the night.

A month earlier, Bob sits in the only glass-enclosed office at one end of a wide, dim office bay filled with aging cubicles. It's on a middle floor of the same stuffy old building where Ruth works. Phones ring. Printers, copiers and faxes whir. The elevator doors stick a bit.

Bob types, talks on the phone and reads from a stack of printouts, all at the same time.

I don't care about overtime hours anymore, he says. You better believe we're making this deadline. Really? Fine. Call me back in fifteen minutes and I'll tell you again.

He slams down the phone. Across the room, Fitzgerald, an impatient, tubby executive with a three-piece suit and gigantic comb-over, charges off the elevator.

All eyes follow Fitzgerald as he waddles toward Bob's office.

Bob's exhausted Assistant pops his head in Bob's door.

Don't look now, but here comes the Big Boss's head stooge, he says.

By that point, Fitzgerald is right behind him.

Mr. Fitzgerald, he says. How very lovely to see you.

Fitzgerald passes him by as if he's not even there.

Morning, Bob, Fitzgerald says. How's business?

On schedule and on track, Mr. Fitzgerald, Bob says. How's the executive suite?

Fitzgerald glances over his shoulder at the busy room and chuckles to himself.

Say, Bob, he says. Drop everything. B.B. wants to see you right away.

Just outside Bob's office door, his Assistant pretends to file something and listens intently.

Gee, Bob says. You know, we're, uhm, we've got this deadline coming up.

Bob's phone rings. He ignores it.

Screw the deadline, Bob, Fitzgerald says. Little secret?

Nobody cares.

Funny, Bob says, processing whether this is true.

The Boss heard about your help in sweeping that little accounting fiasco under the rug last month, Fitzgerald says. He's impressed. Very impressed.

Bob's eyes go wide and he hustles to close the thin door before his Assistant can hear any more.

No problem, Bob says. That's, uh, that's why pencils have erasers. Right?

Bob's phone rings again. his Assistant is at his window, urgently pointing at Bob to answer.

And offices have paper shredders, Fitzgerald says.

Both laugh, Bob nervously.

Well, like I say, happy to help in a pinch, Bob says.

Right, right, Fitzgerald says. You've got three minutes.

Bob's phone rings.

Sure, he says. But, uhm . . .

Fitzgerald suddenly loses both his patience and phony grin.

Fuck the deadline, Bob, he says. It's time to join the club.

An hour later at the town's only private golf course, in his work clothes and borrowed shoes, Bob follows Fitzgerald and B.B., both in the most expensive outfits possible, down a short fairway. Caddies follow along with oversized bags.

Bob knows Fitzgerald to be a highly tuned manipulator who bounces between overwhelming praise and fierce temper tantrums. B.B.'s the Big Boss and likes his nickname. His given name is Lyle. And as a born CEO, B.B. doubles Fitzgerald in every way.

B.B. juggles a cigar and three iron, lining up for another shot.

Beautiful day, isn't it, he chuckles.

Fitzgerald looks to Bob to answer.

Sure is, sir, he says.

They reach Bob's ball. Bob lines up and shanks the shot directly into the woods.

Bob knows B.B. enjoys not being beaten. He reaches into his pocket and tosses Bob a ball.

Don't sweat it, kid, he says.

Thanks, Bob says.

Bob lines up and sends the ball down the fairway.

That'a boy, B.B says.

They reach Fitzgerald's ball. Fitzgerald lines up, steps away, lines up, frets, lines up again and steps away.

B.B. sighs, impatient.

Smoke cigars, Bob, he asks.

Here and there, Bob says.

B.B. reaches into his pocket, finds and hands over another smaller cigar.

This one is a fine sinsemilla my young nephew grows in his Mama's tomato garden, the scoundrel, he says. He cuts me in to keep quiet. Good shit, too.

B.B. holds it out to Bob with a lighter.

Don't mind if I do, Bob says.

Fitzgerald is still fussing over his ball.

That'a boy, B.B. says. Say there, Fitzy, how about you and the boys take a walk?

In mid-swing, Fitzgerald stops, grabs his ball and obediently trots toward the green. Their Caddies follow.

Been keeping an eye on you, Bobby boy, yes sir, B.B. says. Hard worker. Record setter in the overtime department. Pretty little family. Nice little house. Those genuine, solid roots I respect so much in a person. Took a pretty big risk on our behalf last month. That client and their damn accountants could've nailed us good. And you. But Bobby boy kept things nice and tidy and signed your name without blinking. Worth a mint, those kind of balls, if you play your cards right. Believe you me.

Well, you know what they say, Bob says. If you ain't cheating, you ain't trying.

B.B. nearly falls down laughing, coughing smoke from the little cigar.

Christ, Bob, he says. I like that so much I'm stealing it right now.

Whatever you say, Boss, Bob says, forcing a smile.

B.B. takes a manic turn toward serious.

Bobby, he says. I'll be blunt. Those dirty Feds are all over us and our subsidiaries, the ones they know about, anyway. All routine nonsense, of course. Cost of doing business. But I need a man with your background in numbers. Your talent. Your dedication. A man that, aw hell, is smart enough to crack skulls all day so he can go home and wipe his ass with hundred-dollar bills. I see this in you, Bob. Down deep, past all this buttoned-down bullshit. Got it?

Bob is listening.

Let me give you an example, Bob, B.B. says. See that fellow over there?

One fairway over, a Golfer from another party lines up over his ball.

Yes, Bob says.

What would you say if I told you I want him dead before the next tee, B.B. asks.

Bob thinks it over. B.B. is impatient.

Gee, Boss, I'm going off the top of my head, here, Bob says. But if he makes that green, I'll go ahead and beat him to death with my five iron. Otherwise, I may have just enough time to get to the unmarked pistol I keep duct taped to the wheel well of my car.

B.B. pounds Bob on the back and takes a long drag of the smaller cigar.

That's my boy, he says. Yes, sir, Bob-o. That's my boy.

Back at the office, Fitzgerald and Bob ride alone together in the executive elevator.

Boy, do I envy you, Bob, Fitzgerald says. I remember my first day upstairs, back in the Wichita office. After a particularly messy episode in which I personally dismissed more than fifteen teamster wannabes in a single afternoon. There at headquarters, you know, it's a whole other story. It was a dicey walk to the car that night, I'll tell you. But now look at me. Sort of like being a made man, right?

Fitzgerald winks, forcing Bob to rethink B.B.'s little jokes. The office elevator doors open quicker on the higher floors. This part of the building is entirely different. Mahogany trim. Fresh flowers. Light overhead music. Calm.

Allow me to go down the list, Fitzgerald says, marching Bob past water pitchers with floating cucumbers and long rows of expensive desks. Excellent perks package, that goes without saying. Company car. Vacation days, well, take whatever you need. The company has a terrific timeshare down in the islands.

Bob follows Fitzgerald past tranquil office doors with executive nameplates and happy underlings standing guard. No phones ring here. One of the multiple Receptionists send over a happy little robot voice to ask if you'd like to take a call.

Here we are, Fitzgerald says.

Bob's new office has the closest thing to an impressive view the town can offer.

And don't worry, we'll get you out of that rat trap you call a starter house right away, Fitzgerald says. So, take a look around, relax, and then go ahead and take the rest of the day off.

Bob's head is spinning.

I don't know what to say, he says, settling in behind his new desk.

Thank you will suffice, Fitzgerald says. And . . . Oh, wait, I almost forgot. You're about to meet the best part of this whole deal.

With a flourish, Fitzgerald stretches his arm to point across the office. Slinking directly towards them, Margarita is gorgeous and pouring out of her classy business blouse.

Who . . .

That, my friend, is your new little helper, Fitzgerald says.

That's alright, I have Howard, Bob says. You met him

down on the fifth floor. He's very good.

And there, my friend, he will stay, Fitzgerald says. And he'll still cover the real work, with a nice raise to keep him quiet, so don't worry about that. Relax. Margarita here is part of those perks we talked about.

I don't understand, Bob says.

Aw, Bob, Fitzgerald says. I envy you. There's so much you're about learn. My advice? Just say yes. One thing's for sure. B.B. takes care of his boys.

By now, Margarita is at Bob's new office door.

Well, I'll just leave you two to get acquainted, Fitzgerald says.

She steps in as Fitzgerald closes the door.

Morning, she says. What do you think?

Bob can't help but admire the view and then looks out the window.

I think they're going to hang me out to dry, Bob says. And I think I'm going to let them.

Margarita leans knowingly toward him across the desk.

Me too, she says. What do you say we enjoy the ride?

As the sun sets, Bob excitedly climbs out of his car, bottle of champagne in one hand, bouquet of flowers in the other.

In the kitchen, Cathy feeds their Daughter in the highchair.

Bob throws open the front door.

Well, hello there, she says. You're sure home early. What's the . . .

Bob sweeps her into his arms.

Later, the tiny table in Bob and Cathy's tiny excuse for a dining room is festooned with candles, delivery Italian food and a couple empty bottles of cheap wine.

In a highchair, their Daughter is covered, head to toe, in sauce and pasta. They let her play. Cathy swirls her glass of wine.

It's about time the rest of the world sees our big strong superhero the way we do, she says.

It's a promotion, not a cape, he says.

Beneath the table, her toes find their way up his pant leg.

Just a matter of time, she says.

Cathy smiles dreamily at Bob. This catches him with a pang. He bounces to his feet.

Here, I'll clear this off, he says.

Leave it, she says.

Bob gathers dishes.

No, no, he says. There's an oregano-flavored handful over there I'm trying to pass off on you.

That'll just take a minute, Cathy says. Go out to the yard and grab me the hose.

Their Daughter launches a clump of pasta across the room.

When the bathtub's running in the distance, Bob dries plates by hand and avoids his own reflection in the window over the kitchen sink.

Sauce-coated child in her arms, Cathy slides up behind Bob and kisses his neck.

What's wrong, she asks.

Nothing, he says as the phone in his pocket begins vibrating. Work thing I was thinking about. Here, let me get the trash.

Across town in the dark office building, Margarita sits behind Bob's new desk completely naked.

I was here working late, setting up your new office, and it seems you took home something from that big project we're working on, she breathes into the phone speaker. Something I need you to bring back to the office right away.

By now Bob stands beside the trash cans in his front yard, smoking a cigarette, phone pressed to his ear. He listens, intrigued, reaches into his back pocket, finds a pair of very lacy panties and hangs up the phone.

Bob appears at the door to the bathroom where his Wife and Daughter giggle and splash.

Bad news, ladies, Bob says. Daddy's got an emergency at

the office.

Now, with Rusty bearing down on him in the dark, Bob cannonballs frantically through the woods. He tumbles, rolling through the dirt and brambles. For a long beat he just lies there, sucking air, as if it's all a terrible dream, confused by the sudden silence. Then a heavy rustle in the distance starts him scrambling again, pushing him deeper into the forest.

At the same time, Junior calmly cruises a winding country road in his oversized sedan, flipping around on the radio for a song.

In her bedroom, Ruth snores beneath thick covers. The circle of light hums as it appears on the carpet. Ruth opens her eyes, excited.

Well, hello there, she says.

The spotlight moves to her door and stops. Ruth climbs out of bed and it leads her down the hall.

Ruth's front door opens. She follows the spotlight into her yard. The wind whips up. She pulls her housecoat tight over her nightgown. Her slippers have bunnies on them.

Are we going far, she asks. Because . . .

The circle continues down the road. Ruth shrugs and follows.

Officer Carroll sits at his kitchen table in the dark. He pours himself another shot of liquor from a dusty, mostly empty bottle. The kitchen light pops on. Mrs. Carroll is half asleep.

What are you doing, she shrieks.

Not tired, he says.

She rushes over and grabs the bottle away from him.

How many times are we going to go through this, she demands.

For emergencies, he says.

On the table in front of him is a page he smuggled from the police department file room. It includes the mugshot of a greasy, local thug, a rich kid slumming it, sneering at the camera with numbers below his chin. Carroll stares, stares and stares at the photo.

She's had enough.

Well, I'm leaving you, she says. How about that for an emergency?

He doesn't hear her. She dumps the bottle neck down in the sink and storms out, bedroom door slamming behind her.

Carroll's mind stays focused on the photo as he reaches blindly to find a cookie jar in a high cabinet. He sets it on the counter and opens the lid. Inside, a revolver, another pint bottle and a box of bullets.

Not far away, but deep in the brambles, Bob blindly charges on.

Nose to the ground, Rusty's somewhere close by.

Suddenly, the ground beneath Bob falls away. He plunges down a steep bank into a murky creek. The fall takes the wind out of him. He climbs painfully to his feet. Rusty paws and sniffs along the top of the bank, debating whether to jump.

Along a wide, nearby road, Bob drags himself through underbrush to a clearing. Limping, he crosses the road, not a vehicle in sight. Gasping, he picks a direction, but doesn't get far. Again, Rusty's barking, and again it's getting closer.

Bob spots headlights on the horizon. The barking is closer. The headlights are an eighteen-wheeler at full steam. Rusty appears at the wood's edge and spots Bob on the other side of the road. His body becomes a missile. Bob screams at the truck, arms flailing. Rusty charges Bob, teeth bared and snarling. Bob is frozen, beaten, exhausted. Their eyes lock. Only gaining speed, jaws wide, Rusty reaches the center line and leaps for Bob's throat. The truck grill swipes Rusty from mid-air with a half-thump, half yelp, and passing roar. The wheels never slow. Bob shivers beside the road, alone in the dark.

Swerving his family station wagon, Carroll loads his pistol and steers with his knees.

At a lakeside campsite, teenagers snuggle around a dying campfire. A bright flashlight. Heavy boots kick at sleeping bags to a chorus of shouts and screams.

Ritchie, Carroll yells. Where are you, now? Talk to me!

Ritchie, a scraggly teenager, stumbles out of a nearby tent.

Hey, he says, oblivious. What's going on?

Panicked kids scatter into the night.

In street clothes and a ball cap, Carroll grabs Ritchie by the neck. He shoves him back against a tree, the bright flashlight in his face.

Where's Julie Carroll, Carroll says, exhausted.

Hold on, Ritchie says. Who? I don't know anybody. Whatever it is, I wasn't there.

The girl you impregnated last summer, Carroll says. That you dumped off at some clinic downstate.

Fine, Ritchie says. What about her?

Carroll cocks the revolver and places the barrel between Ritchie's eyebrows, his voice like ice.

For the second time, Carroll says. Where is she, you piece of shit?

Bob hurries as he nears the same gas station from before his capture. With relief, he hustles inside. Cooling at the pump is Junior's gigantic Cadillac.

Nobody's behind the register. Bob bangs on the safety glass.

Just a minute, the Clerk calls from the storeroom.

Phone, Bob yells. Do you have a phone?

I said just a minute, the Clerk shouts back.

Junior steps into line behind Bob.

Hey there, Junior says.

Bob bursts from the gas station doors in a slow, painful run, Junior close behind.

Junior walks over and calmly opens the Cadillac's gigantic trunk. Inside, Rusty, dead. In a few long steps, he has Bob off the ground. He wrestles him toward the trunk. Bob's flailing feet hook the bumper and kick hard against the license plate. Junior slams the lid. The Cadillac's tail lights fade quickly into the night.

At the lake, Carroll has whimpering Ritchie by the neck, fully ready to spread his brains out against the tree.

Cops don't do this, man, Ritchie sobs for his life, snot bubbles popping.

I'm not a cop right now, Carroll says.

His phone rings. The moment is broken.

Mrs. Carroll calls from their kitchen phone, too tired to cry.

I found Julie's phone, she says.

She holds a cell phone to the house phone receiver: You have fifteen new messages. First new message: Julie! Where are you? We're up at the lake! Call me!

It's Ritchie's voice. Mrs. Carroll presses a button.

Second new message: Julie! What? Are you still grounded? Call somebody!

She presses the button again.

Third new message: Julie. Baby, come on already. You're so missing it! Where are you?

Carroll leaves Ritchie weeping against the tree.

Junior's basement is pitch black until the door opens at the top of stairs. Junior has Bob by the neck.

I really want to get through this without getting angry, Junior says. Alright?

Slumped, Bob doesn't answer. Junior gives him a shove.

Bob bounces down the stairs and lands squarely on the basement floor. Junior wants an answer.

Seriously, Bob, he says. What do you say?

Through the light from the door, Bob can see Julie, gagged and bound to a toppled-over chair. He gathers his strength, blood pouring from his nose.

Alright, Bob manages. Fine.

Good, Junior says, relieved. Good to hear. Well, get some sleep. Big day in the morning.

Junior closes the door.

The newspaper office is mostly shut down for the night. Stan clicks on a desk lamp. Yawning and a little frazzled, he searches his desk. He pulls drawer after drawer and then again searches his pockets. Finally, he finds his keys.

Across the room, the printer spits out a new fax. Stan makes his way over and examines the pages. The first one is a missing person report for Henderson.

On his desk, Stan lays it side by side with the missing person report for Julie. He sits down in his chair and slides off his coat.

Ruth patiently follows the circle of light along the road. The light stops. Ruth picks up a crumpled photograph. It's Bob and his family in the studio portrait. Ruth studies the photo, concerned.

She continues on, exhausted, her mind wandering.

Ruth's earliest memory is of her Grandparent's farm, the sun rising across the little cluster of buildings. The farmhouse, silo and barns are brightly painted clapboard anchors between fields of wheat and corn. A dozen cousins shuffle, yawning, through their chores.

In the farmhouse kitchen, Ruth and Rudy's Grandmother washes dishes at the sink. She watches her family through the window and smiles. A sudden pain. She drops the plate in her hands. It shatters on the counter. She grips the counter edge, knees buckling. With trembling hands, she pulls open a drawer and fumbles for a tin of pills. She pries open the tin. Pills spill to the floor. On her knees, her fingers find one. She slips it carefully under her tongue. Recovering, she climbs to her feet. The side door bangs open.

Five-year-old Ruth and Rudy skip happily into the room.

Hi, Grandma, Ruth says. The duck eggs hatched. But I didn't touch them. Just like you said, I didn't pet them. I just let them be. But they're so cute. And Daddy says in a couple days, if we're real lucky . . .

Their Grandmother slips into a chair at the long kitchen table.

Ruthie, my little chatterbox, hush for a moment and help Grandma sweep up her pills, she says.

Rudy holds out the tin piled with pills.

Here they are, Grandma, he says. This is all of them. Are you alright?

Right as rain, Rudybear, she says. Right as rain. See, Ruthie, eyes open, mouth shut. That's what gets the job done, hmmmmm?

Ruth nods, bursting to speak.

Fine, her Grandmother says. Very quickly. What is it?

Well, Ruth says. Well, I mean, I was just thinking that, maybe, when the duckies are old enough, I mean, I know we don't have a pond at our house, but with my blow-up pool, or maybe Daddy could dig one in the yard or . . .

Their Grandma takes a difficult breath.

Kids, she says. Come with Grandma a moment. I've got something for you.

In the farmhouse bedroom, Ruth and Rudy follow their Grandmother to a broad shelf filled edge to edge with collectable figurines, jumping, running, playing, fishing from toadstools. She carefully picks two and holds one out in each hand.

Now, you know how special these figurines are to Grandma, she says. I want you each to have one.

Trembling, she hands the boy with the bucket to Rudy and the girl with bows in her hair to Ruth.

Please keep them safe, and I want you to always remember Grandma loves you, she says.

Rudy and Ruth handle the figurines like snowflakes.

Now, Rudy, Grandma wants you to always look after your Sister, she says.

Yes, ma'am, Rudy says.

And Ruthie, she says.

Their Grandmother turns a key at her lips and throws it away.

A little more listen and a little less chatter, she says. Understand?

Yes, Grandma, Ruth says. Because . . .

Grandma wobbles.

Alright, she says. Alright. Now you kids go play.

Ruth and Rudy skip down the hall, toward the back door.

Oh, oh, wait, one more thing, Ruth says.

Ruthie, Rudy says. Come on. We have to help in the barn.

Ruth runs back toward the bedroom.

Grandma, she chirps. I was just wondering, are these like Jack and Jill, because Rudy and I are just like Jack and Jill and . . .

Grandma is face down on the floor. Ruth freezes, words caught in her throat.

Rudy is right behind her. He drops his figurine of the little boy and the bucket. As it hits the floor, a chip breaks from one ear.

Ruth stares, words caught in her throat. Rudy runs for help. Everything's in slow motion.

Their Mother and a half dozen other adults flood the room, pushing the kids out of the way.

Call a doctor, they shout. Mom? Mom!

Ruth picks up Rudy's figurine and holds them side by side.

It's going to be alright, Ruthie, I promise, Rudy says.

40

This echoes in her memory as Ruth finds herself shivering many miles away from her house, in a manicured backyard she's never seen before. The spotlight stops and for a moment grows brighter. She reaches blindly into thick grass and finds Henderson's glasses, caked with blood and bugs. Ruth studies them, fascinated.

Two decades to the day after their Grandmother died, Ruth waits in a tiny Human Relations office, hands folded, petrified, hiding behind giant glasses.

A smiling HR Manager strides in and takes a seat across a wide desk, too big for the room.

So sorry to keep you waiting, Ms. Morgan, he says. This place is a zoo today. Let's see.

He opens Ruth's file.

From the looks of things, we're lucky you came to us first, he says. With your accomplishments in graduate school, I'd say you're looking for a place in the executive suite someday. Heck, maybe I'll end up working for you. It's happened before.

He smiles. Ruth smiles back in a cold sweat.

Right, so, the thing is, I have to ask you a just a couple of these dumb questions, he says. Sorry about that, but they'll have my neck if I don't fill out the forms, you know how it is. Ready?

Unsure, Ruth nods.

Alright, he says. Uhm. Where do you want to be in five years?

Ruth stares back at him, wide eyed. She can't find the words.

You're right, he says. That's a silly one. I always hated that question. How about, what is the number one thing you'd recommend about yourself?

Ruth stares at the floor. She quietly hyperventilates.

The thing you'd most like to change, he asks.

Tears stand out in her eyes. He sees her pain, reaches into

a desk drawer and finds a different file card from the one he was prepared to hand her.

Hey, he says. Listen. I did read your file. My Uncle is a lot like yourself. Still waters run deep is what we say in our family. Why don't you start Monday anyway. Please report to this office. Now, it's in the basement. And an assignment a little below your level, quite frankly. But maybe with a little time and encouragement. Who knows? Right?

Ruth takes the assignment card and flees the office, leaving the HR Manager scratching his head.

Outside, Ruth crosses the parking lot. It's the office building where she still works in the basement.

Twenty-something Rudy waits next to their car.

How'd it go, he asks.

Ruth heads straight for the passenger side, slamming the door. Rudy climbs in.

Well, he asks.

Ruth takes a deep breath.

In five years, I want a house, kids, a job I love and a man who loves me, she says, exasperated. My best assets are organization, number crunching, puzzles and problem solving . . . And in the name of all things holy, I want for just once to speak clearly and loudly to anybody I choose.

Fists clenched, Ruth pounds the dashboard.

Rudy is never interested in the negative part of things.

But did you get it, he asks.

Yes, Ruth says.

Then let's get some dinner, he says. Your treat.

Thrilled, Rudy starts the car and drives away.

Fifteen years after that, in a back booth at the local diner, Ruth and Rudy sit quietly as a Waiter approaches.

Evening Councilman Morgan, the Waiter says. What can I get for you all today?

Hi there, Rudy says. I'll have the special, please. Ruth would like the club sandwich, but on rye, no mustard and extra tomatoes. And if you don't mind, we're running late for tonight's meeting . . .

No problem, the Waiter says. I'll have that for you right away.

Across the room, Stan Reynolds hustles in and finds his own way to a nearby table.

Well, look who's here, Rudy says.

Ruth turns, sees Stan, and tries to turn invisible.

Hey, that's Stan Reynolds from the newspaper, Rudy says. Have you met Stan? Great guy. You'd like him.

Rudy raises his hand to wave Stan over. Ruth pulls it down.

He's such a good reporter, Rudy says. I wonder if he knows you've been in love with him since high school.

Stan spots Rudy and ambles over.

Well, hey there, Stan says.

Ruth stares a hole through the table.

Hey Stan, Rudy says. You know Ruth.

Uhm, yeah, Stan says. Didn't we used to have chemistry together?

I always thought so, Rudy says.

Ruth glares at Rudy, dizzy from holding her breath.

Stan chews on this but lets it pass.

Quick bite before the meeting, he asks.

You know it, Rudy says. Got to keep the strength up for public comment hour.

I'll say, Stan says. Ready for that road-widening measure?

No comment until after the vote, Rudy smiles.

Rudy and Stan share a laugh.

Well, I'll leave you to your supper, Stan says. Nice to see you, Ruth.

Ruth's eyes are about to pop out of her head.

See you there, Rudy says.

Stan heads back to his table.

Ruth kicks Rudy under the table as hard as she can.

That night, thunder and lightning fill the sky above the local Town Hall.

Rudy sits at the center of the dais in the small, wood-lined council chambers, filled to capacity. His eventual Pallbearers flank him on either side. More thunder echoes through the windows.

An Elderly Voter leaning on a cane, spit flying, veins bulging, rants at a podium.

. . . and I remember that it was in nineteen eighty-one . . . I think, he says. Not long after they finally got around to paving the logging road, so it must have been then, anyway. I stood in this very spot, and I made it clear . . .

Alright, Rudy says. Thank you. Duly recorded. We do remember the logging road example from last time.

The Elderly Voter flips through scribbled-over notes.

Is that so, he mutters.

Yes, Rudy says. It was very well said.

Then I relinquish the rest of my time, the Elderly Voter says, waving over his shoulder as he turns away from the podium. Thank you.

Stan sits in the third row, flipping through his notes. A few rows back, Ruth watches him, moon-eyed.

Thank you, Rudy says. Alright. The big clock on the wall says that's enough for one night. Folks, the ladies' auxiliary has punch and cookies out there in the hall. And speaking of punch, if we may enjoy them without fisticuffs, I call this meeting adjourned.

Rudy taps his gavel once to polite laughter.

In the hallway, constituents mingle with plastic cups and shortbread cookies. Rudy finds Ruth hiding in the corner sipping punch.

Hey there, hot stuff, Rudy says.

Ruth rolls her eyes.

Say, Stan's got some questions for me, he says. I told him I would connect him with my press representative. But he'd have to give her a ride home.

Ruth is confused. It sinks in. She punches his shoulder. Rudy leans in close.

Come on, now, he says. You're ready for this. Take your time. Make it happen. See you at home!

The sky rumbles outside. Ruth is equally furious. Rudy slips away into the crowd. She gives chase but spots Stan pushing his way toward her, too late to hide. As Rudy ducks out the door, Stan has Ruth cornered.

Hi there, Stan says. Listen, Rudy said you could help me with a couple details from his upcoming projects. Won't take a moment. First off . . .

Stan swings open his notepad.

Ruth looks like she's going to swallow her tongue.

I have to pee, she mutters to no one.

Stan looks up from his notes. Ruth is gone. He scans the crowd. She's nowhere to be found. He shrugs.

Rudy is practically skipping as he climbs into their car and drives away. Ruth rushes from the building just in time to see him round the nearest corner. Around her, heavy globs of rain begin striking the ground.

At their house, Rudy parks and slides happily through the front door. He breathes deep, grateful for a moment of privacy, doffs his raincoat and saunters over to the living room stereo.

Dancing to club music in his bedroom, Rudy starts opening drawers. Hidden deep beneath winter sweaters, socks and bedsheets is a cornucopia of sexual devices. They land one after another onto the bed. As the music plays, Rudy slyly sings along.

He steps in front of a full-length mirror in a mismatched bondage outfit.

Looking fine, Mister City Council, he says, peering through little eye-holes in a tight mask, open zipper across the mouth. Look-ing fine!

He hooks a complex choking collar to the frame of the closet door and clicks a series of remote controls. Across the

room, a television leaps to life with porn. He fast forwards to
the spot he wants and pauses the video. Slipping his neck
into a dangling harness, Rudy realizes he needs a bit of a
height boost. He looks at the clock.

Leather squeaking, he makes his way down the narrow
hallway, past the dining room and into the kitchen. In the
pantry he finds a wobbly old kitchen stool. He digs through
a junk drawer for a screwdriver to tighten the legs. Minutes
slipping away, he looks to the kitchen clock and hurries.

Back in his bedroom, Rudy uses the stool to climb back
into his contraption, neck first. The lower half of his outfit
hits the floor. As he pauses to collect his thoughts, a stool leg
snaps. Rudy's feet dangle and twitch.

For a while, the music floats through the house for no
one.

Through rain like an artillery barrage, Ruth trudges
home alone. Eventually, she stomps through the front door,
sopping wet, and hears the stereo. This pisses her off more.

Rudy, she shouts. Damn it! If you want to be alone, I'll go
to the fucking movies!

Ruth stomps down the hallway. She throws open Rudy's
door and gasps. It's far too late.

Oh, Rudy, she says.

Now, up early with sleep in his eyes, Stan parks outside
Henderson's house and double checks the address against
the missing person report. With his notepad and pen, he
crosses the lawn, finds the front door and knocks. No
answer. He goes around the back, admiring the landscaping,
not three feet from where Henderson died.

Approaching the gas station, Ruth shivers in her
housecoat and yawns. She squints into the sun. Her spotlight
fades into the dawn. Trudging along, she spots something on
the ground at her feet. It is the broken-off bottom of a
decorative license-plate frame. The plastic reads: *If You Can*

Read This.

Morning light drips through the leaves of Junior's
backyard. He sets Bob, gagged and bound to a heavy dining
room chair, at the edge of the lawn. In a mismatched chair
next to him is Julie, also bound and gagged, drifting in and
out of consciousness.

Junior drags his favorite shovel behind himself, admiring
his plants. He's in a really good mood.

I'd hoped to do this the easy way, Junior says. Should've
known better.

His shovel head makes a deep cut in his pristine lawn.
Bob struggles, eyes bulging.

I'm gonna explain a little bit right now, Junior says. And
here's the first part you need to know. Last year, a doctor
told my Dad he was dying of cancer. Like, a lot of cancer. But
Dad didn't tell me this. He just said let's go fishing in
Florida. Tells everybody the same thing. We're going fishing.
Like every year. A little early in the season. But an annual
trip just the same.

A year earlier, Senior Mazurski, aging but spry, as small
as Junior is huge, polishes the hood of his Cadillac. Junior
stows the green cooler in the gigantic trunk, alongside
various camping supplies.

Across the street, Officer Carroll rakes his lawn.

Have fun in Florida, fellas, Carroll yells. Send us a
postcard if you get a chance.

Hey, Carroll, come over here, Senior says. You'll get a
kick out of this. Senior leads him to the back of the Cadillac.
Written upside down, the plastic license plate frame reads: *If
You Can Read This, Flip Me Over!*

Both men laugh.

To Junior, it was only a blink of an eye later that the
Cadillac is flying south, a bright blur of green sliding by the
huge, open windows, Senior happily prattling on as he rolls

his eyes.

The hole in the yard is growing larger. Junior keeps digging. Bob keeps struggling.

Whole way down, he goes on and on about, well, I don't know how to say this, Junior says. He had this sort of fascination with using, I mean, with, uhm, mulching people. Essentially. As fertilizer. Truth is, if you do it right, the perfect food for plants of all kinds. His favorite trivial subject, you could call it. Then one night, we'd fished all day, tired, and he tells me the thing, you know, about dying. His body was sick through and through. Then he starts in again talking about his yard. Only important things to my old man were me and this yard. All at once I knew what he meant. It all sort of clicked, what he wanted me to do. I didn't know he had a gun.

Beside a roaring fire in a Florida swamp, the Mazurskis relax after a dinner of cooked fish.

I love you, Son, Senior says.

I love you too, Dad, Junior says. Want another . . .

Senior Mazurski puts a revolver to his head and squeezes the trigger before Junior can even blink.

The next day, alongside the dazzling Florida water, Junior sets the cooler in the Cadillac trunk. Rusty jumps in the passenger seat. They head for home.

Soon, Junior mixes chemicals at home on his workbench, still in shock, suddenly noticing his blood-drenched gloves.

Now Bob is listening. Junior leans on his shovel.

I told people a gator got him, Junior says. Because most of him did end up that way. The bigger parts. Rest came back in the old fish cooler. Worked out good, space-wise. Just a little guy, my Dad.

Junior's shovel attacks the soil. He's getting upset and the hole is growing quickly.

We got here, Junior says. I followed his instructions. He just wanted to be a part of his yard. Part of the soil. And, man, does it work. Never grew this way out here before. Not like this. He'd've been so happy. Only problem is, something happened I don't think my Dad would have expected while I harvested his remains for plant food.

Junior's shovel pauses. Bob's eyes: What?

I liked it, Junior shrugs.

Ruth wanders through the front doors of the Police Station in the middle of a sleepy early shift, shivering in her housecoat. The bustling station barely notices her. Clutched in her hands, the items she found throughout the night. Ruth stands at the front desk and tries meekly to get someone's attention.

Excuse me, she says, clearing her throat. Excuse me. I'm looking for Officer Carroll. Excuse me.

It goes on like that for a while.

Then Ruth stops. She takes a deep breath, stomps her foot and finds the top of her lungs.

Hey, she yells. One of you bring me Officer Carroll! Now!

Locked in his bathroom, Carroll vomits over the toilet. Mrs. Carroll knocks, not in a sympathetic way.

There's somebody from the station here to see you, she says, and is gone.

He finds his face in the mirror and barely the strength to unlock the bathroom door.

Across the street, Junior loosens Bob's gag and goes back to digging.

There now, Junior says. That better? Obviously, you scream and I kill that little girl. That's just the way it is.

You said there's nobody around for miles, Bob says.

Just the same, Junior says. Shush.

My family, Bob says.

Don't worry about your family, Junior says.

Let this girl go, Bob says, feigning confidence.

Oh, she's in the right place at the right time, Junior says. Aren't you, honey? Can't tell Julie Carroll where to stand. You know, her Mom and Dad are good people. Put her in those fancy rehabs. So expensive they signed loans. Ruined their retirement. And they still take her back every time she runs off. No end of misery. These are quality people.

Junior digs on.

To look at it from the outside, though, this little girl couldn't have picked a worse time to get caught out late on a school night, Junior says. I only had about a paint can of the good stuff left in the shed. The last of this drifter I ran into who had it coming. That's another story. But you put yourself next in line for the soup, young lady. I mean, if Mr. Henderson hadn't come along.

Julie blinks, eyes foggy.

Great, Bob says. Fine. I get it. But I'm tired of this. You seem to have a plan. Let's hear it.

Junior reaches into his back pocket and finds Senior's revolver.

Good, Junior says. Back to business. I like that. I dig you, Bob, pun intended. I think, with the right pruning, you might just be a good guy. Get it? So here's what happens next. First, I'm going to untie you. Then you are going to take this pistol and shoot me dead.

In the Police Station's interrogation room, Ruth sits with her objects carefully placed on the table in front of her.

In street clothes, Officer Carroll wafts in with the Captain and others in tow.

Whoa there, sailor, Ruth chirps.

Her confidence catches Carroll off guard.

Sorry about that, Ruth, he says. Rough night. What have you got?

Two of these items are connected to missing people, the

Captain says. She says the glasses were found in the yard of a Chet Henderson, reported yesterday. The other is a photo of a guy named Bob Stubbs. Got the call on him when he didn't come home last night.

This one is important too, Ruth says. She hands Officer Carroll the plastic printed with *If You Can Read This.*

Carroll's eyes go wide.

I need a medical unit and all available cars rolling right now, he shouts.

No one moves. All eyes are on the Captain.

The Captain looks him over.

What are we talking about here, Carroll, he asks.

Officer Carroll digs a medicine vial from his pocket. His voice is even and his eyes are clear.

If I don't get this into my Daughter's arm in the next few hours, she'll fall into a coma and stay there for rest of a short life, he says. Please. There's no time. Across the street from my house. Let's go.

You heard the man, the Police Captain yells. Move!

Testing the ropes binding him to the chair, Bob warily studies Junior.

So, you want to give me that pistol in your hand right there so that I can shoot you dead, Bob says. That right?

Yes, Junior says.

Done, Bob says. Untie me and hand it over.

And then you'll make me a part of the soil.

I'll what, Bob asks.

Look, Junior says. If I'm going to end up the creepy guy up the street with bodies in his yard, fine. But I want to be a part of this ground. Like my Dad is a part of it. Not the same, but close enough for me. Please.

Fine, Bob says. Whatever. Give me the gun.

Wait, Junior says. Promise me.

No problem, Bob says. I promise. Give me the gun.

Yeah, but see, Junior says. I tried to trust you once. Didn't work out so well, did it?

Well, look, sorry about that, Bob says. But I understand what you're doing now. And I respect it. So let me have the gun.

Junior tucks the gun into his belt and unties Bob. Bob struggles to his feet.

I'm not worried, Junior says. I have a hunch you're gonna want to help me. Junior holds out a small padlock key.

Why, Bob asks. What's that?

It's the key to the padlock on that big freezer over there, Junior says.

A long, large, coffin-shaped, industrial freezer sits beside the house. It's locked tight.

So what, Bob asks.

So that old freezer's gonna make sure you split me open and spill me into this hole, Junior says.

How in the hell is it going to do that, Bob asks, growing frantic.

By running out of air soon with your Wife and Daughter inside, Junior says. I suggest you use the end of my shovel. I sharpened it for you early this morning, before I swung by to pick them up.

I don't understand, Bob says.

Junior places the key on his tongue and swallows.

A year earlier, Senior sits patiently in a colorful waiting room, flipping through a copy of *Boys' Life* magazine. He's not nearly as tall as the kids on the cover.

A Nurse approaches with a clipboard.

Mr. Manorski, she calls.

Senior grins.

May I bring my magazine, he asks. I'm not finished with the jumble.

The Nurse rolls her eyes.

Follow me, please, she says.

In the examining room, she hands him an intermediate-sized paper gown, covered in giraffes and pandas.

Leave your clothes here, she says. Mr . . .

Just call me Senior, he says. Please. After all these years. Senior.

He smiles. She gives him a blank look.

Fine, she says. Come on out whenever you're ready. Please leave your underclothes on this time.

Fine, he says. This time.

In only the gown, Senior obediently follows the Nurse through taking his blood pressure, weighing and other lab work. The more cross she is with him, the happier and more polite he becomes. Finally, she hands him a plastic cup, guiding him into a bathroom. He pops his head back out the door as she hustles away down the hallway.

Nurse, he says.

What is it now, she asks.

You didn't specify, he chimes. Want that regular or diet?

The crowded nearby waiting room rumbles with appreciation of a good, loud joke.

In the MRI room, as he slides into the gigantic machine, Senior suddenly doesn't find this all so funny anymore.

In a separate room, two Specialists examine Senior's results.

The masses are large, multiple and spreading, they agree.

At the back of the room, the Nurse is losing her favorite patient.

Now in his street clothes, Senior seems to grow smaller and smaller as he trudges down another long hallway to receive his fate from another Doctor in a white coat, whom he's never met.

Please shut the door, the Doctor says.

Later at a nearby bar, Junior's laughing with the Bartender. Senior slides up beside him. The Bartender sets them up with scotch without being asked.

Thank you kindly, Senior says.

I was just talking to Junior here about trimming my trees

this weekend, the Bartender says. How's that sound?

Sorry, Senior says. We're going fishing.

The next day, Junior slams the trunk lid shut on the Cadillac. Rusty and Senior climb in and they tear off down the street, pulling a small bass boat.

Along a wide, rural Florida road, the Cadillac barrels past endless swamps.

Junior drives as Senior prattles on, Rusty in the back seat, windows open, wind in their hair.

See, Senior says. The key would be getting the PH balance just right, because . . .

I know, I know, Junior says. Gross.

Gross, sure, I agree, Senior says. But interesting.

Junior shakes his head.

May we change the subject, please, he asks. I got it.

You got it, Senior says. But do you got it?

Junior looks over, suddenly concerned with no idea why. Senior yelps and points at the road. The old Cadillac screeches to a stop.

Two station wagons, both overflowing with kids and beach equipment, are entwined nose to nose in the middle of the road. The Kids are hanging out of every window as their furious Fathers argue violently.

Junior and Senior leap from the Cadillac.

The Mazurskis' eyes are fixed on gasoline pouring from beneath one of the cars and a small fire wafting from the other.

That's fuel, Senior says.

Junior is already at a full sprint, gathering an impressive amount of speed for a man his size.

I see it, he says.

The arguing Fathers don't notice as the Mazurskis pull their children from the vehicles.

Shut up and run, you morons, Senior shouts.

Junior is sprinting away, terrified kids piled on his shoulders and tucked under each arm. Senior drags away a smaller portion of the same.

The Fathers now close behind, they all barely reach the Cadillac, safe and sound, as the station wagons explode.

Later, in a dark roadside diner parking lot, Rusty sits patiently in the passenger seat of the Cadillac, wagging his tail and watching the Mazurskis through the restaurant window.

Junior is lost in his meal, hands still shaking.

What do they do now, he wonders out loud.

Senior slips strips of bacon into his napkin for Rusty.

Son, he says. Let me tell you something. When your Mother left, I had a pretty tough go of it. You were just little. Well, you were never little, but you know what I mean. After a while, I started to realize, and you know I'm not a spiritual man, that sometimes the world simply takes a weird bounce. The universe, I mean. Life. The things that happen. Anyway. You lays down your monies and you takes your chances, sure. But some things, you can't start and you can't stop. The only thing you can do is play those cards best you can.

Junior tosses another strip of bacon into Senior's napkin.

Come on, he says. Let's get to a motel. At this rate, we'll still be fishing by tomorrow.

Out in the car, Rusty watches them and waits patiently for his cut of the bacon.

The Mazurskis reach their Florida campsite around mid-morning. Junior grabs the green cooler from the truck. Senior hides his revolver under some papers in the glove box.

As Junior sets up camp, he watches his Dad pull on a hook-covered fishing cap and grabs his pole, staring at the water like he's a six-year-old.

Junior launches the boat off the trailer, and together, along with Rusty, the Mazurskis motor out across the glass-topped water.

Now outside their house, police and fire units mobilize,

pouring onto the street. They follow each other in a long, flashing row.

In the backyard, Bob rushes to the freezer.

You said not to worry about my family, Bob panics.

I lied, Junior says. Worry.

Bob claws at the lock.

What the hell is wrong with you, he screams.

You know, I'm doing both you and Julie a real favor here, Junior says.

Bob leaves the lock bloody.

Fuck you, buddy, Bob says.

Hey, Junior says. I could've juiced her. I should've, the little brat. But I didn't. I remember her as a descent little kid, and I believe in people. So now she goes through this and maybe next time she thinks twice before breaking her parents' hearts. Of course, you let me down and I put a bullet between her eyes.

Why me, Bob asks.

When Cathy hired me last week, I saw your picture on the fridge, Junior says. So happy. I thought, now, this is a guy with the world on a string. What I wouldn't give for your life. I mean that. I hope you appreciate that. And think of me next time you hug your family while considering whether or not to stick your prick in some lady on a coffee break.

Junior throws the gun at Bob's feet.

As the emergency vehicles swarm the asphalt in front of the Mazurski house, Stan arrives in his beat-up sedan. Carroll is already in Junior's driveway.

The upside-down writing across the broken plastic frame on the Cadillac's rear license plate says only: *Turn Me Over!* Carroll matches the missing: *If You Can Read This!*

Junior and Bob listen to the sirens. The gun is on the ground between them. Junior plops himself backward into the big hole in the lawn.

Bob, Junior says. Come on. Right? Come get your key.

Open that lid. Hug your child. Once those deputies get ahold of me, put me in a nice warm cell, with the crap I eat, we might not see that key for a month. And those guys running in here don't have the right tools to cut into that thing fast enough to get them air in time. It's double reinforced. Bob? Won't you do whatever it takes to save your family?

Out front, Stan pokes around among the growing crowd.

Anybody know what's going on here, he asks.

Hair tussled, no glasses, housecoat clinging, Ruth catches Stan's elbow. Their eyes meet.

I do, Stan, Ruth says. I do.

Both smile. Chemistry indeed.

A gunshot from the backyard startles everyone.

Officers draw their weapons as Carroll leads the charge into the house, front door wide open.

Julie, he shouts frantically. Julie!

Carroll and the rest burst into the backyard. He finds Julie and pulls the gag from her mouth.

Weapons drawn, Deputies pour in. The first thing that stops them is the smell. Quickly they realize Bob is dark red to the shoulders, digging deep into Junior as the giant's jaw falls slack, life gurgling out into a thick pool.

Down on the ground, buddy, the Captain shouts. Now!

Julie struggles to stop them.

Wait, she says.

Bob finds Junior's key.

Julie summons her strength.

Don't, she yells. Daddy! Don't shoot! Let him do this! Please! Please! It's important! Please! It's alright!

The Captain looks to Carroll, who looks to Julie, dismayed.

Carroll waves them all back, an eye on Bob as he readies his Daughter's syringe.

Weak-kneed, Bob stumbles to the freezer and finds the lock. He fumbles with the slick key.

PEOPLE MAKING DANGER

Across the yard, everyone holds their breath.
Bob throws opens the freezer lid and screams.

OPERATION DRAGONHEAD

A town confuses Army training exercises with an extraterrestrial invasion

Based on a true story.

Earth, 1959 . . .

A quaint little farmhouse in the middle of the night in the middle of America. Bottomless stars above endless vegetable fields. Remote, dark, and quiet, except for all the crickets and fireflies.

In a floral-print room at the top of a long, creaky set of stairs, a snoring Farmer sits up in bed, instantly alert, jostling his Wife.

Go back to sleep, Merl, she says. Whatever it is, you're dreaming.

Hush, he says. Hear that?

No, she says. Don't wake me up. Go to sleep.

The Farmer is on his feet in his nightshirt. He finds his shotgun under the bed.

Shhhhhh, he says. Gonna go look.

You stay away from that bottle, she yells as he creaks down the stairs, past the front door and down to the basement. Outside in the bright moonlight, something heavy hovers silently past the front windows.

In the musty basement, the Farmer pulls the cord on a naked lightbulb. He digs through a cluttered shelf above a grimy workbench and finds a liquor bottle. The bottle is empty, with a note stuck to it: *Go back to bed!*

Cursing under his breath, he pulls the cord and the bulb goes out. But the room's still lit. Bright light from outside pours through the basement windows, then flutters and goes out. The Farmer reaches for his gun.

He sneaks cautiously out the back door in just his long johns and hunting cap. He waits, listening. The crickets suddenly stop. Emptiness bears down on him. He whistles a little to test his own hearing.

Jittery hands on the gun, he creeps into the darkness. A few steps later, he stops again with a sudden lurch, listening. Nothing.

Hovering directly behind him, a plump flying saucer, about double the size of a big, round minivan. Slowly, the Farmer circles the farmyard, listening. The animals stare, wide-eyed and hushed.

The saucer circles with him, silent and out of sight. The Farmer shrugs, takes a deep breath and shuffles off to the barn.

The Farmer's Wife is almost back to sleep when the barn door bangs shut in the wind. She hauls herself out of bed, throwing open the window.

Merl, she hollers. Get away from that jug!

In a far corner of the barn, the Farmer already has the cork out of a big jug. He steams for a moment and takes the biggest pull he can manage.

Marching out in a huff, gun under his arm, fumbling with the heavy barn door, he turns . . .

You and your imagination, he shouts up at the window.

. . . and is nose to nose with the dark saucer. It begins to glow. He drops his gun. The light grows brighter and brighter. A huge flash, then darkness. The saucer is gone.

The Farmer's stunned Wife whispers, Merl?

Yeah, Merl whispers back.

Bring me that jug, she says.

On a middle floor of the Pentagon, a dozen shiny shoes clatter down a highly polished hallway.

In a large, mid-floor briefing room, various clocks and maps highlight locations around the world. Military Brass pours in and heads straight the coffee pots.

Alright, an Army General says. What is this all about?

An Admiral picks out a cruller from a long tray.

Army didn't call this meeting, he asks.

No, the Army General says. All I heard was Operation

Dragonhead, don't be late.

Hammertree's deal, an Air Force General says. Right?

Hammertree, the Admiral says. Always figured that crackpot for the looney bin.

Is that so, exclaims a muffled voice from beneath the table.

They all leap backwards as General Augustus T. Hammertree, a five-foot-tall brawler, hustles from beneath the table as if practicing a high school wrestling drill.

Excuse me, gentlemen, Hammertree says. I often surveil a room before making an entrance. Saved my life many times. Now, tell me. Would a crackpot do that? Precisely.

The Army General rolls his eyes, digging around the coffee pot area for some aspirin.

How may we help you, General, he asks.

Thank you for asking, but I can take the presentation from here, General, thank you, Hammertree says. Lights!

The lights go out and they find their chairs as a clanking projector churns to life. On the screen, a black and grey aerial photo marked Pough River Valley.

It is in times of relative peace, such as these, when we need our strength most, Hammertree says. Yes?

All grunt in agreement.

And it is the sharpest blade that cuts best, Hammertree says.

More agreement.

So, if you don't have somebody to attack, Hammertree says. Might as well attack yourself, am I right?

Say that one again, the Admiral says.

The filmstrip shows a small, bustling town on a lazy river.

What you see before you is an average, small, quiet mountain town, Hammertree says. American in every possible way.

The idyllic photos give way to detailed maps with swooping arrows, troop numbers and timetables.

And as such, the perfect target for a coordinated Communist attack, he says. This town is a hub for the entire region. Powered by its own local hydro-electric dam. A crossroads for rail, telephone and telegraph lines. Yet the enemy could secure this area without breaking a sweat. In a single night, planting their seed deep into the heartland. What makes the average Commie Red's blood sing more than that? So, the strong feeling among many of the executive staff is simply, why not make this an opportunity to keep citizens of fine communities, such as our little town here, on guard? I mean, in a deeply personal way, right down deep in their butt cracks. Always does folks good to leave a round in the chamber, just in case, figuratively speaking. Ike agrees with me that our vulnerabilities are certainly our weakest points. I have his complete faith in that. As a result, this confidential pubic information operation's aim is to win the hearts of the people by frightening their minds as best we can. Officially speaking, the White House fully agrees that it knows nothing about this whatsoever and is in no way involved, of course.

Clandestine nods pass all around in the flickering light. The screen now shows the drawings of the flag and uniforms of an imaginary country, called Aggressor.

Worked these up myself, Hammertree says.

Nice pen work, the Air Force General says.

Thank you, Hammertree says.

So, then, the Admiral wonders out loud. What is Aggressor?

Next on the screen are the battle plans spliced with stock film clips of troop movements from several different real wars and a few classic feature films, as well as actual aerial photos of the town.

A fake Commie country gives folks something to focus on, Hammertree says. Name worked well with focus groups. As you see here, we will descend upon this valley with an overwhelming force. Secure the town, the dam and power plant, the rail yard and so forth. Standard infantry protocol, full air, ground, and tactical, atomic support. All the usual stuff. Then we'll have the local press in to let them witness the devastating swiftness of a potential enemy attack. Next day, the Eighty-Second Airborne will liberate the area. Got a real nice parade planned. And so forth. Questions?

One off the top of my head, the Air Force General says. What about the people?

Hammertree's confused.

People, he says. What people?

The ones that live there, the Admiral says.

This is the farthest thing from Hammertree's mind.

Right, right, he says. Only the Mayor and city government are aware of this exercise. The element of surprise is key. Those weasels in Congress have got to understand. We need more funding. We need more futuristic technology. We need the whole country behind us on this. So, these people? I hope these people of yours crap their pants, General. I sincerely do. Though we will try our best not to shoot them. Naturally.

Yes, the Army General says. Naturally. What sort of futuristic technology?

The lights go on. Startled, the Generals jump in their chairs.

Hammertree now wears a large, round helmet with pointy, metal antennas. Face hidden behind dark plastic, he looks like a metal-headed bug-man.

Beside Hammertree stands Dr. Eugene Percival in a starched lab coat with a big name tag. He grins, eyes wide, mouth open. Insane, but only a little.

Perhaps I should explain, Doctor Percival says.

Whoa, the Air Force General says. When did this guy get here?

Doctor Percival licks his lips and ignores him.

General Hammertree now wears a communications helmet like none other in the world, Percival says. Except for the other ones I made for the Soldiers. Those are the same as this one.

Yes, the Admiral says. Go on.

Anyone wearing a transistor helmet may speak to anyone else wearing a transistor helmet, Percival says. The helmet acts as a gas mask. The helmet contains a day's supply of water. It can operate as a completely functional weather station. Several parts of the helmet may be eaten as food. The helmet contains three Lucky Strike cigarettes, which ignite only upon specific verbal command. There is a hook in the back for storage and opening bottles. It also plays your favorite music.

Percival flips a dial on the helmet and festive music plays.

Looks heavy, the Army General says.

It is, Percival says. Very.

They all exchange impressed nods.

Is it bulletproof, the Admiral asks.

Could be, Percival says. If you aim at it right.

Hammertree removes the helmet and turns off the music.

Well, we'd love to chat all day, ladies, but we attack at dawn, he says.

This operation, whatever it is, the Army General says. It's already on the books? Then why tell us?

Hammertree glares back at them.

Oh, well, I mean, secret mission and all, Hammertree says. Got to tell somebody.

He and Percival rush out. The door closes.

I don't know, fellas, the Marine General says. Would a crackpot do that?

Tell you what, the Army General says. You go tell Ike he picked the wrong guy. We'll wait here. Good luck. Meanwhile, want to watch the movie again?

They do.

Several states away, a tall brick smokestack reads *Home of Pough River Pants*. The sun shines across tidy rows of tiny houses, a store and a school. A Teacher rings the morning bell. Trucks hum through the gates. Workers load raw materials into one end of the Mill and pull heavy crates out the other. Huge windows overlook the workers and the wide, slow river. Henry's Father listens carefully to a squawking telephone receiver.

Yes, he says, patiently.

Henry's Mother hovers at the office door, pencils sticking from her hair. She sees his concern.

Of course, he says. Alright.

She paces as he hangs up.

Another one, she asks.

Our button and zipper man, he says. Called in the whole note.

I don't understand, she says. We always pay on time.

Said he's sorry, Henry's Father says. Said it came right from the top. His Wife has your pie pan.

I'll go by after church, she says. But this can't be. We pay on time. Always on time. Always.

Please don't worry, he says.

Passed worry miles and miles ago, she says. What do we do now?

Get everybody together, he says. I'll find something or other to say.

Across the street from Poughville City Hall, a corner diner hums with a happy breakfast crowd. Darlene sits at the counter. She's the Mayor's only assistant and de facto Chief of Staff, dressed ten years past her age. She studies a dusty ledger covered in miniature, scribbled numbers.

Merva, the diner owner and head cook, whirls out of the kitchen. She's got a spatula in one hand and a coffee pot in the other.

My, my, Merva says, filling Darlene's cup. Only a year out of high school and practically running City Hall already. I swear, I don't know what the Mayor did without you.

I'm sure he did fine, Darlene says. But when they made Little Jim Finty treasurer in this town, Grover Cleveland was president. When they buried him last week, he took any idea how to read this pigeon scratch with him. Mayor's worried. Thought I'd take a look.

Well, anyway, much luck, Merva says.

Thanks, Darlene says.

No, I mean to say congratulations, Merva says, not enjoying the taste of her words. Sorry. Been meaning to say. Congratulations. I'm sure you and big dumb tubby are gonna be so very happy together.

Darlene sips her coffee.

I take it you don't think Charlie's good for me, she asks.

No, and neither's bacon fat, Merva says. I like Charlie Potatoes just fine. But he's been working on you since the second grade. So, why now? This's not how your story ends, lady. I'm sorry, but Charlie . . .

Is here, Merva, Darlene says. Charlie's here. And that happens to be what I like about him.

Outside of town, a good-sized green turtle contemplates a wide dirt road, then goes for it. A half mile away, a Backwoods Hunter in an old pickup rounds a corner, bouncing along at top speed.

Behind him in the truck bed, a set of big bumps send a guitar case, then a duffle bag, high into the air. The next bump is Henry, same school class as Darlene. The three trade positions like a juggling act.

By now, the turtle is in the middle of the road, truck hurtling closer. Rusty brakes lock. Bald tires slide. The turtle braces for impact. The wheels stop just short.

Relieved, the turtle carries on.

Henry gathers his things, hops from the truck bed and knocks on the window.

Thanks, Henry says.

The Hunter is shocked to see him as he winds down the

window.

Who are you, he asks.

You gave me a ride, Henry says. About fifty miles ago.

Thought you fell out, the Hunter says, climbing out of the truck.

I did, Henry says. Couple times.

Well, here you are, the Hunter says. To the Mill, you said, right?

They are stopped at a sign that says *Mill Road*.

Yeah, Henry says. But if you didn't know I was back there, why'd you stop?

The Hunter picks up the turtle and tucks it under his arm.

Soup, he says.

Inside the fabric Mill loading dock, the Workers fill the floor and balconies.

A long while ago, before Henry was born, Mother and I were fortunate enough to buy out our partners in this proud fabric company, Henry's Father tells them. Some wanted to cut corners a bit. But you people are our family. And making pants, shirts, fabric belts, curtains, tents, and other valuable necessities is our life. So, I'm sorry say . . .

He's chocking up. Henry's Mother puts her arm around him.

Courage now, dear, she says.

As of this morning, the Mill is closed, he says to an audible gasp. You'll all get pay for the month. And you all can stay on in the village until the land is sold. We'll keep the school open. But this is that and . . . That's the end of that.

A shudder runs through the crowd.

We borrowed a bit to buy the new equipment a few summers ago, Henry's Mother says. It was time. Couldn't keep up any other way. Last week the bank called that note in. It was unexpected, but we do carry a cushion for such emergencies. Now it's our suppliers too. One by one. Every inch of credit. No explanation why, but it doesn't really matter. This cleans us out. I don't know what to say, except we shook hands with the wrong folks and we take full responsibility.

To keep us going even another week, we'd have to fill a month's worth of orders by tomorrow morning, Henry's Father says. And after that we'd be right back here again. There's been somebody after us for the equipment. Sure showed up at the right time. I'm going up to give them a call.

Upset mutters fill the giant room. Henry climbs up onto the loading dock and drops his bag. His best friend Buddy grows a giant grin.

Hey there, Henry, Buddy says. Have a good trip?

Yep, Henry says. Why the long faces?

All turn, excited to greet Henry.

Hi Ma, Henry waves.

Got orders but not enough time, I guess, Buddy says. Gotta close the Mill.

Orders, Henry says. By when?

Morning, Buddy says.

Well then, Henry says. Let's make some pants!

Son, you don't understand, his Father says.

About what, Henry asks.

How much we're talking about, his Father says.

So, Henry says. How much is that?

Too much, his Mother says.

Too much, Henry says. Well, I've never heard of that, Pop. What are we going to do? Just stand here? How about this? Who's with me?

The crowd is eager.

All right then, Henry's Father says. Let's get to work.

The Mill jumps to life. Henry gives his Mom a big hug.

Welcome home, she says. We missed you.

I better get moving, Henry says.

You're damn right you better, his Father says.

The next day, after the sun rises and while the town still sleeps, the Mill still hums with life. Across the river, high on the hillside, is a towering mansion. Overly ornate landscaping rolls all the way up to an oversized, bronze door knocker with a plaque that reads *Maison de Tuber*.

On the second-floor balcony of the Potato Mansion, patriotic music plays from a huge and ancient radio.

Friends, thunders the big speaker. *I don't have to tell you, these are troubling times.*

Charlie Potatoes, same high school class as Darlene, Buddy and Henry, over-stuffing a bright blue suit, sweeps the skies with binoculars. He works hard to mimic his Father's every gesture. An oversized kid in adult clothes.

Nothing yet, Daddy, Charlie says.

Big Daddy Potatoes is older and larger than his years, with a muscled Male Nurse pushing his struggling wheelchair. Big Daddy generally has a scotch in one hand and a cigar in the other.

Quiet, boy, Big Daddy says. I'm listening here.

Yes, friends, booms a deep voice on the big radio. *As you can plainly tell from these headlines, and more, that fill this big city opinion page, those lashing out at me are attacking you as well. These naysayers. This so-called common good and it's self-appointed representatives aiming to pocket your hard-earned dollar at the end of your long working day. Never forget, it could take no more than one day, that's twenty-four hours, my friends, for a complete collapse of society as we know it to begin in full. Directly before our very eyes. So, remain vigilant. The enemy is among us. Meanwhile, yes, do have heart. I will not stand for this! And you do not stand alone. You have my word. And, folks, mine still means something. Bank on that! And I do all my banking at the United Bank Of The Commonwealth. Trust no other than the down-home UBOTC.*

More music swells. Charlie swings the binoculars across the horizon.

Wait, he says, hopefully. Maybe. No. Never mind.

Quiet, you dummy, Big Daddy says.

Sorry, friends, that's all our time today, the radio says. *But if you're with me, I'll see you here next week for our sunrise meeting. Everybody else? Well, we'll go on and let the Good Lord sort them out. And now let's have the Pure Biscuit Barrel Flour Ladies' Choir leave us in song. One of my favorites. I hope yours too. Oh, and don't forget, those raffle tickets sure are selling fast, so do get your dollars in the mail today!*

A shrill choir begins. The big-armed Nurse turns off the radio.

That was a fine one, Big Daddy says. Give me those.

Charlie carefully trots over with the binoculars.

He sure is right, Charlie says. These days it's us versus them.

The Nurse freshens Big Daddy's drink, relights the cigar, then holds up the binoculars for him.

Shut up, Big Daddy says. Listen to that quiet. The moment before the attack. Boy, remember this moment. An Army base in this town is the start of everything we've deserved all these years. All those hungry mouths to feed. All those new, off-base houses. Think of all the shopping wives! And then they'll simply be forced to move that freeway closer. No choice. National security, after all. That'd show them fools at the state capital to laugh at me. Maybe even run the damn thing right through the center of town if I want them to. Think of it.

I am, Daddy, Charlie says. I'm thinking about it right now.

This exercise's just a big terrain test, that's all, Big Daddy says. Got to be. To try our little valley on for size. Sure. About time, too. I've spread enough money around Washington over the years. Hold on. What's that?

Big Daddy points. His Nurse swings his chair to peer across the river at the Mill, humming with life.

That damn pants factory seems awfully busy this

morning, Charles, Big Daddy says, blood pressure rising. Did you make the calls, as I asked?

Calls, Charlie asks.

The calls, Big Daddy says. About the Mill.

Oh, those calls, Charlie says. Every one of them. Even found a guy to buy off their old equipment.

Equipment, Big Daddy says. What do I care about their equipment? Throw it in the river. Charlie, come here, boy.

Charlie proudly scoots over.

I, I figured it'd help them hurry along, Charlie says. Don't worry, they'll only offer pennies on the dollar, Daddy. Say, that kind of rhymes backwards. Dollar. Daddy.

Big Daddy grits his teeth.

Listen to me, he says. Since this damn federal subpoena and subsequent investigation, I've had to rely on you more and more around here.

Yes, Daddy, Charlie says hopefully.

But there's something I need you to do most of all, Big Daddy says. Something important.

I can handle it, Daddy, Charlie says.

And seeing as a big chunk of this is on your shoulders, Big Daddy says. I mean, you really need to get in there and bring this thing home, Son. So, for me, please . . .

Big Daddy never calls Charlie Son. For Charlie it is a singular and touching moment.

Yes, Daddy, Charlie says, leaning in close. I'm ready. What is it?

Well, Big Daddy says. Could you at least try to fake not stupid? Just for today. It's important, that's all.

I'll try, Daddy, Charlie says.

That's my boy, Big Daddy says. Though, all I can see from here is people making pants. So, tell me now. Can you not handle this, you dummy?

Charlie straightens his tie and stews a bit more.

I'm working on it, Daddy, Charlie says.

Big Daddy motions to be wheeled away by the Nurse.

What a relief, he mumbles into his drink. He's working on it.

Mill Workers pack trucks close to bursting with crates of pants. They disappear one by one into the dawn.

Henry's Mother finds him in a packing room, asleep on a pile of odds and ends in a dark corner. She hangs a new pair of pants over a chair.

Hey, Ma, he says. What's the count? Did we make enough?

You called it, little bear, she says. This'll buy us time. Sleep.

Nah, I'm up, Henry says. I'm up.

Henry's Mother hands him the new pants.

I made these for you special, she says. Those old things you're wearing are filthy. Looks like you wore them halfway around the world.

Oh, they went the whole way around, Henry says.

Seems you were gone so much longer than just a year, she says. Find what you were looking for?

I sure saw a lot, he says.

Don't I know it, she says, flipping on a light.

Pinned across the walls are postcards Henry sent from his travels around the world. Historic places and monuments of every size. Seaports to mountains. Skylines, beaches, carnivals, and smiling faces.

Now, will you look at that, he says.

I started this with the ones you sent me, she says. Then other folks put theirs up too. We all like to take a look in here from time to time. Kind of like we all went with you. So we don't miss you so much.

That's terrific, Henry says. But aren't Darlene's here too?

Oh, well you know, she's busy, his Mother says. Works full time for the Mayor now. Started right after you left.

Can't wait to see her, Henry says.

Lot changes in a year, you know, she says. So much more

now that you kids are all grown. Some thought, once you found the world, you'd never come back.

Well, here I am, Henry says.

On a ridge above the town, General Hammertree, Percival and their Office Staff blink through heavy binoculars, none wearing the experimental communication helmets.

Hand me that thing, Hammertree says. Doctor Percival passes him an oversized radio receiver.

Men, Hammertree begins and stops. Doesn't seem to be working.

Push the button, Percival says.

Which button, Hammertree barks without looking.

There is only one button, Percival says patiently.

Hammertree glares at him and finds the single, bright red button on the receiver.

Stuffed into trucks, tanks and airplanes, speakers in the Soldiers' oversized helmets crackle to life as they bounce toward town in full invasion gear.

Men, Hammertree's voice echoes. It is at times such as this your country needs you most. I'm proud of you. America's proud of you. So do not screw this up.

Hammertree hands back the receiver.

Touching, Percival says.

Attack, Hammertree says.

Breakfasts are cooking in the little village. The whirring machines are shutting down. Weary workers head home to sleep.

The Farmer, still in his long johns, stumbles up to them in the middle of the road. Hair on end, a wild look in his eye, he grips his empty jug for dear life.

Space aliens, the Farmer says.

Hey, Merl, Buddy says. You walk down all the way from your place?

Aliens, the Farmer says. From space. I saw them.
A crowd is forming.

Aw, sure you did, Buddy says. Come sleep it off at my place.

Flying saucer, the Farmer says. Came this close.

His eyes cross at the tip of his finger.

Come on, now, says one of the Mill Workers. Now why would we believe that?

Because I saw it too, the Farmer's Wife says, just as frazzled, only a few steps behind him.

Henry stands in the loading dock doorway, admiring his new pants. There is a roar of distant aircraft. He glances up and stops. Suddenly, from over the horizon, bombers and parachutes fill the sky.

By now the crowd is growing frenzied and panicked. Buddy returns at a sprint from his house. He holds a *True Science* comic book.

Hey, Buddy says. Did they look like this?

On the cover, a flying saucer. Emerging from the saucer, a space alien in a remarkably similar uniform and equipment to what the Army is wearing, with a round helmet and antennas.

Maybe, the Farmer says. But their spaceship was exactly like that one.

Henry runs up, more planes high above them. One parachute is far off course and heading for trees not far from the Mill.

It's a full-on invasion, the Farmer's Wife says.

Buddy, come on, Henry says.

Buddy jams the comic book in his pocket and follows him.

In the woods outside the Mill gates, an Army Paratrooper dangles just inches from the ground in a uniform with patches that have black lightning bolts instead of flags. His helmet is the same plastic bubble with aerial antennas poking from the sides. Disoriented, he flails a little, his parachute latches jammed.

Buddy and Henry peek from the bushes. They agree that the space alien on the magazine cover looks an awful lot like the Army Paratrooper dangling from the tree.

The Paratrooper reaches a boot knife, cuts his straps, and drops free. It takes a moment for him to climb to his feet, his helmet making him a little wobbly. He picks a direction and marches. Henry and Buddy follow.

The main road into town is a flood of troop trucks with big lightning bolts on the sides. All of the troops wear the same plastic bubbles with antennas. They also wear bulky backpacks and thick rubber gloves.

The lost Paratrooper waves down a truck. It stops to pick him up. Buddy and Henry hide in the bushes, studying the comic book.

It's space aliens alright, Buddy says.

Heading straight for Darlene, Henry says.

They run back toward the Mill.

In her office at City Hall, Darlene stares at a photograph on her desk. It is a picture of her and Charlie Potatoes, smiling beside a lake with a dangling fish.

A speaker box on her desk squawks: *Darlene? Have you seen my coat? I'm not wearing it and I don't remember taking it off.*

She pushes a button on the box.

Behind the door, Mayor, she says. Be there in a minute.

Darlene slides open a drawer. She finds a matching photo, same lake, similar fish, different year. This picture has Henry in it. She closes the drawer and goes to help the Mayor.

At the Mill, Henry and Buddy return, out of breath.

Close the gates, Henry shouts, and a handful of Mill Workers jump into action. The rest gather around Henry and Buddy.

It's aliens alright, Buddy says.

I don't know, his Father says. Could that possibly be, Henry?

Never seen anything like it, Henry says.

I have, Buddy says, waving his *True Science* comic book.

A helicopter swoops low over the Mill, dropping leaflets. Henry's Father grabs one.

You are now participating in a military exercise, he reads out loud. Stop what you are doing and proceed calmly to City Hall for further instructions.

It's a trick, Buddy says. A trap. So they don't waste time hunting us down. Diabolical.

This can't be, Henry's Mother says.

Whatever it is, keep those gates locked and lay low, Henry says. Buddy and I'll slip into town and see what's what.

Henry, no, she says.

Mother, let him go, his Father says. Everybody else, go grab what you need. We'll lock ourselves in the Mill. Go on, now. Let's move!

Tanks, jeeps with machine guns and crowded troop carriers roar through the center of town. More leaflets flutter down from choppers circling low overhead. As the trucks unload, the boots of Aggressor troops fill the streets, flooding out of nowhere, herding shocked citizens.

Loudspeakers on the helicopters repeat the same message: *Do not panic. Report to your City Hall. Do not panic. Report to your City Hall.*

Helmeted troops enter each house on one side and emerge shoving a sleepy-eyed family out the other. Soldiers block streets with barbed wire and pile sandbags on corners for machine-gun nests.

Buddy and Henry join the confused crowds.

In City Hall, Darlene helps the elderly Mayor on with his

coat.

I don't know, Darlene says. You should have told me about this first. Won't people be scared?

No, no, the Mayor says. Not at all. You think so?

Yes, I certainly do, she says.

Charlie bursts in.

Honey, they need the Mayor downstairs for pictures, he says.

Charlie, Darlene says. Give us a minute. Please.

Excuse me, Charlie grins. Miss Samuels, forgive me. Is his Mayorship ready to address the public?

Don't be sharp, Darlene says.

Charlie, the Mayor says, now concerned. Do you think this whole business will frighten people?

Not a bit, sir, Charlie says. They are going to love it. Who doesn't like a parade? Now let's go meet the General.

A real-life General, the Mayor says. How exciting!

Buddy and Henry push their way through the growing crowd and duck into the empty diner.

Henry, Merva says. Welcome home!

Hi Merva, Henry says.

I got your postcard, she says.

Saw the Eiffel Tower and right then thought of you, Henry says.

I am a French kind of classy, Merva says. Hey, what in the world is happening out there?

Buddy thinks it's aliens.

No, Buddy says. I know it's aliens.

Well, I'm glad you're back, she says. And don't worry about Darlene. There's still time. If you hurry.

This stops Henry cold.

Time before what, he asks.

The door bangs open and a row of Soldiers barge awkwardly into the confined space of the restaurant.

You are now participating in a military exercise, chants a radio frequency broadcasting through a tiny speaker mounted on the side of every helmet. *Stop what you are doing and proceed calmly to City Hall for further instructions.*

The Soldiers paw and shove them out the door.

Whatever they are, they're rude, Merva says.

Hold on, Henry says. Time before what?

At the curb in front of the diner, the Town Mechanic, in greasy coveralls, eyeballs an oversized Army Squad Leader and his complicated helmet.

What sort of contraption is that, he asks.

Doesn't concern you, the Squad Leader says through his mask with an electronic growl, his view an analog version of how a bee sees the world. Move along.

Never seen anything like it, says the Mechanic, reaching out to touch the helmet.

The Squad Leader catches him by the wrist.

I'm not surprised, the Squad Leader says. *Move. Along.*

Yeah, the Mechanic says, yanking his arm free. Got it. Geez.

A smaller convoy of armed vehicles rumbles toward them. An open jeep screeches to a halt, a loud speaker on the hood playing traditional marching music. General Hammertree and the Doctor climb out. As the Doctor stops the engine, the music warbles and falls silent.

Mayor, a pleasure, Hammertree says, putting out his hand.

Yes indeed, the Mayor says, saluting.

They switch, twice. Charlie is quickly between them.

Charles J.K.W. Potatoes Junior here, sir, Charlie says. President of the Chamber of Commerce. And, may I mention, a Senior Warden at the local Mason lodge. So, anything you need . . .

Charlie gives him a knowing wink along with an odd, wiggling hand signal. Hammertree has no idea what he's talking about and doesn't care. He brushes past Charlie on his way to a podium. Newspaper Reporters and Military

Press, in classic hats, coats and cameras, push forward.

Ladies and gentlemen, your nation thanks you for your cooperation today, Hammertree barks into the echoing microphone. This is a valuable opportunity for our fighting men to test new equipment and also stay sharp in the likely case of emergency and so on. But let's get to the point, here, shall we? Yes, this is a fine town with fine people living in it. Today we will tour your fine town and show the world how fine it really is. So that soon, America will realize how terrifyingly fast our small force conquered you without firing a shot. Think about that while resting in your comfy beds later tonight! I pray that you do.

The microphone squeals. The crowd is stunned.

Awkwardly, a military band begins. The General's Staff rushes him through the front doors of City Hall. Smiling, Charlie and the confused Mayor follow close behind. Henry spots Darlene. She looks very concerned.

Look, Henry says. There's Darlene! Let's go.

Yeah, Henry, Buddy says. About Darlene . . .

Suddenly, the Squad Leader towers over them.

Report to the big green tent beside City Hall for ice cream, hotdogs and currently popular films, the Squad Leader says.

They try to go around him. He moves with them, ready to strike.

I repeat, the Squad Leader says. *Report to the tent beside City Hall for ice cream, hotdogs and . . .*

Got it, pal, Buddy says. We're on our way there now. No problem here. Easy. Easy. Thanks a bunch.

They slip away with the crowd, the Squad Leader eyeing them closely in the helmet's bee-vision.

I have to talk to Darlene, Henry says.

Simmer down, Buddy says. How far are the two of us going to get, running in there all the sudden? I mean, look around. They've got everybody fooled but us, right?

The crowd follows the Soldiers.

Some of them have regular human heads, Henry says.

What about that?

Those are real humans, Buddy says. They always mind-zap a couple people, like top human leaders and a marching band. Can't do everybody, but the scam wouldn't work otherwise. Remember, first rule of Saucer People is, always have a master plan. And, from what I've seen, it's definitely going to be a weird one. We gotta find a weakness, quick.

Alright, Henry says. Follow me.

They fall out of line and dive into some bushes.

Inside City Hall, the General's Staff and the Press pour into the Mayor's office, flash bulbs popping. Hammertree's Staff, in neatly pressed uniforms, anticipate whatever the General may require. Though they don't wear communication helmets, they function as a single unit. If Hammertree's happy, they're happy. If he's sad, they're sad. Right now, they aim for stern and confident for the cameras.

Mister Mayor, Percival says. If you'll just take your seat, there. And sign this where notated.

The Staff hands the Mayor a document and pen. The General points sternly at the paper and squints a practiced smile for the cameras.

The Mayor adjusts his thick spectacles.

What is this, he asks.

Merely the official surrender, of course, Hammertree says. For the cameras.

He forces a laugh that doesn't carry.

The sovereign nation of Aggressor, the Mayor says, signing his name. Never heard of them.

That's the idea, Hammertree says. Pretty good name, I thought.

His Staff agrees.

The Mayor squints at the papers.

For a moment there, I thought you said surrender, the Mayor says.

Harmless, bureaucratic, technical jargon for the normal

legal mumbo jumbo and State Department red tape, Percival says, flipping through the pages and nudging the Mayor along. Great. And twice there at the bottom as well. Perfect, perfect. Now the date. Very strong upstroke, by the way. Says more than people think.

Dazzled by the flashbulbs, the Mayor signs in several places. Then more.

Whew, he says. That's all of them!

Alright, Hammertree says. Take him away.

The Soldiers seize the shocked Mayor, dragging him and Darlene from the room. The Press follows, cameras clicking.

Stop that, Darlene says. Let him go. What are you doing?

As I said before, ladies and gentlemen, Hammertree says. Without firing a shot. Thank you all for your cooperation.

When everyone is gone, Hammertree props his feet up on the Mayor's desk. As the door slowly closes, Charlie is hiding behind it.

Hold it right here, champ, Hammertree says, drawing his boot pistol.

Wait, Charlie squeaks. Wait! I'm on your side! A true patriot! I applaud what you are doing here in our region. I have something to offer . . .

Alright, Hammertree says. Go on. But I'll warn you, I've always wanted to strike down a bloody coup.

Duly noted, General, Charlie says, straightening his hair. I needed to warn you somehow. Your instincts are correct. There are subversive elements afoot.

Now Hammertree's listening.

Subversive, eh, he asks.

Yes, Charlie says, steadying himself. This little town's not at all what it seems. You will definitely need somebody you can trust.

Hammertree raises his eyebrows.

Are you sure, he asks.

Charlie raises his.

Are you not, he asks.

Excellent point, Hammertree says. Sit down.

Soldiers lead the Mayor and Darlene to a basement jail cell, Doctor Percival trailing close behind.

Darlene struggles.

Who said you could do this, she asks.

Your Mayor did, Percival says.

No, he did not, she says.

It was all a part of the paperwork he signed, Percival says. Near the bottom on the third page. Through our studies, we've found that gullible local leaders are a prominent fixture in today's modern cities.

This is ridiculous, Darlene says.

The cell door slams, leaving Percival glaring through the bars.

May I bring you hotdogs and ice cream, he asks. Our studies show that all good-hearted Americans enjoy hotdogs and ice cream.

One with mustard and also a scoop of chocolate, please, the Mayor says.

No, thank you, Darlene says.

And a lemonade, the Mayor says.

Hmmmm, Percival says, eying Darlene suspiciously as he leaves.

At the nearby rail yard, Soldiers in helmets line up to get their picture taken, all pointing seriously at a train car piled high with coal.

Mixed into the crowd, Henry and Buddy wear long coats and hats like the Reporters wear. Henry has an old camera. Buddy has a notepad.

These'll work great, Henry says. Like real newspaper and radio guys.

Great, Buddy says. But if the world doesn't end, we've got to get them back to my Aunt's store, or she'll skin me.

Charlie and Hammertree find a commanding spot on a

rail platform, Soldiers and Staff crowded behind them. They smile big for the cameras.

These are central transportation lines, leading to every state in every direction, Hammertree barks. Now that the town is secured, the Aggressor nation could use these rails to quickly move men and weapons wherever they want. With devastating results!

Next, at a large local farm, the group stands in a field, trampling corn. Henry and Buddy mix in with the onlookers.

Food grown in this valley feeds people across the nation, Charlie shouts from a trailer bed.

Hammertree elbows him from the center of attention.

A simple treasure that just simply fell into enemy hands, he yells. Meaning American children go hungry!

They both smile for the cameras.

Later, the group stands on the top of the towering concrete Hydroelectric Dam built into the mountains above town. The river trickles far below.

Our power generators feed thousands of homes, Charlie says quickly and backs away.

Exhausted from talking, Hammertree struggles to work up a good line.

Sure hate to lose her, he tones. Because . . . Because, you know, this is one darn fine dam!

This lands with a thud. The Reporters shuffle away. Charlie and the General fake a laugh, but it's clear their act is stale.

From a side tap in a large barrel on the back of one of the trucks, Soldiers pour water into little wax-paper cups for the Press and Staff.

Well, there they are, Buddy says. What do you think?

I'm still figuring, Henry says.

One water barrel tips and sloshes water over the side,

landing directly between a Soldier's antennas. The spray of water short circuits his helmet, sending sparks in every direction. A wave of interference travels between the Soldiers, stunning them with a burst of feedback.

Buddy grins at Henry.

How about now, he asks.

A crowd is forming. Doctor Percival runs to help. Hammertree is there first, leaning over the twitching Soldier.

Get that thing off him, Hammertree says.

They are locked in place until midnight, Percival says. It's part of the test. Trust me, he's fine. Only slightly electrocuted. If you go with it, it's sort of fun, actually.

Hammertree leans in, concerned.

So the prototype isn't waterproof, he asks.

That's why it's a prototype, Percival says.

Will this not be an operational problem, Hammertree asks.

The Soldier stops twitching.

Only if it rains, Percival says. There. See? The circuit resets automatically. All fine and dandy now.

Hang in there, kid, Hammertree says to the Soldier. There's a medal on the way to your Mother. Everyone else, back to town!

The Squad Leader watches Henry and Buddy, suspicious.

Hammertree stomps by, a fraction of the Soldier's size. I said get moving!

Yes, sir, the Squad Leader says, climbing into a truck that roars away.

First, back to the Mill to work out a plan, Henry says. Then we go get Darlene.

Yeah, Henry, Buddy says. About Darlene.

As Darlene paces in the holding cell, the Mayor tries to decipher a limerick scratched into the wall.

There once was a, oh, the Mayor says, and reads the rest to himself, intrigued.

Mayor, Darlene says. You like Charlie, right?

It takes the Mayor a moment to answer.

Charlie, the Mayor says. Our Charlie?

He can be very sweet, you know, she says.

Sure, I like Charlie, the Mayor says.

I thought so, Darlene says, for the moment, relieved.

But I like everybody, the Mayor says.

Beside the Mill loading dock, Buddy carefully draws the antenna helmet and lightening bolt insignia with chalk on the concrete. Everyone groups around, genuinely concerned.

They're lulling us into a false sense of security, Buddy says. By the time we wake up . . . Bang! They got us. Sneaky. Captain Stratosphere used to fight them all the time. He was one of the top Dynamic Heroes. But that's just silly kids' stuff. It was *True Science Illustrated* that broke the story on the real Saucer People. And those folks will tell you, this is a nasty bunch.

Tell me again what he calls them, Henry's Father says.

Saucer People, Henry's Mother says.

Buddy hands him the magazine, first flipping past sensational photographs and giant headlines to the part he's talking about.

I see, Henry's Father says.

Well, Buddy says. You don't think they just make this stuff up, do you?

Henry, his Mother says. What do you think?

Charlie Potatoes, Henry says.

Oh, Buddy, she says knowingly. You didn't tell him, did you?

Ma'am, somebody had to, Buddy says.

We were waiting for the right time, she says.

Mister and Missus Charlie Potatoes, Henry says.

He'll snap out of it, Buddy says. But I'm telling you, we got aliens and bunches of them. No one in town suspects a thing. They also could be using a mind ray. Hard to say.

The Mill Foreman is tired of standing around talking.

Alright, then, he says. What are we going to do about it?

Don't know, Buddy says. That's Henry's part.

They all turn to Henry, moping in a chair in the corner. He looks at them looking at him, thinks for a long moment, and pulls himself slowly to his feet.

Let's go stop some Saucer People, Henry says, still a little sad.

In the Mayor's office, Charlie has a map spread across the desk. He is boring Hammertree and his Staff to death.

. . . and as you can see, what we have here is a perfect location, Charlie says. In, as they say, the heart of the region. Self-powered, all tucked away up here in the mountains and yet completely connected to the world. Right over here is our high school . . .

Hammertree's daydreaming, studying the burning end of his cigar.

Wait, he says. To do what again?

Uhm, Charlie sputters. Build an Army base? I mean, military installation. Sir. You see. Right here near the river. Perfect spot. Perfect.

Charlie points to a spot currently occupied by the Mill.

Hammertree squints at the map.

What's that you got there, now, he asks. Looks industrial.

Yes, no, Charlie says. Nothing of consequence. Some sort of clothes Mill. I hear they're going out of business.

Hammertree leans across his desk.

So, he says. I look like the where-do-we-put-the-new-Army-bases guy to you?

Charlie shivers at the thought of failing Big Daddy.

Uhm, he tap dances. I mean, certainly a man such as yourself has some influence in these things. Perhaps we could discuss it more over a first-class dinner?

This perks up Hammertree.

First-class, he asks.

Charlie capitalizes.

Of course, he chirps. Daddy had his best cook from the hotel restaurant whip up something very special. And he sent over a bottle of brandy that belonged to town founder, C.M. Lesterhorn Potatoes, whom they also called Charlie! Or actually, Charles. That being his name and so forth . . .

Catching himself jabbering, Charlie fakes his best smile. Hammertree looks him over.

Tell you what, Hammertree says. I'll take the whole thing under advisement and I kindly accept your voluntary accommodations on behalf of a grateful nation. Alright? Alright.

Fantastic, Charlie says. I'll call Daddy. They shake hands. Charlie dances out of the room, a bit over-enthusiastic.

An odd duck, Hammertree says. But I like him.

In the City Hall basement, Darlene and the Mayor are still in their cell. Darlene paces. The Mayor snores in a bunk. Charlie creeps up to the bars.

Hello, kids, he says. How about some dinner?

Darlene isn't pleased.

Let us out, she says. Where have you been?

You bet, Charlie says. Guard?

A Soldier unlocks the door.

Darlene's suspicious of Charlie's sudden control of the situation.

What are you up to, she asks.

Not a thing, Charlie says, batting his eyes.

Now she's really not buying it.

Did you forget us down here, she asks.

I'm so sorry, Charlie says. They had to make a big show of things. I argued and argued. But they do have their orders. Regulations. Red tape. You know how it is.

No, Darlene says. How is it?

Honey, Charlie coos as best as he can manage. Come eat.

She stops him with an irritated look.

What are you up to, she asks.

Charlie smiles. With persistence, he can really charm her.

You already asked me that, he says.

Whatever it is, we're starved, she says. Come on, Mayor. Warden here says it's time for chow.

Night falls. Townspeople fill a large green tent built on the town square, across the street from City Hall. Happy voices and music tumble out from under the flaps. Soldiers stand guard at the entrances. Trucks and tanks thunder past on constant patrol.

Inside, a sci-fi monster movie plays on a screen at one end of the tent, complete with flying saucers and rubber space aliens. At the other end, Townsfolk dance to a record player, eating hotdogs and ice cream.

Henry leads a handful of Mill Workers toward the tent entrance.

Alright, folks, this is it, Henry says. Everybody knows what to do?

The group nods. Soldiers swarm around them. It's tough to tell which Soldier is talking.

Where were you, one of them asks through his fuzzy helmet speaker.

Funniest thing, Henry says. Our knitting circle meets in the church basement. Got to four-stitching and plumb missed the whole darn deal. Get it? Darn.

Henry grins as the Soldiers open tent flaps and hustle them inside.

At the head of a long table in City Hall's formal dining room, Hammertree is in the middle of a well-worn war story. Percival, Doreen, Charlie and the Mayor pick from a giant feast and politely listen.

. . . which is how I lost my big toe, Hammertree tones. But where was I? Oh, yes, battlefield dysentery . . .

The Mayor jumps in to change the subject.

General, he says. In a couple weeks, the kids here are getting married!

Married, Hammertree grumbles. And so young, yet. Well, congratulations and so forth. Not that type, myself. Men like myself and the Doctor, I'd say we're married to our work.

Oh, I'm happily married, Percival chimes, a large glass of wine getting to his head a little. Lovely gal. My high school sweetheart.

You're married, Hammertree asks. All these years?

Very happily, Percival says. We never, ever speak.

Darlene and I are having one of those big, pricey church weddings, Charlie says. And then right off to Niagara Falls. First class all the way. Isn't that right, sweetheart?

Sure, Darlene says, focused on her own glass of wine, not as sure about it as he is.

Mayor, Hammertree says. Would you be interested at all in joining me for a cigar?

Sorry, don't touch them, the Mayor says.

Charlie reaches into his pocket and finds two large cigars.

I was about to have one myself, he says.

This is the after-dinner company Hammertree hoped to avoid.

Terrific, he says. Really? No one else for cigars? No? Alright, then. Fine.

Inside the big tent, Mill Workers hunker down in different groups around the room, spreading the word about aliens invading their town.

Henry is surrounded by Firemen.

Wait, he says. Then who's over at the Firehouse now?

Rufus'll bark if there's trouble, the Fire Chief says.

Nearby, Buddy huddles dramatically with another group.

Now, don't panic, he says. Don't scream. Don't even blink an eye. But I'm here to tell you, your very living lives are all in terrible danger!

My goodness, the Town Barber says. That's all there in

your picture book?

Page fourteen, Buddy says, pointing. See for yourself.

The Barber flips through Buddy's magazine. The print and pictures clearly outline what Buddy is telling them.

That's what it says alright, the Barber says.

Amid the chaos of the huge tent, nobody in their little group blinks, frozen in terror.

Now listen up, Buddy says. Henry's got a plan. So, nobody panic.

Soon, Buddy and Henry meet in the middle of the tent floor as whispers and panic spread through the crowd.

Guess it's all or nothing now, Henry says. Ready?

Henry, Buddy says, placing a comforting hand on his friend's shoulder. In this life, everyone is given one very special skill. Something they do better than anybody else. This here, what I'm about to do, is mine.

True enough, Henry says. Good luck.

Buddy limbers up.

Pal, he says. I don't need it.

They head off in different directions.

While the music thumps inside the tent, the Soldiers outside look bored. Suddenly, arms flailing, Buddy runs from the tent in only his underpants, whooping at the top of his lungs. Confused Soldiers chase him in circles.

Henry and the Firemen sneak out the back of the tent.

Still a little tipsy in the City Hall Map Room, Percival studies historic, regional maps lining the walls. Darlene frets over a large model of the entire town, complete with the railroads and hydroelectric dam. The Mayor snores on a chair in the corner.

I am fascinated by your mountain life, Percival says. But there is nothing like the desert at night. Our work, our research, the General and mine, it requires we be there. But I'd stay anyway.

I would have thought attacking small towns was your

full-time job, Darlene says.

No, no, Percival says. Not at all. Politics and games. Such a waste of time. No. The General and I, our main mission is a more important one.

Oh, I see, Darlene says. Feeding starving people?

No, he says. I cannot speak of the details.

Oh, something medical, she says. Curing a disease?

Percival is getting steamed.

No, he says. Nothing like that.

Oh, I see, Darlene says. You men clean water for poor kids.

Young lady, Percival says. There will be a day, very soon, in the not-too-distant future, when our world is attacked by another. Our overall mission is focused in this area. In fact, you might go ahead and thank me right now.

Happy to, Darlene says. Except, what am I thankful for, again?

Oh, you'll see, Percival says.

You mean, like, another planet, Darlene says. Like Mars?

Who has spoken to you about Mars, he sputters.

Mars, why, no one, she says, egging him on. Why do you ask?

Percival eyes her suspiciously.

No reason, he says. Though, may I add, for your sake, please do keep it that way.

Along a marble balcony on the City Hall roof, Hammertree holds an unlit cigar as Charlie chatters along.

. . . how the people of our proud county would prosper if only that section of freeway was but a few miles closer, Charlie says. All my Daddy is suggesting is that perhaps your friends in Washington could . . .

Hammertree's eyes glaze over.

Got a light, he asks.

Of course, Charlie says, patting his pockets and finding nothing.

Let me guess, Hammertree says. No match.

No, Charlie admits sheepishly, dashing off. Wait here. I'll go find us one.

When he's gone, Hammertree chuckles and lights his cigar with a fancy, oversized lighter from his pocket, sauntering across the roof, looking proudly over the town, the floodlights, the Soldiers, the trucks, and tanks.

Now hovering directly behind him, out of sight of both the ground and Hammertree, is the dark, bulbous, SUV-sized flying saucer.

A couple blocks over, across the street from the Firehouse, Henry and the Firemen hide in the bushes. Blocking their path, a huge, idling tank.

What now, the Fire Chief asks Henry.

Guess I'll go talk to that tank, Henry says, popping up and striding into the street.

The tank turret turns with surprise, like the head of a great elephant.

Hello, the big, green loudspeaker between the floodlight and machine gun announces. *You are outside the designated area. You must report to your City Hall for instructions. Immediately.*

Henry stands on his toes and speaks directly into the barrel.

You bet, Henry says. No problem.

He walks the wrong way. The heavy barrel follows him.

You are now going the wrong way, the tank loudspeaker says.

No, I'm not, Henry says.

A mumbling conference inside the tank, echoes through the loudspeaker. Meanwhile, the Firemen sneak one at a time across the street.

Yes, the tank loudspeaker says. *You are in fact traveling in the incorrect direction.*

Sounds good, Henry says with a wave, continuing in the

wrong direction.

The big, green tank follows like an oversized puppy.

Halt, the tank speaker says.

You said go to my City Hall, Henry says. Right?

Yes, the Loudspeaker says. *Poughville City Hall is due east of this position.*

Exactly, Henry says. See, I'm from Albertsville. My City Hall's this way. I get what you're getting at now. My mistake. Sorry to be a bother. Here I go. Have a good night, now.

Henry again walks the wrong way. The tank lurches behind him.

Halt, the tank loudspeaker says. *Proceed to the nearest City Hall. Now. Please.*

Hearing please, Henry stops.

Alright, then, he says. But so that I have it right. That one over by there or this other one right near here?

This one, the loudspeaker says. *Wait. Hold on. Yes, this one.*

Ah, Henry says. See, I thought you meant that's the other one. Sorry for the mix up. Have a good night.

Henry again walks the wrong way. The tank rolls forward with him. A hatch pops open on top of the tank. A frustrated Tank Commander pops out, antennas twitching, and points.

Go that way, the Tank Commander says through his helmet. *Now.*

Sure, Henry says. How far?

The Tank Commander pauses and is handed the map from below.

Give me a moment, he says, studying the map.

From inside the Fire House, a fire engine roars to life and leaps into the street. Henry jumps on as the truck passes the tank.

Never mind, Henry yells. I'll just ride with these fellas.

The shocked Tank Commander drops his map.

Inside City Hall, Darlene catches Charlie rifling through

her desk.

Looking for something, she asks.

A match, Charlie says.

Sorry, Charlie, she says. I think I quit.

Quit, Charlie says, suddenly worried from her tone. Quit what?

Smoking, she says, and doesn't mean smoking. I quit smoking.

Nonsense, Charlie says. The higher quality smoke soothes gently and naturally loosens phlegm. What? You like being full of phlegm? Not me.

He keeps digging through her desk.

Come here, she says. Look me in the eye.

I'm a little busy right now, he says, searching.

She's serious.

Fine, he says. What?

They stand eye to eye.

You say a lot of words, Charlie Potatoes, Darlene says. Do you ever mean any of them?

Charlie grins darkly and holds up the picture of Darlene and Henry.

Now who's asking who now, Charlie says. And about what?

Fine, she says. Now stay out of people's desks.

This chump is gone, Darlene, Charlie says, holding up Henry's photograph. Long gone. Left all of us. So now let him go. Alright already?

I know, she says, reaching for the photo. He tucks it in his jacket pocket.

No, no, he says. You won't be needing this. Believe me.

Darlene puts out her hand.

Charlie, she says.

He returns the picture.

Fine, he says. But I think it's high time for all of us to appreciate all the great things we've got right here.

She kisses him gently. His face turns red as a beet.

I'll admit it, Darlene says. You can be sweet when you want to.

Fire sirens wail in the distance.

You bet, he says, easily distracted. Hey, what's that?

Outside, the fire engine roars around a corner on two wheels, dodging barbed wire, water hoses spraying like machine guns. Henry points the way. Buddy runs past in his underwear, Soldiers close behind.

This's it, everybody, Buddy shouts. To the Mill!

The huge tent suddenly empties, Townsfolk fleeing in every direction. At first, the Soldiers scramble to catch them. Then water from the fire truck hits the first set of antennas. Feedback screeches between their helmets, dropping them to the ground.

Percival bursts onto the City Hall roof. The squelching sound of chaos rising from the street below.

General, he says. We are . . .

He finds Hammertree frozen, eyes wide, nose to nose with the dark floating saucer as it begins to glow.

I knew it, Hammertree says, ecstatic.

Flash. Darkness.

When Hammertree opens his eyes again, he's flat on his back. Percival leans over him, stars bright in the sky. Hammertree sits up, vindicated.

Doctor, he says. Was that . . . A real one?

Yes, sir, Percival says, his eyes welling with pride. That was a verifiable twelve-eleven. Or as you would say, sir, a genuine, dang-old, intergalactic twelve-eleven!

In the City Map Room, the Mayor still naps in the corner. Charlie and Darlene burst in, Hammertree and the Doctor close behind.

Hammertree's Staff stands over a twitching Soldier clutching his helmet.

It kind of tingles, he says.

We are under attack, Hammertree yells. Huddle up!

They circle around the model of the town. Percival throws open a thick binder packed with diagrams and instructions.

This town is infected, Percival says. Protocol one . . . Begin!

Percival, Hammertree and the Staff pull pen-syringes from their pockets. One by one, they plunge them into their own legs, dancing with pain.

Vaccination of key personnel complete, Percival declares. Now we immediately retreat to a secure area. And I suppose that includes the rest of you as well.

Gee, thanks, Darlene says. What's happening?

Lady, Hammertree says. You happen to be looking at the nation's top anti-alien invasion experts. Nothing short of divine intervention brought us here today.

Wait, Darlene says. Is this that Mars thing?

Hammertree eyes her suspiciously.

Who talked to you about Mars, he whispers harshly.

Don't worry, Percival says. She knows nothing.

Henry jumps from the spraying fire engine and rushes past the twitching Soldiers on his way into City Hall. As the water runs out, the hoses fall dead. The siren stops as the fire engine flees into the night.

When their helmets return to normal, dizzy Soldiers begin picking themselves up off the pavement.

Fighting to stand, the Squad Leader chases after Henry.

Inside, Henry hurries through the halls, finding the door he's looking for locked tight. He tries the next door. It opens, but is only a janitor's closet.

The Squad Leader blocks the hallway behind him.

This whole floor's secured, the Squad Leader says, moving forward. *You are completely trapped. I got you.*

Part right, Henry says. Part wrong.

Henry backtracks down the hall, still trying doorknobs. All locked. The distance is closing between them.

I'm the whole way right, the Squad Leader says. *I got you.*

Nope, Henry says. Too slow.

Henry takes off running. The Squad Leader chases him like a rabbit. The hallways lead them in a loop. No way out. They run faster and faster, turning corner after corner. The Squad Leader pushes harder and harder, thundering behind Henry, building momentum.

As they round a corner on the last lap, Henry doesn't turn. Instead, he aims for a dead end with a locked door. Neither slows down.

Got . . . You . . . Now, the Squad Leader says.

Henry grabs a doorknob and swings himself inside the janitor's closet. From the hallway, he hears pounding footsteps fighting to stop.

Wait, the Squad Leader yelps. *Wait! Wait!! Wait!!!*

Crash. Henry opens the door.

The Squad Leader took out the entire door frame at the end of the hall. Face down in the rubble, he groans. Henry hops over him.

Like I said, Henry says. Too slow.

In the map room, Darlene isn't buying Hammertree's story. He pounds the table, waking the Mayor.

You must trust our protocols, ma'am, Hammertree says. Your friends, your family, as you knew them, are gone. Take a moment to accept that. They might look the same, sound the same, but inside, you must believe me, they are horrible monsters programmed for your destruction.

Oh my, the Mayor says. What did I miss?

Let me take a look at these protocols of yours, she says.

Percival and Hammertree glare at her, guarding their overstuffed binder like jealous kids.

You're right about one thing, Charlie Fatpants, Hammertree says, waving a hand over the scale model of the town.

Potatoes, sir, Charlie says.

This is the perfect spot to start an invasion worldwide, Hammertree says. How about that. We were a step ahead of them all along!

Hammertree's Staff applauds.

Question, General, Charlie says. Do these aliens use our same kind of money? Or do they have their own kind of money?

Hammertree dramatically points out the Poughville Hydroelectric Dam on the scale model.

Alright, everybody, get it in gear, he growls. We're redeploying here.

The door flies open. It's Henry.

Darlene, Henry says.

Henry, she says.

You got to be kidding me, Charlie says.

Hold on, Hammertree says. Anybody know this boy?

Oh, my, yes, the Mayor says. Henry's finally home!

I'm here to save you, Henry says. I'll explain later. Right now, everybody, quick, follow me.

Henry grabs for Darlene's hand. Darlene slaps him hard.

I'm not going anywhere with you, she says.

Henry is confused and shocked. The Squad Leader stomps into the room and tackles Henry at full steam, pulling him into a painful wrestling hold.

It's one of them, sir, the Squad Leader says. *I have him now.*

Possibly a communist-zombie-alien hybrid, Percival says. A brand-new strain! Let's keep him to monitor! This is so exciting!

Fine, fine, whatever, Hammertree says. Now move out!

A stream of Townspeople rushes through the large Mill gates as Henry's parents wait to close them.

I think we scared them, Buddy says, pulling on some pants. A bunch piled into their trucks and took off.

Get inside, Henry's Father says. We're worried. Henry's not back yet.

Then he must be right behind us, Buddy says.

Army trucks rumble toward the Hydroelectric Dam high above the town.

Hands and feet tied, Henry bounces along in the back of a troop truck with a handful of Soldiers. Most are joking and goofing off. The Squad Leader is focused on Henry.

Smoke if you got 'em, boys, says one Soldier. Lucky Strike!

On his voice command, a lighter clicks inside his helmet and suddenly smoke curls from the vents.

Good idea, says another. Lucky Strike!

Smoke rises from their helmets.

Say, this isn't so bad, the first one says. Stings the eyes a little. But so very smooth.

Henry struggles to free himself from the ropes. Too tight. The Squad Leader isn't smoking. He glares at Henry from deep inside his helmet.

The truck convoy stops on the long, thin road across the top of the Dam, many stories from the rocks below. Troops pour out. Hammertree and Percival oversee the chaos as Soldiers wheel a giant wooden crate off the back of a truck.

Careful, Percival yells. Careful!

Soldiers drop the box the last few inches with a heavy bang. The General and the Doctor brace for impact. Nothing. They take a breath.

Inside the Dam Control Room, Henry sits locked in a glass-walled office. He looks so sad, he could die. The Squad Leader stands guard. Darlene and the Mayor pace frantically. Hammertree bursts in with his Staff.

You can't keep us here, Darlene says.

Could somebody find something to calm these folks' nerves, please, Hammertree says.

The General's Staff produces several liquor flasks. The Mayor takes two.

Honey, Charlie smirks. Listen to the General. He knows what he's talking about.

Well, you can't keep Henry locked up this way, Darlene says.

We most certainly can, Hammertree says. And will. And the world will be safer for it. Have a belt, young lady. Please. Listen a minute. Please. Please?

What the hell, Darlene says, taking a flask.

What I'm about to tell you appears nowhere in any official record, Hammertree says grimly for full effect. There once was a town called Little Bovine, Nevada. And I say once, because it's not there anymore.

Out of thick, moonlit clouds above sleepy, unsuspecting Little Bovine, vicious, sharp Flying Saucers swoop down like attacking birds. Each saucer lets loose a huge cloud of bubbling green-yellow gas.

It was late one night, a few years after the war, Hammertree tells them. As the good people of Little Bovine slept, an alien menace descended upon their town. The resources of their home worlds dwindling, their aim is to break our rich planet down for parts.

At a Little Bovine gas station, an Attendant absently sweeps up between the pumps.

It was the night owls, Hammertree says. The Bakery Truck Driver. The Cop on the corner. They were the ones who got it first. Poor devils.

As the sickly fog passes over him, the Attendant feels dizzy and drops his broom. He stumbles into the tiny station bathroom, looks in the mirror and just doesn't feel right.

Outside, a cab pulls in for gas. The Attendant comes to the cab window, skin now dead, cheeks sunken, eyes bright, glowing yellow-green, and takes a giant bite out of the Cab Driver's skull.

They were already gone and didn't even know it,
Hammertree says.

In downtown Little Bovine, a Zombie Police Officer
climbs into his car. He turns on the lights, puts it in gear and
swerves the wrong way down the street, hitting sidewalks
on either side.

Zombies only want human flesh, Hammertree says. And
Saucer Men want only power.

In the Little Bovine suburbs, a sleepy Homeowner in
pajamas opens his front door to get the morning paper and
finds a Zombie Paper Boy in a ball cap biting his hand.

A plan so deviously simple it almost worked,
Hammertree says. We were all to be Zombie food. And when
they eat the last one of us, the Zombies will starve. After
that, the Saucer People waltz in here, easy as you please.

A Little Bovine Elementary School bus pulls up to a
crowded stop on a neighborhood street corner. The door
opens. Children hustle up the steps past their cheerful Bus
Driver.

When the door closes, the Bus Driver glances in the
mirror to find a sea of glowing eyes staring back.

By the time the Army got to Little Bovine, the town had
nearly devoured itself, Hammertree says. Many of us vowed
that day, never again. Never again.

Blood pours down the bus steps as she is devoured by
Zombie Children.

In the now quiet Control Room, Hammertree's story has
everyone stunned. Their eyes turn to Henry, locked inside
the glass-walled office. He can't hear what they're saying and
he's too gloomy to care.

Hiding around a corner, Charlie quietly blubbers from
panic.

Not long after this first attack, the good Doctor and
myself took charge of a rather special facility, Hammertree
says. Our mission is to be prepared, should the threat return.

Huge airplane hangars stand out on the desert floor.
Inside, a small city humming with activity.

Led by Doctor Percival, Army Scientists carefully study
star charts and space maps.

General Hammertree inspects the design of futuristic
battle gear and weapons. He picks up a test model of a big
gun off a long rack and fires a bright laser bolt through the
ceiling.

Handles nice, fellas, Hammertree says with a chuckle.
Now how about something with some kick to it!

In the Control Room, Hammertree's Staff applauds.

In fact, this exercise today was largely cover for the field
testing of our latest equipment, Hammertree says. Our new
battle helmets saved lives today. Remember that.

Percival hurries in and whispers in Hammertree's ear.

Good, good, Hammertree says. Alright. We're moving on
to the next protocol. Take them out of here.

The Soldiers and Staff shove Darlene, Charlie, and the
Mayor out into the hallway.

Hey, quick question, Darlene says on her way out the
door. Can I make up a protocol?

No, Hammertree and Percival bark, sitting down at a
desk outside the glass-walled office with Henry locked
inside.

The Squad Leader guards the door.

Hammertree finds the button on a speaker box.

Can you hear this, he asks.

Henry nods.

Push your button to talk, Percival says, pushing the
button.

There is a box with a button in front of Henry too.

Yes, he says, pushing his button. I can hear you fine. Why
am I in here?

You attacked my troops, Hammertree says, pushing his

button.

You attacked my town, Henry says, pushing his button.

Well, I'm allowed to, Hammertree says, pushing his button. Doctor, what we have here is a socialist sympathizer with a level-five alien zombie virus exposure. That makes him just about the most dangerous person in the world.

If I could have only a few hours to study him, Percival says.

No time, Hammertree says. The sooner we wipe this little town off the map the better.

Percival looks down.

You're still pushing the button, he says.

Hammertree lets go of his button.

Whoops, he says.

Henry pushes his button.

What do you mean, off the map, he asks.

Enough of this, Hammertree says. Let's go.

Please, Percival says. One moment to communicate with him.

Alright, one, Hammertree says.

Hammertree hurries out. Percival pushes the button to talk.

You must tell me, Percival says. How does it feel, the zombie virus devouring you from the inside? What is it like to crave flesh? Would you like to take a bite of me right now?

Not really, Henry says into the speaker box.

Ah, too bad, Percival says. You will. And I won't be here to see it. Another time. Or not.

Wait, Henry says. How about a glass of water?

Funny boy, Percival says, leaving the Squad Leader alone with Henry. Guard him closely.

Henry pushes the button on his side of the glass.

This must be embarrassing for you, he says.

The Squad Leader punches his button.

For me, he asks.

Their buttons click back and forth like old friends.

Yeah, Henry says and sits quietly disinterested.

No, the Squad Leader says, cautiously. *I'm fine.*

Wow, Henry says. Really? I'll give it to you, then. You're a pretty tough guy.

Yeah, the Squad Leader says. *What do you mean?*

Henry shrugs.

Just because I'm curious, the Squad Leader says. *What would a regular level of guy like you think about it?*

I don't know, Henry says. I guess I'd think, there's important stuff going on out there, and I'm stuck here with nothing to do.

I'm guarding, the Squad Leader says.

Guarding, Henry chuckles. Guarding what?

You, the Squad Leader says.

Me, Henry asks. There's a locked door guarding me. A confident field mouse could guard me. You're only standing there.

I do not need this flimsy door to guard you, the Squad Leader says.

Still, better keep it locked, Henry laughs. For safety, I mean. Obviously.

The Squad Leader unlocks the door and props it open. He crosses his arms, filling the entire door frame.

Alright, he says. *Go ahead and try something on me now, smart guy.*

Henry stands up.

Alright, Henry says. Sorry about this.

The Squad Leader braces for attack, suspicious.

About what, he asks.

Lucky Strike, Henry yells. Lucky Strike! Lucky Strike!

Click, click, click. Smoke fills the Squad Leader's helmet.

Stop that, he chokes. *Help! Prisoner! Escape!*

Rushing into the hallway, Henry turns one way and hears Soldiers running toward him. He turns the other way. Same thing. But by the time they converge on the Control Room door, Henry's gone. A ceiling panel quietly slides back into place.

The Dam's noisy Generator Room is gigantic and stacked with towering, spinning turbines. Darlene, the Mayor, Hammertree, and his Staff cross the floor amid saluting Soldiers in formation.

The people in that cow town, Darlene says loudly. What happened to them?

Hammertree stops. They all stop.

The solution was simple, Hammertree yells over the machines. The decision made swiftly.

Zombies fill the streets of Little Bovine. Thunder in the distance and an atomic mushroom cloud.

And that is the last anyone ever heard of Little Bovine, Nevada, Hammertree shouts dramatically, continuing across the floor.

This isn't good, Darlene says.

The Mayor pats her hand.

We'll find our way through this somehow or other, he says.

They crowd into an elevator. The doors close. A number dial moves slowly from zero to one.

The doors open outside, on the top of the Dam, near where Soldiers assemble a nest of wires and metal tubes into a large, intricate and imposing atomic bomb.

Alright, she says. But we'd better hurry.

Down in the Generator Room, Soldiers march in more and more intricate patterns. Other Soldiers with overloaded repair carts move through the formations, continuously adjusting and oiling gears.

Henry finds his way to the back of a long line and follows along behind, just below the sight line of the heavy helmets. When that group nears where he might be seen, Henry dives

between repair carts until another line passes. He makes his
way across the floor until he finds himself pinned between
two carts on the elevator, going up.

On top of the Dam, Percival carefully prepares the bomb,
pulling levers and pressing buttons.

You can't do this, Darlene says.

And what is that, Hammertree wonders out loud.

Whatever it is you're doing, Darlene says.

Oh, Hammertree says. Do you mean saving the world? I
beg to differ.

I assure you, ma'am, Percival says. Our protocols are
sound concerning this matter.

That's our town down there, she says.

Your town, as you know it, is already gone, Percival says.
Believe me.

The bomb dings like an oven timer. Everyone but Percival
ducks and covers.

Ah, Percival says. All ready! It is so important to pre-heat.

He digs into a deep lab coat pocket and hands
Hammertree another oversized remote control, this one with
a single, big, round, flashing button.

It's the bright red one, Percival says.

Thank you, Hammertree says. I see that.

The elevator doors open as Hammertree is about to push
the button.

Stop, Henry yells, leaping to grab the remote. He runs for
the side of the Dam as the Soldiers raise their weapons.

The zombie's loose, Hammertree shouts. Shoot him!

Run, Darlene, Henry yells.

Soldiers blindly yank their triggers. Henry dives,
throwing the remote. The guns click all around him. No
bullets.

Out of nowhere, smoke still drifting from his oversized
helmet, the Squad Leader intercepts the remote midair with
a flying catch. He lands hard, then jogs over to Hammertree

with the remote.

Hammertree's impressed.

Play any ball, son, he asks.

Go Army, the Squad Leader says.

That'a boy, Hammertree says.

The Squad Leader jogs back over and picks Henry up like a skinned rabbit. Henry struggles, but he's not full of holes.

Now, please, somebody tell me how that commie zombie isn't blown to smithereens, Hammertree says, eying his Staff suspiciously.

Frightened and ashamed, the Staff looks to Percival.

General, we didn't have the heart to tell you, Percival says. The requisition office has some odd regulations about live ammunition in public exercises. I didn't think it would come up, to be honest.

Hammertree is boiling.

Well it did, he says.

I see that, Percival says sincerely. I do apologize.

See that you do, Hammertree says.

Soldiers struggle to pin Henry. He slips free. Again, they tackle him.

Darlene, Henry yells. Run! They're aliens!

Henry, Darlene yells. Stop! They're not!

Henry stops.

Not what, he asks.

Aliens, she says.

All around them, the Soldiers' helmets beep twice. Locks release. The helmets hit the ground everywhere around them. They happily gulp fresh air, then droop, exhausted.

Look at that, Percival says. Midnight. The test is over. Clearly a success, may I add!

Free of his helmet, the Squad Leader gets Henry in a headlock.

Darlene, Henry says, struggling. Good news! They're not aliens!

The Squad Leader gives him a painful squeeze.

107

If you all don't mind, Hammertree says. I was about to do something. Oh, yes.

Hammertree is again about the push the button on the remote. Charlie plugs his ears.

Wait, everyone yells at once. Stop!

Hammertree sighs.

What is it now, he asks.

You're not going to push that button with us all standing here, the Mayor says. Are you?

Hammertree chuckles.

You mean this button here, he asks.

He pushes the button. All but he and Percival brace for impact. Nothing.

Well, Darlene says. I guess if they won't give you bullets, they're sure not going to give you guys a real bomb. Right?

Hammertree looks worried.

Give it a second, Percival says.

A control panel on the bomb blinks awake with a determined-looking row of analogue numbers.

It's the real thing, alright, Percival says. Someone already had the scale model out on loan.

Hammertree is relieved.

This gives us time to evacuate the remaining troops, Percival explains. We're not monsters.

You won't get away with this, Henry says.

It's not getting away with something if it's the right thing to do, Hammertree says. We are moving to the next protocol. Lock them up inside.

Soldiers jump into action. Charlie is frozen with fear.

I thought we were all evacuating, the Mayor says.

With all due respect, Mayor, Hammertree says. You've been exposed to the alien zombie gas. Can't just turn you loose on another community.

So, then, Darlene says. Why bring us up here?

Protocol Five-A, subsection H, Percival says, holding up his emergency protocol binder for them all to see, reading out loud. Take one last look at the world you knew.

This is America, Hammertree says. Everybody gets to say goodbye. Even zombies.

We're not zombies, Darlene says.

Give it time, Percival says.

In the Dam Lunch Room, Soldiers without helmets shove Darlene, the Mayor, Henry and Charlie onto flimsy chairs at wobbly tables. An empty serving counter lines one wall. A door at the far end locks behind the Soldiers.

When we get out of here, you're in big trouble, pal, Charlie says.

Why wait, Henry asks. Let's start now.

They tussle. Darlene pushes them apart.

Quit it, Darlene says. Quit it!

Henry and Charlie retreat to neutral corners.

Now just everyone calm down, the Mayor says.

Charlie switches gears.

Maybe this is all for the best, he says, giving her his most winning smile.

The best, Darlene says. The best what?

Darling, if there are zombies out there, Charlie says. If they've got our town, our people, our Daddies, what can we do? Let's you and me go into the next life together, in each other's arms, like we're meant to be.

Charlie hugs her tight. This crushes Henry, and Darlene can't breathe either.

On top of the Dam, troop trucks load up and disappear into the night. Numbers on the bomb quietly count down. Hammertree surveys the town below them in the moonlight.

Quite a thing, Hammertree says.

Yes, Percival says. The connecting of worlds though violence and mayhem.

You really get me, Hammertree says.

In the Lunch Room, Darlene shoves free of Charlie.

You can't go out there, Charlie says. Are you crazy? You want to see a real zombie? Up close? On purpose?

There aren't any zombies to see, Darlene says.

Charlie pursues her, mainly for Henry's benefit.

Honey, face facts, he says. Why argue in the short time that remains?

This can't be, Henry says.

Shouldn't've come back, Henry, Charlie says. You're bad luck.

First the Mill, now this, Henry says, despondent.

The Mill, the Mayor asks. What about the Mill, Henry?

Bank called in our note, Henry says. Gotta close the doors.

The bank, the Mayor asks. Very curious.

Yeah, Henry says. Vendors too. All of a sudden.

All of a sudden, the Mayor says. You don't say.

Yep, Henry says. Just like that.

Oh my, Charlie says. Behind on the rent, Henry? That's a shame.

What is it, Mayor, Darlene asks.

That's highly unusual, the Mayor says, his eyes on Charlie.

Charlie, what did you do, Darlene demands.

This certainly comes as a surprise to me, dear, Charlie says.

She's on to him.

You're a good boy, Charlie, the Mayor says. No one doubts that. But did you know there is a whole wing out at the State Prison, just for good boys who went and did things their Daddy told them to?

Now Charlie's sweating.

Mayor, please, he says. As head of the Poughville County Banking Commission, it would be improper for me . . . I mean, yes, maybe illegal even if I even considered . . . Oh my . . .

Nobody buys his act. Charlie drops to his knees for mercy.

Oh, Charlie, Darlene says.

Darlene, please, Charlie says. It's Big Daddy! He's obsessed with that Mill. I don't know why. Obsessed, I tell you! So maybe I made some calls. But you know what? If doing right by Big Daddy Charles Winston Potatoes is wrong, then Little Charles Winston Potatoes is wrong. And . . . if Little Charles Winston Potatoes is wrong . . .

Throughout this diatribe, Charlie rises courageously to his feet.

Sit down, Charlie, Darlene says.

Charlie sits.

You know, Henry, the Mayor says. There was a time, not long before you were born, that your parents, myself and Charlie's Daddy all owned equal shares of your Mill. First of its kind in the valley. Modern. Impressive. But Big Daddy always wanted to pay a little less, charge a little more. Had to go one way or the other. I sold to your folks, so Big Daddy did too, happy to finance everything through his own bank, of course. Said they'd fail by the end of that year. Then the next. But there you are. To this day. Still making pants and so forth. I'm glad you're back, Henry. You see the whole world?

Just about, Henry says.

Lots of interesting people, I bet, Darlene says.

No place or any people any better than right here, Henry says.

That's a lie, Darlene says.

No, it isn't, Henry says.

Well then, Darlene says. Why did you never write to me? All those places you visited. All those picture cards you sent to everybody else in town. Even the dog at the Fire House.

Rufus likes volcanoes, Henry says.

But you never sent one to me, Darlene says. Why, Henry? Did you forget me right away? Did you even wait until the train pulled out of town?

I sent you one every day, Henry says. Well, not exactly.

I knew it, Darlene says.

Some days I sent two, Henry says. You never got them?

No, they never arrived, she says, slowly turning to face Charlie, who's caught yet again.

Darlene, Charlie says. As the Poughville Post Master, it would be improper for me . . . I mean, maybe illegal if I even remotely considered . . .

Here, Henry says. Brought you the last one.

He hands her a postcard of a tropical lagoon.

It's beautiful, she says.

I was sitting on that very spot with this fella Prince Elyakauwi, Henry says. At his birthday barbecue. That's his island. Me, his friends, children, and all his wives.

My goodness, the Mayor says. Wives?

Ten of them, Henry says.

My, the Mayor says. Ten.

And he asked me how many wives I was going to have someday, Henry says.

Oh, did he, Darlene says.

And I said to him, I don't know about that, Prince, Henry says. I just want the one. Know what he said?

Do tell, Darlene says.

If somewhere in the world there is a wife worth ten like his, what was I doing there wasting time talking to him, Henry says. So here I . . .

She kisses him before he can finish another word.

Hey, Charlie groans.

I'm hoping you're still alright with a big wedding, Darlene says.

Sure, Henry says.

Good, Darlene says. Because we got one. And what do you think about Niagara Falls?

Don't know, Henry says. Never been there.

Well, how about that, Darlene says. There's a first for everything.

112

At that moment, there is a metallic crash behind the kitchen door. They all freeze in surprise. Then, another clatter of metal.

See, Charlie says. Told you. Zombies.

There aren't any zombies, Darlene says.

Who's that, then, Charlie whimpers. The Army's gone. Is that one of you guy's in there? Sure ain't me.

Nobody's certain what to do. Another bang. Another. They brace for attack. The door flies open. It's Buddy eating a cold chicken leg.

There you all are, Buddy says, jangling a huge ring of keys. I looked all over the place. Lucky I got these. Night Janitor. Side job. Moonlighting, as they say. Saw the trucks and figured they'd bring you up here with them. But they all split. Then I got hungry.

That's great, Buddy, Henry says. But what we really need right now is a key to that door over there. And we're in a bit of a hurry.

No problem, Buddy says, twirling the keyring with precision. Hurry to do what?

I'll explain on the way to the bomb, Henry says.

On the way to the what now, Buddy asks as they open the door and rush out, leaving Charlie behind.

You all hold on a darn minute, Charlie says. I've got something to say.

He realizes he's alone and changes his tune.

I mean, wait, Charlie says. Wait for me!

Outside the door, they find the Squad Leader with no helmet, patiently waiting for them.

I knew it, the Squad Leader says.

You're all supposed to be gone, Henry says.

I took a personal interest, the Squad Leader says.

I admire your passion for the task at hand, Henry says.

Thank you, the Squad Leader says. Extra effort wins the war.

Darlene, Charlie whimpers. What now?

Shut up and stay here, Darlene whispers, recognizing Henry's distraction. Using Charlie's bulk for cover, she slips the other way down the hallway.

Can't fool me this time, the Squad Leader says, completely focused on Henry.

Henry and Buddy square off with him, but the Squad Leader has them outsized. Without his clumsy helmet, they are obviously no match.

Wouldn't think of it, Henry says.

Whump. Clang. Darlene throws a metal trashcan over the Squad Leader's head from behind and whacks it with a mop handle.

Sorry, pal, Buddy says. Good luck with your war.

Come on, let's go, Darlene says.

Split up, Henry says. He'll follow me.

Running, they reach a set of doors and head in different directions.

Doors fly open in the Dam Generator Room. The Squad Leader chases Henry at full speed. The generators are huge, whirring machines full of dangerous moving parts. Ladders and scaffolding reach to the ceiling.

Henry makes it to the elevator. The button doesn't work. He starts to climb the scaffolding, but only makes it a couple feet before the Squad Leader's hand latches onto his ankle.

Not so quick, zombie boy, the Squad Leader says.

Henry kicks himself free and climbs.

Since I'm a zombie, Henry says, running out of breath. You should run away from me.

Nope, the Squad Leader says. I'm gonna getcha. So run all you want.

Will do, Henry says.

They climb higher and higher above the spinning gears, the Squad Leader nipping at Henry's heels.

Reaching another level of scaffolding, Henry is surprised to see Darlene, Buddy and the Mayor staring back at him. Darlene whispers in his ear.

We found the stairs, she says. Keep going.

Henry continues to the next level. They hide as the Squad Leader climbs past them. The Mayor slips a rope around the Squad Leader's foot as Darlene and Buddy pop out and shout, Boo!

The startled Squad Leader falls backward, dangling above the whirring machinery. Never defeated, he struggles to reach the rope.

That should hold him for a minute, Henry says.

The Squad Leader is already shimmying back up the rope.

Nope, Buddy says. Keep moving.

They emerge on the roof, exhausted. The bomb control panel counts down in front of them.

That's not a bomb, Buddy says. It's an elephant. How do you turn it off?

You don't, Hammertree says from the darkness nearby.

He and Percival sit glumly on a bench overlooking the town, passing a flask back and forth. The Staff huddles nearby, doing the same. Hammertree waves his pistol.

Let's just talk this over a minute, Henry says, inching toward the control panel of the bomb.

Hammertree fires into the air. The gun goes off this time.

I promise you, folks, this one's loaded, Hammertree says. And what is your problem with liberty, anyhow?

Nothing at all, Henry says. Maybe we should take a minute and talk about it.

Son, the good Doctor and I know what we're doing, Hammertree says.

In the Alien Confinement Room at Hammertree's desert base, a Saucer Person removes their battle helmet. Underneath is an evil monster with sharp teeth, bug eyes and a long, whipping tongue. It hisses blue steam. Hammertree and Percival boldly stare the creature down from the other side of thick glass. They never flinch.

Swinging his pistol, Hammertree backs Henry away from the bomb.

So, don't tell me my business, Hammertree says.

You'll die too, Darlene says. Why did you stay?

Sadly, our inoculation only covers the symptoms for a short while, Hammertree says. Anybody without a helmet during the attack itself is ultimately as infected as you are. Just as well, really. End of the road for us. This stunt was never going to be enough.

The General droops.

Excuse me, Darlene says. Stunt?

They're shutting our facility down, Hammertree says.

Budget cuts, Percival says. It's our home.

Commie plot, Hammertree says. First we lost the hearts and minds. And now the dollars. Peace is poison.

So, Percival says. The General simply thought . . .

They have no need to know what I thought, Hammertree says. Doesn't matter now. We saved the world tonight. That's what they'll all remember.

Wait, the Mayor says. The General thought what?

This entire magnificent operation was his idea, Percival says.

You said this all came straight from the White House, Darlene says. You swore us to secrecy.

The counter number on the bomb continues to drop.

I'm sorry, Hammertree says. The details are classified.

Can't make that much difference now, Darlene says.

Well, Hammertree mumbles sheepishly. I may not be quite as close with Ike as I've led people to believe over the years. His Aunt is my Mother's Cousin, Gertrude. They are very close. We have met, though. We did. In Berlin, not long after the war. It was a crazy time. Excellent intelligence led me to believe the General'd been killed and replaced by a Nazi imposter.

OPERATION DRAGONHEAD

In a Berlin hotel room, just after the war, Dwight Eisenhower sits in his bathrobe, reading a newspaper. A waiter pushes in a tray of food. It's Hammertree in a poor disguise. He pulls two guns at once and tackles Ike.

The counter on the bomb continues to drop.

Fortunately, I happen to be mistaken, Hammertree says. Would have meant my career, except . . .

Your Aunt is his Mother's Cousin, Darlene says.

Gertrude, Hammertree says.

So, you cooked up a whole invasion, Darlene says.

Percival and Hammertree shrug.

Funny thing about filling out requisition forms, Hammertree says. All of a sudden, it sort of gets away from you. However, I would say, as it so happens, things did work out for the best. And don't worry, everyone. If we all start turning into space zombies, I have bullets enough for everybody.

Hammertree's Staff offers a woeful cheer.

General, Darlene says. I don't know how to tell you this, alright, but there's no such thing as space . . .

She glances up and stops. The plump, dark, flying saucer hovers behind Hammertree. He realizes everybody's now looking behind him. Slowly, he turns. Legs extend from the saucer as it gently lands like a metallic ladybug. Everyone backs away. Doors slide open.

An entire Alien Family pours out: A Mom Alien, Dad Alien and two chubby Kid Aliens, all with big cute eyes, iridescent-green skin and friendly, bouncing antennae. Wearing a variety of space-tourist-trap t-shirts and hats, along with short pants and sandals, they are large, shimmering, vacationing jelly blobs.

Hey, friends, the Alien Dad says. Look, we're not supposed to do this, technically. But I bet the folks at work I'd get a picture with some of you . . . People?

The Alien Mom flips through a hologram guidebook.

117

Yep, she says. How fun!

That's a vocabulary word for the quiz board, kids, the Alien Dad says. People. As in, People are the primitives on the wet, blue planet.

The Alien Kids half listen, giggling and dodging full speed between the stunned, wide-eyed Earthlings.

The Alien Mom wobbles over to Henry.

I like your Earth pants, she says.

Thanks, Henry says. My Mom made these.

Lovely work, she says.

I'll tell her you said so, Henry says.

The Alien Dad waves everyone over in front of the saucer.

This is a good spot, he says.

Please don't make a big production, the Alien Mom says.

I'm not, the Alien Dad says. I'm not. Got to get this, though. They're all just gonna die.

The various humans all gasp and cringe in fear.

No, no, the Alien Mom says. He doesn't mean you. He means his friends at work. Hurry up and take the picture already.

They relax, but only a little.

Dang it, the Alien Dad says. Where's the clicker?

He finds it in a pocket and accidentally clicks the button. The saucer flashes, catching everyone off guard. It's also a giant camera.

Whoops, the Alien Dad says. Sorry. Bumped the button. That'll be a weird one. Everybody right in front, there. And, stand up straight, come on now. And smile!

We are, we are, we are, the Alien Kids chirp in unison.

The Alien Dad pounds Hammertree on the back.

Twins, he says. Weird, huh? They say this talking thing's normal. But, know what? I think they practice. What do you think?

Well, I, uhm, Hammertree says.

Dad, the Alien Kids chime. Hurry up!

I'm just saying, the Alien Dad says. Weird is weird.
Alright. Everybody smile.

The saucer flashes and the family wobbles back toward
the open door.

Thanks, you guys, the Alien Dad says. Have a great
morning.

Will you look around, the Alien Mom says. It's clearly
night time here.

I can't keep it all straight, the Alien Dad says. We go by
smell. Anyhoo, have a great night time.

The door closes and the saucer floats off as quickly as it
arrived.

Ferocious beasts, Darlene says. Doctor, tell us again about
your, what was it, research?

Percival and Hammertree stare at their feet.

And those poor, poor people of Little Bovine, Darlene
says, smirking. What about them?

Zombies, Buddy says. What a way to go.

Hold on, the Mayor says. Buddy, you know about Little
Bovine?

Buddy pulls his *True Science Illustrated* from his back
pocket and finds a page marked *Terror at Little Bovine*.

Well, sure, he says. It's all right here.

Hammertree and Percival know they're caught.

In reality, General Hammertree only commands a large
desert depot for rusting surplus equipment, rows and rows
of odd parts and out-of-date electronics.

Day in and day out, Percival and Hammertree sit across
from each other at desks pushed together amid the acre of
junk. They are the only ones there.

Percival fiddles around inside old radios with a
screwdriver. Hammertree usually naps in his chair.

One day, Percival digs through a drawer and doesn't find
what he's looking for. He slams the drawer to wake
Hammertree.

Will you please look in that desk for my smaller screwdriver, he says. The one with the red handle.

Well, you could have just asked me, Hammertree says.

I did just ask you, Percival says. See if it's there and you can go back to sleep.

Only resting my eyes, Hammertree says, pulling out a drawer.

Something hits the floor beneath the old desk. Hammertree picks it up. It's a dusty *True Science Illustrated*. He turns a page.

Inside is a full-color insert of the scene Hammertree described with a captured Saucer Person behind safety glass breathing blue steam.

A week later, outside the giant depot, Hammertree waits for a postal truck to arrive. It throws off a package. He scurries over.

Soon, he's skipping through the piles of discarded mechanical odds and ends like a kid on Christmas. Percival is already happily working on the first prototype communication helmet, scavenged from spare parts, fashioned after those the Saucer People wear on the cover of the magazine they found. Pages are carefully pasted on a blackboard among Percival's senseless, scribbled notes. They open the first package together: two dozen back issues of *True Science Illustrated* magazine.

On top of the Dam, atomic bomb counting down nearby, all eyes roll as Hammertree and Percival look to each other to plead their case.

Well, Percival says. You don't think they just make these things up out of thin air, do you? It's a known and well-regarded publication. There would have been lawsuits, I assure you.

Doc, I told them the same thing, Buddy says, turning to Henry. So, these fellas Aliens or not?

Not, Henry says.

Well, I'm going home then, Buddy says.

Maybe we all should, Hammertree says.

Whoa, Darlene says. Anybody? The bomb?

The bomb clock counts down.

Stop that bomb, Hammertree yells. Give me the button!

You have it, Percival says.

No, I left it over there, Hammertree points.

The Squad Leader appears at the top of the stairs, woozy, bruised and out of breath. He follows Hammertree's finger to the remote perched on the bomb control panel. It is directly between them.

The Squad Leader runs. Henry runs, but is a step too slow. The Squad Leader grabs the remote and backs away from the group.

Hand me that button, Hammertree says.

Sorry, the Squad Leader says. I can't do that, sir. I think you've been compromised like the rest of them.

Yes, well, no one gave you permission to think, Hammertree says, raising his pistol, but not before the Squad Leader tosses the remote over the side of the Dam.

All rush to the edge as the remote disappears from sight. The counter on the bomb counts down past thirty seconds. All brace for a devastating explosion as the flying saucer again flutters down beside them. The door opens and the Alien Dad pops out.

Hi there, he says. Hate to interrupt. But my Wife is worried. You know, you guys are playing pretty close to this thing.

The Alien Dad lays a gooey hand on the humming bomb. It falls silent and the counter stops at one.

There you go, he says. It can't go off now. But be careful, alright? Jeez.

He lumbers back into the saucer, waving as the door closes. It disappears into the night.

The stunned group stares at the sky, silent for a long time.

Now everybody hold it right there, rolls a deep voice

from the trees.

Big Daddy's Nurse wheels him out of the darkness. Big Daddy waggles a giant pistol.

Daddy, Charlie says. It's been quite a night!

Hold on there, boy, Big Daddy says. Word on the military frequencies is zombie flu's got the whole town. So, we came to find you.

Charlie grins.

You did, he asks. Because . . .

I mean, can't have no zombie Potatoes wandering around, Big Daddy says.

He lifts the pistol at Charlie. Click. Click. No bullets. Charlie's on the ground by now anyway.

Don't worry, folks, the Nurse says. Took his bullets away years ago.

Big Daddy balls his fists like a toddler.

When, he demands.

When you shot me, the Nurse says.

I didn't mean that, Big Daddy says.

I don't care, the Nurse says.

My sympathies, sir, Hammertree says to Big Daddy. No way to treat a man, taking his ammunition.

Daddy, there aren't any zombies, Charlie says.

Big Daddy looks to the Mayor for confirmation.

No zombies, Charles, the Mayor says.

Too bad, Big Daddy says. At first, I thought, well, at least the dummy's finally got an excuse.

Little Charlie Potatoes has had enough.

Alright, he says. That's it. Don't you dummy me no more, old man. I run this town for you. And a lot of other things. And I think it's high time you recognize that.

Big Daddy thinks this over for a moment, then aims again at Charlie. Click. Click. Click. Click.

Damn, Big Daddy says.

Daddy, you know full well I'm not a zombie, Charlie says. I am President of the Chamber of Commerce. A darned good Son . . . And I could sure use some breakfast.

Empowered and exhausted, he isn't sure where to take it next. His half-proclamation hangs in the damp morning air. All turn toward home.

That sounds good, the Mayor says. Right after we wake up some bankers.

Charlie realizes he's still in the doghouse.

For a moment, I thought you said bankers, Big Daddy says.

Yes, Charles, the Mayor says. I said bankers.

Leaving Earth's orbit, the saucer passes the Moon.

Inside, the Alien Mom reads her video book. The Kids are jammed in the back with hovering juice cubes, bizarre action figures and 5D video games. The Alien Dad fiddles with the radio.

Dad, the Alien Kids chime in unison. Dad?

Don't tell me you have to go, he says.

We have to go, they say.

I asked you before we left Earth, he says. Didn't I ask you?

We didn't have to then, they say.

Well, he says. You're holding it past Neptune.

Nooooooo, they moan.

Oh, we can stop at Mars, the Alien Mom says.

This is a ploy, the Alien Dad says. They know once we pay for parking we're in for the whole deal. Really. Haven't we bought enough crap for one trip? And you see what they're doing again, right? Scheming.

No, we're not, the kids sing, scheming. Mars! Mars! Mars!

Come on, the Alien Mom says. You still talk about going there when you were young. Everybody loves Mars. It's the happiest place near Earth.

Fine, the Alien Dad says. Guess we're going to Mars!

His family cheers.

HIGH DESERT

Robbing a remote bank full of mob money goes wrong and gets worse

A filthy, rundown filling station, alone in the middle of nowhere. Only dirt, rocks and darkness surrounding a twitching, florescent ball.

An under-powered hatchback with Carolina plates groans to a stop at the pumps. A sweaty Cross-Country Driver has it crammed with boxes and clothes. Stiff and slow, he climbs out and looks around.

Behind the security glass, a Station Attendant clearly minds the distraction from his extremely graphic sex magazine.

The Cross-Country Driver trudges wearily toward him.

Bathroom, he asks.

The metal drawer slides open with a key chained to a brick.

A crooked door opens into the disgusting little room. The Cross-Country Driver tries to touch nothing.

Returning with the brick and key, he finds the Attendant washing his windshield in a much friendlier mood.

Thanks, the Cross-Country Driver says.

No problem, man, the Attendant says. But the register's busted. It's not talking to the pumps right. Don't ask me, it's the robots taking over. Anyway, you'll need to fill up some place else down the road.

Busted, the exhausted Cross-Country Driver repeats back.

Yeah, man, the Attendant says. Sorry. I'm about to shut the lights and head home myself.

Is there a, uh, the Driver begins.

There's a half dozen places between here and Bakersfield, the Attendant says. All just like this one. Can't even tell them apart. You got like a quarter tank?

Light just came on, the Cross-Country Driver says.

You'll be fine, man, the Attendant says. Don't worry.

Alright, the Cross-Country Driver says. Thanks. Soda machine?

Grab one from the cooler there, the Attendant says.

Nearby, there's on old cooler propped on an older tire.

Awesome, the Cross-Country Driver says. I have cash.

He reaches for his wallet, but the Attendant waves him off.

No, no, the Attendant says. My boss hears I put a dollar straight into my pocket and went home, you got no idea what she'd do. So, go on. Pay it forward, man. Have a good night.

They share an uneasy smile.

Sure, you too, the Cross-Country Driver says. He grabs a soda, gets behind the wheel and drives away.

Behind him, an aging, vintage muscle car lumbers up to the pumps. A thumping, creaking, metal dinosaur emerging thoughtfully from the desert night, tattooed with road scars and experience. Hanner, a local junkyard owner and hereditary criminal, climbs out covered in dust and grease, steady and measured, as if tempered and welded from the same steel.

The Attendant spots Hanner and scurries back toward the security cube door, cursing his luck. He finds that the door locked behind him.

Oh, for fuck sake, the Attendant mutters, fumbling for his keys, dropping them twice.

Hanner sees this, amused.

Now, what are you so worked up about, he asks.

The sweaty Cross-Country Driver rolls down his windows and turns up the radio, fighting to stay awake. He reaches into his back pocket to take out his wallet. It isn't there.

He sees that he'd left it jammed between the dashboard and the newly cleaned windshield. He grabs it, frantic. Empty. Cash all gone. The wallet flops hopelessly in his hand. The Cross-Country Driver wheels the car around and roars back the other way, panicked, angry at himself for getting ripped off, too tired to think straight.

Nearing the gas station again, the Cross-Country Driver doesn't expect what he finds. He slows the car, confused.

Hanner stands under the station lights, his car's tank filling at the pump, the Cross-Country Driver's cash in his hand, the squirming Attendant's head under his boot.

Look, man, the Attendant squeaks. If you'd let me explain . . .

Shut it, Hanner says.

The Cross-Country Driver stops his car and gets out.

Hi, he says. Uhm . . .

I'm thinking this is yours, Hanner says.

Yeah, the Cross-Country Driver says. I think so. Thanks.

Relieved, he reaches out for his money a little too quick for Hanner's liking. Hanner stops him with a look.

Hold on now, Hanner says. Don't thank me yet. In my experience, somebody in your spot, somewhat upside down, is usually grateful enough for whatever they happen to get back. Plus the lesson. Am I right?

Hanner's gas nozzle clicks.

Just agree with him, man, the Attendant says, face in the gravel.

Quiet, Hanner says.

Yeah, I guess so, the Cross-Country Driver says.

Don't guess, Hanner says.

No, you're right, the Cross-Country Driver says.

Hanner hands the guy back part of the cash.

Thought so, he says. Fifteen gallons, regular.

Hanner peels off a few bills and drops them onto the bleeding Attendant. The rest goes into his shirt pocket.

Keep the change, Hanner says. And you two have a good night.

The exhausted Cross-Country Driver blinks down at what's left of his cash. The Attendant sits up, picking gravel off his face.

You too, man, the Attendant says.

Hanner waves over his shoulder on the way back to his car.

Yeah, the Cross-Country Driver says. Thanks again.

Hanner's faded, classic sedan churns heavily to life, headlights flaring, and leaps, roaring past them into the night.

As the sun pops into the sky, a matching set of florescent lights shut off along another gas station roof. This one deep in a bustling city.

With great pride, three heavy-set guys in pricey suits prepare their shiny, luxury car for a road trip. They fill the tank and wash the windshield. Double check the tires. All the while, one of them is always arm's length from the car's locked trunk, pistols under their jackets.

Alright, let's go, the Mob Delivery Driver says, checking his watch.

Impatient, they fight their way through heavy morning traffic, eyes on the dashboard clock. Taillights at an infinite crawl. Then the city gives way to an uphill swing into the mountains. Traffic shifts to long-haul trucks and rental cars. Then the highway drops to a slow glide into a wide desert valley. A sea of tumbling underbrush and shimmering tangles of roadside trash.

It's still early when they pull into town. The sun-bleached row of storefronts slowly open for the day. Grocery, small motor repair, pawn shop, bank, diner on the corner. Quiet, except for the wind and a train somewhere way off in the distance.

The conspicuously clean luxury car parks across from the bank. The Guards wait as the Mob Delivery Driver takes a long walk around the block. He eyes the shops and a passing bread truck, then returns with coffee from the diner and a nod: All clear.

The trunk pops open. The Mob Delivery Driver grabs a heavy duffle bag and crosses toward the still closed bank. There he meets the Bank Manager at the door. The Manager takes a nervous look around and locks the door behind him. The two Mob Delivery Guards wait patiently, hands near their weapons. A stray dog trots past. More time passes.

The bank door bursts open, then again locks tight behind him. The empty bag lands in the trunk. They climb into the car, sipping their coffee as the fancy car pulls away.

Everything good, one of them asks.

Clockwork, the Mob Delivery Driver says. Clockwork.

At the edge of the valley, nestled between jagged hills, an odds and ends collection of mining equipment rusts around a makeshift cabin.

Jack, awkwardly somewhere between teenager and twenties, tends a small and growing cooking fire.

That's not right at all, he complains. I've lived here now most of my life.

Jack's Grandfather, whom everybody calls Doc, including Jack, stomps in a circle, kicking at boulders and bushes in short pants and thick boots, wild haired and sunburned.

If you're not from out here, you can't stay out here, Doc says. Not forever, at least. Simple fact. You've seen it yourself.

Doc's feet freeze in place, rifle barrel sweeping the dirt. He changes his mind and keeps kicking.

Jack is genuinely worried.

Where else would I go, he asks.

Can't help you with that, Doc says. Wouldn't catch me dead, all hemmed in, trapped in the middle of some overgrown metropolis. That's only for city-born folks like yourself.

Thanks, Jack says.

Blam. Blam. His Grandfather digs around on the ground and comes up with two fat snakes missing their heads.

Nothing personal, Doc says. Now cut and cook. I'm hungry.

Out on the highway, only a few miles away, three Hipster tough guys from the city gather around their shiny new sports car, vaping heavily. They consult their phone GPS apps, none of which are loading. The most impatient of them is Benny.

This is the time he gave me, he says.

And he said here, one of them asks.

Text said, drive ten miles past the highway sign and stop, he says. That's the best I got.

Suddenly in the distance, Hanner's rusting muscle car appears, as if emerging from a time before they recognize.

That can't be him, the third one says. Think he'll show?

The muscle car nears and stops. Hanner gets out. He's dressed for work in his junkyard, not for style. The Hipsters are the high-fashion version of what Hanner actually is. Intimidated, they double down on their confident stance.

One of you Benny, Hanner asks.

That's me, pal, one says, stepping forward and, with a look from Hanner, immediately regretting it.

Where we going, he asks.

Couple miles, first right, Hanner says. Can't miss it. Go a couple miles, there's another right. Same thing. That road loops back here.

Alright, Benny says. Let's do this. This'll be fun. Your car's a real classic.

This triggers facetious grins from the group.

Let's see your cash, Hanner says.

He pulls a clip of hundreds from his pocket. This changes their tune.

No problem, Benny says, fumbling out his own mismatched stack of bills.

Hanner hands his over.

Great, Hanner says. Tell you what, you hold this. And

ride with me.

What, Benny asks.

You're not going to hand me a thousand dollars to drive away with, are you, Hanner asks. And when I beat you, I don't want to have to chase you all the way back to Los Angeles. So, let's go. Hustle up.

Right, Benny chirps. Of course.

Too proud to back down, he follows Hanner back to his car.

A craggy-faced town Sheriff and his brand-new Deputy crest a hill behind Hanner and the Hipsters' cars. For the moment, unnoticed on the horizon, the Sheriff glides to a stop and waits.

Racers, the Sheriff says.

Happen much out here, the Deputy asks.

Now and again, Sheriff says. Not like it used to.

Better get out in front of them, the Deputy says. They get moving now, we'll never catch up.

Who taught you how to hunt, the Sheriff scoffs.

Hanner pulls his road-worn muscle car up beside the shiny, angular, modern hipster-mobile. Window to window, they rev their engines.

Raise your hand, Hanner says to Benny. Count to three. Loud. Drop your hand. Got it?

Benny lifts a trembling hand. His eyes are in the side mirror.

One, two, shit, he shouts. That a cop?

Relax, Hanner says. He won't start until we do.

The Hipster driving their car glances back and instantly panics.

Cop, he says. Shit! Shit!

He punches the gas and they all start together, tires squealing. The Sheriff hits the lights and siren, quickly closing the distance between them.

The road rolls out for miles ahead, the Sheriff's siren screaming over the engines. Hanner's losing ground.

130

Can't this thing go faster, Bennie squeals.

Relax, Hanner says.

The hipster sports car has a head start and pulls away.

We're getting out of this, the driving Hipster says. They'll grab him and we'll disappear.

What about Benny, the passenger-side Hipster says.

Tough shit, this was all his idea in first place, the driving Hipster says. And that's his weed in the trunk.

By now Hanner's metal grill is large in their mirrors. The little hipster engine whines, topping out. Behind them, Hanner's car isn't struggling a bit.

Are we slowing down, the passenger-side Hipster says.

No, the driving Hipster says. But we're not going any faster.

As Hanner's car gallops calmly past, they see Benny stare back, terrified from the passenger seat.

Inside, Hanner's car rumbles like a rocket. Benny grips the dashboard for dear life.

See, on a long road, what you really want is power and momentum, Hanner says. Almost over now. Take a breath.

The Sheriff gains speed as well, heat of the chase forcing a grin across his normally angry face.

Missed our chance, the Deputy says. We'll never get there in this heavy old thing.

The Sheriff doesn't appreciate the new guy's opinion. He pops open the glove box, flips a switch and punches a big button.

Think so, he asks.

Nitrous oxide fires out the pipes, nearly lifting the old cop car off its wheels. The Deputy laughs.

A little old-fashioned, he says.

The good shit never goes out of style, the Sheriff says.

The square-jawed Sheriff's cruiser roars toward its prey.

Eyes wide, the Hipsters pee their pants until the Sheriff zooms past, uninterested. He's only after Hanner. They slow to a stop, speechless, shaking.

Wow, they both agree. Benny's screwed.

The Sheriff's car close behind, Hanner leaves the road. A long, sideways slide down a gravel wash takes them both out across a rough salt flat, dodging rock outcrops and underbrush, Benny screaming all the way.

The Deputy white knuckles the dash as well.

Jesus, he says. Who is this guy?

Nobody in particular, the Sheriff says. Ah, damnit!

He misjudges a turn, loses momentum, and misses his chance to head Hanner off. Hanner bounces onto a paved service road and crosses train tracks. The Sheriff stops.

The Deputy's confused.

What's wrong, he asks.

Those tracks are the county line, the Sheriff says. Last year, state declared that county an emergency-only area. Budget cuts. Bureaucrats.

Now the Deputy's extra confused.

Isn't this an emergency, he asks.

Call's got to come from in there, Sheriff says.

Bean counters, the Deputy says.

That's right, the Sheriff says.

Keep you from pursuing a suspect, the Deputy says.

The Sheriff turns his car around.

Nobody ever show you how rules make the game more fun, he growls.

No, the Deputy says. How about you enlighten me?

If you manage to last out here, you'll see soon enough, the Sheriff says. We're ants. This hunk of desert will be here long after we're gone. Nothing changes. All that really matters is how you keep score.

Now miles away, Hanner stops the car and holds out his palm to Benny.

Guess I won, he says.

Yeah, guess so, Benny says, handing over all the money, still shaking.

Alright, Hanner says. You get out here. I'll drive off this

way.

Benny opens the door and gets out. They are very much in the middle of nowhere.

Yeah, thanks man, Benny says through the open window. You lead them away. I'll hang out here until my friends catch up.

No, he's done chasing us now, Hanner says.

Benny looks around.

Then, why am I getting out here, Benny asks.

Because I don't like you, Hanner says, driving off.

On another early morning, town still mostly asleep, the conspicuously clean luxury car parks across from the bank. The Mob Delivery Driver takes his long look around the block.

The Bank Manager watches the car pull up in a row of camera monitors across from his tiny office desk. He stands, takes a last sip of coffee, fiddles with his tie and readies a large ring of keys.

The trunk pops open. The Mob Delivery Driver grabs the heavy duffle bag and heads for the bank across the street. The Bank Manager greets him at the door as usual. But this time, they are not alone.

Down the street, one in a small group of Bank Robbers wears a hard hat and tool belt, taking pictures from the top of a telephone pole. Another slumps on a bus bench outside the barbershop. A third watches from a low roof in the distance with just the scope from a deer rifle. They check their watches and keep careful notes.

Inside, the Bank Manager leads the Mob Delivery Driver across the empty lobby and away from the main vault, through a long, dusty conference room, to a hidden door at the back of a fake supply closet, which opens to reveal a large, secret, private vault.

The Mob Delivery Driver opens a second set of thick metal doors himself to reveal a small mountain of shrink-wrapped money bundles. He pulls a heavy stack of bills from the bag and adds it to the pile.

So, by my count, that's makes twenty-three, at present, the Bank Manager says.

Correct, the Mob Delivery Driver says. That's our count too.

Busy year, the Bank Manager chimes.

The Mob Delivery Driver's look says: We're not friends.

The Bank Manager quietly goes pale and quickly leads him back out of the supply closet, carefully shutting doors as they go.

The empty bag in the trunk and the three Mob Guys drive away with their coffees.

They pass the corner diner where a local named Melinda, a little older than Jack, is enjoying a large breakfast with an elderly Tourist Couple, smiling sweetly and lying through her teeth.

When you get back to Washington, you be sure to tell my Granddaddy that little Susan says hello, Melinda smiles.

Imagine meeting you this way, all the way out here, the Tourist Wife says. You've made our entire vacation, young lady.

The Waitress pours them more coffee and gives Melinda a frown. Melinda smiles it off.

Please bring the Senator's granddaughter anything she wants, her barely interested Tourist Husband says. What else can they bring you, sweetie?

You've been so kind already. Melinda says. Though my Auntie would be so thrilled if I brought her one of their lovely homemade pies. She enjoys the custard so much, and this is the day they make them.

Your finest custard pie, please, he says.

I'll get one from the back, the Waitress says.

Oh, and these berries, Melinda says. I'm sorry, but they're just not fresh. Could you bring us some nicer ones?

The Tourist Couple glares at the Waitress.

She smirks, I'll see what we have.

That will affect her tip, the man says after the Waitress is out of earshot.

Oh, please, no, Melinda says. She's a local girl and works so, so hard. Had a little one very young, with developmental issues, as they say. So sad.

Goodness, the Tourist Wife says. A little help now and again never hurts.

I wholeheartedly agree, Melinda says.

Prompted by his wife's sideways look, the man counts out a pile of bills. Melinda glances down, disapprovingly. He doubles it. It's a lot of cash.

We must be getting back on the road, the Tourist Wife says. But it's been a true pleasure, dear. Please enjoy your coffee. I wish all of our granddaughters were more like you.

You really are very kind, Melinda says, pocketing the tip as they settle up at the register.

In the diner bathroom, Melinda fixes her makeup in the mirror.

Well, now, she mutters. That was a real high point, dummy.

When Melinda reaches for her pie in a box on the counter, she finds the Waitress's heavy hand holding it down.

Your berry comment cost me my tip, the Waitress says.

It did, I'm so sorry, feigns Melinda.

I heard you making up all that stuff to tell those people, the Waitress says. Not very nice.

I know, Melinda says, drawing her in. I was just walking by and they started talking to me and mentioned where they're from. They seemed so lonely. I was only having some fun. Here. Here. Take this. It's all I have.

She hands her a couple crumpled singles. A tiny fraction of what she stole from the table.

No, no, the Waitress says. I didn't mean that.

Take it, she says. Please. I feel bad.

Thanks, the Waitress says. You know, they said something funny on their way out. Did you tell them I have a sick kid?

Sick kid, she laughs. No. Why?

The Waitress shrugs and returns to her day.

Melinda carries her pie down the street to the open back door of the little town grocery store, beside a narrow loading dock. Inside, a sweaty Grocery Clerk sits at a cluttered desk. He's pudgy and smiling.

Hello there, little lady, he says.

Brought you something sweet, Melinda says.

Didn't have to do that, he says.

No, I want to, she says. You've been so generous. My research couldn't go on without you.

My pleasure, the Grocery Clerk says. Just remember me when you get to Harvard and Yale and they give you those Nobel Prizes.

Don't think they give out those big awards for tracking the endangered orange-banded brush lizard, she says.

I'll leave the species saving to you, he says. Will my usual contribution to science cover it this month? If you run low on that special lizard hormone, don't be shy. You let me know. We'll get whatever you need.

He hands her a stack of crisp bills in an envelope.

No, Melinda says. Got plenty for now. I hate to say it, but the coyotes dug up my test kit again. Chewed on the motion sensor. Cracked a new lens. Not their fault. The darling things are always so curious about anything shiny. I think I can salvage the parts, though.

The Grocery Clerk shakes his head ruefully.

Got to get that whole unit up off the ground, he says. Drive some four-by-four posts, put a level platform on there. Solid as a rock. Happy to come out and help you. My cousin and I, we'd have that done in an afternoon.

I know, she says. Unfortunately, if I'm going to study them, I need to be right there in the dirt, where they live.

Down in the brush.

He digs around in his wallet for fives and tens.

Alright, he says. That's fine. Here. Take a little more. I can do better for you next time.

She kisses him on the cheek. That's all he was looking for. A short walk away, at the town party house, Melinda knocks on the door. No answer. She pushes her way in.

It's dark, with just joints and video games glowing. A row of local Stoners sprawl across a filthy couch is definitely happy to see her.

Melinda throws money on the cluttered coffee table, picking up a large, ornate bong.

One of you idiots go get the good bag, she says.

That night is deep with stars above a campfire ringed with headlights. Jack drinks beer with his buddies Pete and Merl. They are all tired of listening to another guy they went to school with named Billows. Billows is all wound up with a fresh buzz cut, chattering away.

Ends up more like seven grand, thank you all very much, Billows says. Pure bonus. I leave first thing in the morning. Travel paid.

Sounds great, Merl says. I mean, the you leaving part.

Free food, housing, and my regular salary too, Billows says. Guaranteed special forces tryout. Or maybe even those predator drones. You know they control those things out of Las Vegas? Las Vegas!

Terrifying, Jack says.

You chumps stay out here and crawl by on minimum wage, Billows says. My money's going in the bank.

So you can come back in a new Corvette and wrap your three-year hitch around the first telephone pole, Pete asks. My two Uncles that did that. Corvettes. Both of them.

Headlights in the distance.

Got a car, thanks, Billows says. And here comes my spare, anyway.

So you're serious about racing this guy for your Dad's old car, Jack says. Why?

Not for my Dad's car, which is my car now, by the way, dumb shit, Billows says. For his. And when I get back from basic, I'm going to parade that old turd box back and forth in front of his place all day and all night.

Your party, I guess, Merl says.

And damn right it is, Billows says. I drove out to Victorville last week and my Cousin tuned her perfect.

Hanner cuts the engine and climbs out of his muscle car. They tense up.

Boys, Hanner says.

Let's do this, Billows says.

From the big rocks out to the train yard and back, Hanner says. How's that?

That'll do, Billows says, playing grownup.

They all split off into various cars to follow each other across the desert to the starting line. Jack stops Hanner.

Hey, I got a mechanical question, he says. Mind if I ride out with you?

Sure, Hanner shrugs.

Dust flying, Hanner follows Billows, sizing up his car. It's a souped-up classic from the same era as Hanner's. Clean. Quick. They look good side by side.

Your friend there's got a real problem with me, Hanner says.

Yeah, Jack nods.

Why, Hanner asks.

Ah, you know his Sister, Jack asks. Wanda Billows. Red-haired. Works at the grocery store.

I know her, Hanner says. So?

You didn't screw Wanda Billows, Jack asks.

No, Hanner says. Why?

Seems to me he thinks you did, Jack says.

I meet you before, Hanner asks.

Yeah, I don't say much, Jack says.

You're not from out here, Hanner says.

Moved here when I was nine, Jack says. Turns out, nobody noticed.

And your friend wants my car, Hanner says.

Symbolic to him, I guess, Jack says.

He's got a fair chance at it, Hanner says. You need something from me?

My Grandpa's truck, Jack says. Mostly drives fine but now it rattles a bit going into low. Bothers me enough to ask. I don't want him getting stuck out here someplace. He's getting too old to walk home.

You mean Doc, Hanner asks.

Yeah, Jack says.

Still wandering around looking for gold, Hanner laughs.

Silver too, Jack says. In fact, he'll take anything shiny. You should see his tinfoil ball.

Bring the truck by, Hanner says. I'll take a look.

They reach the starting line. Jack opens the door.

Will do, Jack says.

Hey, Hanner says. I could use some help on the tow truck, fishing for wrecks a couple days a week. Interested?

Yeah, Jack says. I could use the work.

Alright, Hanner says. Monday. Early. And you mean Tina.

Who's Tina, Jack asks.

Billows, Hanner says. Tina Billows. Not Wanda. And all her idea. For the record.

The two cars line up. Engines roar. Jack, Merl, and Pete watch the tail lights shrink.

Billow's Sister's named Wanda, right, Jack asks.

Yeah, Merl says. She works at the grocery store.

Right, then who's Tina, Jack asks.

Tina, Merl asks.

Yeah, Jack says. Is there a Tina Billows?

Just his Mom, Pete says. Why?

139

The next day, Hanner pulls a cover over Billow's car, deep in the heart of his briar-patch junkyard.

Towers of discarded metal parts and skeletons of carefully stacked vehicles fill the yard. He pops the hood on his own rusting muscle car.

A fancy sports car crawls to a stop inside the gate, steam pouring from the engine. A slick city Con Man pops out in an expensive, three-day-old suit.

Hey, the Con Man says. You work on cars?

Hanner takes a moment to wipe off his hands.

Yeah, Hanner says.

Good, the Con Man says. Fix this. We're in a hurry.

Looks like the radiator, Hanner says.

Whatever, the Con Man says. Fix. Quick. Understand?

The Con Man dials his phone and walks away.

From the passenger seat, a beautiful Lady Grifter slides over and pops the hood. Hanner fixes the radiator hose and fills it from an old plastic antifreeze jug. She gets out to watch.

Hi, she says.

Hi, Hanner says.

The Con Man returns as Hanner closes the hood.

Good, he says. Let's go.

That'll be a hundred, Hanner says.

Dollars, the Con Man scoffs. You're a mechanic and a thief?

I also play the piano, Hanner says.

Pay this guy and let's go, the Con Man says.

The Lady Grifter is taken aback.

Excuse me, she asks.

I'm out of cash, the Con Man says. Remember? Give me what you got. I'll pay you back double when we get there.

We made that deal, she says. Yesterday. Remember?

Right, he says, remembering. Right.

I'll take a credit card, Hanner says.

The Lady Grifter and the Con Man look at each other.

They don't have any of those either.

Sorry, she says. Been a busy couple of days.

I'm happy to hold the car here until you figure something out, Hanner says.

You can't just keep us here, the Con Man says.

Tell you what, Hanner says. Race you for it.

My car for a radiator hose, the Con Man says. In what?

Hanner points at his rusted muscle car.

That one starts, Hanner says.

Tell you what, the Con Man says. You've got a deal. Let's make this quick.

On the abandoned strip of asphalt that runs past the junkyard, they pull the cars side by side and get out.

Down this road, it's two miles to the fire station and back, Hanner says.

Perfect, the Con Man says as the Lady Grifter saunters away. Hey, get in.

The Lady Grifter reaches the other side of the road and waits.

No, I've seen you drive, she says.

In a perpetual hurry, the Con Man scoffs.

That the way you want it, he asks.

That's the way I want it, she says.

Fine, he says.

He gets in. The engines grumble. She steps between the fenders and drops a lollipop.

The Con Man's car leaps into the distance. Hanner cuts his engine and gets out. The Lady Grifter steps toward him, the sun setting behind them.

He's not coming back, Hanner says.

Let's hope not, she says. Want to get a beer?

I know a place, Hanner says. She circles the car and slides in.

Soon the Lady Grifter and Hanner cruise the desert floor. Music floating through the radio fades to static. Hanner takes a sudden turn off the road. They wind down into a

picturesque valley, desert twirling behind the tires. The
faded radio signal returns.

When they reach the spot he's looking for, the song plays
clearly. He stops the car, turning down the radio.

Out here there's a bubble, he says. Keeps the rest of the
world away. Go too far in any direction, radio signal fades.
You're leaving the bubble.

They get out. The radio plays from the car.

She studies the huge, dry lake bed.

You've never left here, she asks.

I like this song, he says.

And she likes him.

How about that beer, she asks.

At the nearest roadside tavern, a heavily muscled
Bartender grins as they come through the door.

Hello, pretty lady, he says. Who's the jerk?

Quiet, you, Hanner says.

Forgive me, miss, I'm naturally entertaining, the
Bartender says. Got a dollar?

Hanner has one ready.

Here, he says. Got to put your name on it.

The Bartender finds a pen and she signs the dollar.

I know a good spot for it, the Bartender says.

The Lady Grifter's eyes are on the low ceiling, stapled
with countless small bills. They cover every inch, their edges
fluttering from a small fan turning in the corner.

What's with all the money, she asks.

The Bartender staples her dollar to the ceiling.

There's one for every person who ever walked in here,
Hanner says. That way, you know, at least you're
remembered someplace, I guess.

That's a lot of people for all the way out here, she says.

Got a Walmart now, the Bartender says, a little defensive.

That's terrific, honey, she says without a trace of irony.
You have a phone? I better tell my Mother I'm alright.

The Bartender leads the way.

Here, use the one in my office.

The next morning, Hanner wakes to the sound of the
Lady Grifter stealing his car. His wallet's empty. He takes his
time pulling on his clothes.
The morning sun hangs low over a dusty trailer park.
Hanner lets his door slam and finds his next-door
Neighbor pulling up on a motorcycle.
That lady steal your car, he asks.
Yeah, Hanner says. Worth it, though.
The Neighbor tosses him the keys to his bike.
I'll bet, he says. Here. Go get her.
Full tank, Hanner says.
Deal, his Neighbor says.
By now Hanner's car is back in the parking lot of the bar
from the night before. The Bartender is shot, leg bleeding
into the gravel, a baseball bat beside him. Cell phone out of
reach.
The Lady Grifter is furious.
Why would you do that, she asks.
The Con Man stares down at the small gun in his hand.
He startled me, the Con Man says.
She holds a bag overflowing with torn dollar bills.
What do we do now, she asks.
Run, the Con Man says.
They jump into the Con Man's sports car. As they drive
away, Hanner slides up on the bike. He rushes to the
Bartender.
Don't move, Hanner says.
I'm fine, the Bartender says, more pissed than hurt. I was
sleeping on that old pool table in the back. They broke in
and tore down all the damn money. Emptied out the register.
Found that pistol I keep under the bar. He caught me in the
thigh when I went to smash him. Go on. Go get them. I'm
alright. Hand me my phone.
The Bartender dials an ambulance as Hanner picks up the

bat.

Soon, the Con Man's car appears on the horizon, growing larger through his windshield as Hanner gains steam. He catches up and sticks his grill to the guy's bumper. Never taps or falls behind. Simply hangs there as if motionless. Together they near a sharp set of curves.

The Con Man is in a panic.

What the fuck is he doing, he yells.

Pushing his foot to the floor, he enters the curves too fast and buries the car hard into a towering drift of weeds, sand, and salt.

The Con Man and Lady Grifter stumble out of their crumpled car, banged up and bleeding.

Alright, genius, the Lady Grifter manages through a wall of anger. What now?

Shut up and let me think, he says, pressing a slice across his temple with one palm, dripping blood directly from the other. Here, give me that gun back.

I threw it out the window, she says.

Oh course you did, he says.

Stumbling back toward the road, they find Hanner leaning against his car, bat menacingly set high on his shoulder.

Morning, he says.

This was all her idea, the Con Man says. She called me from that bar and said meet her there in the morning. Her idea. Hers. She sees money and can't help herself. It's a sickness.

She ignores him and focuses on Hanner.

I'm sorry, honey, she says. For what it's worth, I had a real good time.

The Con Man pulls his phone from his pocket and dials.

Look, you win, the Con Man says. You take the cash like you never saw us, we'll call a tow truck, no problem. None of us were ever here, right?

Hanner takes the phone, raises the bat and hits it a

country mile. Then he picks up the bag, gets in his car and drives away, angry.

The road curves for a long time before Hanner slows near the top of a tall hill. He climbs onto the trunk of his car as the sun finishes rising over a wire-wrapped prison in the distance.

After being searched and searched again, he waits on one side of security glass. Prisoners and families come and go, reuniting through phone handsets. The chair across from Hanner stays empty.

Alright, a Senior Guard says, hovering nearby. That's an hour. He's not coming out and I got to give that chair to somebody else.

Yeah, Hanner says.

Maybe next time, the Guard says.

Maybe, Hanner says. He doing alright?

Sure, the Guard says. You know how your Dad is. It's the Captain's world. We're just all paying rent.

A few days later, Hanner's tow truck rolls steadily down an endless asphalt ribbon. Sky clear. Sun high and hot. Hanner in a foul mood. Jack watches the horizon, his mind far away.

A beat-up old car sits broken down by the side of the road. The Stranded Driver holds up his phone, searching for a signal, waving gratefully as the tow truck stops.

Hanner shuts off the engine. Jack stares out the window.

Hot today, Jack says.

Hanner laughs.

This isn't hot, he says.

Jack and Hanner get out and greet the Stranded Driver.

Thank you for stopping, he says.

Hanner sizes up the trouble with the car. There's a growing river of fluid from the engine along the ground.

Where you headed, he asks.

San Francisco, the Stranded Driver says.

Long way from here, Hanner says.

I'd settle for a garage right now, the Stranded Driver says.

Got one of those, Hanner says. Tow's two-fifty.

That's pretty steep, the Stranded Driver says.

Feel free to shop around, Hanner says.

Right, the Stranded Driver says. What do you think it is?

Now Hanner sizes up the Stranded Driver.

What happened, Hanner asks.

It was like a loud ping and a bang, and the whole thing just stopped, the Stranded Driver says.

Jack lifts the hood and pokes around. You threw a rod, he says.

The Stranded Driver doesn't like the sound of this.

How much is that, he asks.

Hanner shrugs.

The rod, he asks.

Yeah, the Stranded Driver says.

The rod's like a hundred and seventy-five dollars, Hanner says.

That doesn't sound so bad, the Stranded Driver says.

Now ask me about the block, the valves, cam, and everything else that bent and melted when your engine exploded, Hanner says.

I'm guessing an exploded engine costs more than the car's worth, the Stranded Driver says.

It's a disposable culture, Hanner says.

Let me think a minute, the Stranded Driver says, pacing.

Happy to buy it off you, Hanner says. I can sell the rest for parts.

Perfect, the Stranded Driver says. How much?

Two-fifty, Hanner says.

The parts have got to be worth more than that, the Stranded Driver says. Right?

Far more, Hanner says. Would you like us to leave the car? Maybe a better offer's right there on the horizon. You never know.

146

No, the Stranded Driver says. Alright. Fine.

Get your stuff together, Hanner says. We'll drop you at the bus station.

The Stranded Driver gathers his things from the car. Jack and Hanner pull out the chains to start hooking up the car.

Jack looks back at the Stranded Driver.

Feel good about that one, he asks.

Hanner doesn't.

Didn't you, he asks.

Fair's fair, man, Jack says.

Fair, Hanner asks. Did I lie to that guy?

I didn't say that, Jack says.

But you're saying I misled him in some way, Hanner says. Maybe didn't offer all his options? Forced his hand?

No, Jack says. That was pretty much the size of it.

So, then, fair's a magical pixie providing roadside assistance, Hanner says.

No, Jack says.

Then fair's what somebody's ready to pay, Hanner says. Cuts both ways, trust me. You want to keep getting by out here, you're going to have to realize, it's not about you.

I'll keep that in mind, Jack says.

By the end of the day in the middle of town, only a handful of cars are parked up and down the street. Occasional shoppers come and go. Wedged between the barbershop and thrift store is a tiny town bar and grill, door wide open.

Melinda glances over as she passes the door and stops.

Hello there, Melinda says.

Inside, a smiling New Bartender wipes down the bar.

Hello, he says.

She saunters in and sits at the bar.

Well, she says. Haven't seen you in here before.

Started this morning, he says.

Nice to meet you, Melinda says. I'm Carol. Welcome. Bad

147

news. I'm afraid you're a little too good looking. Gonna stick out in this town.

Not at all true, but he'll take it.

Can I get you some coffee, he asks.

Oh, you know, since I'm already here, how about a scotch, neat, please, she smiles, sliding onto a barstool.

Because you look a little young, he says. You know, for scotch.

She laughs.

I do get that a lot, Melinda says. Thank you. But, no, I'm the elementary school teacher here in town. Can't wait to tell the ladies in the front office you carded me.

She digs through her purse and holds up a convincing fake ID.

Believe me, sweetie, I'm legal, Melinda says.

Cool, he says, handing it back. Then shouldn't you . . .

Summer break, she says, dropping cash on the bar.

Got it, he says. Preference?

Oh, whatever you like, Melinda says. I trust you.

An interstate bus pulls up at a stop outside.

Billows hustles off with a suitcase and, not looking at all for traffic,, charges across the street, bursting into the Sheriff's store-front office, where he sits behind a big desk reading a newspaper.

Sheriff, Billows announces. I've given this a lot of thought. I want to . . .

The Sheriff stands, calmly rounds his desk, grabs Billows by the back of the neck, drags him out the door and tosses him in the gutter.

Alright, the Sheriff says. Want to try that again?

I figure, you know, uhm, Billows chatters. Why go the whole way to the Army when I can kick ass right here at home? I want to serve my community. I want to be your next lawful deputy.

The Sheriff chuckles. He walks into the office and returns with a wooden clipboard he bounces off Billows' head.

That's your application, the Sheriff says. Come back tomorrow. Do not bring a gun.

Sure, Billows says. But . . .

The Sheriff notices his actual new Deputy park his cruiser and slip suspiciously into a back alley down the street.

No gun, the Sheriff says, locking the office door.

Fine, Billows says. No gun.

As the Sheriff crosses the street, something else catches his attention. From a nearby doorway, he can hear Melinda laughing.

In the bar, tilting her glass, she flirts with the New Bartender.

How about another, he asks.

Don't mind if I do, she says.

The Sheriff appears at the open door.

Hello there, Sheriff, he says. I'm . . .

Serving liquor to my underage Daughter, the Sheriff says.

Oh, no, I, so sorry, I just started here, the New Bartender says.

Finished, the Sheriff says.

What, the Bartender asks.

You mean you just finished here, the Sheriff says. You don't work in this town. Be gone when I get back. And feel lucky I've got my hands full.

The Sheriff shoves Melinda, kicking and screaming, out the bar door and across the street to his office, past the desks and down a hallway to the lockup in the back. He tosses her in a holding cell.

Will you ever learn, he grunts.

Right back at you, she says.

Funny girl, he says, shutting out the light. Get comfortable.

Crossing the street, the Sheriff traces the Deputy's path from earlier. Rounding a corner down a short alley, he can clearly see the Deputy in a second-story window, in an animated conversation with the entire group of the Bank

Robbers who were watching mob money transfers at the bank.

Aw, donkey shit, the Sheriff says.

Drawing his weapon, he sneaks smoothly up the apartment stairs and kicks in the back door of a dingy apartment.

The place is plastered with maps, blueprints and photographs of the bank, streets and surrounding area. Drapes wide open.

The men freeze, startled to see him. The Sheriff glances around, furious, and puts the Deputy against the wall by the throat.

So, you dick birds think it's this easy to rob a bank in my town, the Sheriff asks.

Let go, asshole, the Deputy says.

The Deputy struggles, but the older man has him expertly pinned.

I am waiting for an answer, the Sheriff says.

Got it, the Deputy chokes. Now let me go.

The Sheriff drops the Deputy, who hits the floor, gasping for air.

Wise up, he says. Close those drapes. Gossip's quicker than lightning.

They close the drapes and gather the pictures.

The Sheriff finds a seat at a little kitchen table and sets his giant revolver down within reach. Slowly, he turns it like the hand of a clock, until it points their way.

Now, the Sheriff says. You're going to get your dirty money. And your people can take this town off of whoever runs things this week. Move whatever shit through it, safe and sound. Frankly, I'm thrilled for the old-fashioned interest in the community. Been a few lean years. But all that still goes straight through me. And I'm not resting my retirement on your combined intellects. So, let's say you go ahead and take it from the top. If we're doing this, the time to impress me is right the fuck now.

The Robbers shuffle pictures and all start pointing and talking at once.

Give us a minute, the Deputy says.

The Sheriff pops open a can of beer sitting on the table across from him.

Take your time, he says.

The next morning, Doc scurries up a rickety ladder sticking out of a deep hole and crouches behind a boulder, eyes shut, hands covering his ears. He waits. And waits. His eyes open. Seems too long. He waits longer. Way too long. He's about to stand up to look, and . . . Boom.

Sharp debris rains from the sky. Jack pops up from behind a boulder nearby.

Are you going to learn to stay down, Jack yells. Or are one of those going to take your head off?

This takes concentration, Doc says. You going to keep nagging or let me work? I'd appreciate some peace and quiet.

What you're doing isn't anything like peace and quiet, Jack says.

I need you to go into town and get me some blasting caps, Doc says.

I don't want you out here blowing up shit all alone, Jack says.

I'm out of blast caps, Doc says. What am I going to do? Wish the rocks to explode? Look for yourself.

Jack opens a lock box and finds it empty.

Alright, he says.

I got plenty to sort through, Doc says. Go to the house. Sleep in your own bed. I'm fine.

Alright, Jack says. I'll go ahead and get food and fuel for the month. See you in the morning.

Gin, Doc says.

No gin, Jack says, starting their old truck.

When he's gone, Doc goes into the old shack and bangs

151

around. He emerges with a brand-new box of blasting caps and a bottle of gin under his arm.

Now maybe I can get some work done, Doc says.

A few miles outside town, the Con Man's car, front end crumpled but still rolling, clanks to a stop in front of a local motel. He gets out, his face fresh from a pretty good beating.

The Lady Grifter wakes up in the front seat and rolls down the window.

What are we doing, she asks.

My head is splitting, the Con Man says. I need to lay down a minute.

No, she says. What are we doing back in this stupid town? We're supposed to be going south. This isn't south.

Quick side trip, he says. That friend of yours. I'm going to give him a piece of my mind. And then we're on our way. Promise. Alright?

No way, she says. You shot a guy here.

His word against mine, the Con Man says. They got their money back. Look around you. It's like cowboy times without the hats. Nobody cares.

He's already stumbling through the door into the motel lobby. The Motel Clerk eyes the wrecked car out front, along with the Lady Grifter in it.

One please, the Con Man says.

Double occupancy is more than what the sign says, the Clerk says.

No problem, the Con Man says.

Up front, the Motel Clerk says.

Yeah, see, thing is, a local friend of ours will be picking up the bill, the Con Man says. His treat. He's not here yet. As you can see, we've had quite a time. Love to get cleaned up and sort things out. Come on. Your parking lot is empty. We're maybe staying for a couple days. Bone tired. Don't make us go down the road. Bird in hand, right? If we could wait and settle our bill then for double . . . Mitch, is it?

The card in front of the Motel Clerk reads: *Hello! I'm Mitch!*

Sorry, the Motel Clerk says. No.

The Con Man wobbles a bit, exhausted.

Which part, he asks.

No, Mitch is the night guy now and, no, I need money up front, the Motel Clerk says. So, I guess, both parts.

The office door flies open and the Lady Grifter flutters in, reading the room. She digs a pair of earrings from the corner of her bra.

Hi there, she says. Sorry to barge in. My, you have a kind face, Mitch.

Thanks, the Motel Clerk says, as she takes his hand and curls his fingers around the earrings.

Honey, my Mother gave me these, she says. If she had any idea how bad my week's been, she would have me hand them to you and say, get this young lady to a shower. I clean up real nice, Mitch. What do you say? Can't you help us?

He slides a key across the counter. She smiles.

I certainly can, the Motel Clerk says.

The exhausted Con Man clutches his swelling face.

Great, he says. Ice machine?

Broken, the Motel Clerk says.

Of course, the Con Man says.

Scattered across Doc's small compound on the edge of town, abandoned machines of dubious value guard a rambling ranch house. Some of it still works, though much never will again. Most of a washer-dryer rests on a four-wheeler chassis with no wheels. A pile of telephone switch boxes snake the dirt with cascading wires. A fading yellow school bus is bolted to a large, rusting Quonset hut.

Jack parks and goes inside.

Inside could be a functioning historical museum for the entire area. Every shelf and surface covered with aging, commemorative trinkets, school pennants, brass figures and election buttons. That, and a lot of desert taxidermy.

Jack finds a beer in the fridge and a seat by the window. Staring out at Doc's scavenged junk menagerie, he needs a quiet moment to think. But the house is too quiet.

In the air conditioning of the town grocery store, Jack wanders the aisles, pushing a wobbly cart, mind elsewhere, buying provisions by the pound and gallon.

Red-haired Wanda Billows takes his money at the register.

How you been, Jack, she asks.

About the same, Wanda, he says. You?

Wanda rolls her eyes.

Nothing ever happens around here, she says.

Yeah, Jack says. Starting to notice that.

Melinda wakes to find herself still in the holding cell. Body stiff, she's been in there overnight. The door is open. She looks out. Nobody around.

There is a full food tray outside the door. She ignores it, then goes back and pockets whatever she can.

Melinda finds her way down the short hallway to the bathroom and showers. She starts the water. Not her first time here.

Melinda shuffles out of the holding area, across the office toward the front door. The place is empty, except for the Sheriff, feet up, reading the paper at his desk.

She almost says something, but doesn't. The door closes hard behind her. He never looks up.

Ungrateful, he says.

Jack's friends Merl and Pete work at a corporate gas station and convenience store on the edge of town. They wear matching uniforms with their names on them.

Jack fills a giant can in the back of his truck.

How do you know that, he asks.

Billows' Mom told my Mom, Merl says. It happened right

before they shaved his head. You know how he gets.
Standing in line, all wound up, talking everybody's ear off
the whole way. Finally, some doctor tore up his paperwork.
Sent him home on general principal.

Even the military doesn't need that kind of aggravation,
Pete says.

Didn't shit himself, Jack says. Technically, he is
improving over time.

You'll do a whole lot better when you finally go, Jack,
Merl says.

Me, Jack asks. Go where?

Wherever people go in the rest of the world, Pete says.
Out doing whatever it is they do.

Walk around malls or whatever, Merl says. Go
swimming. Stare at your lawn. I don't know.

That's not me, Jack says.

Don't think it works that way, Merl says.

But you two are all set, Jack says.

Only until we invent something, Merl says. Plus a solid
investment plan that rolls keno into scratchers into power
ball.

All you got to do is diversify, Pete says.

Melinda flies past them, heading away from town on a
little blue motorcycle. Suddenly the bike sputters and glides
to a stop. She climbs off and kicks it.

After a while, Jack rolls up in Doc's old truck. By now,
Melinda is sobbing, pushing her broken-down bike out of
town with just the clothes on her back.

Hi, he smiles from the driver-side window. Mix up your
stories again?

She doesn't stop. He rolls alongside her.

Thanks for that, she says. Go away. I'm busy.

Seriously, he says. You're not getting anywhere this way.

Didn't ask you, she says. I'm leaving.

Terrific, but headed this way, you're hiking up into the
mountains, he says.

She stops and gets her bearings.

Shit, she says.

Come on, Jack says. Give it a rest for a minute.

Melinda watches Jack roll her bike up into the back of the truck on an old plank, finding a rope to tie it down. They drive away together.

Around then, the Sheriff and the town's Ex-Mayor sit on the porch of a small, weathered hillside mansion with a million-dollar view of nothing.

They pour glasses from an unmarked jug of liquor, well past drunk.

Citizens band radio, the Sheriff says. The whole world right there in front of you. All you had to do was listen. Analog. It all meant something. Then the computers. Mobile phones. It's the joy that went out of the whole thing. The fuzz sound when you came on the line. That squelch. And then off to the races. That's what's missing. We made choices when we saw fit. Because we, you and me. The Captain. We were the law. No satellites tracking your position. That's the difference. I was born too late, that's all. Too damn late. Historically.

I was the last grinning Mayor of a place now coordinated by two different at-large committees and a state board, the Ex-Mayor says. Who meet hundreds of miles away from each other, on videotape. Don't you lecture me about the many punishments of progress.

The Ex-Mayor wears a heavy home-arrest bracelet.

When that grand jury sent you home, I suppose progress called it even, the Sheriff says.

We did have it all there for a minute, the Ex-Mayor says. Didn't we? Once you have money, power, women. Privacy. What else could there be?

Time, the Sheriff says, pouring himself another.

You certain about this outfit you're all mixed up with, the Ex-Mayor asks.

Not even a little, the Sheriff says. But if not now, when? Right?

Sure, the Ex-Mayor says. Well, please enjoy any nice extended vacations in the future. Safe travels and all that, if there happen to be any.

I shouldn't brag, the Sheriff says.

Please don't, the Ex-Mayor says. Wouldn't want you to shoot me on your way out of town.

He flashes his official election-season smile. They laugh and drink some more.

The sun is down. Doc's truck is parked on a bluff. All the stars are out. Jack's making a fire. Melinda sits on a blanket, eating from tins of dried rations, drinking cheap wine.

I have to think she knew she was dying, Jack says. Somehow. So we ended up out here. Mom's safe place, I guess. Here with Doc. Now, all the sudden, everybody's sure I'm leaving. Like I missed a meeting.

Takes a big man to complain so much that people care about him, Melinda says.

That's not it, Jack says.

It's your turn, that's all, she says. Anybody can see that. Except you, I guess. You're always lucky. You'll make it. No matter how many times I leave, I bounce right back. Though, I swear, one of these days, I'll make it stick. I hate this place.

There's got to be worse, he says.

You and your sunny disposition, she says. It's aggravating, you know that? All these years, growing up. You even stuck up for me a couple times. When I needed it. Why is that? Why'd you do that for me?

Oh, you're not bad, Jack says. Just bored. Anybody can see that.

She kisses him and they spend the night together on a blanket under the open sky.

Outside the Sheriff's office the next day, Billows paces in

a brand-new polyester uniform with creases from the
hanger.

When the Sheriff jangles his keys, Billows jumps a foot
and salutes.

What do we got today, boss, he chirps.

Stop that, the Sheriff says.

Billows bounces into the office behind the Sheriff.

Sit down, the Sheriff says. Don't move. Don't talk to
anybody. Especially me.

Hard on the new guy, Billow says. Awesome. I get that.
But if . . .

Tell me you do not have a gun, the Sheriff says, flipping
through a stack of mail.

Of course not, Billows says. I promise.

Not out in your car, the Sheriff says. Not at home. You are
to remain unarmed.

Yes, sir, Billow says. No, sir. Not me. Sir. I do look
forward to the day you will trust me with one, though, sir.

The Sheriff eyes the clock on the wall.

Don't move, the Sheriff says. Don't talk. Just sit.
Understand?

Yes, sir, I do, Billows says, finding a chair. Tough on the
new guy. So worth it.

At a booth in the big picture window of the corner diner,
the Deputy makes a big show of finishing his coffee and
nodding to everyone on his way out the door.

He crosses the street as the Sheriff glides past, pointing
his cruiser out of town.

Out on the highway, the Sheriff spots the luxury car with
the Mob Guys making their normal run. He hits the lights
and whips his cruiser around.

They pull over and roll down the windows, guns out of
sight, but ready. The Sheriff takes his time getting to the car.

Any idea why I pulled you over, he asks.

The Mob Delivery Driver shrugs.

No idea at all, The Sheriff asks.

Speeding, the Mob Delivery Driver offers.

Oh, the Sheriff says. You were also speeding?

I didn't think so, the Mob Delivery Driver says.

The Sheriff takes a long moment to glare through the car window.

Is that what you want me to write down here, he asks. You didn't think so? License and registration.

The Sheriff heads slowly back to his cruiser.

Be cool, the Mob Delivery Driver says. Let the hick cop have his fun. He just likes my car.

In town, the Bank Manager checks his watch and the camera monitors in his office twice. Nothing yet. He's not alone this time, turning his attention back to his much-younger Secretary, half-dressed on the couch. Family photo face down on his desk. Empty bottles in the wastebasket. They had a whole night of it.

I suppose we have another moment, the Bank Manager says.

They embrace until the luxury car appears. He drops her and straightens his tie, finding his keys, trying to focus his eyes.

The Bank Manager hustles across the lobby and opens the door for the man in a suit at the door with a duffle bag.

The Manager nervously scans the street. Moving a little slow, he's startled when the luxury car suddenly pulls away.

Where are they going, he asks.

Now the Boss Bank Robber has a mask on and a gun in the Manager's face.

Take a deep breath, he says.

The Bank Manager vomits across their shoes. Furious, the Boss Bank Robber leads him toward the back of the building.

You don't know what you're doing, the Bank Manager says.

Bet your kids on that, the Boss Bank Robber asks.

They're not even in town, the Bank Manager says.

We heard, the Boss Bank Robber says. Who timeshares in Sarasota?

The carefully researched detail hits its mark.

Just tell me what you want, the Bank Manager says.

Business as usual, the Boss Bank Robber says.

Hiding behind the desk in the Bank Manager's office, the Secretary watches them on the monitors, wide-eyed.

The actual mob luxury car pulls up outside. The real Mob Guys go through their normal routine, agitated, behind schedule and in a hurry.

The Bank Manager meets the Mob Delivery Driver at the door as usual. He leads him through the conference room to the hidden vault doors. When he fumbles with the code at the secondary vault, the Mob Delivery Driver notices for the first time that the Bank Manager is nervous, well past pale, and sweating bullets.

Hey, the Mob Delivery Driver says. What's with you?

There's now a pistol at the base of his skull. A much larger duffle bag lands at his feet.

Easy, big fella, the Boss Bank Robber says. We're just sending a message. Be smart and we'll have you on your way. Now fill the bag.

You're going to beg for your Mother, the Mob Delivery Driver grunts. You dumb . . .

For this, he gets a crack across the skull.

Half-dressed, the Secretary sneaks out of the office and crosses the lobby, slips out the front door and runs, screaming, down the street.

Gathered around the car, the Mob Guards look to each other and can't believe their eyes. Something's very wrong. Before they can reach for their guns, silenced rifle rounds bounce at their feet. They dive for cover.

The Second Bank Robber rounds the corner with a pistol in each hand.

Alright, he shouts. Calm, cool and collected, guys. You know what this is. My friend's a good shot, but his mind

160

wanders. So, stay put. The drop. That's all we want. Nothing else.

Through a rifle scope, crosshairs follow as the screaming Secretary sprints for the Sheriff's Office.

Billows is in the office, watching the clock hands as if wondering what might happen next, when the half-dressed Secretary rushes in. He tumbles from his chair in the corner.

They're robbing the bank, she shouts.

The bank, Billows echoes, even louder. This is it!

Billows props his ankle on the desk and pulls back his sock, where he finds the holster for a little pistol, much smaller than his hand, possibly even an antique of some kind.

Let's go, Billows says. Follow me!

I'm going to stay here, she says.

Good idea, he says, hurrying out and down the street, tiny pistol first.

The Boss Bank Robber shoves the Mob Delivery Driver towards the front door, giant duffle bag over his shoulder. The Bank Manager hands over a much smaller bag, half-full of money.

That can't be all from the regular vault, the Boss Bank Robber says.

So much is online these days, the Bank Manager says.

The Boss Bank Robber tosses the Bank Manager a zip-tie.

Hook yourself to the counter, the Boss Bank Robber says. Hands where I can see them.

The Boss Bank Robber shoves his hostage into the street as their getaway car pulls up. Billows rounds the corner, out of breath, pistol ready.

Bank robbery, Billows screams. Freeze!

He fires wild and dives for cover.

The Mob Guys draw their pistols, but the Bank Robbers are already firing.

Shopkeepers up and down the street emerge from doorways and windows with shotguns and rifles.

The Mob Guys get the worst of it. All three are killed, falling in different directions.

The Bank Robbers are hit but manage to reach their car and pull away. The getaway car bounces hard off a telephone pole on the corner. A head cracks a side window as the car limps off.

Down the street in street clothes, the Deputy takes a moment to collect himself, catches his breath, packs up his rifle and slips quickly off the low roof.

Way outside town and up in the hills, the Sheriff waits at his old hunting cabin with a second getaway car, one eye is on his watch. They're late.

A clunking engine in the distance. The Bank Robbers appear, both vehicle and occupants beat to hell.

The Sheriff directs them into a dilapidated work shed.

What a mess, he says.

They pile out of the car, bleeding, full of broken bones and bullet holes, dragging the money bags behind them.

Your little Deputy came around the corner and started shooting, the Boss Bank Robber says. It all went to shit from there.

Alright, well, you all got to get out of here, the Sheriff says. Right now.

They are dazed and in shock, wandering dumbly in circles. The Sheriff sees they are not going anywhere.

Fine, he says. Drag your asses inside.

As they haul themselves into the cabin, the Sheriff spots the smaller bag of money.

What the hell is this, he groans, cold with frustration.

That's all there was in the main vault, the Boss Bank Robber says.

You weren't supposed to take this, the Sheriff says.

So what, the Boss Bank Robber asks.

So, rip off the mob and nobody knows anything, the Sheriff says. Except whoever gets killed for it. Rob a real bank, and the Feds come to town.

We're all about to disappear, mutters the second Robber. Who cares?

So, disappear already, the Sheriff says.

Your guy shot me, the Boss Bank Robber says. Some sort of cap gun, but it still hurts.

The Robbers collapse in the corners of the little building. The Sheriff rolls back a rug and lifts a couple floorboards. He unzips the large bag and locks one of the money bundles into a hidden floor safe.

Hey, the Boss Bank Robber says. What the fuck are you doing?

Taking my cut, the Sheriff says. Do you mind?

The Sheriff replaces the rug and boards, then opens a large cabinet of emergency medical equipment. He tosses one of them a first-aid kit and another a bottle of pills.

Here, he says. Take twelve. Best I got for now. Let me go figure this out. I'll be back.

The Boss Bank Robber lifts his pistol.

You better, he says.

Or what, the Sheriff asks.

He takes the smaller bag. The Bank Robbers all object.

Where you think you're going with that, the Boss Bank Robber asks.

To fix your mess, the Sheriff says.

The door slams behind him.

Out on the highway, Hanner and Jack are out in the truck, looking for wrecks. The Sheriff passes them fast, going the other way.

He's sure in a hurry, Jack says.

Trouble for somebody, Hanner says.

They pass the Con Man's fancy crumpled car in front of the motel.

Look at that, Jack says.

Hanner is amused to see the Con Man's broken car.

That, he says. That there's more trouble than it's worth.

Now parked beside the back fence of Hanner's junk yard, the Sheriff opens his trunk and finds a large pork bone. Then he uses the car hood to climb the fence, the small bag of money slung over his shoulder.

Large dogs come running, but they seem to know him. He tosses the bone, which they happily fight over, then quickly pass out.

Good boys, the Sheriff says.

He searches the yard for a place to stash the bag, finds Hanner's old muscle car and pops the trunk.

Outside the bank, back in uniform, the Deputy stands helplessly by as a dozen FBI Agents in suits take measurements and photograph the area. Cars and lights everywhere, ambulances leave with the bodies.

The Sheriff parks and jumps from his car. The Lead Agent intercepts him. Their eyes meet in a shoving match.

Sheriff, she says. Glad you can join us.

My pleasure, the Sheriff says. Now please hurry up and get your people off my street.

She lets that go without comment.

So, she says. Neither you nor your one grownup Deputy here were anywhere near town when your only bank was robbed?

As I said, traffic duty, the Deputy says.

Budget cuts, the Sheriff says. Spreads us pretty thin.

Billows sits on the curb, feigning bumps and bruises, surrounded by fawning town folk, the new local hero.

Oh, the Lead FBI Agent says. I see. Thin? Look around you. Let me tell you about thin. Every person in my entire office, that's every agent in this part of the state, is right here, on your street, leaving the world-at-large unprotected against significant crime because you two can't keep your eyes on your little bank, full of, what? Twenty grand?

A Junior FBI Agent pipes up.

A little over forty, the Junior Agent offers.

The Lead Agent's look to the chirping underling is: Don't ruin my punchline.

Per regulation, my office was manned the entire time, the Sheriff says.

The Lead Agent flips through report papers in her hand.

By Deputy Dipshit and his cute little lady gun, she says. Correct?

He was instructed not to be armed, the Sheriff steams.

See, without that moron, these guys would have skated off someplace and hid, the Lead Agent says. Never so harmless in their lives. They'd spend it fast and it'd be a computer at the interstate office's problem by now. Insurance pays the bank. Lord knows, they got it. No trouble at all. But now my staff is here cataloguing a shootout with multiple corpses, about to chase armed suspects into crawl spaces, garage attics, and wherever else they can waste our time. You ever arrest a person for protecting their only nephew? You have no idea the paperwork that comes with that. Not worth the people hours, plain and simple. Not to mention, at exactly five-thirty, I'm missing a divisional little-league game back in the land where roads have curbs. So. Now. My considerable training dictates we ask the questions like why here? Why now? Small time robbers are always going to pick a target close to home. If they're hurt, they didn't get far. In fact, they're already right back where they feel safest. Folks. I would like to lock someone up and sleep in my own bed tonight. I personally don't care who. And my experience is, you local boys always have somebody around that thinks they're ready for the big time. These things usually begin and end with the first moron on the right. So, let's start there. Here's your chance to solve the big case, Sheriff. What do you have for me?

Practice that on the way over, the Sheriff asks dryly. Or is it mostly the same speech every time?

In front of his junkyard, Hanner and Jack unhook a

broken-down car as Melinda pulls up in Doc's truck.

Your business, Hanner says. But you sure she's the best person to lend your truck?

Working on a trust thing, Jack says.

Melinda slides the truck to a stop.

Somebody robbed the bank, she says.

Wow, Jack says. How's your alibi?

Solid, she says. Yours?

Can't be much in there, Jack says.

You'd be surprised, Hanner says.

They walk into the junkyard, a careful maze of metal.

Haven't been inside this place in a long, long while, Melinda says.

Try to keep your hands in your pockets, Hanner says. We prosecute shoplifters.

Hey, another fan club meeting, she says.

So, I gather you know each other, Jack says.

Our Dads fought together in the Army, Hanner says. That makes us like cousins.

Not the regular Army, though, Melinda says. Make no mistake. He means the government's very special, super-secret forces, with the unmarked planes and no patches. Toppled leaders and burned villages from Asia to Kabul to South America and back again.

Then they came here, Hanner says. And miss it every day. I'm sure you read the rest in the paper.

Wrote a two-hundred-word essay for current events class in middle school from an article in some big magazine, Jack says. A Desert Paradise For Crime, it said. Teacher cut the whole article out and hung it on the classroom wall. Big news.

Wasn't all that long ago, you'd think the sky had to ask the two of them if it's time to rain, Hanner says.

That day the judge gave the Captain life, my Dad didn't explode like I thought he would, Melinda says. He came home, took off his suit, sat in our kitchen and stared a hole through the wall. In his underwear, drinking. I ran away and hid for as long as I could manage. Because I figured, next time he stands up, he's going to break everything he sees. I was right that time. Their whole crooked business fell apart after that. The Sheriff lost everything but his dumb job.

Wasn't life, Hanner says. They gave him ninety-three years. But you watch. The Captain'll live it out, just to spite them.

Magazine said somebody ratted, and whoever it was, prosecutors kept it off the books, Jack says.

Would've had to've been someone everybody trusted, Hanner says. I mean, to really put the old man away. To shut the whole thing down for good.

Yep, somebody just like that, Melinda says.

There's a rumble in the distance that echoes across the top of the car piles. Hanner climbs onto a truck hood to get a view of the road.

Here they come, he says.

Who, Jack asks. Why?

Hanner disappears into the junkyard.

Does it matter, he yells. Come on, let's go.

Sheriff in the passenger seat, the Lead Agent steers a thundering line of SUVs toward the junkyard. Billows is in the back seat, just thrilled to be along for the ride.

You know that Hanner's got to have a back way out of his hole, Billows says.

Quiet, the Sheriff says. Go around back.

The Lead Agent rounds a corner to find Hanner leaving out the back gate in his muscle car.

That your guy, she asks.

He's running, isn't he, the Sheriff asks. Get us to the main road. And we'll need a helicopter.

You want a helicopter out here, get yourself a real bank to rob, she says.

The chase grows louder and faster as the Sheriff surrenders, sits back, and enjoys the ride.

Hanner takes them off the road. The city SUVs can't follow him through salt dunes at that speed. The Lead Agent's SUV rolls, tumbling with a moan, like a great elephant in battle. They crawl from the wreck as Hanner disappears into the distance.

Next time, I drive, the Sheriff says.

A few hours later, a newer and much nicer luxury car parks in front of the Sheriff's office. Two very tough Mob Lieutenants in designer suits get out and look around. Work Crews are still cleaning up the crime scene and hauling off vehicles.

The Deputy sits behind the Sheriff's desk. The Mob Lieutenants glide in, then lock the door behind themselves.

Sorry, the Deputy says. Sheriff's not here. FBI's out doing, I don't know, whatever.

Beneath the desk, he carefully draws his pistol.

Not interested in him, the First Mob Lieutenant says. You are the future, aren't you? Old guys all got to retire someday, don't they?

They menacingly circle the room.

I wouldn't know about that, the Deputy says.

Heard about all the excitement today, the First Mob Lieutenant says. Rushed right out from the city. It's quite a drive. We represent certain business interests in the area. Want to make sure everything's all fine and dandy. And so forth.

Business interests, the Deputy says. The shoe repair? The liquor store?

Something like that, the First Mob Lieutenant says. Like I say, this morning we heard all about your little bank robbery incident. Ruined my breakfast, sorry to say. Some friends and I eat together now and again. Normally the highlight of my week. Special little place. Out of the way. Enjoyable. Not this morning. Because this guy at the table. This little runt of a guy. We send him out and all around all the time, sort of

keeping an eye on things. I don't know what all. Mostly it's
to have him out of the way as much as possible, I guess.
Cousin of somebody. You know how it is. So, we're there at
the table, and start hearing about this robbery of yours, and
he pipes up and says, hey, I know that piece of shit town.
That's where, the other day, he sees a guy he remembers
from Florida. Florida. Of all the fuck. And we put together
the guy is part of this group that ripped us off in, let's say,
Tallahassee, all those years ago. Weird, huh? And now
there's you, all dressed like a genuine officer of the law.
Completely official. Look here. He even took a picture with
his phone. Now, how funny someone would make that kind
of connection, on the fly, so far away, and so completely ruin
my breakfast. Funny, right? On such a nice day. I will forever
remember those uneaten waffles.

He holds up a phone with a picture of the Deputy in
uniform, strolling out of the Sheriff's office with a big smile
on his face.

Handsome, the Deputy says.

We checked around and, yeah, you got a face some
people remember, the First Mob Lieutenant says. And here
you are. How about that? Important for us to know about.
What, with our local business interests relying on us to make
sure their goods and services move through this shitburg in
a timely fashion. Unmolested.

Your business interests, the Deputy says. The shoe repair,
you must mean. Or the liquor store. Maybe the auto parts
shop?

That's right, the First Mob Lieutenant says. And,
unfortunately for me, last week, this dumb chump, for
whatever reason, he sent me your exact picture. Only me.
Smart phones. Social media. Out of nowhere. Why me? Ask
his phone book. Time stamped and everything. Boom. And I
thought, this can wait. You know how people do? Screw this
dumb prick. I'll take care of him later when I'm good and
ready. Right? Much later. Right? Well, now it's later. And I'm

on the hook for this whole mess. You asshole. Not something our associates take lightly. My friend here is in charge of making sure things get solved properly from this point forward. In a managerial sense. We were pulling into town just now and he says to me, so where to first? And I said, let's go see what our great old friend from Florida can tell us about it. So, hello. Friend.

I have no idea who you gentlemen are, the Deputy says. Or what you want. If you need assistance, please dial the emergency number.

That's one way to play it, the Second Mob Lieutenant says.

Look, the First Mob Lieutenant says. Professional courtesy, alright? You got something to help yourself out of this thing, speak up now. Speak loud. Because whatever you had in mind, pal, it sure as hell wasn't supposed to go down like this. Throwing you a rope here. It's still gonna hurt. But not as bad. Or long. I promise. Interested?

I'm not sure I understand, the Deputy smiles. Is there some way I can help you gentlemen?

Never say we didn't try, the First Mob Lieutenant says.

They leave. The Deputy locks the door behind them and pulls the shade. Then he runs to the toilet to vomit.

The nearest abandoned truck stop is a huge swath of concrete, outbuildings, a boarded-up restaurant, empty pumps, and a sea of storage units. All long bankrupt and forgotten.

Jack and Melinda wait in Doc's truck. Hanner drives out of the desert through a gap in the back fence.

How did you know I'd come here, he asks.

I would, Melinda says.

Lock that thing up, Jack says. We got to hide you.

Hanner pulls his car into one of the countless storage units. He's about to close the door, but has a thought and pops the trunk. The smaller bag of bank money sits open, front and center.

Now, how'd that get there, Hanner says.

Only way to get that kind of luck, Melinda says. Piss off the Sheriff.

Seems so, Jack says.

Look, Melinda says. I know my Dad. Not killing you after the trial just means he's holding out to really enjoy it. When he hangs this robbery on you, there are people inside that owe him in an ugly way. I don't know why you didn't run all those years ago, or why the cops didn't hide you, but now you got to get going and quick.

Thank you for your concern, Hanner says. Like I told them then, this is where I live.

That night, Doc's truck is parked outside the Sheriff's cabin as he bandages the injured and pissed-off Bank Robbers. The Deputy and Sheriff pace, frustrated.

Scrapes and bruises, Doc says. Couple broken bones. I got a bullet out of this one. Other ones went straight through. You'll all walk funny, but you're going to be fine eventually.

We need to move them soon, the Deputy says. How long?

Got these boys mostly held together with duct tape and spit, medically speaking, Doc says. Give it a couple days or so, or nobody's getting far. After that, no jogging. That shit really will kill you.

Doc stands, gathers his things, and finds his way to the door with a nod.

I'll be back tomorrow with food, the Sheriff says, following Doc out.

The Boss Bank Robber waits for the door to close.

What the fuck was that, he asks.

You're not bleeding to death, the Deputy says. Are you?

Outside, Doc climbs into his truck.

Like old times, he says.

Yeah, the Sheriff says. Thanks.

171

Didn't do it for you, Doc says. Did it because somebody had to. But these days I realize, maybe it was me that kept the ball rolling for you monsters all those years. Kept all that blood from leaking out where the world can see. Old times, I said. Not good times.

Guess somebody had to, the Sheriff says.

Inside the cabin, they listen as both drive away. The Deputy pours the Bank Robbers each a tall glass of liquor.

Alright, he says. Let's stick with the plan. You only got to get to the meeting place. They're going to wait as long as they need to. You know what to do from there.

Let's go right now, the Boss Bank Robber says.

No, you listen to the crazy desert doctor, the Deputy says. Rest up. And when that Sheriff walks through that door tomorrow, make sure it's for the last time. Then be on your way. I'll handle the rest of everything.

The Deputy finishes his drink in a large, urgent gulp, sets a box of bullets on the table and leaves.

Out at Doc's goldmine, Hanner, Jack and Melinda watch a campfire, worried.

Doc pulls up in his truck, slams the door and stumbles over to dig around in his shack until he finds a bottle. No takers.

Evening all, Doc says, sitting and offering it around. Such a pretty night. Nice fire and the night air. Hear you found yourself some trouble.

Some, Hanner says.

You've been gone a while, Jack says.

Doc ignores him.

Well, Doc says. Truth is, without a little trouble now and then, where's the fun? Or at least that's how it seems sometimes. Now, if you'll excuse me, it's been a long day.

His emotions get away from him a little bit. Doc solemnly stands, bringing the bottle with him, closing the shack door behind himself.

Took his medical bag out to the Sheriff's cabin tonight, Jack says. Hasn't touched that thing in years.

Gee whiz, Melinda says. Wonder who could be all shot full of holes and hiding out there?

We're the ones with the bank money, Jack says. That'll be all anybody's going to come after.

That's not your everyday bank, Hanner says. And this isn't all the money.

The next morning, back in the Sheriff's office bathroom, the Deputy is a pale sheet of worry in the filthy mirror. A hard knock at the door.

Busy, the Deputy says.

He quickly washes his face and takes a deep breath.

Out front, the Sheriff parks his car as curious townspeople watch through their store windows.

Alright, the Sheriff shouts at them from the middle of the street. It's all settled but the paperwork. Nothing more to see. Go on, now.

They don't seem so sure.

The Sheriff walks in to find his office transformed into an FBI command center. Computers, radios and maps fill the loud, crowded room. Billows buzzes back and forth, thrilled by all the action.

Hi, boss, Billows chirps. Coffee? These guys so have the best coffee ever.

The Sheriff ignores him. He spots the Deputy slumping in the corner, putting up a poor front.

Well, the Sheriff barks.

Nothing new, the Deputy says.

Well, then, everybody try and make themselves at home, the Sheriff says.

The circus continues uninterrupted.

At the highway motel, their Con Man escapes the room as something inside shatters. He's halfway down the stairs when the Lady Grifter flings open their door.

And cigarettes, she says, slamming it closed.

Of course, my dearest, the Con Man says.

An Upset Guest from a neighboring room pokes her head out a door in annoyance.

A little loud, don't you think, she demands.

The Con Man makes sincere eye contact.

I certainly do, he says.

Driving the souped-up, classic sedan Hanner won from Billows, Jack drops Hanner at the storage unit where his car is hidden.

Good luck, Jack says.

You too, Hanner says.

Jack speeds off. Hanner opens the unit and grabs a flashlight from his back pocket. He pulls the door closed behind himself.

In the car's trunk, he finds a set of old gloves, dumping out the stacks of bills. One by one, he removes the bands and piles the cash back into the bag.

Walking distance from the motel, Melinda enters a cluttered pawn shop and studies the handguns under the glass.

At the counter, the Con Man is furious with the Pawn Shop Owner.

I paid a grand for this watch, the Con Man says.

I understand that you did, the Pawn Shop Owner says. Not sure why. Right now, I'll give you a hundred for it. In cash. So, what's happening?

The Pawn Shop Owner counts twenties across the counter. Angry, the Con Man scoops up the money and turns, tumbling over Melinda and into a row of hocked musical equipment. The Owner rounds the counter to help her up.

Sorry, the Con Man says. I didn't see you.

Get out of here, the Pawn Shop Owner says. My
insurance doesn't cover clumsy idiots.

In the motel parking lot, the Con Man stands next to his
bent-up car, searching every pocket. But then his car lock
chirps. Melinda walks over and tosses him his keys.

You dropped these, Melinda says.

I apologize, the Con Man says. Son of a bitch got me all
flustered.

That old guy is so cheap, Melinda says. Everybody
knows it. You're not from around here.

In town on business, he says.

And short on cash, she says.

The Con Man laughs.

Who isn't, he says.

I can maybe help with that, Melinda says. I need an extra
set of hands real quick. Even split. Nothing complicated. I
just want to grab something and go.

Tell me more, he says.

The Lady Grifter is sprawled on the bed reading a trashy
magazine when the Con Man bursts into their hotel room.

Get moving, the Con Man says. We're back in business.

Billows backs out the door of the corner diner, arms
stacked with takeout food for the FBI. He carefully heads
toward the Sheriff's office.

Down the street, Jack walks out of the grocery store,
climbs into Billow's car and cruises slowly past.

Son of a bitch, Billows says, eyes wide, jaw slack. Jack's
driving my car. Hanner gave that guy my damn car. Why
would Hanner give Jack my car? Son of a bitch! That's my
car! And Jack's driving it! Son of a bitch!

Now Billows can't help but drop everything as he reaches
the walkie-talkie on his otherwise empty uniform belt. A
spray of food and drinks covers the sidewalk in front of him.

He squeezes the button, running.

Son of a bitch, he shouts. Hello. Over!

From the walkie-talkie: *Who is this?*
Deputy Officer Billows, Billow says. Over!
From the walkie talkie: *Who gave you a radio?*
I am currently in pursuit of the suspect, Billows yells.
More news when I have it. Stay tuned. Over!
Billows starts an old scooter and pulls on his helmet.
From the walkie talkie: *Where is our lunch?*

The Sheriff parks outside his hunting cabin and looks
around for a while. Nothing moving. He digs a bag of
groceries out of the back seat. Before opening the cabin door,
he unbuttons his revolver.
Opening the door, he drops the bag and draws his gun.
The Bank Robbers are all dead and piled in one corner.
The big bag of money is in the other corner.
The First Mob Lieutenant is at the table, in full view of
the Sheriff, gun drawn. The Second stands out of sight
against the near wall, gun at the Sheriff's head level.
Come in, the First Mob Lieutenant says. It's nice to meet
you.
Your friend with the pistol by the door, the Sheriff says.
He know that?
The Second Mob Lieutenant steps into view.
Only being cautious, the Second Mob Lieutenant says.
Never know what kind of wild animals you'll find out here.
Right?
The Sheriff walks in, holsters his weapon, grabs a glass
from his cabinet and pours himself a drink. He takes a seat
at the table.
You got to know, where we come from, you're a bit of a
legend, the First Mob Lieutenant says. Most don't believe
you even exist. We waited all day to meet you. This whole
bank nonsense, we know it wasn't really about you. Times
change. Makes for hard choices. We can recognize that. I got
about a million and a half things I could ask you. So, let's
relax a minute. We got all the time in the world.

No thanks, the Sheriff says.

The Sheriff cracks one guy's skull with the chair he's sitting in, while giving the other a mouth full of glass. Both Mob Lieutenants fire, but in close quarters only hit each other. Wounded, angry, they pounce on the Sheriff.

Nobody stops swinging, fists, knees and elbows, broken table legs and bottles, until the Sheriff is the only one standing. He kicks the knobs off the stove and stumbles out as the cabin fills with gas.

The Second Mob Lieutenant pulls himself into the doorway and raises his pistol as the Sheriff fires twice into the gas meter. The cabin erupts into a pillar of flame.

A mile outside town, Billows and his scooter are distant in Jack's mirrors. He turns up the radio and taps the steering wheel in time with the road.

Billows realizes he's following Jack toward the storage units.

Should have known all along that Hanner and Jack would team up, Billows yells into the walkie-talkie, never letting go of the button. They're both such smug pricks about everything. They know we're looking for him. No place for them to hide out here. Except that old, closed-down truck stop. On my way there now at top speed. Hello? Copy? Over!

In the Sheriff's office, Billows' voice drones through a speaker on a table: *Do you copy? Oh, sorry, I'm holding down the . . . You can reply now . . . Hello? Over!*

The Lead Agent searches for the place on a wall map.

Turn that thing off, she says. Where is this idiot talking about? What truck stop?

The Junior Agent flips through another set of maps.

Found it, he says. It's not anywhere on the current maps. Must be closed a long time.

Great, the Lead Agent says. So, nobody's been out there yet? That's our spot. I'm sick of this room. Let's get out of here. Everybody. Go. Now. Move.

Amid the rows of the abandoned storage units at the ancient truck stop, the Con Man steers his crumpled car past identical doors. They get out. He's got a unit number scribbled on a piece of paper. The Lady Grifter is not pleased at all.

I can't read this dumb chick's writing, the Con Man says. I think it's this one.

He pulls open the door and finds Hanner leaning against his car.

Hello, Hanner says.

The surprised Con Man waves a short hunting knife.

How about that, the Lady Grifter says. You do make an entrance.

Knew somebody'd be here, the Con Man says. Wasn't expecting you, though. Save us a trip out to your giant pile of garbage. See? Back on the road before we know it.

Great, the Lady Grifter says. Let's go. And put that dinky thing away. Where did you get that?

Grabbed it at that pawn shop, he says.

You've been hanging around that pawn shop, Hanner says. Let me guess. Little birdie tell you which of these doors to open?

Never mind that, the Con Man says. You have no idea at all, the resources I got. Ears on the ground and so forth.

No kidding, Hanner says.

Thanks to you, we missed our appointment, the Con Man says. The huge pile of cash we thought we'd make, we now owe. Funny how life can turn that way, right? Given the circumstances, I thought it'd only be fair if you chipped in. Something meaningful, at least. Though, she's got a point when she keeps telling me this guy's just desert trash. What are we going to get out of him? I admit, not much.

Just hurry up, she says.

The closed bag of money is on the trunk beside Hanner.

That'll be a good start, the Con Man says. Pick it up and put it in our car. Slow.

Hanner takes the bag and stands by the Con Man's trunk. The Con Man shuffles through his keys.

The Lady Grifter is losing what's left of her patience.

What's your problem now, she asks.

I lost my door clicker, the Con Man says. Must've fell off.

Give me those, she says, taking the keys and unlocking the trunk for Hanner, leaning in close.

Hello there, he says.

I don't think you're desert trash, she says.

No, he says. I am. But I'm great at it.

She smiles. Hanner dumps the loose money into the trunk.

Hey, the Con Man says. What the fuck?

Oh, Hanner says. You want the bag too?

Hanner tosses in the bag and shuts the lid.

You know, I should leave you bleeding out here, the Con Man says. They wouldn't find you for weeks and weeks.

Oh, quit while you're ahead, the Lady Grifter says.

You know, you're welcome to stay, Hanner says.

She thinks about it. The Con Man laughs, stabbing Hanner's back tires.

Maybe another lifetime, sugar, she says.

They climb into their car and drive away, passing Jack in Billows' car halfway across the giant parking lot.

Hold on, the Lady Grifter says. Who's that?

The Con Man can't be bothered with details at the moment.

Who cares, he asks.

Jack pulls up to the storage unit as Hanner shuts the door.

Got sandwiches, Jack says.

Excellent, Hanner says, getting in. I'm starved.

Jack drives through a gap in the back fence and disappears into the desert.

The FBI SUV convoy meets the Con Man and Lady Grifter as they pull out onto the road. He stops the car and raises his hands.

Idiot, she says, raising her own.

Relax, he says. They're not looking for us.

The Junior Agent taps on the window, badge on his belt, other hand on his gun.

Shut off your engine, please, he says.

The Con Man complies, waving the keys.

No problem, he says cheerfully. What's up?

What were you doing in there, the Junior Agent asks.

Uhm, the Con Man says. Looking for gas, officer?

We are so lost, the Lady Grifter says. Point us in the right direction?

Wait here, the Junior Agent says, hustling back to the lead SUV.

Billows catches up on his scooter.

Guys, he yells, desperately pointing to the storage units. He had to go that way!

In the distance, the Con Man sees Doc's truck approaching with the regular traffic. Then he notices Melinda is driving. As the Junior Agent waves the traffic slowly past, Melinda smiles, her arm out the window, the Con Man's door clicker in her hand.

Hey, the Con Man says.

What now, the Lady Grifter asks.

That's my clicker, the Con Man says.

Melinda pushes a button and drops the clicker as she rolls past. The Con Man's eyes follow his clicker to the pavement as his trunk smoothly opens. Desert wind catches the loose bills, swirling them into a green and white cloud as the Agents draw their weapons.

Idiot, the Lady Grifter says.

The Sheriff waits with a big coal shovel beside his smoldering cabin. Everything is gone, down to the concrete foundation. He digs out the area around his floor safe and opens it. His cut of the money is intact inside, untouched by the heat. Battered, bleeding, and completely out of patience, he takes his money, climbs into his car and aims for town.

The FBI is gone from Main Street. The Sheriff arrives to find the Deputy waiting for him in front of his office and the street quiet in every direction.

The Sheriff stops at the center line and gets out.

Didn't think I'd see you back here, the Deputy says. One tough bastard. That's for sure.

Their hands hover over their holsters.

A few loose ends, the Sheriff says. Not much more. Then I'll be on my way. You know. How we planned.

Plans change, Deputy says.

Oh, the Sheriff says. Is it the Mob right on top of you or the Feds way ahead of you?

Either way, the Deputy says. I got to feed them both something. Or somebody. And it looks to me that . . .

Blam. Blam. Blam.

The Deputy crumples. The Sheriff never blinked. He stands over the Deputy and gives him three more.

Wouldn't have lasted a year out here, the Sheriff says.

Shopkeepers and town folk appear at their doors and windows. A dozen sets of shocked eyes.

Nothing to see, the Sheriff shouts. Move the fuck on!

Hanner pulls up in Billows' car.

I can see you're busy, Sheriff, Hanner says. But you got a minute?

I'm on a roll today, the Sheriff says. Why not?

Terrific, Hanner says. Want to take a moment and reload?

No, the Sheriff says. When I catch you, I'm going to do this with my bare hands.

Halfway to his car, the Sheriff stops. He turns, calm, and walks over, planting both hands on Hanner's door. Hanner doesn't flinch.

Kid, the Sheriff says, low and serious. Real quick before

we go. Thing I got to know is, did you sleep any better after that? After little-old you succeeded to wipe out this whole, incredible fucking money maker, which I helped to build with the sweat of my own two balls. I always wanted to leave you home. Lord knows you should have been in school or something. But your Daddy'd say, now's the time for him to learn. Put him in the truck. I knew it'd all go bad. You got no stomach. Little whiner. Never did. Held you off as long as I could. Day you got born, the Captain got weak. And you grew on him like a tumor. And he just got weaker. Because of you. And now there he sits. To rot. In a cement and rebar box painted lime-fucking green. Because of you. So, as somebody who once powdered your delicate behind, I got to know. Did your declaration of personal justice finish off those nightmares of yours? With the people in their filthy, rat-covered trailers. Their eyes and teeth on fire. Trapped. Screeching. Screaming. Did fucking over me and everybody who ever cared about you make reasonable peace with your own great, big, giant share of the same ugly shit?

Hanner's engine revs with a heavy growl. The Sheriff leaves a horrible laugh the whole way back to his cruiser.

They fly out of town together into the hills, engines pounding. Hanner and the Sheriff are side by side, fighting to shove each other off the road. Their cars scream across every rising ridge line, through hairpin turns and quick, sharp drops.

The Sheriff collides with Hanner from behind. Hanner pushes Billows' car faster and faster. In Hanner's mirror, the Sheriff's eyes are like fire. With this, Hanner loses his focus and slides, nearly losing his car over the steep, rocky edge.

The Sheriff follows close, ready to go over the edge himself if it means Hanner goes with him. He slams Hanner again from behind, pouring pure anger into the steering wheel at every turn.

Nearing the top of the ridge, they collide hard and the Sheriff loses ground. Hanner manages to stay on the road.

The Sheriff fights to catch up as Hanner disappears around a blind corner.

The Sheriff follows, engine roaring, gaining ground. Then he finds himself face to face with Hanner, powering back towards him, blocking the road like a growing wall.

Eyeball to eyeball, it's the Sheriff that blinks.

Jack and Melinda follow in Doc's truck, far behind.

In the distance, an explosion of fuel, glass, and metal. A dense column of smoke rises. They share a worried look.

Jack pushes the truck through the same tight curves, searching for Hanner behind each one, finding nothing, again and again.

Finally, they round another bend to see Hanner sitting on the hood of Billows' car.

In the valley below, the Sheriff's car is burning. The twisted wreck seems unsurvivable. Melinda gets out and stares, numb.

Come by my yard in the morning, Hanner says. And I'm sorry about your Dad.

Thanks, she says. Now let's go. Nobody needs to see us hanging around here.

Clinging to a narrow rock ledge, the bleeding and battered Sheriff hauls himself painfully to his feet. He doesn't subscribe to the idea of unsurvivable.

Farther downhill, his smashed car burns, though not hot enough to destroy all the evidence inside.

He finds an old-fashioned grenade in a go-bag he grabbed on the way out of the car and tosses it, spinning the pin in his hand. The car explodes again and bounces away.

Pick through that, you jerks, the Sheriff says.

The Sheriff pulls the survival kit onto one shoulder and his bag of money onto the other. He scurries down the rocks and quickly out of sight.

The next morning in his junkyard, Hanner crawls out from under Billows' car as Jack and Melinda pull up in Doc's truck.

This thing's like a tank, Hanner says. Tightened a couple bolts here and there. But she's all ready to go. Or he, if that's your thing.

Go, Jack asks. Go where?

You'll figure it out, Hanner says. But I need you to do me a favor.

Alright, Melinda says.

Hanner disappears into an old shed, digs around and returns with a brand-new surfboard.

Ordered this from a magazine when I was fourteen, Hanner says. Not sure why anymore. You should have seen people's faces when the mailman brought it down the road, sticking out the back of his truck, like the thing came from outer space. Shame for it to sit here. Go use it for something.

Alright, Jack says. That all?

Maybe a postcard, Hanner says.

Will do, Jack says.

Melinda and Jack head for the horizon in Billows' car, surfboard strapped to the roof.

Hanner opens a beer and sets it in the dirt next to his rusting muscle car. He pops the hood.

PAGANINI

A violinist plays so magically the world assumes he must be pure evil

Expectant murmurs travel through a velvet-draped Italian opera house in the early nineteenth century. Huge candles flicker across the empty stage, long shadows looping through the heavy air, from footlights to balconies.

As if flowing from the curtains, Paganini steps carefully into view. Head to toe in pitch black, he smiles a sharp set of gold teeth.

Sharp breaths then growing applause.

He stops to consider the faces blinking back at him through the din. A master at the end of his years, still venting fire. Thin, oddly angled. Long black hair framing sharp features. In a suit he slept in a while ago. Violin at his side. Showing no cards. Drawing out the moment.

Samael, somewhere between menacing and handsome, settles into the last seat in the last row.

All at once, Paganini's violin roars. Shouts. Cries. Screams. Stops. Then begins again. No sheet music. The orchestra jumps into place with Arabian drums and fights to hold its ground. Notes rise from both of Paganini's hands. Harmonics bend the light around him. In the audience's eyes, the music takes life. Flames rise from his strings. Shadows become faces. The curtains flow blood.

Paganini drops his hands. The stunned audience is not responding. At least, not enough. He stomps toward them and sharply coughs, looking for a reaction. He wobbles, sickly. Then confident. Then sweating, cold, hot, and clammy all at once. The audience swoops forward: Don't stop.

That's the urgency he was looking for. Paganini smiles. Again, notes flicker like fireworks above the crowd.

Samael stands. Tall, broad, benevolently evil, his face and eyes always smolder. Right now, they are distraught.

Outside the opera house, Samael flags his carriage.

Music pours from the building. Two Gentlemen Passersby stop, drawn to the music.

Paganini, says one. My Wife's Sister saw him perform. She was quite taken.

They exchange a telling look.

Interesting, says the other.

Sorry, sport, Samael says. This is his last.

Samael climbs into his carriage and is off.

Again, Paganini stops on the head of a pin. The audience hangs mid-air, the halted chord spooling out before them. They can't help themselves but reach forward to grab for it.

A single bead of sweat takes a long journey down his nose. He is coiled steel, violin and bow locked mid-note. Limbs at unthinkable angles. Again, soaking in silence.

His deep-pool eyes are weary. Strained. He blinks softly. Mind drifting through a moment that isn't this one. Paganini plays a line. Tears away a string. Plays a line. Rips a string. Then again. Down to the final one. The final note. The theater erupts.

He steps to mid-stage and calmly bows. The audience sweeps down the aisles. Paganini strides confidently into the wings. As he passes from the stage, he crumples to the ground.

Morning in the Genoa streets. A stately apartment house stands out among its neighbors. Bandif, a priest with twisted posture and a limp, scurries to the front door and knocks. Waits. Then knocks again more urgently.

Shutters of an upstairs window fling open.

Father Royer, distinguished, sharp and angry, glares down in his night clothes.

What do you want this early, he asks.

In the distance, the Cathedral bells sounds.

No one told them to ring those bells, Royer says.

Paganini is dead, Bandif says.

Royer tightens himself against a wave of joy.

Finally, he says.

Sir, Bandif repeats louder. Niccolò Paganini . . .

I heard you, Royer says. Now quiet those bells.

The shutters slam.

Nearby, a marketplace of food and goods overflows with life. Two lady Servants dawdle a bit, doing the day's shopping.

I'm told he died without sacraments, one says.

Fitting, says the other. The man's soul was as dark at the night he was born.

Fair trade for such music, says the first one.

Don't say such things, says the other.

You can take my word for it, says the first. I remember once, quite a while ago, there was a small dinner. Paganini arrived late. Very drunk. It was so exciting. A vase broke. He had something to do with that. I was in the kitchen. But I still remember the sound of his heels tapping so oddly on the floorboards. And then the house filled with such music. As if the air caught fire. We all stopped. A dozen or so. Closed our eyes and heard from where we stood. At times it was like two playing at once. I swear to you, and anyone else there would as well, there was a voice. A woman. Crying out. And a sudden flock of birds, as if in a panic. Never'll be sure how, but there it was.

Nonsense, says the other.

Believe what you will, says the first one. I can tell you that night I had the most fantastic dreams. Such wonderful, wonderful dreams.

The other servant spits.

And now Paganini burns in hell, she says.

He certainly does, says the first one.

The next day in his study, Royer paces in his vestments, pulling at the bridge of his nose with a continual migraine. Bandif rushes in.

The ship is arriving, Bandif says. Achille Paganini brings

the body alone.

Fine, Royer says. Do as I told you. They cannot know our eyes are on them. Go on.

On the city docks, Germi, Paganini's lawyer and friend, hides his strain behind a scarf. A small ship nears.

Not long now, Niccolò, Germi says quietly to himself. Not long.

Tall and strong, Achille Paganini waves from the bow.

Soon, Achille leads a horse-drawn cart on foot, small group of Workmen walking warily to either side. Paganini's handsome child is purposefully dressed as a gentleman. Germi, a little plump and grey, bounces slowly along beside him.

Careful now, Germi says.

I am, Achille says, enthusiastically, then thinks for a moment. Of any one thing in particular?

We're about to find out, Germi says.

Niccolò Paganini's simple coffin is strapped to the cart. His name tumbles through a crowd growing behind them.

Bandif hurries to stand guard at the locked cemetery gates. With him, a group of thugs in expensive clothes. Achille and Germi stop their procession.

Greetings, Germi says.

Hello, Bandif says.

Achille steps forward.

This is the body of my Father, Niccolò Paganini, he says. For burial, as he wished.

You may not pass, Bandif smiles.

To Achille, this does not compute.

Perhaps you didn't hear me correctly, Achille says.

I heard you perfectly, Bandif says. I know who you are. You may not pass.

Germi rushes forward.

Do not do this, he says. Please.

I'm not doing anything, Bandif says. Not anything at all.

Germi pulls Achille away by the shoulders.

Come with me, he says. Quickly.

I don't understand, Achille says.

Royer, Germi says. This dolt's master. He and your Father. A long time ago . . . They met.

Oh, Achille says. May I assume they did not get along?

Yes, you may, Germi says. So, right now, we must hurry. If Royer holds sway, your Father's body is not safe.

Germi leaps with all of his might upon the horse with the cart and coffin. He pulls Achille up behind him. They disappear into the baffled crowd.

That night, Achille stands at a window in Germi's study, looking over the city. Germi enters and moves straight to pouring himself a drink.

It is done, Germi says. This is insane, and not the Genoa we all once knew. Royer and others like him, they've taken leave of whatever civility we all pretend to. I am so very sorry. I should have seen this. I should have been more ready.

I need to know my Father's body is safe, Achille says.

And I need you to trust me, Germi says. Please rest. Much will be happening very soon.

I don't understand, Achille says. My Father died with this one simple wish. Every morning of my entire life he had me read him his psalms. Why is his faith now some sort of question that you must bring to trial?

I don't know, Germi says. A thousand nights seducing the wives of Europe's most powerful men? Egos bruised. Fortunes gambled. Often from the wallets of other people. Jealous men like Royer.

They cannot do this, Achille says.

Remember that they can, Germi says. There is a handmaid in Nice who claims she brought a priest and that your Father chased them both away. Violently, she is telling people.

Achille is weary of this story.

I assure you, my Father made a confession, he says.

To whom, Germi asks.

To me, Achille says. He confessed to me.

Germi nods. I will wake you when the time comes, he says.

Soon, wind and rain whip the city. A carriage hurries through the sudden storm. Men in dark clothes, leather gloves and masks, bounce along slick cobblestones. Hoofs pound to a halt outside the gates of a huge sanitarium.

An Elderly Nurse carefully carries a very full chamber pot from a room as lightning and thunder fill the windows.

At the other end of the long hallway, a Fat Doctor emerges and waves oddly. From the shadows behind him, two Masked Thugs. Four leather gloves grab the Fat Doctor.

The chamber pot bounces off the floor. Before she can scream, another leather glove clamps across the Elderly Nurse's mouth.

Down many flights of stairs in the morgue, keys jangle. A door swings open. The Fat Doctor leads them through a room stacked with corpses.

This way, everyone, the Fat Doctor says, rubbing his shoulder. Why so rough?

Behind him, Royer removes his mask.

The performance was your idea, Doctor, Royer says.

Yes, well, the Fat Doctor says. Someday, Achille Paganini will come for his Father's body. As the head physician, I have the only key. So if that goat didn't see you capture me, she would point me out first of all. We have history, she and I. But do take care, please. I am not one of your mongrel street rats, gentlemen.

The last word drips condescendingly. The Fat Doctor leads them through more locked doors, past more dead bodies in worse and worse states of decay.

I see, Royer says.

The Fat Doctor glances back.

Shouldn't you cover your face, friend, he asks. I don't know what you have in mind. And I do not want to know who you are.

As the Fat Doctor drags open the last, heavy door, he and Royer find themselves nose to nose.

Don't worry, Doctor, Royer says. I trust you.

The Fat Doctor recognizes Royer and is instantly frightened.

Ah, the Fat Doctor says. Father Royer.

Open the door, please, Royer smiles, cold, vicious and pleased with this response.

The Fat Doctor fumbles with the keys. The crypt door opens. Empty.

But I placed Paganini's body here myself, the Fat Doctor says. My apologies. This certainly is a mystery. Beyond my control, I assure you.

Yes, I can see that, Royer says, taking a deep, angry breath and turning to leave.

Though, Father, the Fat Doctor says. Things as they are, since I did bring you down here at my own considerable risk and could still potentially face discovery . . . Perhaps a small amount of the silver you mentioned would be appropriate?

Royer nods, reaching into his pocket to find a few coins. He patiently hands the silver to the Fat Doctor with one hand and knocks him unconscious with the other.

In the inky-dark harbor, Paganini's tightly wrapped coffin is lashed to the deck of a ship slipping quietly into a storm. Rain whips the deck. Achille finds a seat next to the coffin. Germi pulls his coat tight against the wind.

You should go below, Germi says.

Perhaps in a moment, Achille says.

Neither are ready to let go.

Does us no good to sit here watching that box, Germi says.

I don't like this skulking around, Achille says.

Nonsense, Germi says. Your Father loved to skulk. He

191

would also now instruct me, as his trusted representative, to find you a drink.

They crawl below deck. The small ship plunges into the night.

The sun rises across Ile St. Honorat, a red, jagged outcrop of rocks on the open Mediterranean. Thick, beautiful flowers grow from the soil between the thorny stones. Achille and Germi slosh a smaller boat toward the rocks with a handful of Workers, the long wooden box tied down between them.

Together, they haul the coffin up the rock face. The work is hard and slow. When they finish burying the coffin, the sun is setting again. Exhausted, they sit and look out at the sea, passing a bottle between them. By now they are tired and approaching drunk.

Nice a spot as any I've ever known, Achille says.

Though, you know, your Father would have loved to visit America, if only once, Germi says.

Yes, Achille says. He spoke of it often.

They lean over the mound of soil, addressing the coffin.

Well, Father, Achille says. Here we are. Just to hide you a bit until Germi makes his case. Can't hold us off forever.

Forever hits like a lead weight.

But in the meantime, we thought you might want to wait it out here in America, Germi says. New York, I think. If you could only see for yourself.

New York, Papa, Achille says. How wonderful.

There are all shapes of women and every one of them knows your name, Germi says.

Too sad to continue, they gather their gear and descend in silence.

Under the cover of midnight, Achille and Germi slip off the ship again in Genoa, arguing passionately.

Enough, Achille says. I don't want to hear of this again. Please.

You are not safe here, Germi says. Not at this moment. I will stay, and I will see this through. There are powerful forces taking a prideful interest in your Father. People with no fear. Please. When this matter is settled and all is well, you may immediately return.

A horseman draws to a stop beside them. Caprechi, out of breath, is a more slovenly version of Germi.

The messenger, he barks. Our man in Royer's office has word.

Caprechi slides to the ground.

Lower your voice, Germi says.

Messenger, Achille asks.

This is an associate of mine, Germi says. Don't mind him.

Hello, Caprechi says, all but bowing. I am Caprechi. I was, I am, a great, great admirer of your Father. We fear this messenger carries a package. Letters. From nobles of every sort. All opposing your Father, be . . .

Caprechi's mouth out ran his mind for a moment. A look from Germi drags him to a stop.

Achille, Germi says. Over the years, Royer has kept a certain guild of those our Niccolò thought to taunt and tickle more than the rest. We are covering every route we can. We will sort this out.

I insist I help, Achille says.

Excellent, we can use another set of hands, Caprechi says, finding a roll of paper in his coat. I marked this map myself.

Achille grabs the map, climbs onto Caprechi's horse and gallops away.

Caprechi, I am angry with you, Germi says. I'll give a day to produce a list of reasons why.

Germi stomps off, leaving Caprechi to panic.

The moon hangs bright and full in the Italian countryside. A wide lane leads to an open break amid dense trees.

Achille enters the clearing on horseback, exhausted after

a long sprint.

It is no matter to me who you are, Achille says out loud to no one. Or even from what foul place.

He climbs down and draws a long sword, unfamiliar with the weight. He is tall and dashing, but no fighter.

My name is Achille Paganini, he says, testing his voice again, this time with a sword. And your message will not pass.

Achille takes a long, deep breath and droops, resting for a moment.

Then, a voice from the darkness: It just now struck me. You don't know. Not for sure. Do you?

Startled, Achille drops his sword. He finds it and confronts the trees.

Who is there, he commands as best he can muster. Show yourself!

Not just yet, the voice continues. I prefer you wonder a bit. What sort of messenger carries your Father's fate, little Achille? Is it human? Is it evil? Is it old Samael himself?

Show yourself, Achille says.

A figure moves among the trees, laughing deeply, with a sharp, harsh cough.

So that you can stab me with your terrible long sword, the voice continues. Achille! Are you ready to swing wildly at whatever demon your Father's past drew out for you tonight? Well, fine then.

The voice grows, booming around Achille as the figure darts through the underbrush. Ready yourself! Find that fury! Here it comes! Here it is! ARRRGH!

Achille grips his sword with both hands. A loud crack as a rock breaks a dry branch at Achille's feet. He spins and again drops his heavy sword.

The shadowy figure boils with laughter.

Little Achille, why don't you put that heavy thing down before you hurt yourself, he says. I am unarmed.

Achille can't quite make him out in the dark.

Who are you, he asks.

The dark shape digs into his coat and finds a candle and match. Light hits his face.

Achille gasps.

Father, he says.

This is Orfeo, small and ugly with a distinct likeness to Niccolò Paganini as a young adult. He laughs.

No, Orfeo says. Your darling older Brother.

I don't have a Brother, Achille says.

This slight sours Orfeo's cheerful, false front.

We've met before, he says. I am Orfeo. Certainly, you remember.

I remember, Achille says. And I don't have a Brother.

Only one of us is so often mistaken for our Father, Orfeo says. And that isn't you. So if it is true he only had one child, then may I ask, what are you doing here, Achille?

You do resemble my Father, Achille says. Only weaker and smaller.

You shouldn't make jokes, Orfeo says, waving a bundle of letters from his pocket. After all, Father's enemies will steer his legend now. Enough about that. Come give your Brother a hug! We'll read through these together and have a laugh! You'll see! Let me show you.

Achille backs away, sword rising. He tries to echo the definitive tone he heard at the cemetery gates.

You will not pass, Achille says.

Achille, please, you do not know the man described in these letters, Orfeo says. If you did, I doubt you would carry yourself so proudly. Let him burn.

I knew the true man, Achille says. And you will never have the pleasure.

They circle each other, Orfeo empty handed, Achille pointing his heavy sword.

Brother, I am going to do you a favor, Orfeo says. Because I do believe you would kill any messenger who will act to condemn our Father's soul.

Of course, Achille says.

Orfeo holds out the bundle of letters. Achille lowers his sword. As a short, pointy knife hidden in Orfeo's sleeve lands with a whisper in Achille's side, he stumbles. Orfeo dances away.

Though that would cost you, little Achille, your own place in heaven, Orfeo says. Would it not? Yes. I could never abide that.

Achille raises a blood-stained hand. Orfeo eyes Achille's horse.

Now I will reach Genoa in a hero's style, Orfeo says.

Raising his sword, Achille blocks Orfeo's escape.

I said you will not pass, Achille says.

Orfeo aims his knife.

Is that so, he asks. Well, then. I suppose we shall see . . .

Many years before in Genoa, a bright sky towers with puffy clouds.

Teresa, a teenager in a uniform from a local church school, braids flowers into her Grandmother's hair. A huddle of Teresa's Classmates sit at her feet.

Oh, her Grandmother says. I don't think I should tell you girls such stories.

Please, Teresa says, charming her. Please.

When I was your age, Teresa's Grandmother starts slowly. There was one very long and hot summer. I went to the country with the family of my friend from school. One day her cousin stopped on his way to Rome. Very handsome. He told us he had a dream. And in the dream, the Devil himself offered a trade for his very soul. And right then he picked up his violin and played something so excruciatingly beautiful we fell as if in a trance. I will never forget that day.

Who was he, the girls beg.

His name is no matter, Teresa's Grandmother says. My friend's Father did not like the boy's story. Then that summer, he slipped beneath an ox cart. Such music. I so love music.

I do too, Grandma, Teresa says.

A distant church bell rings.

Soon, the students file up stone church steps. Teresa dawdles. The sound of hoofs and shouts flow into her own private concert.

Martina, same age, in the same school uniform, talks with two rough-edged teenage boys across the street. Antonio holds a mandolin. Bruno only has eyes for Martina.

Wait right here, Martina says.

Right here, Bruno says.

Martina plunks at Antonio's mandolin.

And don't worry, she says. My friend Teresa is just crazy for music.

She skips across the street, joining Teresa and the other girls filing up the steps. The bells stop. Bruno and Antonio wait, impatient.

Let's go drink and come back, Antonio says.

No, no, Bruno says. Wait. See?

A coal shoot door beside the church pops open. Martina and Teresa vault out. The girls skip across the street and take the boys by the hand.

Quick, Teresa says. Run!

Along a slow river, Antonio's music is the hit of their little party. As he sets down his mandolin, Teresa wraps herself in his arms.

You will be an important musician, she says.

I am a serious musician, he says. So, yes. Someday.

Then our children will be serious musicians, she says.

Antonio is off guard. This is important to her.

Every single one, he says.

Teresa grins.

Play some more, she says.

A decade or so later, a heavy, low sun beats across a crowded street in a crowded neighborhood. Adult Antonio carries his mandolin under his arm, well dressed in an old suit, drenched in sweat. He lands hard on their front stoop.

Teresa waddles out of the house. She is very pregnant, a young child and toddler in tow.

How long were you hiding out here, she asks.

The time shows in their faces.

A joy to see you as well, Antonio says, following her inside.

The other three of their five children, ages two to eight, tumble and fight.

Carlo, Antonio says, grabbing the oldest. Did you practice?

Yes, Carlo says, lifting a tiny, weathered violin. He plays, terribly. Antonio yanks at his thick belt and chases the boy. Teresa rubs her belly.

Down to you, little one, Teresa says.

In the blink of an eye, Teresa is screaming in an upstairs bedroom. A grouchy Midwife thrusts a newborn into her arms. The hallway is crowded with Antonio's loud, drunken friends.

Well, tell us, Antonio insists, hovering in the doorway.

Boy, the Midwife grunts.

The hallway mob cheers and rushes downstairs, led by Antonio.

Don't worry, the baby is fine, the Midwife says, slamming the door.

On an unbearably hot night, windows open, drapes dead still, Teresa carries the thin, colicky infant from room to room. At one end of the house, loud, cranky, arguing children. At the other, Antonio drinking and grumbling alone. Baby wailing all the way.

Go bother the neighbors, Antonio shouts.

Teresa steps onto the doorstep with the fussing baby. Suddenly, a small, refreshing breeze whips past.

Hush, Nico, Teresa says. Enjoy the fresh air.

Beneath sharp moonlight on the corner is Samael,

precisely as he appears on the day of Paganini's final performance.

Evening, he says.

Teresa nods and bounces the baby.

Such heat, he says. Poor thing must be miserable. What is his name?

Niccolò, she says.

Greetings, Niccolò, Samael says. Very nice to meet you.

Samael holds a violin.

May I, he asks.

Please, Teresa smiles.

As Samael plays, Niccolò falls quiet. Teresa nods thankfully to Samael, who continues to play as she returns inside. The music rises through the curtains, along with thick, cool air. Where the music and comfort find a child, they sleep. Teresa tiptoes through the house. Antonio snores in his chair. She lays Niccolò in a basket and collapses into sleep beside him.

In the basket, baby Niccolò is wide-eyed at every note of Samael's wonderful music.

In her mind, Teresa finds herself alone outside an old theater, elegantly dressed. She rushes up steep steps to the theater door. Skirts in hand, she steps down the aisle amid the growing thunder of the single violin. Huge flames gush from every chandelier. The musician performs with his back to her. The flames spread, guided by the music. An orchestra of demons erupts. The violin fights them back. The performer turns. It is Niccolò, a wild-haired adult, smoke rising from his violin. Dust and debris tumble from the ceiling. Teresa looks up. Angels peel back the ceiling to show clear blue sky. She rises into the air, laughing. Below her, Samael conducts the orchestra. All perform a variation on the song he played outside the house.

In the morning, Teresa wakes up on the floor. Sun pours through the windows. House still snoring. Music gone. Baby Niccolò sleeping.

When Niccolò is a toddler in short pants, Teresa leads the family like ducks into a church pew. Gaunt, he alternately coughs, whines and cries.

Niccolò's too noisy for mass, Antonio says. Let me take him home.

Yes, maybe you two could go wait at the tavern down the street, she says.

Mass begins. As the music starts, Niccolò falls quiet. Antonio shrugs. Beside them, Niccolò pulls himself to his feet. His huge eyes dart to find the source of the music. His skinny fingers wiggle in the air. The choir begins. The air around him vibrates with sound. Niccolò trembles like a high-voltage wire. The passion of the music sends him into convulsions. Teresa rushes Niccolò from the church, family in tow.

In their front room, a Doctor worries over Niccolò's motionless body. Poking, prodding, listening, thumping. For once, his brothers and sisters are quiet. Teresa weeps on Antonio's shoulder.

A growing procession waits outside the family's door on a cloudy morning. Niccolò's little, open, shroud-covered coffin is passed, hand to hand, along the top of the crowd.

A Neighborhood Band gathers. As the music reaches the box, skirting across the top of the crowd, Niccolò's eyes open. He sits up, searching for the source of the music. The thin death shroud covers his face. He pulls it away. A sea of heads turns with shock. A gasp travels through them. They set down the coffin and back slowly, silently away as Teresa descends gratefully upon Niccolò.

When the kids are five years older, they trail behind Antonio as he leaves the house with his mandolin. Teresa follows them out the door with Niccolò.

Here, she says. Take the baby.

Don't call him a baby, Antonio says. Niccolò is catching

up. I can tell.

Good, then, here, she says. Take him with you. I have things to do today.

He is still too small to go out in the streets, Antonio says.

Painfully thin, Niccolò smiles up at his Father and takes his hand.

Make up your mind, Teresa says. And find a job.

Hungry and bored, the children follow their Father through bustling streets. Antonio carries his mandolin, searching for work. He knocks on one theater and tavern door after another, shut out each time. Niccolò is frail and struggles to keep up, lost in his own world.

To Niccolò's ears, the hoofs, wheels, and shouting, much like for his Mother, are coordinated musical sounds.

Antonio straightens his clothes outside another theater.

Carlo, he says. Where is your violin?

Carlo was daydreaming. He holds out the instrument.

Here, Papa, he says.

Antonio turns over a box beside the door.

Well, get to playing, he says. The rest of you, look hungry. Coins come directly to Papa. Mind Niccolò.

Carlo stands on the box and plays his violin. Antonio disappears into the theater. Carlo stops and sits on the box, watching his siblings argue in the street.

Niccolò picks up his Brother's violin and plays along with the motion all around him. At first just picking out pieces. Then weaving a mesmerizing tapestry. Antonio is shoved out the theater door.

No, the Theater Owner says. No. And no again! And don't come back in here anymore! You have my answer.

Should anything change, however, Antonio protests. You know I am competent. You know I am . . .

Antonio and the Theater Owner stop. It takes them only a moment to realize that little Niccolò's body is a fluid extension of his bow. Father and Son's eyes meet. Niccolò halts and puts down the violin.

Sorry, Papa, Niccolò says.

In a bedroom of their house, Niccolò perches like a tiny bird on a big wooden chair, his giant eyes wide with focus. His delicate fingers twitch on the bow. Antonio forces Niccolò's arms into playing position, painfully placing his fingers along the strings.

Lessons in this room are between Niccolò and Papa, Antonio says.

Yes, Papa, Niccolò says.

Teresa clears her throat from the doorway. Antonio slams the door.

Outside a crowded neighborhood tavern, Antonio stands on his knees to straighten a replica of his own suit, fitted to slight, pale Niccolò. Thick hair stubbornly combed, Niccolò looks like a regularly proportioned, middle-aged man seen from a great distance.

Now, Niccolò, these men are very important, Antonio says. You will not embarrass Papa. Correct? No? Yes?

Niccolò studies Antonio' eyes, his nose and beard. The words flutter past him like butterflies.

I don't think you even hear me, Antonio says. Maybe Papa's wasted too much time on you and your silly violin.

Niccolò hugs his instrument. Satisfied by this response, Antonio takes his hand and drags him through a smoky, knee-high obstacle course, then hoists him up through the forest of limbs to an orbit just above the foul crowd inside the tavern.

Gentlemen, Antonio shouts. And the rest of you!

Scattered laughter. Antonio wears a showman's grin. He captures half their attention. Antonio stands Niccolò on the bar top, the violin clutched nervously in his arms.

Gentlemen, please, he says. Simply listen.

Grumbles from the crowd. Antonio leans in close, where only Niccolò can see or hear, and drops the nice act.

Do you hear how I boast for you, he asks. Do not shame me.

I won't, Papa, Niccolò says, determined to the bottom of his little feet.

As Niccolò places his violin under his chin and bursts into song, rapt silence spreads through the crowd. His huge charcoal eyes burn like fire. His body twists into an uncomfortable seeming, but to him perfectly natural posture, directing all of his energy through his violin.

Across the hush and narrow light of the crowded tavern, Niccolò launches notes that bounce like grasshoppers across a field.

The child takes on the appearance of a small demon, his violin sending sparks through the air. The Theater Owner who refused Antonio earlier now catches his arm.

Leave it to a flop like you to have a child this talented, the Theater Owner cackles drunkenly. Or did you move a rock and find a goblin? What do you feed it?

I teach Niccolò myself, Antonio says. He knows just as I know.

Doesn't play as you play, the Theater Owner says. This is natural ability. Someone needs to build on that. Improve his education and the young man is welcome on my stage at any time.

The Theater Owner fades into the crowd, leaving Antonio to stare bitterly as Niccolò happily performs.

All Niccolò can see are thrilled faces in every direction. He lowers his bow and bows to cheers. Antonio yanks him from his perch and out of the room.

Antonio and Niccolò walk home together in silence. Niccolò is visibly pleased. Antonio is sour.

Well, Antonio says. Did everyone enjoy the music this evening? Did little Niccolò do well?

Yes, Papa, Niccolò says.

I am sorry you feel this way, Antonio says. I suppose your

ambition is only to amuse a room full of drunks. If you consider that satisfactory, I have wasted my time.

No, Papa, Niccolò panics.

Antonio lifts Niccolò up onto the front step of their house.

You embarrassed your Father tonight, Antonio says. We will continue to rehearse together. But tomorrow we will find a new professor.

No, Papa, Niccolò says.

Yes, Niccolò, Antonio says. I am sorry. Though we certainly cannot spare the money, this is the position in which you place the family. Now what do you suppose will happen if your new professor were to see a performance as pedestrian as the one I saw tonight?

Niccolò rushes into the house, past his waiting Mother. He strips off his miniature suit jacket and shirt. Beneath his sleeves and collar, sharp bruises stand out on his ivory skin. Niccolò stands on his chair, hoists his violin and begins to play. Teresa rushes to the bedroom door, but Antonio is ahead of her. He shuts it hard.

A nervous Music Professor's Assistant slinks into a large and cluttered library, a grand piano at the far end.

The Professor plunks one note at a time, very seriously noting each one on papers spread across the piano top. He ignores his Assistant, inching toward him until their wigs nearly touch.

He can wait, the Professor says.

His Father will need to leave for an urgent appointment, the Assistant says.

Then he can wait alone, the Professor says.

The Assistant dashes from the room. The Professor plunks and writes. Plunks and writes. Time passes. The sun sets. The Assistant lights candles all around the room.

The Professor sets down his pen. He is pleased. He plays a passage, smiles to himself and sorts his papers.

PAGANINI

From a distant corner of the silent house, precisely the same passage echoes on violin. The Professor and Assistant stare at each other.

The Professor plays again and stops. Again, the violin repeats the same notes. He plays a more complex version. The violin matches. Angry, the Professor plays his new piece, from the top, ink still drying on the page. The violin stays perfectly in step. A gust of wind bursts from a forgotten open window. All the lights blow out.

Bright notes from the tiny violin ricochet through the darkness. The Professor lights candles, swishing his candelabra around the room, out the door, and down a hallway to the front of the house. At first he finds nothing. Then he looks lower.

At their feet is paper-thin Niccolò, playing his little heart out. In his miniature black suit, long curls and large eyes, he looks more like a gargoyle come to life than a small boy. The effect is unholy.

Tell his Father I am convinced, the Professor says.

In the balcony of a small theater, Samael watches a matinee crowd file in.

Behind the curtain, a Stagehand stands little Niccolò on a stool before a mirror.

Hold your breath this time, the Stagehand says.

Niccolò isn't listening. He studies himself in the mirror, violin in hand. Posing, he smiles to himself. For this, Niccolò gets a mouthful of makeup powder. Coughing, when his big eyes pop open, he is thrilled at the effect.

Drawn by the excited murmur of the crowd, the Theater Owner peeks out from behind the curtain.

Another sellout, the Theater Owner says. A week straight! I retained the orchestra for the entire rest of the season!

The whole season, Antonio muses. Well, oh my! Continuing with our current terms? Is that what I should assume?

Well, yes, the Theater Owner says.

Well, then, no, Antonio says. You'll need to offer better than that.

The Stagehand barrels toward them.

Has anyone seen the boy, he yells.

In the filthy theater back alley, Niccolò stands on a crate and plays for a group of appreciative tramps and beggars. They sit mesmerized. It is here that Niccolò is at ease, pouring himself into the violin. The notes he plays are his own variation. The violin squeaks when Antonio grabs Niccolò by the neck and hauls him inside. The door hangs open. Inside, the packed theater cheers.

Teresa marches the family into high mass, crowded shoulder to shoulder beneath the statues and Latin carvings. The choir sings, incense swinging, smoke dancing in the light, Niccolò at the edge of his seat. Teresa is thrilled by his concentrated attention. The rest of the group is sleepy and distracted. Mass ends but the music continues. Parishioners genuflect and file out.

Teresa and the rest get to the aisle before they notice Niccolò is still in his seat.

Come along Nico, she says. I'll come back with you again this evening. I promise.

Niccolò spends his favorite days alone beneath a low tree, near a bubbling brook on the Professor's estate, amid the birds and wildlife. He absently picks out and matches individual sounds with eerily similar musical runs on the violin.

The Professor and Antonio watch him from a distance.

Raw talent is just that, the Professor says. He much work to do.

Practice is a wasted performance, Professor, Antonio says. His current level of study is clearly sufficient. I have no

more musical education than that myself and I certainly
know from where I speak. I warned you. Niccolò is in great
demand all over the city. Soon we will tour. I will not allow
you to pollute him with frivolous music theory. I see no use
for it. His purpose is to play, Professor, for as many people
as possible. You can have him once a week, in the morning.
That is a time he normally wastes with his Mother.
Understand?

I understand completely, the Professor says. Please take
him and go.

Antonio flashes furious.

What did you say, he asks.

I have no interest or time to debate what musical
education this child requires, the Professor says. It would
break my heart to participate in souring this genius in the
way you recommend. Antonio, you are about to leave my
house. Take him with you or leave him for his lesson, on my
terms, and continue to profit from the growth he finds with
me here Your choice.

Greed tops pride. Antonio leaves.

Niccolò carefully pushes open an ornate door to the
Professor's music library, crammed with books.

And this is where they live, he asks.

Yes, the Professor says. All the sounds. And their
families. Right here.

Niccolò is confused. He listens, but hears nothing. The
Professor draws a large text down from a high shelf. He
opens it carefully.

No, Niccolò, the Professor says. In here.

The Professor tips open a large book full of musical notes
and illustrations. Niccolò's smiles, running his thin fingers
down the page.

In a distant town outside another theater, Niccolò hides
behind his Father's legs as Antonio accepts congratulations

from an enthusiastic mob. Niccolò's eyes are on Carlo, nuzzling a Local Girl behind them in the theater doorway. Niccolò wants whatever his siblings have.

Later that day, Antonio and Niccolò climb the steps of a giant cathedral. Royer steps sharply into their path, much younger but already quaking with a deep, focused anger. He pretends to smile as he looks them over.

Good morning, Father, Antonio says. We are traveling musicians and heard about today's audition. For the festival. Would you please direct us?

Yes, the Paganini boy, Royer says. Much talk about you. Be careful, young man. The Devil plays the fiddle. Very sorry. But the audition was yesterday.

Niccolò is stricken.

That can't be, Antonio says. Listen, his Mother will be very angry with me. This was very important to her.

Royer looks bemused.

Pity, he says.

Inside a rehearsal chamber, an impossibly high and lovely note from soft, pouty, rouged lips. They caress and tease the sound with feminine assurance and round faces. The gaggle of plump and rosy Castrati warm their throats with astounding trills, giggling at private jokes in frilly outfits, rigorously trained and freshly powdered, the foie gras of singers.

Robed priests help a yawning Bishop in heavy vestments to an ornate chair. Royer strides into the room, glowing with anticipation, and bows. The Bishop mumbles quietly to his Priests, who share a subtle laugh.

Castrati, the Bishop says to Royer. Always with the Castrati. Is there nothing else?

Not of such quality, Royer says flatly.

At his direction, the Castrati leap into song. Their voices rise like sparrows. The Bishop is pleased.

Then a breeze flows through the windows, carrying a note that pierces the Castrati's rising tone. Then another. And

another. Royer is frozen with confusion and rage. The
singing and violin join, swirling together. The voices stop.
The violin draws the Castrati to the windows. The Bishop
motions. Priests help him to his feet.

In a courtyard below, Antonio holds Niccolò over his
head. Niccolò plays as if standing on solid ground.

Hello, the Bishop yells from the window. That's sufficient.
Very nice. What is his name?

He is Niccolò, Antonio says. Niccolò Paganini.

Congratulations, Niccolò, the Bishop says, turning to
Royer. The boy will perform.

But rehearsing both together could take weeks, Royer
says. Months.

Oh, no, the Bishop says. Just the boy. We have singing
every year.

The Bishop leaves, robed priests in tow. Royer walks
solemnly to the window.

There he finds both Paganinis grinning up at him in
victory.

In another dark theater, as his fingers fly across the
strings, Niccolò's eyes wander to the faces of the crowd.
They seem frightening. Both delighted and sinister.

In the wings, he finds Antonio in his usual spot. Glaring.
Niccolò's mind returns to his work.

Backstage, Niccolò sits outside an office, feet dangling
from a chair bigger than he is.

On the other side of the door, both the Theater Manager
and Antonio are red faced.

You stood people in the aisles, you grinning bastard,
Antonio yells. That wasn't part of our deal. So, I'll have my
share, thank you.

Let me stop you right there, the Manager says. Now, if
you think the likes of you can stand there and . . .

Antonio grabs him by the throat.

As Niccolò waits, a pretty Chorus Girl wanders past in

half a costume and no makeup. Little Niccolò looks exhausted to the bone. Hearing the struggle behind the door, she wraps the boy in her arms. He wasn't ready for this, but does not protest.

Poor thing, she says. That pretty violin of yours must get awfully heavy.

Niccolò smiles, snuggling close. Then closer. Suddenly, she isn't so sure this isn't an adult in disguise.

Months pass. Antonio paces around little Niccolò on his chair, hunting viciously for a slouch, an itch, a relaxed moment. Niccolò's bones and joints painfully form around the violin. This posture becomes second nature. His fingers twist awkwardly to reach distant strings. Though his eyes show agony, his hands become infinitely flexible and fly through scales in his sleep. Day turns to night and back again.

As Niccolò outgrows him, Antonio grows cold. At first, he just watches and drinks. Eventually, he leaves entirely, locking the door. Now little Niccolò explores the violin on his own, alone, pacing the room, day and night, carefully watching a clock tower in the distance. As the bells toll, they lend counterpoint to Niccolò's frenzied musical experiments.

Growing his first chin hairs, gangly limbs particularly awkward, Niccolò strides across another in an endless tour of stages. He stumbles on a nail, fumbling the violin, catching it just above the floor. The grumbling audience waits, their negative tone washing over him. His heart pounds. Niccolò raises his bow and plays. A string breaks. Sour notes tumble through the room as he screeches to an ugly halt. Niccolò winces. The whipping string left a tiny trickle of blood across his cheek. He finds he likes the sting. Grumbling grows to shouts and boos. Niccolò is frozen. To him, the crowd noise is a great angry wave, rising up to crash across the stage. He looks to the violin. His string is broken. How can he play? Niccolò retreats for the wings. But then he stops. Straightens. He sees that Antonio is off somewhere, distracted. Mind whirling, he looks again to the violin and grins.

Niccolò steps to center stage and begins again, audience against him. Carefully at first, then stronger, he recalculates which notes to play on fewer strings. The crowd is turning. Soon they are with him. Niccolò's confidence grows. Suddenly, he tears away another string. The audience gasps with delight. He plays on, then tears away another, finishing the piece on a single string with the crowd in the palm of his hand.

As they cheer, Antonio appears in the wings, horrified at the wasted strings. Niccolò lingers in the stage lights for as long as he can manage before marching off to his punishment.

Dawn again, and Teresa jostles awake the pile of kids who long ago outgrew their tiny room, Niccolò still smallest among them.

Stumbling down the hall, he hears Antonio shouting from a nearby room. Niccolò peeks from the doorframe. Antonio, in bed clothes, grips a heavy strap. Carlo stands before their Father in his clothes from the day before, eyes bloodshot, head pounding. Now in his late teens, Carlo is far bigger than Antonio. This doesn't matter. The strap falls hard across Carlo's back again and again. Carlo fights not to crumple. But he doesn't fight back.

As the family scatters after breakfast, Niccolò backs down the hallway and sneaks from a side door. Outside, beneath the front steps, he finds his violin carefully bundled. He moves quietly as he can, but not very. A cough behind him. He droops, turns, caught. It's Carlo.

I thought I might take a walk, Niccolò says.

A walk, Carlo says. Yes. Well. If you ask me, you should make it a long one.

211

Carlo stuffs coins into Niccolò's hand.

I must go, Niccolò apologizes, face flashing the burden of his choice. Or else Father will press me like a berry, and I won't be any good to anyone at all. Where did you get this?

Don't worry about that, Carlo says.

Father will know, Niccolò says. He'll be angry.

Well, this one I will enjoy, Carlo says. Goodbye, Nico. Write to Mama.

Carlo disappears into the house.

Niccolò turns, tucks his violin under his arm and walks all night, putting as much space behind him and home as possible. When the sun rises, he finds himself in a little country town.

The street is smaller and different from the city he is used to. More friendly and quaint. Hungry, he follows a vegetable cart past a bakery. Huge and wonderful cakes fill the window. Counting the coins in his hands, he confidently strides into the bakery and emerges biting into an oversized cream puff.

Soon, grimy head to toe, he taunts foot traffic, mocking people's size and gate with tricks on his violin. His audience is a crowd of cheering beggars and rabble.

Drunk on both wine and the moment, Paganini enters a brothel through one door and emerges on the other side, literally aged ten years.

Now in his teens, stumbling drunk down a side street on a sunny afternoon, Paganini spots an old parlor chair someone left out with the garbage. It is identical to the one his Father used to teach him. Paganini stops. The way it blocks his path, it is as if the chair is staring at him, waiting. He picks it up.

Deep in the forest, Paganini sets the chair in the center of a small clearing, violin tucked under his arm. Paganini sits in the chair and stares at his hands. Then at his violin strings. And for a long time, the bow. He stands, looks at the chair, sits back down. He plays a piece, then plays it backward. Then with just the bow. Then just with his other hand. As the sun sets, animals pass by, ignoring him. At dawn, Paganini is still working, pacing around and around the chair, his mind at full steam, dissecting the violin. Then he stops. Something clicks. Paganini steps up onto the chair. He plays. The harmonics are so far advanced compared to his previous music, it scares him a little and he stops. He starts again. Paganini plays as the sun breaks the horizon. The air melts around him. Time slows. This is a quantum leap in his work. Paganini finishes, climbs down and kicks over the chair, leaving it behind in the clearing, whistling the music he just created.

Lost in a summer rainstorm, full-grown but still boyish, smiling at the door, Paganini wanders his way into a local Luthier's workshop around suppertime. His violin charms the Luthier's Wife into feeding him and lending him her husband's skills for an evening that stretches into a week.

I'll help you build a fiddle, Paganini, the Luthier says, hovering in his workshop doorway. As long as you keep your eyes off the lady of the house.

Waving him off, Paganini plays a piece on his violin and sets it on a work table. Slowly and violently, he deconstructs the instrument, prying open and studying even the smallest aspect of the tiniest part, as if wringing out every grain of magic. Then he directs the Luthier to copy each one a size bigger and stronger. Working their way through the room of exotic tools, both seem as if possessed. Hours, then days, pass. Plates of food come and go untouched. Paganini's limitless focus drives the Luthier past exhaustion. When they are done, Paganini holds a meatier, more powerful version of the same violin. It nearly hums in his hands. He raises his bow and a long, low note bursts across the room like an electric charge.

The Luthier's Wife throws open the door workshop door.

What kind of violin is that, she asks.

That's no violin, the Luthier grins. That is a cannon.

New weapon under one arm, nearly empty bottle under
the other, Paganini sways into the nearest large town. He
smacks his lips and coughs, transparently pale and thin. He
makes his way to the closest hotel on a busy street corner
and stumbles in. The Hotel Clerk eyes him.

I need a room, Paganini says. How much?

More than you have, I'm sure, the Hotel Clerk says.
Niccolò nods and walks out. From the street pours music
from Niccolò's violin. All traffic and commotion stop.
Niccolò returns, dumps coins onto the desk and collapses.

Fine, the Hotel Clerk says. But you'll also be paying for
the doctor.

In a small hotel room, a Town Doctor examines Niccolò,
barely breathing. He steps into the hallway to find the
anxious Hotel Clerk and closes the door.

My goodness, the Town Doctor says, turning down the
hallway. That man is not well.

Wait, the Hotel Clerk says. Aren't you going to do
something?

No, the Town Doctor says. Seems he's used to it.

In the room, wrapped in a blanket, Niccolò stares out the
window in sweaty agony.

Across the road, a carriage pulls to a halt. A beautiful
widow, Lady Aiden, climbs out in dark, elegant clothes.
Catcalls fly from beggars on the nearby corners.

Helping her to the cobble stones, Lady Aiden's
Coachman, a low and muscled brawler, reacts with a snarl,
rolling up his sleeves. She is caught up in the fracas. Above
them, Paganini throws open his window and raises his
violin. He sends a high, bright note down across her, so
directly she touches her cheek. The Coachman and rest do
not notice, but Lady Aiden's eyes rise to him. Then, as
Paganini plays, faces lift to follow the sound. At the climax,

PAGANINI

Paganini collapses out of sight. Lady Aiden screams.

Paganini wakes in a large fancy bed in a large country
house, wearing a frilly dressing gown.
The Coachman stares down at him.
No funny business, he says.
Paganini shivers, befuddled. The Coachman holds a bowl
of some sort of stew and a huge, hovering wooden spoon.
This is a nicer hotel than I thought walking in, Paganini
says.
This is Lady Aiden's manor house, the Coachman says.
She took a likening to your fiddle. I'm to well you up and get
you scrubbed good. She'll meet you then.
The Coachman shoves the huge spoon into Paganini's
mouth.
Beside a well in the house garden, the Coachman plops
Paganini into a washtub of soapy bubbles and scrubs him
like an oversized spaniel.
That night, on her private terrace, Lady Aiden stands
with her back to the long, open doors. An elegant table is
candlelit behind her. The Coachman sends Paganini onto the
terrace with a shove but remains inside. In an ill-fitting suit
and plastered-flat hair, he stumbles toward her. She laughs.
Oh, my dear, Lady Aiden says. I am sorry. He's protective
of me.
No worry, Paganini says. He reminds me of Mother.
Here, sit, she says. Eat with me.
No, he says. I'm sorry. I'm still full of some sort of stew.
Paganini stares warily at the food.
Oh, then he likes you, she says. I sense you have a very
difficult relationship with food.
It doesn't seem to like me much, he says.
I can't help you with that, she says.
You have already helped me plenty, he says.
I can give you more, though, she says. Things you need.
To help you dress like a gentleman. Hold a fork like a

gentleman. I've heard all about you from friends in town. They say you are no gentleman.

I don't understand, Paganini says. Why?

I would like to hear you play, she says. I need to hear you play.

A guitar rests on a small table nearby.

This is more my Father's instrument, Paganini says. This relationship is complicated as well.

With your Father or the guitar, she asks.

Yes, he says. Both. Perhaps with my violin it would be . . .

Don't argue with me, she says. My husband is dead, and I am going quite mad. Quite mad here alone.

Her mood is mercurial and razor thin.

You are not alone, Paganini says.

She bursts into tears. He moves toward her. She retreats to the other side of the terrace.

Please, she says. He wrote it for me.

Paganini picks up the guitar. Beneath it, sheet music. He plays, tentatively at first, then brilliantly. Lady Aiden seems trapped in the shadows. Tears stream down her cheeks. She strips off her gown and jewels, then crumbles, sobbing. The Coachman collects her in a blanket and strides into the house.

That sounded real nice, the Coachman says.

Paganini pours himself a glass of wine.

Days pass. He plays for her beneath the fruit trees. They run through the fields together. Make love in the rain.

He plays for her by the fire. She lectures him on dining habits, dance steps, clothes. He wakes, coughing, in her arms. She mothers him.

One afternoon, the Coachman hovers over Paganini, hair neatly combed, clothes newly cleaned, as he hunts to place the correct fork into a formal table setting.

Sit down, Paganini says. Won't you?

The immense Coachman sits across from him as Paganini

places silverware upside down and backwards. Amused, the Coachman grins, so Paganini takes the opportunity to change the subject.

You worked for Lady Aiden's husband, Paganini says.

There was a fire, the Coachman says.

I shouldn't pry, Paganini says.

The winter house, the Coachman says. First, I found the lady. Lying on the floor by the stairs. I took her outside. By then it was gone. They were all gone. The mister. The staff. The house. This is all she has left now. This house. Me.

Paganini places a spoon.

There, he says. See? I'm learning.

The Coachman grins.

Not really, he says.

Early on a crisp morning, Paganini rolls over to find Lady Aiden standing at the window waiting for the sunrise. The drapes flutter. Years have passed.

Always with the dawn, he says.

I'm sorry to bother you, she says.

Never a bother, he says. You are a stunning pleasure to open one's eyes to.

She blushes.

Such a happy accident I found you, she says. There is magic in you, Paganini. Always let it burn bright, won't you? Such a rare thing. So wild. Never let them stamp it out. Please.

I promise I never will, Paganini says, stretching and burying his face in her pillow.

Thank you, she says. Now sleep. I'm sorry I disturbed you.

Paganini closes his eyes.

When the sun is up, the birds are singing. Paganini smacks his lips, slides out of bed and tugs on his clothes. A deep moan rises from outside. Paganini rushes to the window. On the stones below, the Coachman pulls Lady

Aiden's broken body into his arms.

That afternoon, the Coachman stops the carriage outside a tavern in town. Paganini climbs out, politely dressed as a gentleman. They embrace. The Coachman drives on.

Inside, Paganini finds a singing, drunk crowd. Paganini steps to the center of the room and raises his violin. He plays Lady Aiden's song. The room slows to a halt. They stand like zombies in a trance. He finishes. They remain perplexed. Paganini wistfully drops a bag of the lady's coins on the bar top.

Drinks for all my friends, Paganini says.

The tavern erupts and the party continues.

In an empty French concert hall, Charles LaFont's violin beautifully leads the orchestra through a rehearsal. He is perfectly groomed and the same age as Paganini. This is a rehearsal, the hall empty except a handful of rich Patrons in aisle seats. They are pleased with LaFont, who plays best in the classic style. Not a hair or note out of place. LaFont bows to the orchestra and the politely appreciative Patrons.

The moment the music stops, Paganini bursts from the wings, dressed in the ragged remainder of the clothes Lady Aiden gave to him, assuming LaFont's turn with the orchestra is done. He's ready to go.

Good afternoon, gentlemen, Paganini says. Sadly, they've left us limited time together. But listen closely and I assure you, this will be simple.

The orchestra stares at him, dumbfounded. LaFont takes Paganini's elbow and, playing it up for the chuckling Patrons, leads Paganini, confused, to the wings.

Sirs, please do not mind my young friend, LaFont says. A little joke between musicians.

Excuse me, Paganini says. They said I was next to rehearse with the orchestra.

You must be Paganini, LaFont says. Give the poor bastards a moment's rest. That was quite a turn I put them through just now.

Paganini protests until LaFont produces a small liquor flask. He leads Paganini down a long set of stairs, into the bowels of the building. There they find a group of musicians, drinking, smoking, and showing off. Ludwig Spohr, a few years younger, finishes a sad piece on the violin. He plays with his own version of LaFont's proper, classic style. Dignified. One note at a time.

Something new, Spohr says. What do you think?

Beautiful, Paganini says. My Mother loves that sort of thing. I will play it for her the moment I see her next.

The room is struck dumb. Spohr steams.

LaFont, he says. Why are you dragging urchins in from the gutter?

Allow me to introduce Paganini, LaFont says and they all laugh.

This ragamuffin, Spohr asks. I didn't believe the rumors were serious. And I was worried. What a relief.

But I said it was good, Paganini says.

Paganini, you do far exceed expectation, LaFont smirks. I, for one, look forward to your performance tomorrow. May I offer some hard-won advice?

You'd be wise to listen, Paganini, Spohr says. If I had LaFont's sort of polish and luck, I'd be sitting pretty in Hamburg rather than wasting time here with the likes of you.

Alright, Paganini says.

I look at you and my advice is that it's long past time for you to embrace the part, LaFont says.

Nods all around.

The part, Paganini mimics dryly.

Yes, LaFont says, losing hope in Paganini. Honestly, how you even got this far, I do not know. You see, these Patrons, Paganini, are your only true audience. And they like to get what they pay for. For instance, an obvious professional to whom they may quietly, smugly even, attach their name.

Who not only looks the part, but truly is the part. From his collar to his shoes. Whose first step into any dinner party is the very essence of, oh look everyone, what fortune, the maestro has arrived. This is the cold business of the thing, yes? That's why they put these little exhibitions together. To choose among the best cuts of meat for their elaborate summer dinners.

I'm fairly certain that playing music is the business of the thing, Paganini says.

Naturally, you must play well, Spohr says.

Paganini hands back LaFont's flask, now empty.

That's a relief, he says. Because, fortunately, I do play well naturally. Now, if you fine fellows will excuse me, I need to find out if our orchestra is up to the task.

Paganini leaves.

They shrug: Poor fool.

The next night, LaFont climbs out of a carriage and finds half the orchestra slumped, exhausted, in the alley behind the concert hall.

What happened to all of you, he demands.

Signor Paganini, the orchestra mutters.

He couldn't have kept you here all night, LaFont says.

I am amazed he let us take a break just now, whines a percussionist.

In front of a hushed and elegant audience, LaFont performs, precisely as before, finishing his piece to polite applause. As the curtain drops, LaFont bows and finds a place in the wings, next to Spohr.

Paganini's next, he says.

From the other wing, Paganini takes his place on stage. The curtain rises.

My goodness, well, I know you're fascinated, but I certainly wouldn't expect much, Spohr says.

Paganini stands like stone in a shimmering suit and flowing gold wig, which mocks every gentleman there. Instead of his violin, he holds a guitar. The audience laughs.

How odd, Spohr says. I suppose he surrenders in advance.

Both find seats amid the amused, condescending rumble of the crowd. More moments pass as feet shuffle toward the aisles. Then a rare smile creeps at Paganini's mouth and his fingers dance across the guitar. At first in short bursts. Then in a torrent, drawing them back into their seats as if on a wire.

Spohr grows pale when he hears his own tune from yesterday. Paganini brings an elegance to the piece Spohr couldn't. Spohr and LaFont exchange blank stares.

Paganini throws down the guitar with a crash and the orchestra erupts. He finds his violin and they battle, back and forth. Paganini stands as if fighting gale winds. The thrilled audience rises.

As Spohr and LaFont watch, huge volleys of flame arc back and forth between Paganini and the orchestra, neither giving ground. Paganini flashes a mouth full of solid gold. In the air between them forms the battle scene from Milton's *Paradise Lost*. Armies of Angels march across a thundering sky, clashing violently. Samael leads the rebels. The rich patrons are out of their seats, shaking their fists at Paganini's wild performance. They shout and threaten to rush the stage.

This Paganini is possessed, Spohr says. LaFont matches his envy.

Dawn breaks on a quiet road along the far side of a high-walled Palace. A coach slides to a halt. Laughter vibrates from inside. A door opens and an expensively dressed but night-worn Duchess Pauline pops out. She is pretty, young and little drunk. With a stumble, she dives through an obscured passage in a large hedge.

She emerges on the Palace side of a thick wall at the edge of a vast and proper garden, then slips down dew-damp paths to a set of back stairs. There she finds Duchess Elisa sitting on the garden steps in her bed clothes, peeling and eating a piece of ripe fruit.

Up early with the birds, Elisa says, taking a bite. She hands a piece to Pauline, who plops down beside her.

I never know if you'd rather judge or envy me, Pauline says. I'll assume both.

Darling Brother sends his regrets, Elisa says. He will not visit us next month. Heavy is the brow of even the smallest Emperor.

Very true, Pauline says. You're up early.

Sometimes I miss Paris, Elisa says. I wander there in my dreams.

Of course you do, Pauline says. Tied to this marvelous place and all the Tuscan nobles you can eat. Your private salon of notable bores. Like so many blocks of wood. How you must envy my freedom to travel at my leisure.

Freedom, maybe, Elisa says. Reputation, not much.

Time to build a proper court, Pauline says. With thinkers and poets and people who know how to live. Two nights ago, I warmed myself by the fire for the longest time before I realized the bench I sat on was actually the sleepy man who plays the harp.

My husband plays the harp, Elisa says.

Does he, Pauline says.

The husband stays, Elisa says. But I have begun drafting my new court.

Then I know just who to bring, Pauline says. They say the soul of an old lover is trapped in his violin. That he played Boroni's newest and most complex composition by ear. That's what you need around here. Fire. The Napoleon of the violin. That's what they say.

Do not liken some fiddle player to a Bonaparte, Elisa says. I know of Paganini. His magic violin. His reported effect on certain aspects of a lady's character. Have you met him? Would you like to?

I have no infatuation with Paganini, Pauline says. The

way they tell it, he looks like an odd insect. Paper skin. Giant nose. Giant eyes. Long stringy curls. No, thank you.

That's what they say, Elisa says. But that's not all that they say.

Enough, Pauline says. Forgive me for trying to breathe a little spark into this gilded trap. I prefer sculptors, anyway.

Duchess Pauline gathers her skirts and storms off. Duchess Elisa finishes her fruit and climbs the steps. At the top, her Palace Servant stoically waits.

Add Paganini to your list, Elisa says.

Yes, ma'am, the Palace Servant says.

A packed theater mumbles impatiently at an empty stage.

Behind the curtain, the stage crew searches high and low. Doors open and close, everyone scrambling. Finally, a storage closet door opens and Paganini tumbles out, a young Chorus Girl tumbling after. They giggle.

Paganini bounces out of the wings and feigns surprise to find an audience there. He finds his violin on a stand along with some music. Paganini pages through the sheet music and yawns to the murmuring, expectant audience. The orchestra waits. Paganini tosses the pages into the air with a flourish and a cloud of paper. As he launches into a musical improvisation, the crowd erupts with applause. The orchestra is perplexed.

From an aisle seat, Elisa's Palace Servant, tartly observes.

Sun rises through deep red curtains at a theater-district brothel. A table ringed with tough gamblers doesn't blink as Eliza's Servant carefully unrolls a heavy rug. In the middle, he finds Paganini, peacefully unconscious. His violin sits at the center of the card table. The Servant shakes him.

Paganini snaps awake, smiling.

Well, good morning to you, he says.

Your presence is requested at the Palace, the Servant says, producing a handprinted card. Paganini's eyes go wide and he leaps awkwardly to his feet, crashing around, straightening his clothes. He bows to the card players, bleary and wobbling. They ignore him.

Gentlemen, please excuse me, I am needed most urgently, Paganini says.

Paganini and the Servant exit together. Out front, Paganini stops. The Servant stops. Paganini is in a sudden panic. He emphatically grabs the Servant's ear. The Servant listens patiently, sighs, draws a small purse from his pocket, and disappears inside. Paganini paces. The Servant returns, violin in hand.

At the Palace, the Servant leads Paganini through hallway after ornate hallway, no one else around.

I guess I forgot about the holiday, Paganini says.

Holiday, the Palace Servant asks. No holiday today.

There are no people around, Paganini says.

There are many people, all around, the Palace Servant says. It's all that large.

I see, Paganini says.

They enter a suite of rooms.

These rooms will be yours, the Palace Servant says. I'll bring something for you to eat. Should I send for a doctor as well?

Paganini straightens his back.

No need, he says.

The Palace Servant rings a bell.

Very well, he says. Use this if you need anything. The auditions are tomorrow evening, following dinner.

I didn't agree to an audition, Paganini says.

A formality, I am certain, the Palace Servant says.

I should say so, Paganini says.

The Palace Servant closes the door hard behind himself, leaving Paganini to survey the room.

In a small chapel on the Palace grounds, Duchess Pauline slips into a pew. Candles burn all around. A disinterested cat sits on the altar. Royer slips in next to her.

Father, Pauline says. How wonderful to see you.

I was already planning a trip to the region, Royer says. When I received your letter, I wasted no time. How may I help you?

This is not the normal stoic Royer. She brings bright blush to his cheeks. He is mad for her.

So, you'll be staying the night, then, she says, taunting him for sport.

If the lady likes, Royer says.

Likes are one thing, Father, Pauline says, sliding slowly past him. Do you know what it is the lady wants? What every princess wants. Absolutely everything she's not supposed to have.

Pauline disappears down the aisle, Royer close behind.

In a side chamber, he falls into her arms. They waste no time. Clothes hit the floor as Pauline kicks the door shut.

A pebble bounces off a high bedroom window of the Paganini family house. From below, Paganini whistles a complex church tune. At a window, Teresa's eyes go wide. A door opens and she embraces her wandering Son.

The moon is bright, Niccolò, she says. Step back from the windows. Your Father would be furious to see you here.

Let the old man shout, Paganini says. I have wonderful news. I am invited to join the Court of Lucca, Momma. Napoleon's own Sister. Momma. I have arrived. Command performance tomorrow night.

I hear her Husband is handsome, she says.

I hear he's a bore, Paganini says.

Play nice, Niccolò, she says.

Always, Momma, he says, handing her a heavy bag of coins. Tell Papa the prices went down at the market again.

She touches his face.

I miss you, Nico, she says.

I miss you, Momma, he says. But I am never far.

Antonio shouts drunkenly from inside.

Teresa, he hollers. Where did you go? Teresa?

She pulls their heads together. Both quietly mumble a prayer of their own design.

There you are, she says, slipping back inside. Dazzle them.

Paganini stumbles into his room, only a little drunk, the Palace Servant a step behind.

Where have you been, the Palace Servant pouts. Dinner is almost over. I do not have the time to chase after you.

Paganini's attention lands on a suit of clothes beside a dressing screen. White and cream from cuff to collar, including a giant powdered wig.

No, thank you, I never eat before a performance, Paganini says. What is this?

Your clothes for the evening, the Palace Servant says.

A little stuffy, Paganini says.

I assure you, this is in the fashion, the Palace Servant says.

Precisely, Paganini says, forcing his eyes to focus.

A nervous Harpsichord Player is flopping before a yawning, overheated gaggle of Tuscan Royalty. Elisa sits at the center of the loosely gathered audience. Beside her, her husband, Captain Felix. He is strong and handsome, with beautiful hair and the jangling, heavy uniform of an accomplished military man. He yawns. This amuses Elisa. She nudges him. They snicker together. Pauline slides into the seat beside her. A large group of Musicians wait with their instruments. Each wears an outfit unmistakably similar to the one given to Paganini. Paganini isn't among them.

You've dressed them the same, Pauline notices. Why?

Because I hope that they play well, Elisa says. But I know they must remember who it is they are playing for.

Very well, then, Pauline says. Which one is Paganini?

None of them, Elisa says. Truant, it seems.

226

PAGANINI

I was told he arrived yesterday, Pauline says.

He did, Elisa says.

The Palace Servant trails Paganini into the room, practically shoving him into place beside the other matching musicians. Paganini looks around with a combination of horror and panic. He looks and feels ridiculous in his costume. Pauline and Elisa eye him.

Oh my, Pauline says. He is even homelier than we thought.

Certainly is, Elisa says.

Slowly, Paganini turns. His sharp ears pick his name from amid the harpsichord notes ricocheting around the room. The three exchange an awkward look. The body language is unmistakable. Paganini is now recalculating the situation.

Samael, with a crooked smile, mixes easily with the audience, seated in the back row. He is amused, watching this moment unfold. The Harpsichord Player finishes to moderate appreciation. The next musician hauls himself into place.

Alright, enough, Pauline whispers to Elisa. Let us hear from the Napoleon of violinists.

Elisa makes a sour face and motions to the Palace Servant, who politely interrupts the current Harpsichordist and summons over the waiting Violinists, Paganini among them. The Palace Servant places sheet music before them. The nervous Violinists hustle to sort out their music and get a glimpse at what they will be expected to play by sight. Paganini looks to his violin and droops. Elisa clears her throat. The Violinists take the hint and all at once begin, competing to shine among the other identical players. There are tears in Paganini's eyes. He does not play. Almost mournfully, he tightens his strings. Barely looking at the music before him, he launches bitterly into the piece.

His notes fly, brighter, above the rest. Paganini's eyes locked on Elisa and Pauline. Both ladies suddenly float, transfixed. Enchanted. The Violinists stumble with their

227

bows, stunned by the brilliant outburst. Suddenly, Paganini stops. Silence. The ladies drop back to their seats. Paganini steps forward.

Please forgive me, Paganini says, rushing from the room, leaving jaws agape. I am suddenly not well. Thank you.

Paganini slams the door of his empty room, frantic with anger. Alone, he struggles to think. The drapes are blowing at the open window. But there is no wind. As he stares at them twirling there, a chair behind him scoots on the floor. He turns. There he finds Samael, smiling.

Hello Niccolò, Samael says.

Paganini sputters.

How did you get in here, he coughs.

The furious Palace Servant bursts in to lecture Paganini. Samael holds up a hand. The Palace Servant hangs mid-stride, mid-thought. Samael twirls his fingers. The Servant backs mechanically out the door, full reverse, gently shutting the door.

My friend, Samael says. How is your Mother? Did she ever tell you that once she had the most wonderful dream?

Every day, Paganini says. I know who you are.

I'm certain you do, Samael says. Tonight I would like to offer you something of tremendous value. I want to do you a favor.

Spare me your favors, Paganini says. I believe I play quite well.

Yes, I agree, Samael says. No chance for the likes of me to improve upon a gift like that. No. Paganini. I would like to free you. From your body. The pain in your stomach. In your arms. In your back. Your brain. The sort of ironic condition that proves my overall point, in a sense. Don't you think?

In fair trade for what, Paganini asks. Exactly?

You don't understand, Nico, Samael says. In the end, your throat will close. Your lungs will fill. And all too soon. They already believe your music rises from some demonic place. Why not embrace the part?

Paganini opens the door and waits. Samael stands.

I am hearing that too often, Paganini says.

Very well, Samael says. I am nothing if not patient, my friend. Just say the word. Even if only in your heart. And I will be here. But please, waste no more time.

And you believe I will, Paganini says.

Yes, I expect you will, Samael says, stepping from the room.

Then you do not know my Mother, Paganini says, closing the door.

A few days later, the now intimidated Palace Servant creeps to Paganini's door with a large tray, heavy with food, and carefully knocks. Frantic music from inside stops. Paganini throws open the door.

Ugh, Paganini says. Thank you. Leave it in the hall. I'll pick at it later, but I just can't stand the smell.

Duchess Elisa inquires whether you will be emerging today, the Palace Servant says.

Excellent question, Paganini says. Did you bring what I told you?

Yes, the Servant nods.

Balancing on the tray with everything else is a large glass jar of dark liquid.

She is quite upset, the Palace Servant warns to no interest.

This is India ink, Paganini says, shaking the jar, suspicious.

Yes, the Servant nods.

Really, Paganini says. And there isn't any darker?

No, The Palace Servant says. Sir, the Duchess asks . . .

Yes, Paganini smiles reassuringly. Please inform the Duchess, both of them if you like, that Signor Paganini is embracing the part.

Paganini slams the door. Pondering this, still balancing the tray, the Palace Servant slowly tips, corrects too late, slips and falls beneath a shower of dishes and silverware. The

229

door locks.

That night in a Palace ballroom, Captain Felix and
Duchesses yawn their way through a performance by
another small ensemble.

No sign of the magical Paganini again this evening,
Pauline says. How much longer will the maestro remain
here with us in residence?

Let him hope it does not rain tomorrow, Elisa says.

In his room, Paganini stands on a chair in his
underclothes, rehearsing scales and finger movements, just
as he did for Antonio years before. He struggles. Sweating.
Joints aching. Guts twisting. His long, dangling curls are
now black as the ink. In the corner, the suit of clothes
provided for him by the Servant now drips black as well.
The ink jar nearby is empty and on its side. Something at the
window catches his attention. He climbs stiffly down from
the chair, grimacing. But when Paganini reaches the window,
he grins.

In the ballroom, the musicians drone on before the
dozing court in their after-dinner formal wear. Paganini
appears in the doorway, in jet black. Heads turn. Politely, he
crosses the room. The faces follow him, stunned. Even the
music stops.

Paganini steps toward large glass, exterior doors,
muscling the heavy drapes aside. He swings them open.

Slowly, everyone stands, following him out onto a large
balcony. They find Paganini with his back to them. The stars
are clear and very bright.

Please forgive the delay, Paganini says. My sickness
erupts at the least useful times. I am sorry.

Only if you would favor us with a bit of your music, Elisa
says.

Paganini lifts his bow and plays. Above him a star falls.
He plays. Another falls. And another, as if Paganini is
pulling them from the sky. All are transfixed. Paganini's eyes

230

turn from the heavens. Seducing one Duchess with a particular refrain, he turns to the other with a second, then back again.

He finishes, leaving them all in a trance. With a satisfied grin, Paganini slips down a flight of stairs into the garden, leaving the crowd staring at the sky.

There he finds Samael, smiling.

Bravo, he says.

That night, Paganini tosses and turns. His door briefly opens, then light footsteps. Framed in the moonlight, Duchess Pauline.

Evening, my lady, Paganini says as she slips into his bed.

The years pass in a flurry.

Paganini leads the orchestra on the Palace lawn. The air is alive with summer.

He patiently instructs both Sisters from musical texts, then adjusts their form at the guitar and violin. They both keep an eye on him as well as each other.

Paganini climbs into a carriage at the Palace gate. Elisa approaches.

Represent me well, Paganini, she says. Return to us safe and sound.

Behind the carriage door, obscured from view, they kiss.

Soon the world will be speaking only of Elisa and her marvelous salon at Lucca, Paganini says.

The door closes, and he is off. Both Duchess Elisa and her Servant watch him go, smitten.

Around holiday time, Paganini arrives late to dinner, dressed in a uniform with spangles identical to the one Captain Felix wears. Felix stiffens. Afterward, as guests file into the parlor rooms after the meal, Elisa pulls Paganini into a dark corner of the parlor for a private word.

Not funny, she says.

I agree, Paganini says. Were they serving us a bird or a fish? Or possibly some combination of both?

This can't continue if I can't control you, Elisa says.

If you could, you wouldn't want me, Paganini says.

Then, one chilly, late-spring morning, Paganini is in his bedclothes, on his knees, a short escape from a low, nearby window. Captain Felix is in his travel clothes, hat and overcoat still in place. He stands at the other end of a loaded and cocked hunting rifle which is pressed to Paganini's forehead.

Brother, Paganini pleads. Friend! How long is it? I believe it may be almost a decade here at the Palace, together you and I, Paganini says. Yes. Cohorts, aren't we? Yes?

Cohorts, Captain Felix says. Then when is my birthday?

Paganini is at a loss.

Whenever it is, they serve us that awful soup, he says.

The Captain's finger moves to the trigger.

Say good night, Paganini.

My friend, Paganini cries. My Brother! Wait!

So, I would return at dawn from extended travels to find either my real friend or my actual Brother sneaking down my own private hallway, Captain Felix says.

Oh my, Paganini says. Suddenly I see the depth of this unfortunate misunderstanding. Forgive me. May I?

Paganini climbs to his feet. The Captain is listening.

Misunderstanding, Captain Felix says.

I'm pleased you never noticed before, Paganini says. But I have the embarrassing habit of walking in my sleep. You can just imagine my surprise to wake just now to find myself here, like this, with you. Ha!

Walking in your sleep, Captain Felix says.

Yes, Paganini says. So glad that is cleared up. Now, let's go find you some breakfast. You must be fainting from your travels.

Captain Felix doesn't budge.

Do not think I forget your vast reputation, Paganini, he says.

Duchess Pauline peeks from her window, panicked.

232

Ah, but don't you see, Paganini asks. Therein lies a great example of why you should trust me. And forget what terrible feelings you quite understandably have underway.

Go on, Captain Felix says.

Forgive me that, in my vanity, I imagined everyone well knew, Paganini says confidentially, leaning in closer. On the occasion when I do take a lover, always with great forward thought and tremendous respect, mind you, I leave my mark.

Duchess Elisa worries from her own window.

Your mark, Captain Felix says, studying the situation with a measured breath.

On the neck, most often, Paganini says. Or elsewhere. A love bite. Don't ask me why. Childish, really. But it is understandable that passionate men such as ourselves lose ourselves to the moment a bit, yes? What am I saying? A hero such as yourself has no time for silly gossip about harmless fiddle players. Forgive me. Go check. I'll wait.

Check, Captain Felix says. Check what?

I'm not sure, Paganini admits. I don't pretend to comprehend all that is in the mind of Tuscany's military leaders. I have no idea what you suspect me of. All I am suggesting is that if you suspect any foul play might have befallen any portion of this house, from the shutters to the cobblestones, check. If you find my mark on so much as a chamber maid, return to this spot and shoot me dead. I will wait right here for you. You have my complete word. I am that confident you will find nothing, and we shall forget this moment and forever remain friends.

Captain Felix lowers his weapon.

Your word, Captain Felix says.

Without that, what am I, Paganini asks. I shall not budge.

Felix spins on his heels.

Panicked, both Duchesses disappear from their windows.

Elisa finds a mirror and desperately powders a large suction mark just below the neckline of her dress. Pauline tears at her skirts and the layers underneath. Paganini left his mark squarely on her left buttock.

Still in his bedclothes, Paganini reaches the garden wall and frantically climbs. Dropping with a thud on the other side, his favorite Palace Servant is waiting with his prized violin. Paganini gratefully takes the instrument.

You will be missed, sir, the Palace Servant says.

Thank you, my friend, Paganini says.

A gunshot and shouts from Captain Felix in the distance. Paganini is off at a sprint.

Far out in the country, still in his bed clothes, he stumbles along with his violin in one hand and a half-empty jug of wine in the other. Beside him trots an unsaddled donkey. A group of amused Farmers catches up to them on foot.

Hello, a Farmer says. Why did you steal my donkey?

That is very presumptuous of you, Paganini says. I will have you know, he stole me.

Half-dressed and drunk, Paganini is more of a curiosity to them than any sort of threat. The chuckling Farmers turn the donkey toward home. They take back their jug as well.

Goodbye, dear friend, Paganini tells the donkey. If you get to the Palace, tell them I would appreciate the return of my pants!

Thunder, lightning and rain pour down as Royer slips out of the night and into the Palace chapel. He finds Pauline alone in the front pew. Glowing, he sweeps toward her.

My darling, Royer says. Why is it so long since you sent for me?

Her eyes are red with desperate tears.

He's gone, Pauline wails. He's gone and not coming back. Here I am with nothing to remember him by. Don't you see? I can't live this way. I can't. Not like this.

Who, my dear, Royer asks. Who is it that's gone?

Paganini, Pauline sobs, falling into his arms.

Royer's heart returns to stone.

PAGANINI

Ah, yes, he says. Paganini.

Preceding a performance deep in the heart of Europe, a famous Music Critic and fawning Wealthy Gentlemen sit amid a murmuring audience. The Gentleman reads from a broadsheet with an advance review of the show, written by the Critic.

Phonies like Paganini may seduce the rest, reads the Gentleman. Does this city not cry out in favor of serious musicians? True art is a gift from the greats. We do not honor them with upstarts and horror shows.

Clearly put, you must agree, the Critic says.

Yes, the Gentleman nods. But was it wise for you to publish this before he opens?

That was an error, confides the Critic. Overeager printer. No matter. I've read numerous reports of this Paganini. I'm not as easily fooled or amused. What a bore. You see one every few years. He's clearly peddling gimmicks to ignorant ears. This city despises a fraud. The very least I can do is help keep the stages clear for genuine performances. Watch closely. It will be just the one night for Paganini.

They nod knowingly to each other as the orchestra begins. Paganini steps to center stage, scans the audience, then pours every ounce of his focus onto the Music Critic.

I don't think he agrees, the Gentleman says.

Paganini launches into a stunning array of notes. The orchestra struggles to keep up, rising to their feet. The Critic is transfixed. Paganini pins him with his gaze, driving the music with growing fury.

Before the Critic's eyes, shapes grow from the shadows. They form frightening animals, blend and shift with the music. The air around Paganini swirls at his command. Hovering above the thrilled faces, the Critic sees his own Mother. And she is very angry with him. The Critic clutches the Gentleman's newspaper, manically tearing it into smaller and smaller pieces.

After another performance in yet another of many cities, in an impeccable and ornate mansion drawing room, a group of sophisticated Noblemen are smug and drunk. The hour is late and candles burn high. Paganini and a Challenger study each other. The Challenger clutches a violin. Paganini balances a wine glass on the top of his head.

In my hands is a composition so new the ink is dripping as I hold it, one of the Nobles says. No eyes, beyond the composer, have seen a single note.

A coin is tossed. Paganini snatches it from the air. The glass shatters.

I submit to your guest from France, he says.

The Challenger bows.

In fact, I am Swiss, he says.

Congratulations, Paganini says.

The Noble leads Paganini into the hall, then into a cellar, shutting the doors behind him.

Nobody could hear a thing down there, he says when he returns.

The Challenger studies the sheet music. He plays the beautiful and complex composition flawlessly. The group is enthusiastic.

The Noble disappears for a moment and returns again with Paganini.

Was it a hundred or thousand, my little wager with your guest, Paganini asks.

Hundred, the Noble says.

I see, Paganini plays to the crowd.

So, then, how about a thousand, he offers.

The Challenger swallows hard. Out of his depth, but confident from the positive response, he nods. Paganini sets the pages on the music stand upside down.

As Paganini plays, the same music takes on new life. The crowd is so moved that they never notice the embarrassed Challenger slip quietly out of the room.

In his private study, Royer slumps against the window frame, back to a room full of anxious and frightened fellow Priests, paper clutched in one hand, softly tapping the glass in front of him with the other.

His angry eyes prod the street below. The room is frozen, hanging on Royer's next words. Bandif rushes in. Body language stops him in his tracks.

A message arrived just now from the Vicar-General, Bandif whispers, as if to himself. Paganini will perform in Rome.

The glass pane beneath Royer's finger shatters.

A deep-black carriage pulled by equally dark horses screeches to a halt outside a small rural inn in the dead of night. Paganini tumbles out into the mud, pale, sick, exhausted. He is a horrific sight.

A small Inn Keeper is immediately at the door, frantically yelling, in German, waving a lit torch. The beautiful Inn Keeper's Daughter appears behind the screaming little man.

My Father says leave this place, she tells Paganini, her body language communicating the opposite. He is very superstitious.

Superstitious, Paganini smiles. Charming.

Teufel, says the Inn Keeper.

I certainly understand, Paganini says, shifting to a more seductive tone. Please. Come here and let me see you. Tell him I mean you no harm. Do you have a room for me? I am more than able to pay. I am a musician. I have a concert tomorrow. Nearby. Somewhere. Perhaps you've heard?

The Inn Keeper's Daughter calms her Father and takes the torch.

Come in, Signor Paganini, she says.

The next morning in his room, she wipes Paganini's brow with a wet cloth as he sleeps. He's startled awake.

Just a dream, Paganini says. Apparently not over. But

certainly continuing to improve. How long have I been here?

You collapsed last night on the way to your room, she says. Don't you remember?

Certainly, he says. I wanted to see if your dear Father could lift me.

I carried you, she says.

My champion, Paganini says, batting long eyelashes.

This makes her laugh.

Is it true what they say, she asks.

Possibly, he says. What do they say?

The soul of a murdered lover is trapped in your violin, she says.

Oh, that, he says. And if I say yes?

She bites her lip, scared, excited.

There are men from the theater downstairs, she says. They want to know if you will be able to play tonight.

Darling, have Father tell them I am staying put right here in your caring embrace, Paganini says.

That is too bad, she says. I would so love to hear you perform. So love. So very much.

Paganini heroically forces himself to his feet, leading her to the door.

Give me a few hours, Paganini says. Please return for me this evening, dressed for the night of your dreams.

But I have no ticket, she frowns.

Paganini laughs and kisses her forehead, closing the door behind her.

Samael now sits on the edge of the bed.

You have no shame, Samael says. Is that all that motivates you?

Paganini finds a water pitcher and dumps it over his long dark curls and days-old clothes. He takes a deep breath.

Yes, he says. What I have, as you enjoy reminding me, is precious time. And though the world may be full of gorgeous daughters, only so many will pass a young man's way.

238

Oh, Samael chides him. Did she meet a young man?

Paganini digs through his luggage and finds a small glass vile full of a putrid liquid. He downs it and winces.

Depends on your point of view, Paganini says.

Ah, Samael says. The latest elixir of oily mud. Delicious?

Leave if you can't be quiet, Paganini says, stepping up onto a chair, as he did when he was a child, closing his eyes, hands locating where a violin and bow should be, but aren't. Playing through his concert just the same. Samael looks over to the closed violin case on a table nearby and groans.

What is turning in that mind of yours, where you believe even a little German Inn Keeper will steal your notes from the air, Samael says.

Not the notes, Paganini says. My thoughts. My ideas. It is not the bow, but the mind that is the value here. Believe what you like otherwise, but believe that. It will take them a hundred years to discover what I do as a matter of habit. Let the old man pay to listen for himself. I gave him far too much for this claptrap room.

Paganini then closes his eyes and rehearses the entire concert, silently, in his mind.

Out in the hallway, the Inn Keeper carefully approaches the door to spy on his guest. He peers through the keyhole, watching Paganini play silently, frantically, alone in the room.

Teufel, the Inn Keeper agrees with himself. Teufel.

On a dry winter day, the streets of Genoa are full and alive. In an upper floor suite of legal offices, violin music, not always in key, tumbles from behind a door and down a crowded hallway. On the other side, Germi, thin and not yet grey at the temples, absently fiddles, pacing and reading from stacks of paper piled on every available surface.

The door flies open. Germi tries to ignore a bookwormish older lawyer, Figari, and continues to fling flat notes around the room. Figari waits.

Good morning, Germi says, finally. What do you want?

It is the middle of the afternoon, Figari says. Come with me. I require . . .

My personal assistance, Germi says.

Call it that, Figari says.

Because you have access to one of the city's brightest judicial minds, who is thus far undefeated in court, Germi says. Go on. You can say it.

Because your brother lawyers would like a few moments of genuine peace, Figari says. And because perhaps I have found a match for that silver tongue of yours.

In a damp prison cell, Figari and Germi find Paganini lying on the cold stone floor, chained. His eyes are closed, arms sprawling in the most melodramatic way possible.

Ahem, Figari says.

Go away, Paganini says and doesn't move. I am in no mood.

Ahem, Figari says.

Paganini sits up and looks to Germi.

I hate it when he does that, Paganini says.

Me too, Germi says.

Hello, Paganini says.

Hello, Germi says.

I would stand up and shake your hand, but I am currently feeling very, very sorry for myself, Paganini says. Trapped here. Endlessly confined.

Since late this morning, Figari says. You are quite a mess.

Let me out of here and that awful little Tailor will have quite a mess, Paganini says. I'll tell you that.

The Tailor whose only, and vastly younger than you, Daughter you transported unsupervised to Parma, Germi says.

Yes, Paganini groans.

With the promise of marrying her away from prying eyes, Germi says.

To be fair, at some point, I tell all of them that, Paganini says.

You poisoned her, Germi says.

That's not fair, Paganini says.

Well then, Germi says. Which of these complaints are not true?

None, Paganini says.

Germi finds a stool and sits eye-level with Paganini.

Then do tell, he says. Do tell.

When I first returned home to Genoa, I feared I would be stuck in a web of troubles remaining from my childhood, Paganini says. But I was wrong. This city loves me. Genoa is my city. This city is mine.

As Paganini remembers, a packed theater and audience are in the palm of his hand. Antonio, now much older, watches from the back row and storms out as the audience erupts.

Then, at a huge formal ball, Paganini floats drunk through the crowd, from female glance to female glance. Angiolina Cavanna catches his eye and dismisses him all at once. Devastatingly pretty, she's got an old soul and a lot of things she wants from the world. Suddenly this includes Paganini.

Looking down on Paganini in his jail cell, Figari ruefully shakes his head.

I suppose I'm never happy until I find someone to ignore me, Paganini says. If we are all to be held to the choices made while our hearts are at the controls . . .

Paganini stops. Germi doesn't blink.

I am making an excuse, Paganini says.

I am aware of that, Germi says.

I have no excuse, Paganini says, thoughtfully. And I don't usually admit to things like that.

Perhaps your conscience likes me, Germi says.

Months before, in Parma, Paganini and Angiolina tumble out of a coach in front of a small hotel, entwined. He holds his hands over her eyes as they enter an adequate, but not fancy room, with a flourish. She twirls around and all at once her happy countenance turns bitter.

Paganini, Angiolina says. Will I have to beat your cheapness out of you?

Serves you right, you old letch, Germi grins through the bars. Figari looks to Germi, horrified, but Paganini laughs.

It was a perfectly nice room, Paganini tells them. Father always said, endlessly, that people have money because they keep their money.

That night, Angiolina sits at the window, arms crossed in a snit, watching Paganini sleep. Her stomach hurts and she is very uncomfortable. She kicks the corner of the bed. He stirs. She kicks again. He sits up in a half-sleep panic.

At dawn, inside the town apothecary shop, Paganini shoves a crumpled piece of paper into the Chemist's hand.

I need some of this, Paganini says. For worms or bad root vegetables or some such thing. I've had both and never complained at all this much. As you can imagine, it is urgent.

The Chemist turns to the shelves of jars and bottles behind him.

How big, he asks.

I don't know how big they are, Paganini says. It is a frightening fact that they exist at all.

Not the worms, the Chemist says. The horse.

Horse, Paganini asks.

Mule, the Chemist asks. Pig?

Stop naming animals, Paganini says. She's a girl. A woman. She's a woman.

Oh, I see, the Chemist says, reexamining the paper. And she sent you for this? Worms indeed.

Yes, Paganini says. To cure her of whatever is driving us both insane.

The Chemist winks at him.

Not sure how to respond, but eager to get moving, Paganini winks back.

The Chemist finds a different package and hands it to Paganini, leaning in close.

You don't want those, the Chemist says. You want these. Mix it all with some water. She better take the whole thing and eat nothing else for a day or so.

Whatever does the job, Paganini says, paying him and turning to leave.

The job indeed, the Chemist snickers. Good luck.

Half out the door, these words land ominously across Paganini's back.

Paganini mixes the powders as Angiolina sprawls across the bed. He then slips into the street, crossing the Hotel Owner's Wife's cold glare, and drinks the night away.

The next morning, Paganini finds the Hotel Owner's Wife waiting for him. The door to their room opens to reveal Angiolina curled around a bucket on the floor. She trades off shrieking and vomiting.

What do you expect to do now, the Hotel Owner's Wife demands.

Call the Constable, Paganini says. Immediately.

Spinning his story to Germi and Figari, Paganini absentmindedly waggles his chains.

I paid them enormously to take her home to her Father right away, he says. Where I assume she recovered safe and sound. So, I am sorry for the trouble. But can we not put this behind us?

She didn't go home to her Father, Germi says. For whatever understandable reason, she didn't want to face him. She slipped away. Months later, her Father found her in the mountains. Half frozen, sleeping in some barn. The baby didn't survive.

This last shot lands just as Germi intended it to. Paganini drags himself to his feet, chains and all.

I need to be alone, Paganini says.

On the busy sidewalk outside Ferdinand Cavanna's Tailor Shop, Germi watches customers pass in and out. Out of nowhere, Germi finds Royer beside him, also staring at the shop door.

Such a shame, Royer says. How this poor family was tortured by that awful, evil violinist, don't you think?

Hello, Germi says. And you are?

Forgive me, Royer says, extending his hand. I am the neighborhood Priest. Looking to finally replace that old suit?

I am now, Germi says.

Well, you are in the right place, Royer says. This is a fine man and an excellent tailor. A credit to the community. Why, I bounced little Angiolina on my knee. And I am certain justice will see fit to punish this Paganini to the end of his considerable wits. I follow his career closely, and I assure you it is one rolling scandal. A menace. Paganini is a menace. Ask anyone.

Ferdinand Cavanna, A kindly older man steps out of the shop, wiping chalk dust on his smock and warmly embracing Royer, who gives his best smile.

Germi sits across from a deflated Paganini in his dank prison cell. Figari is there as well, positioning himself beneath a tiny window facing only the sky, uncomfortable in the sad, moldy room.

Mister Cavanna has agree to terms which he feels will give this matter, and his family, some peace, Germi says. His words. Not mine.

Germi finds a square of paper in his pocket, crumbles it and tosses it to Paganini. Chains rustle as he reads.

This is outrageous, Paganini says.

That must be a fraction of your accounts in this city alone, Figari says.

I will thank you to not concern yourself with my accounts, Paganini says, trying to toss it back and remembering his chains.

It is this or a trial, Germi says.

There is something more sinister to this duo than the facts let on, Paganini says.

Those damned untrustworthy facts, Germi says.

You are fired, Paganini says.

And you are skewered, Germi says. Either too proud or too stupid for your own good. Pity. I never heard you play.

Germi stomps away, leaving Figari to deal with the raving musician and vice versa.

Wait, Figari and Paganini say together. Come back.

Too late, Germi's gone.

In a stuffy chamber of the local Court, presided over by a steely-eyed Magistrate, Paganini, his head in his hands, stands with Figari. Figari is delighted by the drama.

She ran and hid from shame, Ferdinand Cavanna's voice quivers. Shame that this violinist drew down upon her and our family. I understand that now and blame her not at all. I searched months for her. To bring her home. When finally I received word, I hurried into the mountains.

Cavanna rocks woefully on his feet as he describes a dramatic scene to the stuffy, crowded room, Angiolina nodding emphatically with every detail.

On a deep mountain pass, bundled against the frigid cold, Cavanna reaches a dilapidated farmhouse in a small clearing, then falls to his knees in prayer that he might be there in time.

He heroically throws open the door and finds Angiolina giving birth on the floor, hours later stumbling back out into the snow, exhausted and covered with blood.

My Daughter survived, Ferdinand Cavanna tells the Court. Her child was lost.

The spectators gasp. Angiolina fails to stifle a moan.

Behind them, a door opens. Germi rushes in, hustles over, and whispers in Figari's ear.

Don't say a word, Germi tells him. Our guests will arrive momentarily. I hope. So pretend I am speaking very seriously. Alright? Fine, just nod. Now would be good.

Figari eventually catches on, adopting his best attempt at a knowing gaze. Germi can't help but roll his eyes. Their conversation draws the muttering room's full attention.

If you would be so kind, a disinterested Magistrate says.

Apologies, Figari says. Another moment, please.

On cue, the door opens again. Two men hurry into the room.

At the sight of these men, Ferdinand Cavanna looks nervously to his Daughter. Her eyes are wide.

Germi continues to whisper. Two more enter. Same reaction from the Cavannas. Germi motions them all forward.

Witnesses, Germi makes a point of whispering loudly. For the defense.

The Cavannas are ready to faint. Two more enter.

The Magistrate tires of Germi's interruption.

Does this man represent you, he asks.

He is talking to Paganini, who stares wide-eyed at Germi, trying to understand his game.

He's talking to you, Germi says.

Paganini half stands and bows.

Yes, please, Paganini says.

Two more men enter. Ferdinand Cavanna bolts to his feet.

We withdraw, Ferdinand Cavanna says. We withdraw my complaint. We are free to go. Let's go.

Ferdinand Cavanna and his Daughter flee the room to stunned silence. Confused looks all around, except Germi.

Well then, the Magistrate says. I suppose that . . .

Sir, if I may, Germi says. In light of Mister Cavanna's understanding, Paganini would like to bestow twice the amount of the complaint to the church orphanage.

Paganini is red-faced with anger. But when the room explodes in applause, he softens and accepts, shaking Germi's hand.

Paganini dances into the street, Germi a step behind him. Royer calls from the shadows.

I hope you are proud of yourself, Royer says.

All is well, Father, Germi says. Thank you. Is this part of your neighborhood as well?

Yes, Royer says. They all are.

Then I'm sure you're aware this credit to the community and his Daughter have collected several private settlements from quite a few drunken gentlemen, Germi says. These men didn't mind providing a message as long as they would not be asked to speak themselves. Sort of on odd fraternity, actually.

Royer is boiling.

I was under the impression you were fired, he says.

I was, Germi says. But this suit. It fits just awful.

Paganini is now in the distance, dancing with passersby, singing at the top of his lungs.

Hurry now, my good friend Germi, Paganini shouts. Your celebration is getting cold!

Germi smiles and starts after him.

Paganini is a sickness in the eyes of the Church, Royer calls after him. A public hazard. You did your part to spread that sickness today. That disease.

Well, one must do one's part, Germi shouts back. Good day.

Germi bows and skips off after Paganini. They hurry together into the closest restaurant. Royer watches, bitterly.

In reality, Ferdinand Cavanna did drop to his knees from exhaustion in front of the mountain farmhouse, much as he described. But reality is different than his testimony.

A gruff group of Cousin Cavannas burst from the farmhouse, dragging him inside. Ferdinand Cavanna finds his Daughter painfully giving birth on the floor. His first instinct is to beat her. The Cousins restrain him. Later, Cavanna stumbles out into the night, exhausted, covered in blood. A baby cries inside.

From the darkness, Royer lifts a lantern. Cavanna is startled but recognizes Royer.

Mother and child well, I presume, Royer says.

The baby is sickly, Ferdinand Cavanna says. Weak. The girl is fine until I get ahold of her. You wasted no time.

Bring me the child, Royer says, holding a large bundle of money to the light. Cavanna disappears inside and returns with baby Orfeo wrapped in blankets. Royer takes the baby carefully, tossing the money into the snow. Cavanna dives after it.

This child died today, Royer says. Say it.

He, Ferdinand Cavanna stammers. It . . .

Say it, Royer says.

The baby died, Ferdinand Cavanna says. Everyone is very upset.

Alone in the chapel, Duchess Pauline paces, impatient. Royer appears at the door, carrying what appears to be a bundle of blankets.

You should not have contacted me this way, she says.

You said you needed a part of him, Royer says. I promised to bring you whatever you need.

He throws back a blanket. Pauline studies Paganini's baby like a necklace of fine gems.

You do not disappoint me, Marcus, Pauline says.

That's all Royer was looking for.

During a tour through Spain, Paganini sweats in bed, guts twisting. Samael sits at his side, waiting patiently.

PAGANINI

I appreciate the company, but you waste your time here, Paganini says.

Paganini, you frustrate me, Samael says. Why should we not stand and walk out of here together?

As the door flies open, Samael is gone. A Hotel Manager rushes in and points at Paganini.

Doctor, please do not let this man die in my hotel, he says.

An Elderly Doctor enters and pulls up a chair. The air in the room reflects Paganini's long and sickly stay.

He's been here for weeks, the Manager says.

I pay my bill, Paganini says.

He is right, the Doctor says. This is not a hospital.

Paganini attempts to pull himself up, but fails.

I see, he says. It will be a lecture, then.

The Elderly Doctor smirks.

Heavens no, he says. I'd trade a few years here at the end for a night on the town with the likes of you. However, there is no need for a man of your means to suffer this way. There are great minds at work, Paganini, pushing the bounds of human science. It is a cure you need and you are in luck. Put your faith in the newest medicine. Come with me and surrender to the cure.

This has a nice sound to Paganini.

The cure, he says brightly. Could it be?

They are already expecting you, the Elderly Doctor says, extending an ornate invitation card.

Samael stands in the corner, shaking his head, unnoticed.

Bring my coach around and send someone to pack up this mess, Paganini tells the relieved Hotel Manager.

Rain pours down as Paganini's coach winds up a long, sharp path toward the giant and imposing front door of a remote sanitarium, tucked down a long stone-walled lane in a dense, ancient forest.

In a basement laboratory, Paganini stands naked as a

team of Academics measures every inch and angle. More look on, sternly taking careful notes. They carefully lower him into a giant copper vat of thick and smelly liquid. Paganini can hardly breathe and it stings his eyes. Lifting him, they hustle across the room toward a second vat, losing their footing, dunking him hard as they slip and fall.

Later, Paganini is placed against a long bed standing upright and is strapped tight, his arms straight out. A group of pretty Nurses enters.

Hello, ladies, Paganini flirts. To his horror, the Nurses apply leeches.

Another door opens and a Sanitarium Doctor carefully balances in a tray of vials.

Drink this, the Sanitarium Doctor says, pouring one vial after another down Paganini's throat. Then drink this.

When all are empty, he hands Paganini a bucket.

Thank you, Paganini says. What is this for?

By now they usually vomit, the Sanitarium Doctor says, leaning away expectantly.

Who vomits, Paganini asks, concerned.

Patients, the Sanitarium Doctor says.

Then I should vomit, you're saying, Paganini says.

Don't you want to, the Sanitarium Doctor asks.

There is worry in the Sanitarium Doctor's eyes.

What happens if I don't, Paganini asks.

I don't know, the Sanitarium Doctor says.

They both shrug, sit quietly together, and wait.

Later, a heavily muscled Orderly unlocks and opens a big, heavy door. Behind it is a tiny, otherwise dark, stone room with a roaring fireplace. Inside, Paganini is strapped to a chair, drenched in sweat. The Orderly unstraps him.

Thank goodness, Paganini says. I thought you forgot me in here. I need you to tell them, this treatment is entirely too hot.

The Orderly helps him to his feet.

Thank you, Paganini says. I'll tell you. This all may be

working. Right now, I am absolutely famished, and I can't remember the last time I had any appetite whatsoever.

The Orderly leads him down the hall to another small stone room, this one with no fire. He sits Paganini in an identical chair and straps him down.

Very refreshing, if a little cold, Paganini says. Very cold, actually. I cannot believe that it is supposed to be this cold in here. Is this correct?

The Orderly closes and locks the door.

In the laboratory, a huge board of sketches and measurements divide the room. The Sanitarium Doctor paces back and forth in front of the Academics.

The peculiar symmetry of his limbs, he says. His unbalanced posture. Odd lengths. Strange angles. Remarkably flexible and powerful. Organs fighting like cats in a bag, of course. A calamity of a corpus, gentlemen, but perfection wrapped around that violin. Nearly useless for any other purpose and killing him as well. Some would be happy to burn this creature at the stake. Hard to say that wouldn't be a relief to him.

On a warm, sunny day in the Sanitarium Garden, two Orderlies hoist Paganini by his armpits and walk him back and forth, his feet barely paddling along. A pitcher of water sweats on a table near the gate.

The weather today, Paganini says. Unbearable. Go on and get yourselves a drink, boys, leave me here for a stretch. I'm not going anywhere.

The Orderlies leave Paganini dangling from a low tree limb and get their water. When they turn back, he's gone.

Paganini bursts into the nearest tavern, still in his hospital clothes. The bar is crowded.

The Tavern Keeper laughs as she finds Paganini's violin case below the bar. She sets it down with a bottle beside it.

Back sooner than I thought, the Tavern Keeper says.

Paganini opens the case to find a hidden wad of bills. He throws a few across the bar.

I tried it their way, Paganini says. I guess I'll stick with mine. Here. For your trouble.

A Drunk Customer bumps into Paganini. They are the same size.

How much for the pants, Paganini asks.

At a brightly lit mansion along a wide, slow river, exquisitely dressed guests file in and out of a huge party. An orchestra plays on the lawn.

Paganini bursts from his coach with a stumbling flourish and charges inside. All around him, whispers of his name.

Carefully posed at the top of a long flight of stairs, dazzling, pouting in a couture dress, Antonia Bianchi's eyes circle for prey.

She floats down into the music, people, laughing and flirting.

A puffy Industrialist takes her hand. My dear, the plans are set, he says. In the morning, my private ship will take us wherever we like. London. New York. I will show you the world.

Paganini appears at a large doorway with a flourish. No one takes note except Antonia. Paganini waits. The costumed Doorman doesn't notice him. Paganini takes a giant step forward and summons a deep voice.

Attention, attention, I am extremely pleased to now present to you, the assembled Ladies and Gentlemen of this ballroom, the globally acclaimed virtuoso and widely acknowledged grandmaster of the violin, Niccolò Paganini!

All turn, surprised. Paganini bows. Antonia grows flush.

I know Paganini, the Industrialist boasts. Care to meet him?

As Paganini brushes past, the Industrialist stops him. Hello, my great friend, he says, reaching for Paganini's hand and missing. It is excellent to see you.

Paganini is about to shrug him off when he spots Antonia.

252

You're that wealthy hunter with the giant house and all the big dead animals hanging all over, Paganini says.

Yes, the Industrialist says. My trophies. I hosted many parties for the Duchesses. We were thrilled when you chose to play.

This aims to impress Antonia and misses.

Yes, Paganini says. Well, I would very much enjoy hearing your technique for trapping birds.

This is aimed at Antonia as well.

My expertise is large game, the Industrialist scoffs.

I wouldn't take that from him, Paganini smiles at her, drifting into the crowd.

So then, the Industrialist says. Where were we?

You said ship, she says.

Yes, of course, he says. Finest in the world.

I'm sorry, my dear, Antonia says. But you know I become terribly ill at sea.

We've planned this for weeks, the Industrialist says.

Whatever you say, darling, she says, squeezing his hand, leaving him dumbfounded. Please, contact me the moment you return. I do want to hear all about it.

Antonia falls into step behind Paganini. He turns with a smile.

Sir, I do not believe you've met me yet, she says. Paganini is taken.

Months later, dawdling around his private library, Germi stares into the fireplace, nursing a pipe. Caprechi enters with a big bundle of letters.

These were all delayed together, Caprechi says. Arrived just now. Sat accumulating somewhere. Storm in the mountains, maybe. Perhaps a ship sank. Or something.

Well, at least we know the facts, thank you, Germi says. Have you located none of the passages I asked you for this morning?

Yes, Caprechi says, fumbling through a stack of law

books. I have them. One moment.

Germi opens one of the letters at the window.

Paganini writes that he is finished with love, he says.
Another deathly serious spoiled affair.

Well, perhaps with time, Caprechi says.

Germi reads on and shrugs, then opens another letter.

Well, then. Paganini is in love.

To Germi's surprise, Caprechi closes the books and makes
himself comfortable.

What are you waiting for, he asks.

Well, go on, Caprechi says. Open the next one.

At another in an exhausting tour of theaters, Paganini
pauses amid his normal routine, lowering his violin to the
disgruntled clamor of his audience.

Enough of that, Paganini says. I would like you to meet
the voice which fills my heart.

He motions to the wings. No response. Antonia stands
behind the curtain, feet frozen, eyes wide. Paganini is
enchanted. He takes her hand and leads her, terrified, to the
center of the stage. Paganini plays. Antonia sings. She is not
perfect. Paganini urges her on. With his effort, they
intertwine.

That night, Paganini and Antonia throw open giant
windows at the top floor of a very fancy hotel. The lights of
Naples stretch before them.

For you, my love, Paganini says. All for you.

She collapses into his arms.

Finally, she says.

The Papal Palace throws long shadows under afternoon
sun. Paganini waits alone in a long private hallway full of
antiquities borrowed from all of history. He studies his worn
invitation again, not sure if he's where he's supposed to be. A
tall door opens at the distant end of the hallway. Pope Pius
appears, also alone, peeling off a heavy hat and top robes.

PAGANINI

Baron Paganini, Pope Pius says, taking his hand. Thank you for waiting. These ceremonial meetings are endless.

No, I certainly must thank you, Paganini says. When you once arranged for me to perform on the sacred days here in Rome, it was my Mother's proudest day.

Niccolò, Pope Pius says. Even then some saw you as a threat. I hear it even more now. And this always amuses me. I see the man beneath. I see the effort you work so hard to hide. I fear you not, Paganini, and I want you to know that.

Thank you, Paganini says. I can not describe what that means.

Yes, well, I've brought you here to make you a Chevalier, Pope Pius says. Consider it your gift to me. Let their tongues wag at that.

Paganini's small set of rag-tag apartment rooms are barely furnished and messy, top to bottom. It is mostly a place to sleep when he isn't touring, which is rare. He wakes to Antonia leaning over him.

I do not understand, she says. How often are you sickly this way?

It is not how often I am ill, my love, Paganini says, closing his eyes. It is how often I am well. And on balance, not often enough.

When he opens his eyes again, she is gone. Then soon, again, he wakes to find her leaning over him.

Get up, she says. I have the answer.

Antonia drags Paganini through the entryway of a large, empty house on a grand estate.

Really, my dear, Paganini says. I must rest. Where are we? Who lives here?

We do, she says.

An Estate Agent stands expectantly at the top of a long flight of stairs. Standing behind him, Paganini's new Housekeeper, Cook and Driver, well dressed and confused.

The Estate Agent hustles toward them.

Greetings, he says.

Paganini is dumbfounded.

Yes, Antonia says. Signor Paganini is happy to sign whatever documents you require.

I need to roll over and open my eyes, Paganini says. I am dreaming too vividly.

Hush, Antonia says. This will be more to our standards. Won't you feel better in a proper house?

I wasn't aware we had standards, Paganini says.

A side door opens. Delivery Men haul in a line of furniture.

You've been busy, my love, Paganini says.

You've been boring, she says. I am off.

Appointments, no doubt, Paganini says. Busy, busy.

Yes, she says, handing him a bundle of letters. And I took the liberty of accepting these invitations for us to perform. Do be prepared. With all these expenses, we really must keep working, darling.

She kisses him lightly and leaves Paganini with the Estate Agent and his new House Staff. He nods up at them, wide-eyed and friendly, though unsure.

Hello, Paganini says. Very nice to meet you all.

The Estate Agent clears his throat. He does have a bundle of papers for Paganini.

Well, then, the Estate Agent begins, his smile halted by a cold stare from Paganini.

Yes, I am just now getting to you, Paganini says.

It is a beautiful morning in the gardens at the Palace at Lucca. A Palace Teacher leads a group of very well-dressed and polished Students through lessons in their grammar books. The one sore thumb among the angelic faces is Orfeo, now five. Orfeo looks like young Paganini. A tiny, pale, black-haired bird with angry eyes. He does not fit in and feels it through and through.

Alright, the Palace Teacher says. That is enough for now.

The children run off to play. As the Teacher gathers and stacks the books, she looks up to find a Palace Guard running towards her. Soldiers rush for the gates.

Gather the children, he shouts.

Behind a large hedge, a group of geese has surrounded little Orfeo. They peck at him mercilessly. The other Students laugh and taunt him, throwing handfuls of bread at him to attract the birds.

The Teacher and Guard search frantically. They hear screaming, then silence. They rush behind a hedge to find Orfeo surrounded by dead birds and horrified children.

Perhaps that one is a Bonaparte after all, the Palace Teacher says.

That night in the chapel, Pauline finds Royer waiting. Cannon fire echoes in the distance.

Thank goodness you are alright, Royer says. I was so worried.

She drags Orfeo from behind herself.

Here, she says. Take him.

Outside, her armed guards wait impatiently beside carts overstuffed with expensive goods. Royer is confused. She is half-disguised in a scarf wrapped around her head.

Napoleon is finished, Pauline says. We are leaving. Take him.

This boy isn't some trinket you can just return, Royer says.

No, trinkets don't bite, she says. You brought him here, didn't you? I only sent for you because I have no other choice. Please. Take him.

He nods. She leaves in a flutter of skirts.

The horses stomp, dragging the carts away from the church. Royer stares down at five-year-old Orfeo, a tiny scale model of Paganini, his archenemy, and reaches out his hand. The child takes it.

Come with me, Royer says. We will find you something

good to eat.

Paganini is on his knees in the hallway of his new home.
Behind a door, Antonia screams his name.

Unbearable, Paganini says to the ceiling. Release me from
this moment. I am trapped. Please. I am lost. Isn't there
something? Some purpose? Some post by which to guide
myself?

Samael is nowhere to be found.

A baby cries. The door opens and a newborn infant is
thrust into Paganini's arms. At first, he is stiff and distant,
then melts as the baby smiles, pure light, a shock of hair
across his forehead. This is Achille.

Ah, Paganini says. I see it now.

Antonia is exhausted on the bed as a Local Doctor fusses
over her. Paganini brings the baby to her.

Look, my dear, he says.

I smell that perfume, she says. Where have you been?
Who were you with while I lay in agony?

Here with you, Paganini says.

I didn't see you, she says. Where did you go?

Quickly back on tour, an audience roars as Paganini
raises his golden Achille into the air. Antonia appears on
stage, stepping between them and the audience, somehow
crowding he and Achille out.

This, Paganini doesn't like.

The next winter, Germi stands at the window in
Paganini's huge, ornate drawing room, admiring a table
covered with newspaper clippings.

Impressive, he says.

Paganini sits across the room, bouncing chubby and
happy Achille on his knee.

We conquered, she and I, Paganini says. Wherever we
went. Like a windstorm. My violin and that angelic face.
These last several nights, completely in her honor.

Paganini's Housekeeper appears at the door.

As I said before, Germi says dryly. Congratulations.

Ah, Paganini says. It's time. Follow me.

In front of the house, they find a carriage overloaded with fine goods and luggage.

You have a beautiful child, Germi says as they make their way out the door. An impressive home, infamous around the world, why not take time, rest, forget all of this travel a while?

Out of the question, Paganini says. I rest only when forced. And then strictly under protest. Time is shorter than you give credit.

Did you not once tell me you'd finally found your anchor, Germi asks. Your orbit? How many Irishmen's yearly pay must you jam into your pockets?

Paganini lifts baby Achille into the sunlight.

Never enough, Paganini says. You understand, don't you, my boy? Of course, you do. Tell the silly man, nothing is nearly ever enough. Yes indeed.

Antonia appears at the front door. She is dressed to travel, eyes shooting daggers at Paganini. Silently, she approaches, mouth opening, aiming to fire.

Ah, Paganini says. Hold steady, dear girl. Remember our bargain.

She bites her tongue and without a look to Achille, climbs angrily onto the carriage. It pulls away.

I feel it was a generous settlement, Paganini says. She will understand better in time. You will make sure she's comfortable, won't you? And far from earshot?

The assembled House Staff watch her carriage disappear. It doesn't break their hearts to see her go.

Of course, Germi says.

Now, let's get you a bath, Paganini says as Achille giggles.

Paganini's black carriage and horses jangle to a stop in yet another town. Paganini emerges with Achille, now eight and dressed as a miniature gentleman. The stronger Achille grows, the more Paganini shows his age.

On one side of the street is a town theater. On the other is a secondhand clothes shop. Inside, Paganini fumbles through a stack of worn, black coats, Achille in tow. I need a jacket, he says.

Ah, the Shopkeeper says. Funeral?

Performance, Paganini says. These seem reasonably clean.

Performance, the Shopkeeper says. Signor Paganini? Sir, there is a fine tailor shop just up the road.

How many of these, do you suppose, could I buy for the cost of just one from this tailor of yours, Paganini asks.

The whole stack, I suppose, the Shopkeeper says.

Then please do not speak to me anymore of tailors, Paganini says.

The local Concert Promoter ducks his head into the shop and is thrilled to find Paganini. What a pleasure. I am surprised to find you here.

Me too, Paganini says.

I am pleased to say the theater sold out immediately, the Concert Promoter says. A packed house!

Immediately, Paganini asks, peering out the shop windows. How immediately? This is a nice town. You made a mistake. They can pay more.

The Concert Promoter clearly doesn't follow what Paganini's saying.

They can pay more at the door, Paganini says. Must I tell you your business? See to that. Otherwise, you may find me at whatever sort of hotel you have here. I am not feeling well today, which also puts this performance at a premium.

Paganini finds a cheap suit coat he likes, holding it out like a dead fish.

I'll take this one, he says. Should I ever play again, it will do fine. Do you have any very black ink?

I'm certain we do, the Shopkeeper says. I'll look in the

back.

Folks won't like this, the Concert Promoter says.

In his little room at a small nearby hotel, Paganini lays prone and in agony as Achille reads from his Bible. Paganini's huge Carriage Driver sits in one corner. The new jacket drips ink, hanging in the other corner.

Take the boy and get him a meal, Paganini says. I am not going anywhere. Thank you.

As the oversized Carriage Driver and Achille leave a nearby café, they find the street filled with a groaning and angry mob chanting Paganini's name and pounding on the hotel walls.

Wait here, the Carriage Driver says, darting into the crowd. Don't move. Wait here.

Achille, always a good boy, waits. The crowd grows in size and fury, focused on the building. All, except one small face, which is turned to study Achille.

Hello Achille, says Orfeo, a far smaller facsimile of Paganini. Orfeo grins at him through horrid teeth.

You know my name, Achille says.

Yet you do not know mine, Orfeo says.

I don't understand, Achille says.

When misplaced brothers meet for the first time, all is forgiven, Orfeo says, throwing out his arms with sinister welcome.

Achille backs away.

Leave me alone, he says.

I intend to, Orfeo says. But I was told it is important that we meet in person. I see why now. To put a face on all that is cheated from me. And though, for now, it is again goodbye, I do pray we see one another again soon, Achille.

Nearby, Royer enjoys watching this moment unfold.

Fists pound the door of the hotel until violin music explodes from the windows. Silence.

Paganini bursts from the doors, perched on his Carriage Driver's shoulder, playing his heart out.

The crowd parts triumphantly as they head for the theater. The Carriage Driver scoops Achille up under his other arm.

They set the place on fire, my boy, Paganini grins. No sense to argue with that! The proletariat has spoken! What a review!

Thrilled by the whole spectacle, Paganini plays on.

Joy becomes panic below another hotel window a few years later, as a flood of terrified citizens fill the streets of Paris. A rapidly aging Paganini is distracted by his own troubles. Rossini, a fellow musician, hurries to his door.

My friend, why did I agree to travel so alone, so far from home for so long, Paganini says. Never again. Every one of these journeys feels like a hundred years without my Achille.

You'll be home soon enough, Rossini says. It is time to abandon Paris, my friend. Cholera is spreading. Gather your things.

Paganini considers this.

No, you go, Paganini says, realizing the trouble surrounding him. I'll be fine for now. Go. It's alright.

Stepping into the street, Paganini moves upstream, against the current of people, until he finds himself at an overflowing hospital.

There he finds the sick and dying covering every inch of floor, writhing in a way he is very familiar with.

The room falls still as Paganini melts into his violin.

Not long after, Paganini coughs desperately into a hallway mirror, fighting just to breathe.

That the best you've got, he grumbles at his sickness.

His drawing room door flies open. Paganini bursts into the room with a big smile and bottle of wine, as if nothing were wrong at all.

Here you are, he says. Found what I was looking for. This one will certainly be worth the wait.

PAGANINI

A Business Speculator smiles back at him from across many empty bottles. Papers and contracts spread out before them on the table. Paganini opens the wine and pours.

The brilliance, sir, is you need never set foot in the place, the Speculator says. Except, of course, that you'll want to. It will become a cultural home for all of France, and indeed the world. Music, literature, art. Poetry. Dancing. Every manner of relaxation and enjoyment. All right there along the Seine.

And all you need to borrow the capital is my name, Paganini says.

Correct, the Business Speculator says, pouring more wine. In exchange for this enormous consideration. And do not forget our ship leaves for America the moment you desire. Certainly, we would encourage you to conquer other continents as well. They will love you there.

Indeed, Paganini says. There is much I can do with this money. I'll buy presses in Genoa. I will battle back all these horrible things they print about me. Teach the world my technique. Which will change music forever. And I will make a fortune.

Another fortune, the Business Speculator says.

One can never have too many, Paganini says.

To the Casino Paganini, says the Business Speculator, as they raise their glasses.

Better yet, Paganini says. To freedom.

Locked tight in their coach on another tour, Paganini and Achille bounce along, weary. Rain pounds the roof. Paganini is sickly, showing his age more than ever. Achille, in his late teens, reads from his Bible.

Won't be long now, Father, Achille says. We are nearly there.

Always nearly, Paganini says. Nearly, nearly, nearly. Without you, I couldn't even try.

Rest, Father, Achille says.

That night in his dressing room, Paganini sits, exhausted,

absently rubbing at his throat. Achille helps his Father to his feet.

They stand in the wings, Paganini crumpled and weak, Achille holding him up. As the curtain rises, Paganini creeps slowly onto the stage. A roar of applause. He straightens, full of life, and plays with his usual fire.

Afterwards, he limps back into the dressing room with the help of stage hands and finds Achille holding a letter, tears rolling down his cheeks.

The first shovel of dirt is thrown on Teresa's grave. Nearby, Paganini is a swaying tower of grief. Rain pours down.

His Brothers and Sisters turn to walk away, leaving Paganini and his Father on either side of the grave, staring bitterly at each other.

One morning in his study Paganini sits with a window open, mournfully playing for a collection of birds gathered outside.

The door opens, changing the light in the room. There stands Achille with his beautiful new fiancée.

Father, this is Penelope, Achille says. We are to be married.

The pretty girl in the sunlight draws Paganini from his funk.

My dear, he has told me so much, I feel I already know you, Paganini says.

He kisses her hand.

Soon Paganini, Penelope and Achille sit laughing together in the garden.

Paganini's Housekeeper leads Germi to the gate.

Delightful, Paganini yells. My friend, why did you not tell me you are traveling this way?

Penelope smiles. Paganini is enchanted. The look in Paganini's eye, studying the girl, stops Germi cold. He looks to Achille, who is oblivious to this connection. Germi continues his urgent mission.

Join us, Paganini says. We were discussing our upcoming trip to the Americas. Imagine that! Oh, for once, my friend, I am calm and ready to enjoy every little thing.

Germi throws a newspaper down on the table between them. Penelope picks it up.

Paganini dead, she reads. Violin sold at auction? That is not very funny at all.

In his drawing room, Paganini is distraught.

It appears rumor is fit enough to print these days, he says. Madness. How many piles of paper does this scheme sell? Who will their advertisers kill next? Do they not understand what damage this could do?

Germi holds a letter out to Paganini.

Your investors insist you appear three times a day and perform, Germi says. To prove to their backers that the Casino Paganini is properly named for a living legend.

That was not our arrangement, Paganini says. Tell them I refuse. I have retired.

I would, Germi says. But they are nearly bankrupt themselves. Workers unpaid. Materials stolen.

So, what do I care about their losses, Paganini asks.

When their pockets turn up empty, your own debts will grow like mushrooms, Germi says. And when these new, great friends disappear into the night, their debts will become yours.

Paganini straightens his coat. He is not well, but it is time to go back to work. He takes a rough, deep breath.

Please inform the children, Paganini says. America is postponed. For now.

Yes, Germi says. Of course.

Another audience, though captivated as he plays, can see that Paganini is worn thin, his time growing short. The mechanism performing perfectly, the parts swiftly breaking down.

Then his eyes open to find this was a dream and Penelope leans over him, wiping his brow. She smiles.

Good morning, he says.

Afternoon, she says. I am so happy you are awake. Achille just left for the theater to discuss last night's receipts. I'll fetch him back.

No, no need, Paganini says.

His voice strained, Paganini watches as she fills a glass from the water pitcher. He looks to her, then his violin. Shame crosses Paganini's eyes. The battle is lost.

My dear, it hurts to speak, he says. Please hand me my violin. Would you like me to play for you?

In the carriage on their way to the theater that night, Achille reads aloud from his Bible. Penelope and Paganini's eyes are drawn like magnets. They struggle not to let their connection show.

Finally too sick to travel, Paganini rests in a dark bedroom, alone.

Outside, Paganini's Housekeeper beats rugs in the garden. A Local Priest beckons her from the bushes.

As I've said, I don't understand how I can help you, she says.

We must shatter the Paganini myth, he says. He must repent, to me, today, so that the world may witness no profit from this brand of evil.

I see no evil in this house, she says.

Of course not, my dear, he says. And how could you? It is part of the very air you breathe. From where I stand, I see it all around you.

This puts her in a panic.

What do I do, she asks.

Only what is right, he says. For both his soul and yours.

The Priest slips out of Paganini's garden into an alley. Royer is waiting for him. They stride off confidently

266

together.

And now, the opening scene. Paganini's final
performance. Packed house. Mouths open, eyes wide. A few
notes from completing a feverous concert, he stops on a
pinhead. The audience hovers midair. He stares back at
them. His deep-pool eyes are weary. Strained. He blinks
softly. Mind drifting through a moment that isn't this one.
Paganini plays a line. Tears away a string. Plays a line. Rips a
string. Then again. Down to the final one. The final note.

The theater erupts. He steps to mid-stage and calmly
bows. The audience sweeps down the aisles. Paganini strides
confidently into the wings. As he passes from the stage
lights, he crumples to the ground. Achille scoops his Father
into his arms and rushes for the exit.

The black carriage hurries to a stop behind Paganini's
house. Achille lays his Father on his bed. Paganini is in
agony, guts twisted, fighting to breathe.

Rest now, Achille says.

Paganini reaches for water. He cannot speak. The pitcher
is empty. Achille grabs it and rushes from the room.

Paganini's Housekeeper appears at the door, her Priest in
tow. They slide quietly into the room. Paganini opens his
eyes to find them praying over him.

Confess now, Paganini, the Priest shouts. Declare your
league with evil. Much is at stake! No time to be fiddling!

Eyes bulging, Paganini does everything to scream, except
actually make a sound. He struggles to his feet on pure
adrenaline, shoving the elderly Priest from the room, hurling
any object in reach after him down the hall.

Achille and Penelope come running. They wrestle
Paganini into his bed. The Housekeeper hides in the corner,
then slips out the door.

Father, please, Achille says.

Paganini looks into Penelope's eyes. She is truly frantic
that he is dying. Achille's fiancée is more in love with his

Father than anyone she's ever known.

Paganini's Housekeeper appears at the door with a slate and chalk in her hands. She inches toward them.

Please, she says to Achille. For us all. He must repent. His soul is at stake. All of our souls. Please.

Paganini holds out his hands. She gives him the slate. He smashes it against the wall. The Housekeeper runs, screaming.

What could you possibly confess, Achille laughs.

Penelope and Paganini's faces now show the affair Achille has been missing. Achille looks from one to the other as the fact soaks in.

Unable to speak, this fatal regret stands out in Paganini's eyes. He reaches out. Achille recoils.

Samael appears between them, Penelope and Achille frozen at the sudden sight of him.

Good night, Paganini, Samael says. You stubborn, brilliant fool.

Paganini breathes his last. Samael closes Paganini's eyes, nods to Achille solemnly, and disappears. Penelope collapses. Achille backs from the room.

Deep in the Italian countryside, Achille and Orfeo face each other down in the moonlight. Achille's sword is heavy. He bleeds from his side. Orfeo is unhurt but outsized with his dagger.

So then, Orfeo says. What will it be then? Brother.

Achille droops.

Only what is right, he says. Brother.

Orfeo softens. Acceptance is more seductive than revenge.

Tell me what you mean, Orfeo says, warily.

I can see it all so clearly, Achille says, throwing down his sword.

He opens his arms. Tears fill Orfeo's eyes and he drops his knife. They embrace.

Orfeo sobs while Achille reaches beneath his own coat and finds his own dagger. He presses it to Orfeo's neck, holding the much smaller man tight. A trickle of blood.

You do bleed like a Paganini, Achille says, slapping Orfeo to the ground. Achille takes the bundle of letters and a match from Orfeo's pocket.

You read these, Achille asks.

Yes, Orfeo says.

All true I'm sure, Achille says, lighting the pages and walking away.

Wait, Orfeo says. Please. Help me know him. It's only right. You have to.

I imagine your precious letters told it all, Achille says.

Not nearly, Orfeo says. Not nearly.

The fire burns bright as Achille climbs painfully onto the horse.

Then your opportunity is gone, Achille says, and rides for Genoa.

Many years later. In a cold bath at an expensive bordello, hands clutching his chest, Royer is dead. Footsteps. A woman screams.

Now older than his Father was when he died, Achille patiently hurries through the streets of Genoa in the rain.

Germi is on his own deathbed, still with a gleam in his eye. Achille sits beside him.

I did so look forward to this annual trip of ours, to the proverbial gates, to stand up for your Father, Germi says.

The door remains open, Achille says. You fought bravely for him all these years. I've never fully thanked you.

My pleasure, young man, Germi says.

Neither is a young man anymore.

At the office of the Archbishop, Achille enters and stiffly bows. He looks around, confused and concerned. A Baby-Faced Priest sits behind a huge, ornate desk, as if a child broke in and put on robes.

It stopped raining, the young Priest says. What's the matter?

My appointment is with the Archbishop, Achille says.

He is very busy, the young Priest says, friendly but disinterested. I assure you, I am qualified to meet with you.

He glances though a stack of paper before him.

Alright, Achille says. And Father Royer . . .

Father Royer is dead, the young Priest says. Two nights ago. In some bordello, they say. What theater is that! Ha!

Very well, Achille says. I am here to speak with you about my Father.

The young Priest drops a heavy stamp onto the paper.

The wondrous Paganini, yes, he says. I've heard of him. Not very musical myself. Here you are.

The young Priest holds out the stamped paper.

I don't understand, Achille says.

The young Priest shuffles again through the pages.

Look at this, he says. So much time has passed, the ink has faded. I, for one, see no reason to spend any more. This is a new age, Signor. Best to be done with old business. Yes? Consider the matter closed.

Yes, Achille says. I agree. Yes. Thank you.

He gratefully hurries from the room.

At Ile St. Honorat, the jagged, red outcrop of rocks on the open Mediterranean. Thick, beautiful flowers stand out among the stone outcrops.

Achille supervises as his Father's coffin is lifted from the ground.

The sun is shining in Genoa as Achille leads a cart carrying the coffin, finally, through the cemetery gates.

The monument reads: *Niccolò Paganini, who drew from the violin divine music.*

Achille Paganini sits at his Father's side, raises his own violin, and plays.

YARDLEY COUNTY

A dead convict goes home on the day his criminal career began

Across a sun-cooked prison yard, broad shoulders part crowds of cons at recess. A head taller and a scrap-iron pile of muscle, this is Lenny. Lenny gets a wide berth.

Somewhere in his past, Four-year-old Lenny smiles, drenched in sunshine. Wrinkled hands reach out. Lenny giggles as they lift him. His Grandma Edna swings him through the air.

His Mother's voice echoes back across the years.

Always such a happy baby, Lucinda says. Hard to remember that sometimes. That little boy would just shine. So bright. Like looking at the sun.

Edna sings, Moses, Moses on the mountain, Moses on the mountain at the back door again.

The front door of their small house slams.

I did my best, Lucinda continues. Lord knows.

A young, pretty, and overly manicured Lucinda darts from the house. She's dressed for a party.

I told you this morning I was thinking about going to town, she shouts. And none of your pouting when I get back.

Wendell, skinny and bespectacled, mopes onto the front porch.

But, Lucinda, Wendell sputters and blinks. Sincerely. Please. Wait.

Little Lenny smiles and squirms, reaching out for his Father.

Lucinda's floating words grows bitter.

His Father, she says. Wendell. No good at all. He run off when Lenny wasn't five, even. Just gone. After that, well, no room to help that boy. None. All-consumed. Like a stone. That's my Lenny.

Wendell grins as he lifts Lenny into his arms.

Approaching a sliver of shade thrown from a high prison wall, Lenny's shoulders drop. He finds a Huge Inmate kicking a much Smaller Inmate, huddled, bleeding before him.

Please, the man on the ground begs. No more.

The stomping continues. Other Cons mill around, tossing a basketball, laughing and joking, concealing the brutal beating from the guards.

Lenny reaches down and drags the bleeding man to his feet. Everything stops. The beaten prisoner flees into the crowd. Lenny nods. The Huge Inmate nods.

I had him too young, a now much older but still heavily painted Lucinda continues into a scratchy prison microphone, adding an extra hitch to her voice. I know that.

A larger, staged commotion explodes across the prison yard. A shoving, shouting diversion. The Huge Inmate and Lenny grapple.

Guards squint from their towers. Machine-gun bolts snap.

The Huge Inmate pulls a sharpened screwdriver from his sock. Lenny buries it into his gut, breaking the man's hand in the process. Pain and confusion cross the Huge Inmate's eyes as he crumples.

But we gave him a loving home, Lucinda confidently lies to the impatient Parole Board. Lenny's Stepfather and me. Roy. Bless that strong man. Anybody could see we tried. Made no difference. One look at little Lenny and you just knew. This little boy's a hundred years old.

Prison sirens blare as the bloody weapon drops among shuffling feet. The broad shoulders turn. Lenny's face is a standing stone of detached anger. His eyes far away. His mind searching for answers without a clear question, desperate to silence a clanging drumbeat somewhere in the distance.

As always in his world, Lenny simply walks away, chaos erupting behind him.

In the humid and dusty meeting room at the far end of the prison, Lucinda clutches a handkerchief and sobs.

Across a long folding table, a prim Parole Board Chairman leans into his microphone, unimpressed. Ancient speakers scream with feedback. He shoves thick glasses into place.

Ma'am, please answer the question.

Lucinda's sharp eyebrows do not like his tone.

Excuse me, she snorts.

The question, he says. The exact same question directed to you every time we meet. Please.

I am, she says, tartly. I'm answering.

Good, he says. In that case, then let me just urge you to be as brief as possible.

Alright, she begins slowly, only getting an audience like this every couple years. Do I think . . . That my . . . Poor, poor little Lenny . . .

Correct, he cuts her off, squinting into a file folder before him. Can you sit there and look me in the eye, look any of us in the eye, and honestly say that your . . . Leonard Jacob Smith, convicted arsonist, thief and all around violent criminal . . . Is or ever can be rehabilitated?

Lenny's Mother blows her nose and folds her handkerchief.

No, she says.

Well, that's lunch everybody, the Chairman chimes.

Inside a lonely hamburger stand located on a quiet road somewhere in the 1970s, Sixteen-year-old Lenny holds a huge revolver on an overweight Manager. The gun barrel droops with uncertainty. Lenny's face is bruised and cut from fighting. The Manager is smiling at Lenny, moving behind the counter, reaching for something. Lenny shouts too late.

Gunshot. Then a flash bulb pops.

A number bar hangs across Lenny's chest. A Local Cop chews gum and winds a well-scuffed camera.

Name, he says. Date of birth.

Nearby, a Secretary taps at a typewriter. She's not that much older than Lenny.

Leonard Smith, Lenny says. And today . . . I'm sixteen today.

The Cop grabs him by the neck.

Happy birthday, she smiles as the heavy door slams hard behind them.

Out of thick darkness, a peephole snaps open. A bar of light crosses Lenny's eyes, glaring calmly back. The hole snaps shut.

Locks turn and clank. The door swings open. Prison Guards in tactical gear stand warily, batons in hand, as if preparing for a riot.

One brave Guard steps forward.

Alright, big fella, he says. Let's move it. Nice and easy.

Lenny is soon shackled to Lucinda's chair. The Parole Board sneers at him. This time, a handful of Reporters are there with cameras and notepads.

Lenny, my release to the media covers many of the particulars of your, aw, let's call it a career, says the Parole Board Chairman in full-theatrical mode.

A sneering snicker passes down the Parole Board table.

And ladies and gentlemen, please allow me to point out for the record that the majority of the following events occurred during the mere twenty-six-or-so months of freedom Mister Smith has enjoyed, via several violent escapes, over the course of more than four decades of

274

incarceration, he says. Turn him, boys.

Guards grab and turn Lenny's chair. A side gallery of angry faces stare back at him.

Alright, let's start small, the Chairman says. Smash and grabs. How many? Who knows? Here's one. Arson. Clerk in Alabama asleep in back of his store? You came in the front. Remember him, Lenny?

A woman in the second row breaks down in sobs. A disfigured man sits mute in a wheelchair beside her.

Well, here he is, the Chairman says. This is his Wife, Lenny.

Arms move to comfort the woman. Lenny doesn't flinch.

In fact, we've invited a few of the families you've shattered to be with us here today, the Chairman says. We thank you, folks, especially as many of you traveled some distance to be here. Baltimore, Seattle, Austin . . .

Angry, accusing, pained expressions cross the room.

The Chairman draws out the moment for effect, then continues to knowingly read from a file in front of him.

Countless assaults, he says. Armed robbery. Auto theft. Destruction of property again and again. Twenty-two guards hospitalized. As for fellow inmates, we've about lost count, haven't we? But another one this morning just for good measure, right, Leonard? Maybe we'll get lucky and he won't pull through. Anyway, countless warrants. Trials. Prisons, jails, work camps. Escapes. Manhunts . . . Arson. Arson. Arson . . . Arson. What is it with you and fire?

I'm doing my time, Lenny says.

The Chairman makes sure to capitalize on this with a flair of outrage.

Your time, he says blithely. His time, ladies and gentlemen. Lenny, let me ask a question. On behalf of the good people of this state, whom I pledge will soon not need to fear scum like you should they choose to make me their Lieutenant Governor this fall!

The Chairman points and squints dramatically. A camera

clicks, missing his cue by an awkward moment or so.

Son, he says, chewing each word roundly. I need to ask. Are you even a little bit sorry?

Lenny thinks this over.

You ask me, sorry never does a whole lot for anybody, he says.

A condescending grumble rolls through the room. The Chairman throws Lenny's file at him, papers fluttering onto the smudged tiles between them. The camera clicks again, again a twitch late.

Alright, the Chairman says. Parole denied. Big surprise there. No, the real news of the day is a sight better than that. You're taking a ride, Lenny. Got you a bed in that brand-new, maximum-security facility upstate. Designed specifically to break irredeemable losers like yourself. Break them into little, itty-bitty, tiny, tiny pieces. So that a rightfully disgusted public can sweep you away and never need be bothered with your poison ever again. I look forward to stopping by soon to watch the process.

The parole room rattles with applause.

Lenny gives them nothing.

A cool and pleasant day. Children laughing.

A new town water tower throws a long shadow across an overgrown field. Treetops along the edges sway.

Four-year-old Lenny runs, all smiles.

Don't you peek, Annagrace, he yells. Run, Dub. Run!

Lenny's best friend, about a week younger, whom folks call Dub, isn't the quickest on his feet or in any other category.

Five-year-old, pigtailed Annagrace covers her eyes, spinning.

. . . ninety-nine, she yells. A hundred!

Lenny and Dub hit the ground, faces in the weeds, giggling.

Dizzy, Annagrace drops her hands and looks around. I'm

going to get you boys!

Annagrace listens carefully, smiles and starts to run.

Lenny's laughter is giving him away.

At one end of a muddy parade ground, revelry explodes from a huge speaker on the mess hall roof.

Sixteen-year-old Lenny sits bolt upright in the juvenile work camp bunkhouse. Bug-eyed, he drips sweat and can't catch his breath as a passing Bunkhouse Guard cracks a broom handle across his feet.

Boys burst from the door. Bleary, Lenny is the last one out.

A uniformed Work Camp Sergeant in dark glasses takes note.

In long lines, the delinquents drag telephone poles from a truck bed alongside a remote country road. All at once, Lenny and two dozen others hoist pole to their shoulders.

The sun heats them to the metal in their belt buckles. Armed Guards drip sweat and daydream. A Thug behind Lenny kicks at his heels.

Whoops, the Thug says.

These poles don't move themselves, young turds, a Road Guard shouts. Tighten it up.

Another kick at Lenny's heels sends him stumbling. The line lurches forward. The pole tumbles to the ground. Lenny shoves the Thug. The Thug shoves back. They are too tired to even wrestle.

A shell snaps into a shotgun chamber. All freeze. The Sergeant's face grows sharp beneath his glasses.

Now, you both are new, he says. So, I imagine you ladies probably think I'm about to lose my temper. Shout and curse. Give you extra time out here under this sun. Call you ugly names. Hurt your little feelings.

No one makes eye contact with the Sergeant, except Lenny.

But on my line, you start something, you finish it, the

Sergeant says. Let's go.

The other boys circle up. Lenny and the teenage Thug look to each other with a shared flash of worry. The sweating Road Guards share amused looks and wager in a low grumble.

I said get to it, the Sergeant says. Lenny and the Thug square off. Lenny walks into a straight right. Then a left. He hits the ground.

The Sergeant grabs Lenny by the back of his shirt, lifting him. They are nose to nose.

What kind of sadness is that, he says. I heard you killed somebody. Doesn't show.

The Sergeant shoves Lenny back into the ring. They square off again. Lenny catches a hard cross and lands in the arms of the cheering Road Guards.

There's a whisper in his ear.

Got five dollars on you, one Road Guard says. Lose and I cut your nose off while you sleep.

Lenny finds his footing and decks the Road Guard hard, sending him to the gravel. Silence. Flat on his back, the Guard looks to the Sergeant, ready to tear Lenny apart. The Sergeant's eyes say stand down.

Well, well, seems we've got a contest, the Sergeant smiles.

Lenny steps forward. He lands a shot to the Thug's nose, then another. The crowd is with him. The Thug wobbles, swinging blind. Lenny sidesteps, landing his fists in a series. Each throw draws blood with a sickening thud. After a while, faces can't help but turn from fright. Soon, the Thug is a lump at Lenny's feet, blood pooling beneath him in the dirt.

Nobody moves. Lenny stumbles over to the pole, reaching down and struggling to lift it. It doesn't budge. In silent awe, a handful of boys hustle over to help him. They shove to stand beside him.

Halt, the Sergeant says.

They do, the pole painfully frozen on their shoulders.

Sure showed him, he says. Didn't you, boy?

All eyes move to the ground, except Lenny's.

Take his shoes, the Sergeant says.

Guards leave Lenny barefoot on the jagged gravel.

Alrighty, young hero, the Sergeant grins. Now, move it.

Lenny nods. Together, the boys march. Lenny doesn't flinch.

Remember, young turds, I got you either way, the Sergeant says, a touch of worry behind his mirrored glasses. Stronger you get, more fun I get breaking you.

The prison peephole snaps open, waking Lenny, stretched out across the concrete floor. The hole shuts. Locks grind and the heavy door opens slowly. The Prison Guards twitch, batons in hand. Again, the brave Guard steps forward.

Morning, sunshine, he says.

Down a dim prison hallway, Lenny limps along at his own pace, shackled hand and foot, a small formation of Guards behind him. They near the visiting room door. Lenny stops.

This isn't the way to the yard, Lenny says.

There's a single table at the center of the stark visiting room. Sitting alone is Annagrace Adell, grown but not as worn as Lenny. She frets and fumbles with a circle of metal in her hand, wearing her Sunday best. The clock ticks. Her folding chair squeaks.

The door opens. Lenny sees her and turns to leave. A muscled and intimidating Visiting Room Guard shoves him inside and stands close by.

Hello, Lenny, she says.

Lenny's tongue stumbles as his feet turn to lead.

Sit down, the big Visiting Room Guard barks. Behave yourself.

Lenny stares him down as he sits. Annagrace is pale, shaken by the grim tension all around her.

Hello Annagrace, Lenny says.

You never came back for this, she says. Thought I'd bring it to you.

She sets a plain gold ring between them on the table. Lenny reaches for it with manacled hands. The Guard steps forward and pockets the ring.

I'll hold onto this for him, ma'am, he says. Don't worry.

Annagrace nods, wiping at her nose with a handkerchief.

I know you told them you don't like visitors, she says. So it took me a long time to work out a way to see you, Lenny. Long time. Years. Letters and phone calls. Wardens. Parole boards . . .

Lenny searches for words.

I don't know, he says. I guess, you could say that somewhere along the way . . .

Went to the capitol a couple times, she says. Met the Governor, even. Finally, I just told them . . .

. . . I lost the privilege, he says.

. . . I'm dying, Lenny, she says.

This thuds onto the table between them.

I keep, uhm, I keep newspaper clippings, Annagrace says. You're sure famous.

In a big crochet bag beside her chair, she finds a thick, dogeared book stuffed with yellowing newsprint.

I guess that's part of it, Lenny says.

She turns the pages.

The person you became, she says. The person you are. You've done a lot of awful things, Lenny.

Each headline and photo shouts another offense.

I know, Lenny says.

And people ask me, Annagrace says. All the time. My kids. My husband. They say, why're you always saving those stories? All the terrible stories.

Then, Lenny says. Why do you?

Because, she says. Because the person you became isn't the person I know. The person you are. This isn't you. Did

280

you ever find him, Lenny?

Who, he asks.

Your Father, she says. Wendell.

No, Lenny says.

Annagrace can't accept this.

Didn't you look, she asks. Don't you care?

No, he says. That was a long time ago.

Mister Jenkins, she says. Remember him? The janitor at the high school?

I guess, Lenny says.

Passed on last year, she says. I volunteer at the hospital sometimes. I was there his last couple days. My Dad. Your Dad. Mister Jenkins. They all grew up together. So I asked him. I asked him, who would know where your Daddy went. Who could find him?

What'd he say, Lenny asks.

He said that, besides your Mother, the only person left that knows is you, Lenny, she says.

Me, he says. Me?

What does he mean, Lenny, she asks.

Lenny doesn't know. Annagrace closes her book and stands.

Well, I suppose you better figure it out, she says. There's something you lost somewhere, Leonard Smith. Something I don't know how to get back for you. But I do know where you start. Find your Father, Lenny. Find yourself. Find my Lenny. Please.

She stands. The visiting room door swings open from the outside. Annagrace leaves Lenny shackled alone with the Guard, staring down at the scrapbook.

Across a barbed-wire parking lot, Lenny and five other shackled prisoners march together. Guards point the line toward a heavily armored van.

Conner, a scraggly con behind Lenny, leans forward.

My Brother damn near bled to death, Conner says.

Thanks to you. I knew he'd make it. He's always been the tough one in the family. Of course, I'm the mean one.

One by one, the cons are locked to their seats. He and Lenny are the last two in, closest to the door as it slams shut.

The oversized van roars down a wet, rural highway beneath a clearing sky.

Between the Cons and two Guards in the front seats is a web of steel grating. A small door connects the two compartments.

An hour and not a word out of you, Conner says. Something on your sweet, little mind?

Lenny watches the world slide by as much as he can through the van's barred windows.

Enough, Conner, says the Guard in the passenger seat. Enough.

Moses, Lenny sings low, eying Conner. Moses on the mountain. Moses on the mountain at the back door again.

Conner grins.

Singing me a song, precious, he grins.

Very slowly, Lenny is overtaken by a violent coughing fit. The Passenger Guard glances back with only vague concern.

Jesus Christ, Conner says. Don't die before I get my hands on you.

Lenny wipes spit off his mouth with shackled hands and fidgets at his wrists. He smiles for once.

This shakes Conner's confidence.

What're you so damn happy about, he asks.

Lenny's hands are free. He leans over and grabs the shackles at his feet. All too quick for anyone to react, he stands, flicking the bent piece of metal he coughed up and used as a key. It bounces off Conner's forehead.

Hey, Conner yells. Guard!

The Guards don't bother to look back.

Quiet, the Driving Guard says.

Lenny rears back, smashing Conner in the jaw.

Help me, you assholes, Conner groans, teeth, blood and

spit pouring from his mouth.

The Passenger Guard glances back, then turns in horror to see Lenny on his feet.

Holy shit, he says. Call it in.

The Driving Guard fumbles for the radio. The Passenger Guard grabs for a taser on his belt as he opens the cage door. Lenny grabs him by the throat and yanks him through the door. He slaps away the taser and they struggle over the Guard's revolver. The Cons scream and pull at their chains. The gun fires once, burying a round into the Driving Guard's collarbone. Everything inside the van slows, trapped in that moment, eyes locked wide as he slumps over the wheel.

Slowly crossing the center line, the prison van enters a heavy, wobbling skid. Rolls. Flips end over end. And comes to rest upside down in the road. Then, nothing. Not a soul for miles. Except Lenny.

Through a jagged, open door, Lenny crawls from the wreck. Free of the metal and glass, he looks back and stops.

He sees his own dead face staring back at him from among the tangled bodies. Though the van burns with thick chemical smoke, he can't smell it. Can't feel the flames against his skin. The sky is cold, dim. The air silent.

Hoofs scratch at the dirt behind him. A tall horse with no saddle blinks at him and waits. He climbs on, light as a feather. They trot away as the van explodes.

Decades before, Four-year-old Lenny watches his Father paint Yardley across the town water tower, rope around his waist, precariously clutching the metal tank with one hand, brush in the other, dripping can swinging from his belt.

Wendell's Son sees a superhero.

Now the sun sets on Lenny staring up at the fading tower, letters disintegrating. The horse carries him slowly past.

Main Street is empty, dusty and tired. Single-story

storefronts along cracked, scarred, ancient sidewalks are locked tight and forgotten until tomorrow.

A pickup rumbles through, ignoring the only stoplight. An open sign blinks on and off. Above it, dim bulbs twitch: *Roy's Bar & Grill.*

Lenny climbs off the horse outside a thrift store, bloody prison clothes reflecting in the front window. He turns down the alley. The horse wanders away.

Glass shatters in the distance. The front door swings open. Lenny emerges wearing street clothes and crosses the street in front of Roy's Bar. Unsure, he steps inside.

Empty stools. Empty tables scattered nearby.

A dingy light covers local high school sports memorabilia. Photographs, trophies, ball gloves and more, all nailed in a scatter-shot pattern along the walls. A rabbit-eared television delivers a snowy baseball game.

A thick-necked man behind the bar curses under his breath. The bar light gleams off his thinning flattop.

This is Curtis Mahoney, a high school athlete gone to fat. The door slams as Lenny enters.

Well, hey there, friend, Curtis grins. Pull up a stool. Yes, sir. Have a seat. Whataya drink?

Lenny is startled to see him.

Rye, he says.

Haven't touched that shit since high school, Curtis chuckles. Whataya say we make it two? Yes, sir.

He sets up two glasses and digs through the bottles behind the bar. He finds the one he wants and pours.

I tell you what, Curtis says. This damn game's going to be the death of me. Another five bucks gone over slow feet and foul balls. Know the feeling?

Lenny doesn't have an answer. Curtis drains his glass.

Not much of a talker, Curtis says. I know how that is. Let's start a tab. Whataya say? Yeah.

Curtis pours again. Lenny looks across the town photos lined up over the bar. Holiday parades. A couple epic floods.

Grainy faces long gone. One is Lenny as a kid, standing with Lucinda in the street out in front of the bar, shielding their eyes on a bright day.

Lenny downs his drink.

Where's Roy, he asks.

Couple years late for that, Curtis laughs. Caught a grabber right where I'm standing. Widow sold to me and moved out of the state. Sweet deal, really. I never bothered to change the sign. Know how much new neon costs these days? Damn crime. What do you want with him?

The television picture changes. A News Anchor extends a serious look from behind a lime-green desk. Behind him floats a picture of the smoldering prison van, surrounded by flashing lights.

Good evening, the Anchor says. Tonight, police report no survivors in a single vehicle crash involving a prisoner transport vehicle headed to the newly opened prison facility outside the town of Yardley earlier today. Meanwhile, good news on the high school sports front. And Bippy, our shelter puppy of the week, has a new home! We have all the details and adorable footage. So, stay tuned for this, wacky weather . . .

A clown dances across a cloud-covered map, honking a horn.

. . . and more, he says. See you back here at eleven!

The game returns to the screen. Curtis pours another round.

Je-zia-us Christ, Curtis says. That damn prison. It's shameful those government jerks could even think about shutting down a perfectly good Army base. Way the world is today. Irresponsible. And the last thing anybody around here wants is a bunch of trash like that a couple miles away, eating three hot meals and playing ping pong on our dime. Ought to line them all up and get it over with. Both the politicians and the criminals. Here's to fire and twisted metal in the meantime.

He holds out his glass to toast. Lenny doesn't budge.

Come on now, Curtis says, truly a little hurt.

They down their drinks. In the mirror behind the bar, Lenny's eyes focus on the sports gear and memorabilia. Curtis takes a long drag on an always-burning cigarette.

I see you recognize real history when you see it, Curtis says. That wall there's all mine. Ladies and gentlemen, your very own hometown hero . . .

Curtis starts to drink.

Mahoney, Lenny says. Curtis Mahoney. I'd completely forgotten your name until right this second. Funny how the mind works.

Curtis chokes on his drink.

Oh, well, do I know you, he asks. We go to school together? Come on now. Give me a name at least.

How about Dwayne Rhodes, Lenny says. Most people called him Dub. Remember that name?

Curtis recognizes Lenny and doesn't like where this is going. He sets his feet.

Lenny's mind travels to find Sixteen-year-old Dub's body splayed across a bank of rocks below the town railroad bridge on a cold afternoon. Blood fills trickling water. Eighteen-year-old Curtis, complete in a varsity jacket and a healthier version of that same buzzcut, seethes with anger as his loyal gaggle of Jocks drag him away.

Curtis seems so much smaller to Lenny now. Without a breath, he has Curtis by the neck, bouncing his skull off the bar.

The street is empty. Lenny drags Curtis out the front door.

Instinctively, Curtis tries to bolt. Lenny kicks hard at the back of his knee and sends him flailing to the ground. He struggles to stand.

Son of a bitch, Curtis says, squaring off. You can't just

come around here and . . .

Lenny catches Curtis with an uppercut that puts him flat on his back. Curtis coughs, adding to the spray of blood across his shirt. The wind picks up. Lenny takes a long breath. Curtis finds his way back to his feet.

Hey, Curtis splutters. Wait. Look. Lenny, right? Yeah. I . . . Your friend . . . Fuck it.

Curtis takes a swing as he rushes Lenny. Lenny steps sideways as Curtis catches the bar door face first. Lenny pounds him again to the ground. Curtis covers and sobs with real fear.

Wait, wait, wait, Curtis says. I'm . . . I'm sorry.

Lenny stares down at Curtis for a long moment, turns, walks into the bar and returns with a bottle of liquor. He takes a deep swig and dumps it all over Curtis.

Good for you, Lenny says.

Lenny has Curtis' lighter already lit. He drops it and walks away.

Curtis moans as he burns. Lightning in the distance. Thunder.

Lenny takes a right at the corner and stumbles down a tight row of small, weathered, sleeping homes. Chimneys lean. Grass grows high with weeds and wildflowers around junked cars. Stray dogs sleep in the dirt. Dim streetlights along a scattered line of crooked poles seem lost in the night air.

Lenny stops. A dilapidated house stares back at him. This one is long abandoned. He steps into the yard.

Four-year-old Lenny stands in that same spot, the sun high in the sky. He smiles up at Wendell beside him, holding his hand. Edna grins from a rocking chair on the porch. Lucinda is at the front door, glaring at Wendell.

A distant rumble. A grimy, rattling, old truck bounces to a halt, trailing dust. Out climbs Roy.

Lucinda bursts from the house, squealing with joy.

Under the streetlights, Lenny plants a foot onto the shallow porch. Then another. The boards beneath him object loudly. He studies the old wooden rocking chair. Lenny reaches out and tips the chair. It rocks steadily back and forth. He tests the arms with his weight. It holds. Lenny sits down. The chair gives way. Lenny sits among the splinters, fighting stubborn tears.

Four-year-old Lenny peeks from the dark kitchen screen door, beside a dull naked light bulb throwing a low haze across the backyard. Music hums from a transistor radio. Lucinda dances cheek to cheek with Roy. Wendell mopes nearby, a broken man.

Now, in dark woods across the street from Lenny, a patch of ground glows red hot, then burns. Sudden flames lick the trees. Lenny finishes off the bottle. He stands and is drawn toward the fire.

Police sirens whine in the distance. Lenny can't hear them over the twirling, roaring fire in front of him.

Decades before, Roy hauls a loaded-down tarp across the street in the darkness, toward that same spot. Four-year-old Lenny follows close behind, dragging shovel.

After Roy digs into the soft earth, his lighter fails to spark. His scar-covered hands try again. It lights across Roy's twisted, drunken, evil grin.

Lenny drops to his knees at the center of the blaze. Tears roll down his face. The fire grows around him.

Stop, he says. Just, please, stop.

Lightning crosses the sky as Lenny bursts into flames.

Dawn spreads across thick leaves.

A hand grips and pulls a bare arm. Another dangles a

needle dripping ink. At the needle's point is a nearly finished lightning bolt.

Damn it, hold still, Dub, Sixteen-year-old Lenny says.

Dub cringes, a skinny, long-haired, jean-jacketed, cow-hearted, wannabe tough guy. A deep bruise circles his eye.

Alright, Dub says. Alright.

Dub flinches again. Lenny, same long hair and jacket, concentrates on guiding the needle.

Hold still, you puss, he says.

Lenny holds out his own arm with an identical tattoo. Measuring a segment with his fingers, he starts again.

Hey, got you a souvenir, Dub says, pulling a brass doorknob from his jacket pocket.

Jesus, Lenny says. That's evidence, dumbass.

It's a souvenir, Dub says. When else are we out this early in the morning?

I'm always awake this early, Lenny says. Around here's a lot better place with no people.

Lenny pockets the doorknob.

Now hold still, he says.

Dub grits his jaw. Lenny goes back to work with the needle.

There, Lenny says, wiping Dub's arm with a bandanna. Done.

They hold their forearms side by side and admire the matching lightning bolts. Both nod in satisfaction.

Now let's go find that bottle, Dub says.

Side by side, the two boys march through the trees.

Lenny notices Dub tenderly poking at a bruised cheek.

How's that eye treating you, he asks.

Don't want to talk about it, Dub says. I'll live.

Lenny won't let it drop.

Tell me what happened, he says.

Don't want to talk about it, Dub says.

There is a long silence between them.

Top was off the ketchup again, Dub says.

Lenny's heard this one before.

Yeah, he asks.

Said I don't want to talk about it, Dub says.

There is a long silence between them.

I was coming around the corner, Dub says. Mom caught me in the eye with the bottle. Said never do it again. Said this'd help me remember.

They cross the rotting, wooden railroad bridge. Below, a muddy, shallow river trickles across sharp rocks.

Dub, Lenny says.

Yeah, Dub says.

You don't like ketchup, Lenny says. Hell, you put mustard on french fries.

They reach an old dead tree and stop.

Didn't say I did it, Dub says. Said I don't want to talk about it.

Lenny reaches deep into the trunk of the tree. He removes a mostly full bottle of rye whiskey.

Yeah, Lenny says. I know.

Lenny unscrews the top and hands it to Dub.

Lenny, I got to get out of here, Dub says.

We've both got to get out of here, Lenny says. Anyplace beats this.

Dub drinks and coughs, eyes watering a bit.

Here's to that, Lenny says, tipping up the bottle without much trouble.

I'm serious, Dub says.

Me too, Lenny says.

He hands it back to Dub. Dub takes a long swig and chokes some more.

I mean it, Dub says. I'm leaving. We're leaving. And we're going now.

Lenny turns to shove the bottle back into the tree.

How's that, he asks.

A gunshot explodes behind him.

This jolts Old Lenny awake in the center of a large

charcoal circle across the street from the house where he
grew up.

Jesus, Young Lenny yelps.

Dub holds a huge revolver like a dead fish.

Young Lenny grabs it away.

What the hell is wrong with you, he shouts.

I, Dub stammers, I didn't . . . I . . .

Young Lenny locks the safety and dumps bullets into his
palm.

You didn't what, he asks. This your Dad's?

Yeah, Dub says. I figured . . .

We're not going to go rob that damn hamburger shack,
Young Lenny says.

Yes, we are, Dub says. Then we'll go and never look back.

No, Young Lenny says. Stop it with that.

You won't help me, I'll do it myself, Dub says.

Young Lenny drops the gun into the hollow tree. He
pours the bullets into a jacket pocket.

Do what you like, Young Lenny says. I'm keeping these.

Fine, Dub says. But you'll see. You got to take what you
need.

Let's go, Young Lenny says. It's late.

The boys head for home. They cross back over the rotting
bridge, emerging from the woods near Lenny's house. The
tiny houses are new and clean. Front yards tidy. Newish cars
at the curbs. A paperboy rides by.

Young Lenny heads toward his house. Dub turns up the
street, peeling back his sleeve.

Hey, Lenny, Dub yells. This really looks pretty good!

Young Lenny's neck tightens. Quiet, already, he whispers.
And don't show people that.

Behind them, Old Lenny steps out of the trees. He didn't
see the boys, but he stares in wonder at the newer houses,
yards and cars.

Young Lenny slips through his bedroom window, then
quietly out of his jacket and shoes. He sits down on the bed.

Sliding open a bedside table drawer, he finds a plain gold ring. He turns the ring over in his hand.

Kneeling beside the water tower, Wendell slides the ring off his finger. A cigarette dangles from the corner of his mouth. He holds the ring out to Four-year-old Lenny. In a move, it disappears.

Here, now you try, Wendell says.

Young Lenny drops the ring back into the drawer and slides carefully into bed. Downstairs, Roy shouts an angry, rolling, muffled roar through the thin walls.

Young Lenny's face hits the pillow. Heavy footsteps on the stairs. Then at the door. He tenses, head to toe. The door bursts open and there is a big hand lifting him sideways off the mattress.

Where is it, dipshit, Roy grunts.

Where's what, Young Lenny asks.

Hand it over, smart fuck, Roy says.

Hand what, Young Lenny asks.

Dipshit, Roy mutters, wiry and brutishly strong, sour-faced and tattooed.

He wheels Young Lenny toward the door, shoving him head first down the stairs.

Young Lenny lands at the head of the dinner table, coiled like a spring.

Lucinda stands in the corner smoking a cigarette.

He didn't take your bottle, Roy, she says.

The fuck he didn't, Roy says, tearing the kitchen cabinets apart.

You must've drank it, Lucinda says. You know you probably drank it. Did you look in your truck?

I smell it on him, Roy says.

You smell you, Young Lenny says.

Roy slaps him off his chair.

Lucinda shrieks for effect, Roy! Damn it! Roy!

So smart, Roy says. So smart.

Roy pulls a lighter from his back pocket and grabs Young Lenny by the neck.

Roy, Lucinda yells, serious this time. No! Roy! Stop!

But she doesn't actually move to interfere. Not a hair.

Roy lights the lighter with one hand and holds it to Young Lenny's face. He squirms but can't break free.

You just keep thinking that, Roy says. Keep thinking you can beat old Roy. You just do me a favor and try . . .

Roy holds the lighter closer. Then closer. Young Lenny shuts his eyes and braces. Across the room, Lucinda catches her breath. Roy snaps the lighter shut. He turns and flings Young Lenny into a chair with a thud.

. . . 'cause that's the day I'm waiting on, Roy laughs, stomping from the room.

Young Lenny grits his teeth, shaking with rage. Behind him, his Mother reaches to touch his shoulder but draws back.

Go on now, she says. Get on to school.

Young Lenny bounces to his feet and gathers his school books. Lucinda sits down at the table, the end of her cigarette shaking. Roy's laughter flows from upstairs.

Edna, years fading, nearly blind, rocks in her chair on the front porch.

Moses, Moses on the mountain, she sings. Moses on the mountain at the back door again.

Young Lenny bursts from the house.

Hey, Grandma, he says.

Penelope's in the weeds, she says. Go get her, now. She's off in the weeds.

Young Lenny sets down his books to tie a shoe.

Penelope died, Grandma, he says.

She's off in the weeds across the road there, Edna says. Go get her.

Roy stomped your rabbit, Grandma, Young Lenny says. She died.

Roy exits the house, kicking Young Lenny's books into the front yard. Papers scatter across the crab grass.

Vandal, Edna says.

Mumble in English, old woman, Roy says. He climbs into his filthy, rattling truck and tears off.

Come here, boy, Edna says. He does. She touches his face.

Build your house on the tracks, sooner or later, you get the train, Edna says. Understand?

No, Young Lenny says.

You will, Edna says. Give it time. Go find my rabbit now.

Young Lenny catches up to Dub on Main Street. A handful of people and cars mingle among the stores.

You're sure quiet, Dub says.

Grandma's rabbit, Young Lenny says.

The one Roy stomped, Dub asks.

Yeah, Young Lenny says. Roy kicked it every day. Every day it shit in his shoe. Never the same shoe. Kept it interesting. Up until that last one Roy stomped her with.

My kind of rabbit, Dub says. Hey, hold up a minute.

They are standing outside the town thrift store.

Dub, I'm not going in there again, Young Lenny says.

Come on, Dub says. One last time for the rabbit. And also you got to learn to stand up for yourself.

Dub strides into the store. Young Lenny follows.

A beady-eyed Thrift Store Clerk leans behind the counter. A handful of lurking Local Kids the same age wander the candy aisle and look at magazines.

Why do some never learn, the Clerk barks to no one.

Dub marches over to the counter. He eyes a shelf of fire crackers in a glass case behind the Clerk.

One of each, please, Dub says.

Out, the Clerk says. I do not have the patience for you today.

Dub pulls a crumpled fist of bills from his pocket.

I asked politely, Dub says. And this is actual money.

Told you, the Clerk says. I don't sell those things to

children.

We're not children, Dub says.

I know a dozen kids you sold them to, Young Lenny says. You do it all the time.

Yeah, well, none of them are you dirt balls, the Clerk says.

Dub twitches with rage. He takes a sorry slap at a display rack on the counter. Everyone in the store watches in slow motion as it weakly teeters and then tumbles with a clatter.

The Clerk is on his feet. Dub and Young Lenny are already out the door. In a full sprint, they disappear down the street toward their school. The Clerk follows them out onto the sidewalk, already out of breath from rounding the shop counter, and heads the wrong way.

I swear, Clerk shouts. You little freaks!

Old Lenny stands in the mouth of the alley nearby, not sure what to make of the world around him. He didn't see Dub or Young Lenny run the other way. The furious Clerk smacks directly into him.

Move, you jerk, the Clerk shouts before tumbling over Old Lenny's outstretched foot.

Damn it all, you transients, the Clerk growls, for a moment rolling on his back in the dirt like a turtle. Why don't you go bum your way back where you came from?

The Clerk takes off down the alley. Old Lenny grins as he ducks into the store.

Happily, Dub and Young Lenny march side by side toward the town high school. They catch up to Sixteen-year-old Annagrace Adell, walking just ahead.

Hey there, Annagrace, Dub says.

Stop it, Dub, Young Lenny says.

Don't you tease me Dub Rhodes, she says, walking faster.

I said, hey there, Annagrace, Dub says. Lenny, I think maybe that poor girl's gone deaf!

Annagrace smiles and doesn't look at them.

I said stop it, Young Lenny says.

How's she going to know she likes you unless she looks at you, Dub winks. Wait, he shouts. I remember. I did know you're deaf, Annagrace. I heard you sing.

She stops, angry.

You shut your ugly mouth, she says.

There, Dub mutters to Young Lenny. See? Work it or jerk it.

Dub waves his arms at Annagrace.

It's a miracle, he shouts.

Alone in the store, Old Lenny pockets candy and a hunting knife. Then he slips behind the counter toward the fireworks.

Down the street, he passes the Clerk coming the other way, boiling.

Too fast for you, Old Lenny asks.

That's it, let's go, funny guy, the Clerk says, grateful for a fight he can finally throw his weight into.

Behind them, the store crackles with a dozen tiny sticks of dynamite. Glass shatters. Something heavy hits the ground. A long pause. Then a second and third round of popping and crashing.

The Clerk shakes his head and goes straight for Roy's bar.

Annagrace, Young Lenny and Dub only make it as far as the parking lot of the school, three stories of squat, square, towering brick surrounded by patches of grass in the dirt. Rather than filing in through the front doors, a crowd of students pool out front. Dub is beside himself.

Hmmmm, Dub says slyly. A commotion. What could it be? I should find out.

Dub takes off toward the crowd.

Annagrace eyes them both.

Got a secret to share, Lenny, she asks.

Nobody's got a secret in this town, Young Lenny says.

Why do you two idiots act so tough, she asks.

Not so tough, Young Lenny says.

Nothing wrong with fitting in, Annagrace says.

Fit in, Young Lenny laughs. Here? With these creeps and their Army base? Raised right. Trained right. Yes, sir. No, sir. They'll be in Germany and Guam and Japan in six months. And we'll be here. My Mom and Dub's Mom doing their laundry. Roy pouring their booze. Dub's Dad pumping their gas. You too, sitting in your church, worrying over everything. Face it, Annagrace. None of us are going anywhere. They're the ones that should try fitting in.

Annagrace narrows her eyes.

What's a nice girl like me bothering with trouble like you, anyway, she asks.

Young Lenny smiles. He pulls the doorknob from his jacket pocket.

She takes it from him.

What's this about, she asks.

Wait, he says. You'll see.

She drops the knob into a deep pocket in her skirt.

Almost forgot, she says. Happy birthday.

Young Lenny isn't sure what she means.

Who said it's my birthday, he asks.

Miss Roosevelt, in third grade, she says. Your family didn't forget your sixteenth birthday, did they?

Young Lenny smiles bright.

Annagrace, he says. Even I forgot.

She kisses his cheek and whispers in his ear.

Remember that for next year, she says.

Curtis Mahoney, only two years older but a world larger than Dub and Lenny, proudly wearing his varsity jacket on a hot day, pushes toward them. He and Young Lenny stare each other down.

Looks like the place is shut tight, Annagrace, Curtis brays. What do you say we meet up under the bleachers in ten minutes?

Annagrace blushes. Young Lenny's neck tightens.

You watch yourself, Curtis, Annagrace says.

I'm only watching you, Curtis says.

Annagrace sways away into the crowd. Curtis and Young Lenny both watch her go.

Got eyes on you too, inbreed, Curtis says.

Half his size, Young Lenny's ready to launch himself at Curtis.

Watch where you put those, Young Lenny says. Don't want to lose one.

A short, furry arm parts the two. Coach Tullus, squinting, tubby like a boulder with limbs, clutches a megaphone in his other hand.

Save it, Curtis, Tullus says. This shit ball'll get his soon enough. Because don't think for a moment I don't know who's behind this.

The megaphone squawks as he walks away.

Alright, Tullus screeches. Alright. Everybody settle down.

Throughout the hallways, angry Teachers pace outside their classroom doors. Not a single knob among them, all are shut tight. Students crowd around, thrilled at the distraction.

Principal Barton pulls on the jacket of a mismatched suit, shoving his way through the throng.

Alright now, Barton says. Alright. Settle down.

He spots Jenkins, the school's half-drunk, unshaven, wild-eyed custodian, leaning against a locker, chuckling at the chaos.

Get a screwdriver and get these doors open, Barton commands loudly, so all can hear. Now!

Jenkins rolls his eyes, trudging toward his basement supply room. Barton reaches his own office door and is relieved to find a doorknob in place. He reaches for it. It comes off in his hand.

Damn it, he seethes. Hell! Damn! Tullus!

Tullus scurries out the crowd.

Yeah, Bob, he says.

Barton hands him the knob.

Get to the bottom of this and hurt somebody while doing it, Barton says. Now.

At Lenny's house, Lucinda has her head on the kitchen table, staring out the window, ice melting across a half a glass of gin, an almost empty bottle nearby.

No use fretting now, Edna says from the doorway. Train's come and gone.

She has a cane and wears a tattered fancy hat.

Didn't ask you, crazy old woman, Lucinda says.

Shouldn't talk to me that way, Edna says. Wendell never let you.

Well, look where that got Wendell, Lucinda says. And just what did you expect me to do? Live here alone with an insane old woman and ungrateful child the rest of my life? At least Roy's a man. I'll take the good with the bad.

Don't see any good about it, Edna says.

Lucinda flings the glass at Edna. Bad throw. Booze shatters against the wall. Edna doesn't blink.

I'm going to go find Penelope, Edna says. Find your senses before I get back.

Your rabbit's dead, old woman, Lucinda says. When're you going to get that? Dead. Hear me?

Ignoring her, Edna leaves Lucinda searching the kitchen for a new glass.

Inside a school classroom, a screwdriver prods the hole where a doorknob should be. The door swings open, Jenkins is on his knees in the hallway. He waves his hand with a flourish.

There we are, he says.

A prim Civics Teacher shoves past him, followed by students.

Of course, step right this way, Jenkins says from stiff knees. Never you mind the old jackass.

Students fill the halls, all well-groomed, except Dub and Young Lenny. Half the doors still stuck shut, Teachers try in vain to herd students and restore order.

Ah, Dub says. Sweet mess.

He heads toward the basement stairs.

Young Lenny continues on. Jenkins falls into uneven step beside him.

Got them chasing their tails today, Jenkins says.

Young Lenny plays dumb.

What, he asks. I don't know what you mean.

Don't what me, Jenkins says. I'm the one who spends all my time wiping your damn lightning bolts off everything in this place. I know that kind of energy. Had plenty myself. It's inside you. Crime. Take it from somebody who left a lot of life behind the walls. Powerful thing. Useful if you need it. But once you let it out, no putting it back. Believe you me.

Young Lenny hustles away.

And quit scratching up my furniture, Jenkins shouts as Barton's voice returns, somewhere in the distance.

Why in heaven's name are these doors still closed, he yells.

Jenkins slumps down the hall.

Dub slips into Jenkins' basement supply room and yanks the light cord. He lifts a ring of keys from a hook and draws a matching key from his pocket. He almost has the key back on the ring when he hears Jenkins grumbling outside the door. Dub grabs the light cord and dives for cover as the door opens.

. . . no use to rush a man, Jenkins growls. What's going to get done is going to get done.

Jenkins yanks the light cord. He digs around on a workbench until he finds a long, flat screwdriver. Then he reaches beneath the workbench and finds a flask. He takes a long pull and shoves it back into place.

. . . an ounce of thank you, Jenkins says, never hurt a

person . . .

Yanking the cord again, he leaves.

Dub switches the light back on, replacing the key. He then digs beneath the bench until he finds the flask. He pockets it after a long swig.

The school Civics Teacher prowls the front of the classroom.

Alright, folks, she begins. In light of this morning's events, let's get right back to where we were. Yesterday we discussed the fundamentals of life in a rational, modern society. Which assumes an understanding, ladies and gentlemen, that you are all capable of comprehending the difference between right and wrong . . .

In the back of the room, Young Lenny rolls his eyes.

A similarly prim Math Teacher prowls the front of her own room in the same irritated way. A complicated equation plasters the chalkboard.

So this presents a problem, she says. And how do you solve a problem? That's right. Follow. The. Rules.

In the back of the room, Dub ignores her and scratches a large, detailed lightning bolt on the back of the chair in front of him.

The Civics Teacher turns toward the board. No chalk.

The Math Teacher turns toward the board. No chalk.

The Civics Teacher reaches for her top desk drawer.

The Math Teacher reaches for her top desk drawer.

Principal Barton walks down the empty hallway.

Finally, he says. Everything back to . . .

At the far end of the hall, the clatter of doorknobs hitting the floor. A teacher screams.

The Civics Teacher pulls the drawer. The drawer bottom is gone. It is full of doorknobs. They clatter to the floor.

The Math Teacher pulls the drawer. The drawer bottom is gone. It is full of doorknobs. They clatter to the floor.

The clatter of doorknobs emerges from every classroom

in every direction. Principal Barton covers his ears.

Young Lenny grins.

Dub grins.

The classroom loudspeaker crackles to life.

Dwayne Rhodes and . . .

Barton covers the microphone with his hand.

Who's the other one, he asks.

Tullus leans against the doorframe, arms smugly folded.

Smith, Tullus says.

Oh yes, Barton says. And Leonard Smith . . .

Young Lenny is already on his feet. Students around him cheer.

. . . report to my office, the speaker fuzzes. Now!

Young Lenny exits his classroom and finds Annagrace carrying a heavy wood block marked *Bathroom Pass*.

Well, Annagrace says.

That's a deep subject, Young Lenny says.

She pulls the doorknob from her skirt pocket.

I'm impressed, tough guy, she says. Funny.

More where that came from, he says.

This will suffice, thank you, she says.

Young Lenny turns and floats toward Barton's office. As he rounds a corner, Tullus catches him by the neck.

Well, well, well, Tullus says.

In Tullus's other hand is the base of Dub's skull.

Screw you, fatty, Dub says.

Can it, Tullus says. This is the end of you two.

They turn down a steep row of stairs.

Sorry, Coach, Dub says. Got an ear infection. I can't hear bullcrap.

They speed up.

Oh, I think you heard me, Tullus says.

Tullus shoves. Young Lenny and Dub crash to the bottom of the stairs. The flask bounces from Dub's pocket in one direction and a bullet from Young Lenny's pocket tumbles in the other.

302

Tullus sees the flask and swoops.

Hmmm, Tullus says. What do we have here?

Young Lenny reaches out and scoops up the bullet before Tullus notices.

In a work shed beyond the school's overgrown practice fields, Jenkins fiddles beneath the hood of an ancient lawn tractor. Old Lenny throws a shadow across the open door.

Jenkins looks to see that an ax handle is in reach, but doesn't turn around.

Can I help you, friend, he asks.

Maybe, Old Lenny says.

Jenkins laughs, stretching his back, digging through tools on a rotting workbench.

Maybe I can or maybe I will, he asks.

Somebody better, Old Lenny says. Looks like you're it.

What do you say we start again, Jenkins says.

I'm looking for somebody, Old Lenny says.

Out of sight of Old Lenny, Jenkins reaches slowly for a sharpened screwdriver beneath a pile of rags.

What's it to me, he asks.

You knew Wendell Smith, Old Lenny says.

Jenkins stops.

Barton is behind his desk, picking through a tin of tiny pills. Tullus perches in the corner. Curtis leans against the closed door.

This does not happen, Barton says. Hear me? Not at my school.

Barton swirls the pills in his hand and dumps them in his mouth. They go down wrong.

Not on my watch, he chokes, gulping at a glass of water.

Not after we get done, Tullus says.

You sure it was them, Barton asks.

Absolutely, Tullus says.

How, Barton asks.

Tullus feigns confusion.

How what, Tullus asks.

Barton is suspicious.

How are you so sure, Barton asks.

They're the rotten apples, Bob, Tullus says.

Bad seeds, Curtis says.

Both adults ignore him.

Got a couple every year, Tullus says. The long hair. Patches on their jackets. Smoking in the john.

And that thing with your car, Curtis says.

Tullus cringes.

These the kids that spray-painted jackass on your car, Barton asks.

Yeah, Tullus says. Yes. Fairly sure that was them.

Barton is losing his patience.

What is it here you can't control, he asks.

Bob, Tullus begins.

They're inbred, Curtis says.

Will you please shut up, Tullus says.

But they are, Curtis says.

Now Barton's interested.

What are you talking about, he asks.

Lenny's Mom is married to her brother, Curtis says. It's true. Ask anybody.

Tullus is ready to throw Curtis through a wall.

Now how would you know that, he asks.

My Dad drinks at his Dad's bar, Curtis says. Roy. Roy's bar. Any time he gets too drunk, Roy tells everybody all about it.

Barton is at the window, staring down at the playing fields.

Yeah, he says. Evidently, he's her Uncle. Anybody else know?

Everybody, Curtis says. I make sure they do.

Barton lands hard in the oversized chair behind his desk, considering his options.

What about the other one, he asks.

Just as rotten, Tullus says. Leave this to me.

Jenkins is sitting on a low stool, sipping clear liquor from a jelly jar. He wipes at his mouth with the back of his hand.

Haven't seen Wendell Smith in ten, twelve years, Jenkins says. People say he took off one night. Never sat right with me. Nobody goes nowhere like that.

You two grew up together, Old Lenny says. You never asked?

Jenkins' eyes are swimming. He's long past drunk.

Did, he says. At first. Plenty of ways to answer a question. Sometimes folks say nothing. Look right through you. Right through the wall on the other side. All they see is something wicked bouncing back through their mind. Car falls off the jack. Body fished out of the lake. Gun goes off. Lucinda. That Mother of hers. That kid of theirs, Lenny. And that Roy. All of them. You see that look in somebody's eye, they've been someplace. Seen something.

The kid doesn't know, Old Lenny says.

The hell he don't, Jenkins says. Now beat it. Some of us are busy working for a living.

Old Lenny yanks a wrench from the wall and clears the cluttered workbench with a long, frustrated swipe.

Listen to me, he says. He was too young. He doesn't know.

In a single move, Jenkins throws the liquor across Old Lenny's eyes and has a boot knife against his neck.

So, you like to break things, Jenkins says, calm and steady. How about that. Now, I don't know you. Don't care to know your troubles. But understand me that something happened. Something ugly. What Wendell or the rest of them had to do with it, I've got no idea. And I don't care to wonder, either. I'm just a tired old con with a field to mow.

Jenkins climbs onto the tractor. The engine whines, then roars.

Find out what bit that boy, you'll find Wendell Smith, Jenkins shouts.

The tractor engine sputters and stalls, the sudden silence spreading into the wind.

And let him know I asked about him, Jenkins says, cranking the engine back to life and lurching out of the shed, leaving Old Lenny behind.

Young Lenny and Dub watch the School Secretary count a huge pile of money from one side of her desk to the other. Mrs. Pinkle is older than the town. She works very deliberately, with no haste.

The door to Barton's office flings open. He walks over to a large filing cabinet, fishing keys from his pocket.

Almost through, Missus Pinkle, he asks.

She's not nearly even close. He picks her carefully notated tally off the desk.

My goodness, Barton says.

Twice last year just so far, she says. Biggest ham raffle ever.

Barton yanks open a file drawer and removes a heavy wooden paddle.

Well, get it counted and into the safe, Barton says. I have letters for you to type.

He levels a finger at Dub and Young Lenny.

You two. In my office, he growls. Move.

Soon Curtis marches Dub and Young Lenny beneath the football bleachers. They grimace and limp from being paddled.

Smells like piss down here, Dub says.

Tullus shoves trash bags into their hands.

Get used to it, he says. You're mine all day, all week, all month.

Curtis chuckles.

Asshole, Dub says.

What'd you say, Curtis demands.

First, I said ass, Dub says. Then hole.

Curtis pushes Dub to the ground. Young Lenny pushes Curtis.

Hey, Tullus says. Enough.

You heard him, stupid, Young Lenny says.

Shut it, inbreed, Curtis says.

Curtis pulls Young Lenny into a painful half-nelson.

Hey, Tullus says. Stop.

Inbreed, Curtis says.

I said, enough, Tullus tells him.

Young Lenny stops squirming. Curtis drops him.

Now get picking or I'll have you running the track 'til Thursday, Tullus says.

Dub and Young Lenny drop their heads and peel off their jackets.

Tullus grabs Dub's arm and squints at the freshly inked lightning bolt showing through a makeshift bandage.

Now, there's got to be a rule against this, Tullus says. What about you?

Tullus grabs Young Lenny's arm.

Couple of funny boys, Tullus laughs, walking away. Get working.

Curtis follows him.

Fuck this, Dub says.

You said it, Young Lenny says. Got a cigarette in my jacket.

Across town, Old Lenny looks up at the sparkling clean Yardley tower.

He remembers standing in the same spot many years before, watching Wendell finish the tower's first coat of paint.

Wendell spots Four-year-old Lenny and scrambles down a ladder, worried.

My goodness, he says. Now, what are you doing here?

307

Your Momma know you're out of the house?

Do the trick, Four-year-old Lenny says. He stares at the wedding ring on Wendell's finger.

One time, Wendell says. He slides the ring off his finger and holds it out. In a move, it disappears.

Here, now you try, Wendell says.

He hands him the ring. Little Lenny waves his fingers. Nothing.

Practice with it a while, Wendell says. Right now, we'd better head home.

Wendell picks up his lunchbox and takes his hand.

Dub and Young Lenny sit on the top row of the bleachers, passing a cigarette.

Tears stand in Dub's eyes.

Why's he always saying that, he asks.

Young Lenny gives him a moment to recover.

Inbreed, he asks.

Yeah, Dub says.

Damned if I know, Young Lenny says. He probably doesn't even know what it means. He likes to repeat back words he hears other people say. It's funny except for when he broke my nose about it.

That son of a bitch is on my list, Dub says.

What list, Young Lenny asks.

My shit list, Dub says.

Young Lenny laughs. I've got one of those.

We ought to get that guy, Dub says. Beat his ass. Leave him in the woods.

Not worth it, Young Lenny says.

You never want to settle the scores that really matter, Dub says. I'm tired of doorknobs and spray paint.

Is this about pissing on Missus Arbidor's lawn, Young Lenny asks.

No, Dub says. In her mailbox. It's not going to kill you. I can't fill it alone.

I don't care if you think your English Teacher's evil, I'm not screwing with some old lady, Young Lenny says.

Evil, Dub says emphatically. And mean about it.

I'm sure she is, Young Lenny says. But look, you give, you get. Got it? And that goes double points for screwing with old ladies.

Fine, Dub says, studying the end of the cigarette for a moment.

Can't run every time somebody beats your ass and call you names, Young Lenny says. Where would you end up? Our right time will come.

Well, that time's coming sooner than later, Dub says. And we'll need cash or we're not making it anyplace.

Yeah, maybe so, Young Lenny says.

Slowly, elderly Mrs. Pinkle emerges from Barton's office with a large green money box and makes her way down a long flight of stairs.

She crosses a dim, giant basement cafeteria and silent industrial kitchen, then reaches a small office. There she moves aside a framed health certificate to reveal a hidden, imbedded safe. She turns the dial.

Tumblers click inside the dark wall safe. A bolt pops. Light floods in as the door swings open and a cotton gym bag slips over Mrs. Pinkle's head.

Old Lenny steps into the front yard of his childhood home. Lucinda is passed out in the rocking chair on the front porch, empty glass at her feet.

Mom, he says.

She blinks awkwardly awake.

Je-sus, buddy, she says. Thought you just called me Momma. Though, uhm . . .

She smirks and looks him over.

You can call me anything you want, she says. New around here? What's your name? You look familiar. You a

309

salesman? Been through here before? Sit on Mamma's lap
and tell me all about it.

She cackles, reaching for her glass, sliding out of the chair
with a thump.

What I meant to say, Old Lenny says. Is your Mother
home?

Lucinda leans back on the porch boards and hiccups.

The hell you want with her, she laughs.

I'll take anybody sober enough to stand, Old Lenny says.

Oooh, she says. You're the sharp one. Sorry. She's busy
chasing dead rabbits. My husband's at work. Ungrateful
child's at school. We're alone, stranger. Come on in. I'll fix us
some refreshments.

Lucinda cackles, head drooping. Old Lenny backs away.
She coughs and passes out, drooling. He scoops her into his
arms and sets his Mother down on the living room couch.
She smacks her lips and blinks at the ceiling.

Lenny, hon, she says. Get me my drink.

Old Lenny walks out. He returns, setting her glass on the
coffee table. He digs around the kitchen for a bottle, returns
and pours. She happily reaches for it. He helps her sip.

That's my good boy, she says.

Some people say people can change things, Old Lenny
says. Like if they only dig deep enough, they'll find some
good hiding out amongst all the garbage. What do you say
about that?

Lucinda snores.

Yeah, he says. Me too.

Barton scurries down an empty hallway with the School
Librarian in tow. She has a gaunt, angry glare.

. . . my point is that I'm continually and extremely
disgusted, she says.

Yes, of course, Barton says, spotting Tullus heading
toward them, waving him over.

Tullus makes an effort to escape around a corner.

Tullus, Barton says. Freeze.

Tullus trots over.

Yeah, Bob, he asks.

Seen Missus Pinkle, Barton asks.

No, Tullus says.

She's wandered off again, Barton says. Walk with us. We were just discussing our process of processing, uhm, complaints.

Multiple complaints, the Librarian says.

Yes, Barton says. Multiple complaints.

They cross the dark, empty cafeteria.

Lunch staff closed up hours ago, Tullus says. She probably dozed off back here somewhere.

They cross the empty industrial kitchen toward the cafeteria office.

. . . harsh persistence, the Librarian continues. That's what's missing at this school. Hear me? Harsh. Brutal. Persistence.

Quite right, Barton says. Certainly, we can . . .

The Librarian screams. Barton gasps, as does Tullus. Mrs. Pinkle is tied to a chair in the office, bag over her head, snoring. Lightning bolts are painted in mustard on the floor. The wall safe hangs open. The money box is empty at her feet.

The Librarian faints, hitting the ground with a thud. Neither man moves to catch her.

Young Lenny and Dub shuffle around under the bleachers, pretending to pick up trash. Dub glances up.

Ah, shit, Dub says. Here they come.

Curtis leads a dozen other Jocks, charging across the field.

Keep your head down, Young Lenny says. Look busy.

Think it's too late for that, Dub says.

A Police cruiser screeches into the school parking lot, lights flashing.

Dub drops his bag of trash.

How do you feel about running now, he asks.

Grab your jacket, Young Lenny says.

In the parking lot, barrel-shaped Deputies Miller and Jones lean against the hood of their cooling car, lights still flashing.

And the money, Miller asks.

Gone, Barton says. Every dollar.

They drew lightning bolts with mustard, Tullus says. Same kind tattooed on their arms.

That so, Jones says.

These hoodlums won't get away with this, Barton says.

They'll probably say they don't know anything about any money, Tullus says.

Curtis and his gaggle of Jocks rush up to them.

They're not there, Curtis says.

Tullus stomps a foot.

Darn it, he chimes. They're running for it!

The Deputies amble back to their car.

Don't worry, Miller says. They always go home eventually. We'll find them.

Siren blaring, they tear out of the parking lot.

They'll cut through the woods, Curtis says. Let's go, guys.

To class, boys, Barton says. Schools still in for another hour.

But, we know where they go, Curtis says.

That's enough for today, Barton says. Let the adults handle this. Back to class.

Curtis drops his head and turns toward the school with the rest, mustard caked around the heel of his shoe.

Dub and Young Lenny sprint through the woods as if their lives depend on it.

Holy crap, Dub says. Holy shit. Wait!

They stop, panting.

Let's go, Young Lenny says. Don't quit now.

Got to catch my breath, Dub pants.

Come on, Young Lenny says. Go to your house. Grab stuff. Meet me at that hollow tree.

Right, Dub says, stumbling off in a hurry.

Young Lenny heads for his house.

Roy pushes RayRay, the town drunk and his best customer, out the bar door.

Come back after an hour, Roy says. Got to eat my lunch.

RayRay puts up a fight.

Never heard of packing a sandwich, he asks.

Roy locks the front door behind himself, climbs in the same old truck and clatters away.

Inside, the doorframe around the bar's back door splinters at the lock. The door swings open. Old Lenny drops a cinder block.

Already home, Roy climbs out of his truck, slamming the door.

Upstairs, Young Lenny slips in through his bedroom window. He reaches into the drawer for Wendell's ring.

Damn it, Lucinda, he hears Roy thunder downstairs.

Sprawled across the living room couch, Lucinda looks around, confused, hair plastered to her face.

What, she mutters.

Roy grabs her by the shoulders, lifts and shakes her.

What is the matter with you, passed out drunk in the middle of the day, Roy shouts. Where's my lunch?

I don't want any lunch, she hollers.

In his room, Young Lenny stops and listens, his eyes closed. He can't move.

Roy slaps Lucinda. She bounces to her feet. He slaps her again. Disoriented, she picks a direction and runs, bouncing off furniture and walls along the way.

Come back here, Roy yells.

Lucinda stumbles out the front door with Roy close behind. Roy gets her hard by the arm, dragging her back toward the house as Young Lenny's teenage fist lands square on his chin without much effect. Roy is delighted.

What in high hell, he grins.

Let her go, Young Lenny says, reeling back for another one. He misses. Roy drops Lucinda and grabs Young Lenny by the throat.

I see it's finally about that time, Roy says.

The Police car pulls up. Miller and Jones climb out.

Hey there, Roy, Jones says.

Hey there, Bill, Roy says. Jerry.

Roy, Miller says.

Come for the boy, Jones says.

Roy still grips Young Lenny.

That so, Roy says. Some kind of trouble?

Yep, Miller says.

Well, just finishing up here, Roy says.

We can wait if you want a moment to speak with him, Jones says.

Lucinda is a sobbing mess on the cracking concrete walkway. Roy turns Young Lenny loose.

Take your best shot, Roy says.

Young Lenny rushes Roy. Roy catches him on the jaw and sends him down. Young Lenny climbs back to his feet.

You got bad genes, boy, Roy says. Momma's a drunk. Father's a pansy.

Young Lenny snorts, blood smudged across his mouth, and rushes again, catching another combination on the way to the ground.

Roy grins over him.

What kind of sadness is that, he asks.

Please, Lucinda says. Won't you just stop?

She climbs to her feet, tears streaming, and shoves a hand into both their chests. Makeup drains down her face.

Damn it, Lenny, she says. Can't you behave?

It's this that finally wobbles Young Lenny. Roy shoves Lucinda away. Another combination bloodies Young Lenny.

He doesn't feel a thing.

You're like your old man, Roy says. Soft. Kind that gets chewed up. Spit out.

Another combination. Young Lenny drops his hands but stands his ground. Roy jabs. Young Lenny blinks and sways.

So, you going to fold like him, Roy asks.

Another jab.

Whine like him, he says.

And another.

Cry like him, he says.

And another. Young Lenny spits blood and charges again. A quick hook to the ear from Roy sends him tumbling five feet. This time, Young Lenny stays down.

That's enough, Miller says.

Jones and Miller move to collect Young Lenny from the ground. He scrambles to his feet, slips through their hands, then charges, limping across the road, disappearing into the woods.

Christ, Jones says. I'm in no mood to be running after the garbage today.

Let's get the other one, Miller says. He'll tell us where they think they're going.

With a tip of their caps, the Deputies tear off in their car.

Roy laughs as he steps over Lucinda and starts his truck. He's still laughing as he pulls up outside his bar. Roy climbs out so happy, he's out of breath.

He throws open the door and steps in, a smile on his face as he strolls behind the bar, chuckling. He reaches for a bottle. Footsteps behind him. A strong hand knocks the bottle the ground. Roy finds himself face to face with Old Lenny.

Hello Roy, he says.

A lifetime ago, Four-year-old Lenny smiles up at Wendell, holding his hand in their front yard. Edna waves from her rocking chair on the porch.

A beat-up, old truck whines to a stop. Roy pops out with a suitcase.

Hey, hey, Roy shouts. Look who's home!

Oh, my goodness, Roy, Lucinda chimes with a giggle, bursting from the house. You got out!

She runs over and throws her arms around him.

Afternoon, Edna, Roy says.

Thought they'd lock you up for good this time, Edna says.

You got no luck, dear, Roy says.

Little Lenny sits at Edna's feet on the porch.

Roy, this is our Lenny, Lucinda says, her tone a little funny. Isn't he something?

Well, hey there, little shit, Roy says. Shake.

Roy's hand eclipses his. Lucinda disappears into the house.

Listen to me, Lenny, Edna says. Stay clear of this fool, now. He's the baby in our family. Came along years after the rest of us. My Sisters. My Brothers. Not our fault he turned out just as ornery and mean as they come. Never did grow out of it, like that doctor said he would. Did he, now?

She aims her words like arrows as Roy grins back. Lucinda returns with an oversized camera.

Shut up, old woman, Lucinda says.

Truth's truth, Edna says.

Quietly, Wendell pushes closer and closer to them.

And this, this is Wendell, Lucinda sighs. I wrote you about him.

Wendell puts out his hand.

How do you do, he says.

I do fine, Roy says.

He and Lucinda snicker. She pushes little Lenny toward Roy.

Come on now, she says. Let me get a picture of the men together. Wendell inches his way into the frame.

Sure, Wendell, Lucinda laughs. You too.

316

The flashbulb pops.

Old Lenny stands over a bloody and broken Roy
sprawled across the floor behind the bar. Roy's eye is swollen
and lip split. He gasps for air.

What the shit, Roy sputters. Old Roy kiss your Wife?

Sorry, mac, lady's choice.

Wendell Smith, Old Lenny says. What happened to him?
What did you do? You did something. And he left. What did
you do, you piece of shit?

This name brings Roy another happy chuckle. Old Lenny
pulls him to his feet and presses his face to the bar top. Roy
moans in pain. He releases him and rounds the bar.

Ha, Roy says. Lost your nerve. You look like the type.

Old Lenny sits down at the bar. Roy sets up a glass for
himself and pours.

No, Old Lenny says. Not this time. You and I are having a
conversation. Nice and civil. Then I'm going to leave.

That so, Roy says, gulping.

I asked you a friendly question, Old Lenny says.

Roy pours another, breathing heavy. He laughs.

Right, Roy says, baiting him. Wendell Smith. Halfwit,
yellow-belly. That Wendell Smith?

Old Lenny's fists clench.

I'm not doing this your way, Old Lenny says. Not
anymore. Not your way anymore.

Only saying, he always struck me as a man's man, if you
catch me, Roy says. A touch sweet? That boy of his, about
the same. Weak in the bloodline. Sad, really.

As Roy lifts the bottle again, Old Lenny's fist catches him
across the mouth. A reflex. Old Lenny stares at his hands in
frustration. Roy staggers for a pistol at the end of the bar.

I'm getting awful tired at this party, buddy, Roy says.

Struggling for control, Old Lenny raises his palms.

Let's just start again, he says.

Roy's breathing hard.

317

Son, I know just about everything there is about your Wendell Smith, Roy says. Trust me, not worth your time.

Roy's heart seizes. The pistol tumbles to the ground. He slumps, still chuckling, holding onto the bar.

No, Old Lenny says. No.

I'll be damned, Roy says, growing peaceful. Know what, boy? In this light, you know, you look just like . . .

Don't you die, old man, Old Lenny says. Not yet.

Me, Roy says as his eyes go dull.

Old Lenny bursts out the bar door, passing RayRay on his way back in.

Bar's closed, RayRay, he says.

RayRay stomps his foot.

Damn it all, RayRay says. What's a person to do?

Old Lenny rushes faster down the sidewalk and finds himself nose to nose with the horse that brought him. Gratefully, Old Lenny climbs on and rides away.

Peeking around a corner in the dark living room, Four-year-old Lenny watches Roy, Lucinda, Edna and Wendell at the kitchen table. Cigarette smoke hangs thick in the air.

Lucinda is laughing. Empty beer bottles cover the table.

Come on now, Wendell, Roy says. I was just kidding with you. Don't be sore.

Roy gives Wendell a playful shove. Wendell remains sour faced.

Don't pout, Wendell, she says. We're just teasing you.

Lucy, Roy says. Where'd you hide the hard stuff? Some of us need a real drink.

Wendell doesn't drink liquor, Edna says. Doesn't know from your kind.

Lucinda is already digging into a cabinet.

Time he learned, she absently mutters. Here we are!

She sloshes a jug of moonshine across two short glasses. Wendell carefully lifts one.

There now, Roy says. How about a toast?

A toast, Wendell asks.

To family, Roy says.

Yes, to family, Wendell says, paralyzed deep inside, watching his own slip away.

Dub sneaks in the back door of his house, through the kitchen and into the laundry room.

Behind the dryer, he finds a tattered cigar box. Inside is a collection of childhood treasures. He pockets an army knife, nudie playing card, half pack of cigarettes, and a shiny metal army man.

Overloaded with grocery bags, Dub's Mother shoves her way through the front door, complaining to herself.

As Dub carefully replaces the box, he bumps the washing machine. The open washer lid drops shut with a clang.

In the living room, Dub's Mother halts mid-step.

Dwayne, she says. That you, boy? What the hell you doing out of school?

She stomps into the kitchen and drops the bags.

I heard you, she says. Come in here.

She pokes her head into the laundry room.

Don't you hide from me, Dwayne, she calls.

She stops. Listens. Hears nothing.

Damn it, she says. Come help me get these bags out of the car.

She listens, still nothing, and heads for the front door. When she's gone, Dub pops out of a tiny mop closet.

Dub's Mother steps outside to finish unloading her car, just as Miller and Jones pull up.

Hello there, fellas, she says. What can I do you for?

Inside, Dub creeps over and quietly opens the refrigerator door. He finds the ketchup and turns the cap. He carefully spits into the bottle, shakes it and sets it back as his Mother leads Miller and Jones into the house.

That little bastard, she says. Knew it would be something like this. Come on. Now, be quiet. He's hiding in here

319

somewhere. We'll find him.

Dub's Mother leads Miller and Jones as they sneak across the living room. By the time they get to the kitchen, Dub is gone. His Mother wordlessly points Jones and Miller toward different areas of the house to search. They grudgingly obey.

Tullus sits at his desk in the school's tiny, sweaty, cinder block athletic department office. He's reading a horse-racing form. A knock at the door.

Yeah, he says.

Curtis pokes his head in.

It's me, Coach, Curtis says.

I can see that, Tullus says. Come in. Lock that door. Now, about this missing money.

Curtis fumbles with the door handle.

Yeah, Coach, he asks.

Tullus opens a drawer, counting a stack of loose bills onto the desk, making the pile look as big as possible. Curtis keeps fumbling.

Alright, enough, forget the lock, leave it be, Tullus says. Here. That splits it even.

Curtis can hardly contain himself.

How much is it, he asks.

About seventy-five each, Tullus says.

I thought there'd be a whole lot more, Curtis says.

Nope, Tullus says. Small bills, mostly. Go ahead, asshole. Count for yourself.

Naw, Curtis says, not up to the challenge. Naw. That's alright.

Curtis reaches for the money. Tullus shoves him away, reaching for a gym bag. He piles wrestling gear on top of the money in the bag.

Now, Tullus says. You're not going to touch any of this for a couple months, at least, right?

Yeah, Curtis says.

Look at me, Tullus says. Not any of it. Right?

Right, Coach, Curtis says.

And when you do, tell people it's a birthday present from a relative or something, Tullus says. Maybe somebody died in Canada and left it to you. Something simple and believable. Think it through. Think, for once.

Right, Coach, Curtis says, reaching for the bag.

Tullus stops him again with a heavy hand.

I repeat, Tullus says. Do not fuck this up.

Do not worry, Curtis says, as seriously as he can muster. I've got this. No problem here.

And don't go looking for those boys, Tullus says. Let them get shot running.

Right, Coach, Curtis says. You bet.

Now, out, Tullus says.

Curtis leaves. Tullus slides open a desk drawer, where there's a much larger stack of much larger bills, and finds the flask Dub stole from Jenkins. He opens the flask and returns to his racing form.

Too simple to believe, Tullus mumbles.

Below the water tower, Edna sweeps the tall weeds with her cane.

The horse brings Old Lenny here at a gallop. When they reach his Grandmother, the horse stops cold.

Penelope, Edna shouts. Penelope!

Edna swipes at the weeds with her cane.

Where are you, rabbit, she says. Who's there?

Old Lenny says nothing as he climbs to the ground. The horse shuffles away.

Come closer, Edna says. Who's there?

Old Lenny takes a step toward her. She reaches out.

Closer, she says.

He does. She touches his face.

Lenny, she says. That you? It is! How you have grown.

Hi, Grandma, Old Lenny says.

Give us hug, she says.

321

He does. She takes his hand.

Been a long time, I guess, Edna says. Come on. You're helping me find Penelope.

In the school parking lot, letter-jacketed Jocks surround a beat-up, secondhand convertible. Curtis pops the trunk and throws his money bag inside.

All paid now, fellas, Curtis says. Now let's go find some inbreeds.

Out of breath, Young Lenny emerges from the woods at a little country church. Annagrace sits on the back steps, staring into space.

Annagrace, he whispers.

Lenny, she says. Where've you been?

Shhhh, he says. Come here.

She walks toward him. He's clearly beat up.

What happened to you, she asks.

We ran off, Young Lenny says.

You're hurt, she says. Quick, come inside. We'll clean you up.

No, he says. I can't.

She touches his face.

Oh, Lenny, she says. Why'd you do it?

It was just doorknobs, Annagrace, he says.

Everybody knows you took the money, she says.

He doesn't follow what she's saying.

What money, he asks.

From the big ham raffle, she says.

We didn't take any money, he says.

She shakes her head.

Then why did you run, she asks.

Doorknobs, Young Lenny says.

Well, come inside anyway, she says.

I'm leaving, he says.

Where would you go, she asks.

I don't know yet, Young Lenny says.

How are you going to get there, she asks.

Don't know, Young Lenny says.

Too adorable to be a criminal, she says.

I think , he starts, but can't find the right words.

I'm not going with you, she says.

Then, I guess I came to say goodbye, Young Lenny says.

Then, goodbye, Annagrace says.

He starts to turn. Annagrace grabs his face, kissing him, then slaps him across the mouth.

Come back, she says.

Young Lenny places his Father's ring in her palm.

Hold onto this, he says. I'll be back. You'll see. Promise.

Beneath the water tower, Old Lenny and Edna trudge carefully through the weeds.

I remember the day you came home from the hospital, Edna says. Your Daddy was so proud. Wouldn't let you go.

I need to know, Old Lenny says.

He was a good man, Edna says. Good man, and kind. A lot like your Grandfather at his age. I thought that if anybody could straighten your Mother out, it'd be Wendell. You came along. Judge sent Roy away. My happiest days.

Grandma, where did he go, Old Lenny asks.

Edna strokes his cheek.

You grew up so handsome, she says. And so good. I always knew. I always tell people. My Lenny. He's a good, good boy. Always is. Always.

Grandma, Old Lenny says. My Father. Wendell. What happened? Where did he go?

A memory crosses Edna's eyes. She covers her mouth, trembling.

Moving to squat behind a drape in the dark living room, Four-year-old Lenny sneaks closer to watch the adults at the kitchen table.

323

Never had learned to swim, Lucinda says. All grown up and never been near water. Pure shame. Lake's only about fifteen miles away. So Roy packed up the car with lunch and beer and fishing poles. Got me my first little bathing suit.

I do not think your Daddy would have likely approved, Edna says.

Lucinda sloshes her glass.

Daddy, she cackles. For all I know, I'm hatched from an egg.

Nobody means to die in a war, Edna says.

He was sure eager to go, Roy says.

Wendell stares a hole in the table.

And you always make sure to stay high and dry, Edna says.

Roy tops off Wendell's glass.

Hey there, buddy, Roy says. Let's freshen you up.

Wendell doesn't drink, Edna insists.

Sure trying tonight, Roy says.

Lucinda's chair scoots closer and closer to Roy's.

So, anyway, Lucinda says. Roy taught me my first bike ride too.

She puts her head on Roy's shoulder.

First matinee movie, she says.

Wendell downs his drink.

There's a sport, Roy says. Here's another.

Roy pours. Beneath the table, the toe of his heavy boot slips under the bottom rung of Wendell's chair.

First cigarette, Lucinda says.

Wendell drinks deep and holds out his glass.

Watch it, pal, Roy says. Sure you want to go again?

Wendell nods. Roy pours.

Lucinda's hand slips up Roy's thigh. Wendell tips his glass back. Roy's toe leverages the front legs of Wendell's chair from the floor.

. . . and oh, firsts for just lots of things, Lucinda says.

Roy flips Wendell backward onto the floor. Little Lenny

darts up the stairs from his hiding place in the shadows, ugly laughter echoing behind him.

Dub is already reaching into the hollow tree when Young Lenny arrives, running. Dub jumps a foot.

Damn it, Dub says. You scared me.

Well, I'm plenty scared myself, Young Lenny says.

These people need to relax, Dub says. It was just a joke.

They think we stole the raffle money, Young Lenny says. They don't care about the stupid doorknobs.

See, Dub says. They peg us whether we did something or not.

Well, we didn't do it, Young Lenny says. I'm not leaving here with people thinking we did.

Wake up, Dub says. How many times you need to get shit on to know to wipe your face?

Young Lenny can't help but laugh.

Well, if you put it that way, he says.

Dub reaches into the tree and drags out the revolver.

Let's get this cash and go until we feel like stopping, he says.

No, Young Lenny says. Let's hike five miles down the railroad tracks, find a pawn shop, sell that thing, and make sure we never get back here.

Dub waves the gun.

Come on, Dub says. Didn't you ever hear? Teach a man to fish.

Young Lenny takes the gun away from him.

Rather make sure he doesn't shoot his foot off, Young Lenny says.

Tullus locks his office door and trudges toward the parking lot.

Barton appears behind him.

Tullus, he calls.

Yeah, Bob, Tullus says. I was just heading for your office.

Were you, Barton smirks, tapping his watch.

Then Barton looks past his watch and bends, swiping the toe of Tullus' shoe with his finger. He finds dried mustard.

Is this what I think it is, he asks.

Yeah, Tullus says. Sorry. It all happened really quickly.

Idiot, Barton says. Stupid, sloppy, idiot.

Hey, Tullus says. Don't worry. Look. I was just heading to your office. Here. There's your cut. Count it.

Tullus hands Barton an envelope hidden in his racing form. Barton looks over his shoulder and tucks the envelope into a coat pocket.

What about what's his name, he asks.

Don't worry about him, Tullus says. Curtis thinks it was only a couple hundred. I gave him all the small bills and he's happy as a clam. They catch them punks yet?

Soon enough, Barton says. Trouble like them is a drain on society.

Barton leaves. Tullus waits a moment, then he reaches into his coat and finds another, much thicker envelope.

Point, match, Tullus, he says.

Behind his bar, Roy is a still an undiscovered, blue-grey heap on the floor.

In her bathroom mirror, Lucinda's eyes are foggy and surrounded by cuts and bruises. Fighting to keep her balance, she works with a makeup case to cover the mess.

Dub's Mother searches a closet. Miller climbs down from the attic. Jones looks under a bed.

Ma'am, Miller says. I don't think . . .

Don't ma'am me, she hisses. I know that boy. He's hiding in this house somewhere. Wait. I know where he is!

Where, Jones sighs.

In the walls, she says, an unbalanced mind shining from her eyes.

Curtis and the other Jocks find the railroad tracks and
turn in the direction of the wooden bridge.

I know they're back here somewhere, Curtis says.

Old Lenny and Edna sit side by side in the weeds.

Grandma, he says. Please.

I just don't have the words, child, she says. One day
everybody hears the train.

Wendell, mind swimming, tucks Four-year-old Lenny
into bed.

I don't want to go to sleep, he says.

Well, that's not up to you, Wendell smiles.

Is Roy staying here, he asks.

For a little while, looks like, Wendell says.

He's loud, he says.

He is, Wendell says.

He's mean to Grandma, he says. You should make him
leave.

See, Wendell says. Thing about people is, best to just let
them be. You take the time to teach somebody a lesson,
there's a price you're gonna pay for that yourself. It all comes
back one way or the other. So, you got to keep your head.
Hardest thing sometimes. Leveled many a man. But you
promise me. Make sure people don't get to you. They'll try.
Just eat away at you until you snap. But don't give in.
Hardest thing in the world sometimes. Understand? Promise
me.

I promise, he says.

That's my good boy, Wendell says.

Roy's laughter echoes in the distance.

Later, in the backyard, a transistor radio plays a gospel
choir singing.

A dim bulb above the back door glows. Roy and Lucinda
dance cheek to cheek.

Edna is asleep in a lawn chair, beer in hand.

Four-year-old Lenny is out of bed, peeking from behind the screen door. Lucinda giggles as Roy whispers in her ear.

In the far back corner of the yard, Wendell leans against a rusting metal shed, vomiting clear liquor.

Curtis and his buddies reach one side of the bridge just as Young Lenny and Dub reach the other.

Fuck, Young Lenny says.

Double fuck, Dub says.

Hot damn, Curtis says.

Come on, Young Lenny says. We'll go the other way.

Ain't nothing the other way, Dub says.

Yeah, I guess not, Young Lenny says.

Hey there, inbreeds, Curtis waves. You're coming with us.

With that, Young Lenny steps onto the bridge, Dub close behind. Curtis leads his group straight at them.

The hell we are, Young Lenny says.

At the water tower, Old Lenny helps Edna to her feet.

My, she says. You grew up so big and strong. I confess my mind is going. It seems like just this morning I wrapped your sweet-sixteen present and I put it in my . . .

In her pocket, she finds a small square of gift paper and holds it out, a little confused to see it, because this Lenny is clearly no longer a teenager. Old Lenny takes and unwraps the package. It's a photograph of himself as an infant, held by a smiling Lucinda and Wendell. He's dumbstruck.

My birthday's today, he asks.

It sure is, she says.

Four-year-old Lenny hovers at the screen door, hiding in a shadow, watching Roy and Lucinda dance cheek to cheek. Wendell's had enough. He stumbles toward them, trying to cut in.

You'd best be on your way, Roy, Wendell says.

Lucinda pushes Wendell away. He tries again. This time, Roy shoves him. Wendell lands hard on his back in the muddy yard.

On the railroad bridge, Curtis stands ready to pounce, Young Lenny ready to defend himself.

We can do this easy or hard, Curtis grins.

Let's start the hard way, then see what happens, Young Lenny says.

You're done now, inbreed, Curtis says.

The Jocks grunt and shove forward in agreement.

We didn't take any money, Dub says.

Whatever you say, Curtis says. Wasn't even that much. But you're going up for it anyway.

Young Lenny drops his guard.

What do you mean wasn't that much, he asks.

Curtis is confused.

What do you mean, what do I mean, he asks.

Well, Young Lenny groans. We're talking about that raffle money, right? The one the whole town enters. And the Army folks. For an entire cooked hog. On Pinkle's desk, there had to be a thousand dollars.

No, Curtis says, eyebrows crashing together as numbers cross his mind. It wasn't hardly anything. Bunch of ones and fives.

Nine hundred and thirty-two, Dub says. Some change. I saw her write it down.

No way, Curtis says.

Damn it, Young Lenny says. You took it. Didn't you, Curtis? You and Tullus and, who? Barton? Yeah. Bunch of masterminds. And then they ripped you off, you dummy. At least that part's funny.

No, smart guy, Curtis says. What do you know, anyway?

Only that I've had it with you, Young Lenny says.

That so, Curtis says.

That's right, Young Lenny says. You and your stupid jackets. There is a lot of shit I put up with in this town. But you I just can't stand.

How about we settle up right now, Curtis says.

They square off. Dub pushes past Young Lenny, pulling the revolver from his back pocket. The Jocks scurry backward.

Dub, Young Lenny yells. Stop!

Dub steps toward Curtis, shoving the gun barrel toward him.

All I know is, we're crossing this bridge, Dub says.

Curtis can see the empty chambers of Dub's revolver.

Well, I may be a dumb son of a bitch, he says. But that gun's empty.

You don't want to find out, Dub bluffs badly.

Curtis steps forward.

The hell I don't, Curtis says.

Dub stumbles backward across an old iron spike and reaches to catch himself on a missing railing, dropping the gun along the way. Young Lenny dives to catch him. Dub flops, screaming, from the bridge, headfirst onto the sharp rocks below with a sickening thud. Blood pours into the rolling current.

Curtis and Young Lenny scramble for the gun. Young Lenny has it first. Snapping open the chamber, he pulls a bullet from his pocket and snaps it shut.

Run you dummies, Young Lenny says.

The Jocks scatter, Curtis leading the way.

Young Lenny looks down at Dub, broken across the rocks.

Damn it, Dub, he says, hurrying into the woods. Damn it.

Old Lenny reaches the stream's edge and rounds a bend in the creek, rushing to Dub's body splayed across the rocks, eyes frozen wide.

Damn it, Dub, he says. I'm sorry. I'm so sorry.

Four-year-old Lenny tries to slip out the back door, hoping to watch the adults from a better position in the bushes. The rusty aluminum door slaps behind him. Lucinda and Roy turn, clutching each other.

Looks like somebody don't know where they belong, Roy says.

That's alright, Wendell says. My boy. My boy can stay up late sometimes. If he likes.

Stumbling, Wendell tries to scoop little Lenny into his arms, but he recoils. Wendell is hurt by this.

What's wrong, he asks.

You smell like puke, dummy, Lucinda says.

Wendell covers his mouth and shrinks backwards.

Hey, boy, Roy says. What do you think of your old Dad, tossing his lunch in the backyard?

Roy laughs. Lucinda tips up her glass. Edna doesn't stir.

Now get back in that house and go to bed, Lucinda says. Nothing for you out here.

He scurries back inside. A few moments later, his eyes are back at the door.

Annagrace mops a small altar as one of the church doors shuts quietly behind her. She turns to find Old Lenny sitting in a back pew.

May I help you, she asks.

He doesn't answer.

She approaches him slowly. Roy and Dub's blood, caked across Old Lenny's shirt and knuckles, stops her cold.

Don't be scared, Old Lenny says.

I'm not, she says, backing down the aisle.

No, Old Lenny says. Wait. I came to talk to you.

She stops.

Why, she asks.

Please, he says, staring down at his hands.

Well, she says. What is it?

Why are people so damn rotten, he asks.

331

Not everybody's rotten, she says.

I am, he says.

Why are you telling me, she asks.

You're not, he says.

She inches closer to him.

Do we know each other, she asks.

Let's just say we do, he says.

What happened to you, she asks.

Turned bad one day, Old Lenny says.

No, Annagrace says. I mean your clothes. Your hands. The blood.

There's something I came to tell you, Old Lenny says. To save you a lot of time someday.

What, she asks.

Once somebody goes rotten, they're rotten, he says. No changing that. Doesn't matter how they got that way. Remember that. Please.

Old Lenny stands.

Tell me something, mister, Annagrace says.

Yeah, he says.

You hurt people, she asks.

Yeah, he says.

Feel bad about it, she asks.

Yeah, he says.

Well, that's all there is to it, she says. No need to stay rotten. It's all up to you.

Old Lenny stares at her for a long moment. She doesn't flinch.

He leaves the church. Annagrace goes back to cleaning.

No need to stay rotten, she says to herself. No need at all.

Outside the church, Old Lenny finds the horse waiting. He climbs on and they are off.

Inside the hamburger stand at the edge of town, Young Lenny sits in one of the handful of empty tables, sipping a soda. The Manager stares at him from behind the counter.

Listen, pal, the Manager says. I'm not saying this for my health, here. We're closing up early. Time to go.

He walks back to the kitchen. Young Lenny reaches into his coat and draws the revolver.

Outside, Old Lenny slows the horse in the parking lot, watching through the plate glass as Young Lenny stands, gun at his side.

The Manager emerges from the kitchen and sees the gun. Hey. Hey, easy, now, he says.

Young Lenny is paralyzed. The Manager crumples before him.

Don't shoot, he says. What do you want?

Young Lenny doesn't blink, mind spinning.

Hello, the Manger says. What do you want, kid?

The, uh, Young Lenny says. The register.

Take it, the Manager says. It's yours.

They both look to the huge, heavy, metal register.

No, Young Lenny says.

No, you don't want the register, the Manager asks.

Yes, Young Lenny says. No. Open it.

This your first robbery, kid, the Manager asks. It's my third. Shot twice the last time. Want to see the scars?

Out of the corner of his eye, the Manager sees the restaurant's Fry Cook through the service window, frantically dialing a phone. The Cook gives him a thumbs-up.

The Manager reaches with one finger to pop open the register. Young Lenny's focus is on the money inside.

Maybe sixty dollars here, the Manager says. A whole lot of it nickels and pennies. Meanwhile, you're standing there with your thumb in your ass and a gun in the other hand.

I said shut it, Young Lenny says.

The door opens. Old Lenny enters.

Hey great, the Manager says. It's a party.

He said to shut it, Old Lenny says to the Manager.

Nothing happening here, mister, Young Lenny tells Old

Lenny. Beat it.

Give me the gun and walk away, Old Lenny says.

In the house's backyard, Roy and Lucinda melt into each other as they dance.

Wendell grips a pint jar of grain alcohol. He sloshes the deep glass toward Roy and Lucinda, an unlit cigarette jammed in the corner of his mouth.

I want this man out of our house, Wendell says.

Head on Roy's shoulder, Lucida laughs. Edna doesn't stir.

Wendell gives Roy a weak shove.

You dummy, Lucinda says.

Roy's knuckles tap Wendell's chin.

Wendell stumbles back, alcohol spilling down his shirt.

Yeah, Roy says. Dummy.

Wendell raises his fists.

Roy hands Lucinda his glass.

Well, if that's the way it's going to be, Roy says.

Wendell swings, misses, his back to Roy. Roy kicks him in the pants. Now Edna is awake and on her feet.

You two stop it, Edna yells.

You're all wet, dummy, Lucinda says.

Lucinda dumps her drink on Wendell and follows it with Roy's. Roy laughs.

Listen to the lady, Roy says. Enough is enough. Now, go wash yourself off. You stink.

Wendell rushes Roy again. Roy catches him in the ear. A blank look crosses Wendell's face, the bent nub of cigarette still clenched in the corner of his mouth.

Here, dummy, Roy says. Allow me.

Roy pulls a lighter from his pocket and lights the end of Wendell's cigarette. The paper flairs for a long moment. Roy and Lucinda turn to pour themselves another drink.

Wendell bursts into flames.

At the hamburger stand, Young Lenny glances down at

the revolver, heavy in his hand.

Folks are fed up with getting pushed around by you little punks, the Manager says, gaining confidence in the chaos.

I said, shut your mouth, Young Lenny says. The gun barrel is shaking.

Give me the gun, Old Lenny says.

You shut up, Young Lenny says. Now.

Walk away, Old Lenny says. Trust me. Now.

Can't do that, Young Lenny says. Too late.

Old Lenny reaches out his hand.

Hand it over, he says.

Young Lenny points the twitching barrel at Old Lenny.

Who are you, he asks.

I'm you when that gun goes off, Old Lenny says.

The Manager takes a step down the counter. The gun swings his way.

Don't get stupid, Young Lenny says. Everybody stop. Let me think.

Old Lenny turns to the Manager.

Listen to him, he says.

The Manager keeps inching.

Not going anywhere, pal, the Manager says. Let's us just sort this out.

The Manager slides a hand beneath the counter. Out of sight, a shotgun hammer snaps back.

Damn it, Old Lenny yells. Don't!

Young Lenny fires. The Manager's shotgun fires. The counter explodes upward. Young Lenny's shot pins the Manager to the wall. Splinters rain down on Young Lenny and Old Lenny. They are stunned, unhurt.

Shit, Old Lenny says.

Sirens in the distance. The Manager slides to a crumpled heap, blood pouring from his chest, shotgun across his lap.

Four-year-old Lenny stands numb at the back door of the house.

Wendell flails, a screaming pillar of fire.

Water, Lucinda, water, Edna wails, stumbling toward the house.

Piled at Roy's feet, Lucinda pulls at her hair, screaming.

Roy laughs and laughs.

The shrieking Fry Cook bursts from the kitchen. He spots the dying Manager and screams some more, sprinting out the front door.

Young Lenny stares down at the smoking gun in his hand. Old Lenny reaches over and takes it away from him.

What's left of Wendell smolders in the backyard as Edna clutches an empty soup pot, sobbing.

Lucinda gathers herself and disappears into the house, dead silent.

Roy spots Four-year-old Lenny standing beside him.

Come on, kid, Roy says. Work to do.

Beneath the streetlights, Roy pulls a loaded-down nylon tarp across the street and into the woods, to the same patch where Old Lenny was struck by lightning. Little Lenny follows close behind, dragging a shovel.

Good lesson here, boy, Roy says, digging a wide hole. Your Daddy, he was just soft is all. So weak he finally up and drowned in it.

Roy sits down next to him in the darkness.

Listen here, he says. You're in the real world now. Think about what I'm going to tell you, now.

Roy's lighter fails to spark. He tries again. It lights Roy's cigarette.

Rich, poor, Roy says, waving the flaming lighter. Don't matter. Other man wants to take his first. Knock you down rather'n learn your name. So all you got to do to get by in this world, find the biggest son of a bitch and beat him half to death for it. Easy as that.

Little Lenny stares into the flame.

That's the plain truth, Roy says. Live by it. Just always remember. Nobody gets the best of old Roy. And that includes you.

Roy's grin sours as the lighter snaps shut.

A handful of Police cars screech into the hamburger stand parking lot, lights flashing, sirens blaring.

Inside, Old Lenny and Young Lenny stare each other down.

Didn't mean to, Young Lenny says.

Old Lenny raises the revolver.

I know, he says. Doesn't matter now.

A single heavy gunshot thuds inside the hamburger stand as the Police rush in to find Young Lenny dead on the floor, the revolver out of reach.

Old Lenny is gone.

BONUS: VALLEY FOOTBALL

Meet us at the park at midnight. Bring your helmet. Keep your mouth shut.

Dirty, tape-covered cleats pound across mismatched turf in the middle of a bright, clear, San Fernando Valley night, gathering momentum past tumbling shoulder pads and grasping arms until . . .

Yeah, I'm probably kind of old for this sort of horseshit, Dan mentions to himself. But, you know what? We're from the Valley. And, sure, there are lots of valleys. Tennessee Valley. Hudson River Valley. Silicon Valley. Nice enough places, I'm sure. But when people say the Valley, you know the one they mean. So later on, when somebody wonders out loud where it was that somebody realized a bunch of grown adults could be this damn happy to pull on pads and clobber each other in a public park in the middle of the night, they need to know. This all started in THE Valley.

. . . the crash of bodies, pads and helmets. A whistle in the distance meets a chorus of chuckles and happy groans, followed by the sirens of approaching police cars.

A couple days ago, heavy, cold, grey rain thuds against the long, sealed windows of an East Coast office building.

In a third-floor cubical farm, low, beige walls stretch as far as the eye can see. The din of humanity is smothering.

Dan works quietly at his desk with a mountain of spreadsheets and binders piled in front of him. His cell phone buzzes on his desk. He mutes it.

A chipper Coworker pops his head over the thin partition.

Psst, he says. Hey! Dan my man! You hear what's happening?

Dan tries to ignore him and keep working, but his Coworker's grin can wait all day. Dan sighs.

What's that, he asks.

Promotions, his Coworker says, delighted.

Really, he says.

Dan's cell phone buzzes on his desk again. He mutes it.

I'm sure of it, his Coworker says. Company stock is through the roof. We're now the eighth largest independent auditing firm in the whole Mid-Atlantic!

Impressive, Dan says.

I'll say, his Coworker says. This is a fantastic organization of which I am proud to be a vital part. You bet. Just ask my Twitter. And you should post something like that too, by the way. They monitor online stuff for sure. Doesn't hurt to say it out loud as well, like in conversations such as these and around people in the bathroom or elevator, if you think of it. Even if you're alone, still great practice. Just one of those Ten Tips To The Top Floor from my daily blog. Sent you the link. Anyhoo, they've been calling folks upstairs all day to give them the good news. Upstairs! I hear there's one of those awesome, deluxe coffee carts up there. No charge. Double shot. Done. Triple, no problem. None. Oh, man, I'm so psyched for free deluxe coffee service!

Dan's cell phone buzzes on his desk again. He mutes it.

Come on, Dan says. Enough.

If you need to take that, I'd never tell, of course, his Coworker says.

No, Dan says. It's these realtors, all of a sudden. About my Mom's house in Los Angeles. I don't know. Rather not think about it right now. Anyway, who do they want?

The realtors, his Coworker asks.

The people upstairs, Dan says. With all the promotions.

Yeah, yeah, right, his Coworker says. Well, from what I can gather, only those of us with our master's degree. Ooh, maybe I shouldn't have mentioned that. Sorry.

That's alright, Dan says. I have one in business administration. In fact, I'm pretty sure everyone on this floor has at least one master's.

This takes some of the wind out of his Coworker's sails.

They do, he asks.

Yep, Dan says.

An officious Floor Manager appears at Dan's cubicle.

Hey, she says. They want to see both you guys upstairs in ten minutes.

This is it, Dan's Coworker says. I should go pee real quick. Hot damn.

Ten minutes later, the cold, thick rain pours down as Dan and his no-longer-cheerful, now former Coworker exit carrying their desk items in boxes. They stand beneath a narrow awning, only slightly out of the rain.

That went poorly, Dan says.

I don't understand, his former Coworker says. Why would they do this? Why? Everything's going so well around here.

Yeah, Dan says. Too well. A company getting bought up like this usually means layoffs. If they don't consolidate, where's the profit, right?

Dan receives a blank stare.

I don't follow you, his former Coworker says.

What's your degree in again, Dan asks.

Third and fourth-century linguistics, he says.

Dan pulls his phone from his pocket and dials.

Both centuries?

I know, his former Coworker says. I don't mention it much because folks seem to clam up around academics. But we can talk all about that. What a day. Nothing left to do but for two old buddies to go drink drink drink our blues away. You betcha. In fact, I think there's a nice wine café . . .

I need to call my wife, Dan says.

Sure, his former Coworker says. I had one of those once too, but, funny thing . . .

It's ringing, Dan says.

Dan's former Coworker wanders off into the rain.

Right, he says. Of course. Well, guess it's just me off to the old bus stop, once again. Ooh. Nice and cold. Brisk! Perfect weather for the first day of the rest of your life.

Hello, says a male voice Dan doesn't expect to hear from his Wife's phone.

Dave, Dan says. How's it going? Weird. I thought I was dialing Julie.

You did, Dave says, dry and smug. She's right here.

Is that my phone, demands a voice in the distance. Who is it? Hello? Crap. Dave, you stupid shit.

Oh, just tell him already, says Dave, stomping away.

Not like this, Julie says. Dan. I can explain. You know it's been different since . . .

Dan hangs up, stunned but somehow not surprised.

The rain pours down. His phone rings again. He answers.

Look, Dan says. I . . .

Hi there, says Dan's Property Manager through the phone. Dan! Wow. So glad to finally reach you. Ritchie Simmons here at Western Valley Property Management. Calling about your late mother's house. The renters are finally out and they turned in the keys this morning. So, if you want me to go ahead and list that puppy through our excellent sales department, well, now really is a great time to . . .

No thanks, Dan says, surprised to hear himself say this.

If this is about our fees, I can assure you, we are very competitive, the Property Manager says quickly. However, perhaps I can talk to my boss . . .

No need, Dan says. I think I'm moving back in.

Well, the Property Manager says, sputtering. Now, I can assure you that if you try to sell this house on your own, you will simply never . . .

How's the weather there today, Dan asks.

Sunny, the Property Manager says. It rained last week, so really nice.

Perfect, Dan says. Thanks.

Dan hangs up and takes a deep breath. He dumps his box of desk stuff in the nearest trash can. The rain stops.

Jets swarm Burbank Airport, climbing dramatically on takeoff. Nothing but sun above a hazy sprawl rolling up into the hills.

An Uber pulls up to the curb. Dan waves, rumpled in the same clothes, no luggage.

You Dan, the Uber Driver asks.

You bet, Dan says.

Dan gets in and they launch into traffic.

Hey, Dan says. Happen to know if that discount liquor mart off Victory's open these days?

With the big smiley face on it, the Uber Driver asks.

Yeah, Dan says.

Rough landing, the Uber Driver asks.

Lousy takeoff, Dan says.

The Uber leaves the freeway and enters a sleepy residential area. They pass a hodgepodge of blue-collar homes and fading strip malls full of dusty mom-and-pops.

Dan takes a pull off a pint bottle wrapped in a paper bag.

West Valley, huh, the Uber Driver says.

Born and raised, Dan says.

Canoga Park, the Uber Driver says.

Much change, Dan asks.

Never, the Uber Driver says. Lots of new buildings, but as long as new people think Winnetka sounds too far away, the rest of the city seems happy to leave us alone.

Yeah, Dan says. I've always said, it's the 405, not the fucking Alps.

The Uber drops Dan off on his childhood front lawn under a clear, blue sky. The yard is littered with oranges from a perky but unattended tree. He finds the pint bottle of liquor in his pocket, takes a pull, and unlocks the front door.

He finds the house empty and wanders room to room. It's eerily quiet. Dust hangs in the air and flickers in the light through the windows.

He unlocks a padlock and opens the creaky garage door.

Stacks of boxes and the house's original furniture are packed to the ceiling.

One by one, Dan replaces end tables and chairs throughout the house. He manages to shove the couch into place all by himself, now wearing an old high school football jersey.

In his childhood bedroom, Dan hangs classic posters from his youth. He has the bed spread to match, covered with sports heroes in action.

He fills a kitchen cabinet with gas station and fast food water glasses covered in cartoon characters.

He hangs a row of family photos in the light spots along the hallway wallpaper where they once were. The last one is a team photo from Dan's junior league football team. He stares at it for a long while.

The garage is now empty, except for his old bicycle, many sizes too small. Dan jumps on the bike. The tires hold.

An ice cream truck plays its song as it passes. Dan counts the loose change in his pocket, finds he has just enough and pedals down the street, following the truck.

Inside the house, Dan's phone rings on the kitchen counter. It stops. A moment later, his message alert beeps. Another moment and it rings again.

On the screen, eight missed calls, seven messages, and the words *Julie Calling*. The screen flashes as the battery dies. Finally, silence.

Meanwhile, a few blocks away, Dan sits on his childhood bicycle, wearing his high school football jersey, eating a popsicle, listening to the birds chirp.

The ice cream truck pulls away, playing its happy song.

Behind him, a garage door opens and Little Lou, same age as Dan, emerges dragging a garden hose. Lou isn't little at all. More like a low brick wall.

Dan, Lou says.

Little Lou, Dan says.

It's just Louis now, he says.

They hug.

Sure it is, Dan says.

That your old bike, Lou asks.

Yeah, Dan says.

Lou spots Dan's popsicle.

Did I hear the ice cream truck, Lou asks.

You did, Dan says.

Be right back, Lou says.

Soon Dan and Lou pedal through the parking lot of a nearby strip mall on bikes way too small for them, both happily eating popsicles.

So then, Dan says. How was the Navy?

Excellent for a long time, Lou says. But I should have taken the hint long before I couldn't fit through the damn hatches anymore. Pop died and I came back to help run the equipment store. I like it. We still do all the little league uniforms. All the local trophies. Bowling's big again. And we own the whole way to the corner, Uncle Tommy and I. The laundromat. The book store. The bar. The diner.

Wow, Dan says.

Yeah, Lou says. Pop bought the whole thing piece by piece on credit, paid it off over time and didn't tell anybody. Always thinking, that guy. Not out loud, of course. None of them really make much. I figure somebody will come along and make it all a gas station someday. With a fast food drive-thru or whatever. But until then. Here we are.

They arrive at Big Lou's Trophies & More and go inside.

The store is stuffed with local sports history. Newspaper clippings, plaques, photos, trophies, as well as a broad collection of new and used sports equipment in varsity sizes.

Uncle Tommy emerges from behind the counter. He's a larger, rounder, older version of Lou, with a '70s-era porno mag in one fist and an unlit cigar in the other. He juggles both in order to shake hands and they end up in a bear hug.

Danny boy, Tommy calls.

How you doing, Tommy, Dan asks.

344

Can't complain, Tommy says. You back?

Looks like it, Dan says.

Tommy's grin lights up the room.

Well, then, he says. Step into my office.

In a cluttered storeroom, Lou, Tommy and Dan share an expertly crafted joint and talk about old times.

Lou, your Dad would have skinned us if he caught us back here like this, Dan says, which makes Uncle Tommy cough happily.

Well, that's progress, Tommy says.

Pop was a lot looser than he let on, Lou says. Just not in how he spoke or thought or dressed or ever did anything in his whole life. Beyond that, big accepting bowl of jello.

Tommy squints at Dan.

You know, Tommy says, I remember that jersey.

Dan looks down at the old high school jersey he's wearing.

Yeah, he asks.

We went through a ton of those senior year, Lou says.

Tommy digs through a shelf of yearbooks.

But that one, Uncle Tommy says. With the extra stripe on the sleeve. We ordered those special. For the big game.

They look at a picture Tommy finds in a yearbook. There are mustaches and penises on every picture on every page.

He's right, Dan says. There is an extra stripe. Keeping up on your artwork, I see.

It's a passion, Tommy says.

Wasn't that big of a game, Lou says.

Trust me, Tommy says. It was big.

State would've been big, Dan says. That was just the end of the season.

Don't sell yourselves short, Tommy says.

Six points short, Dan says. To be exact.

Was a beautiful throw, Tommy says.

Thanks, Dan says.

You know, Old Stone Hands teaches yoga down at the

park, Lou says. Sells real estate. Rents out a hotel by the airport to do these motivational seminars. He's on every other bus bench. Smiling. Drives me crazy. The prick.

Don't call Reggie that, Dan says.

Prick or Stone Hands, Lou asks.

Stone hands, Dan says. He's definitely a prick. But he caught a lot of balls that year.

Not that last one, Lou says.

Long time ago, Dan says.

Doesn't feel that way, Lou says.

Dan digs around a bin and pulls on a helmet without ear pads, joint still dangling from the corner of his mouth.

Still fits, Dan says. What do you think?

I say we go play some ball, Lou says.

On the tennis courts at a nearby public park, Reggie has a ponytail with short hair. He's head-to-toe in workout gear and skin-tight spandex, leading a Senior Yoga Class, also poured into their outfits.

Exhale, Reggie says. And bend lower if you can. That's it. Lower. Lower . . .

The Seniors drop lower in their poses and gravity takes over. They slowly sink to the ground, twisting downward, and stay there, sprawled across their rubber mats.

Excuse me, an Elderly Student says. Is this the right form?

It isn't. Reggie's phone buzzes, he scrolls, tuning them out.

Fantastic, Reggie says. That's perfect. Be very proud. Alright. Let's call it a day, folks. Super work. Give yourselves a big, big hand. Or, you know, whatever. See you on the bus.

None are in a position to clap, but bravely try anyway. More painful groans. Reggie hears a familiar whistle and looks up.

Over on the park playing fields, Lou lines up to long-snap Dan the ball. They wear mismatched helmets and shoulder pads. Tommy blows his whistle again.

That's a nice sound, Tommy says.

We get it, we get it, Lou says.

Quit stalling, Dan says.

You ready, Lou asks.

I said I was ready, Dan says.

Just making sure, Lou says.

Lou snaps a perfect spiral to Dan.

Nice, Dan says.

Yeah, I'm a natural, Lou says.

You've practiced, Dan says.

Me, Lou asks. Nah.

Every night, Tommy says. Now that's the world's weirdest hobby.

Hey, Lou says. Everybody's good at something.

Nice snap there, Little Lou, Reggie yells, now smirking nearby.

The great and powerful Stone Hands, Lou says. Nice bulge.

You'd notice, Reggie says.

Not really, Lou says.

Alright, enough, Dan says.

In the nearby parking lot, Tommy digs around in the back of the store's equipment van, complete with their logo on the side.

Dan tosses Reggie the ball.

Hey, Dan, Reggie says. How's the East Coast?

Cold, Dan says. Mostly, really cold.

That's what I hear, Reggie says. Playing a little catch? Probably wise to get your friend here some exercise before the diabetes sets in.

That pushes Lou an inch too far. Reggie sees this and backpedals a moment before Tommy shoves a helmet and pads into his hands, again taking an opportunity to blow his whistle.

No goofing around, Tommy says.

Thanks and all, Reggie says. But . . .

Tommy blows his whistle. Loud.

Line up, he yells.

Ah, screw it, Reggie says. I got a minute.

Soon the football floats in a high arch across the sky. It lands in Lou's arms. His legs start slowly, powerfully, like a locomotive leaving the station.

By the fifth step, Lou's at maximum velocity as he collides head-on with Reggie and Dan, who bring him down like a rhino.

Tommy blows his whistle. They help each other to their feet.

That was awesome, Lou says.

My turn, Reggie says. My turn!

The ball again tumbles out of the sky, this time into Reggie's hands. He gains speed quickly, fluidly.

Dan charges toward him, picking a careful angle of attack. At the last moment, Reggie swerves gracefully on his toes and leaves Dan in the grass far behind him.

Sprinting, Reggie takes a prideful glance over his shoulder. As he turns back, he meets Lou like a stack of cinder blocks. The impact sends them sprawling.

Tommy blows his whistle. Laughing, they help each other to their feet.

But they're not the only ones laughing. Three athletic College Kids mock them from basketball courts in the distance.

The former teammates look to each other, then to Tommy. They all see a chance for some fun.

Say, young fellas, Tommy yells. You interested in playing some ball?

Soon, the three College Kids are in shoulder pads and helmets. They face off with Reggie, Lou and Dan. The two teams size each other up.

Alright, already, College Kid #3 says. Let's do this.

Dan holds out the ball.

No, no, College Kid #2. Please. You first.

Alright, Dan says.

Yeah, see, we were always taught to respect our elders, says College Kid #1.

Yes, Lou says. That's probably a good idea.

They line up. Lou snaps Dan the ball.

Lou blocks his guy while the other two go after Reggie. Dan puts the ball right between them and into Reggie's hands for a quick score. The College Kids shake it off and regroup.

That was luck, College Kid #1 says. Give me that ball.

They line up. College Kid #1 takes the snap, dropping back as Lou thunders down on him, his blocker on his back in the dirt. Much quicker than Lou, he flees sideways, but doesn't see Dan blitzing until the moment before a vicious sack.

Dude, College Kid #2 says. Weak. Give me that.

College Kid #2 takes over, lining up for the next snap. Lou again puts his blocker on his back and gives chase, but he has time to throw.

The pass is beautiful and right on target, which Reggie anticipates and takes it back for a pick-six.

I can't play right in half-pads, man, College Kid #3 says. Not at full-speed. That's how you get hurt, you know.

Yeah, College Kid #2 says. These old creeps don't know the science of it.

Easy there, captain science, Reggie says.

What'd you say, old mister ponytail man, College Kid #2 asks.

The ponytail thing hits home.

Hey, Reggie says.

We don't even have cleats, College Kid #3 says.

Us either, Dan says.

Just a friendly game, Lou says.

My ass, College Kid #1 says. What, you do this three-man shit to hustle people?

Maybe, Reggie says. Why? Is that a thing?

I don't know, College Kid #1 says. Geez.

Man, if you gave us a day to put a team together, you'd see what it's all about, College Kid #3 says.

Alright, Tommy says.

What, College Kid #3 grunts.

Yeah, how about seven on seven, Tommy says. Right here. Tomorrow night. I got all the helmets and pads you kids'll need. Shoulder. Elbow. Thigh. Maxi.

The College Kids exchange a look, wondering if they're in over their heads. They peel off their equipment and throw it in the dirt.

Fine, College Kid #1 says. We'll be here. But if you're not, we're coming after you.

Right back at you, kid, Lou says.

Great, old man, College Kid #3 says.

Not for nothing, but your banter really needs work, Lou says.

Huh, College Kid #3 asks.

Exactly, Lou says.

The College Kids sulk away in a hurry.

I know some folks, Reggie says. Receivers.

Couple of my Navy buddies are born blocking backs, Lou says. I'll call them.

Tomorrow night, then, Dan says.

Perfect, Lou says.

They begin to walk their separate ways.

Oh, hey, Reggie says.

Yeah, Lou asks.

This was fun, Reggie says.

They all agree.

In the parking lot, daylight dims as Reggie's class waits anxiously for him on their bus.

That night, Uncle Tommy and his girlfriend Linda watch the television news over loud thwacking sounds coming from their backyard. They both have their own TV remotes.

My goodness, Linda says. How long's he been out there?

From the backyard: Thwack!

Leave him be. Just working off some nerves, Tommy says. He wants to play well tomorrow. Those kids today were jerks.

He volumes up the TV. She volumes it down.

It's nice that Danny's home, she says.

It sure is, he says.

From the backyard: Thwack!

He volumes up. She volumes down.

He'll find Lou a nice girl, she says. You watch.

Linda, he says. Please. Button it. When we lost Gina, it caught him off guard. That's all. Normal to need a chance to regroup after that.

From the backyard: Thwack!

He volumes up. She volumes down.

Next month is six years, Tommy, Linda says.

He doesn't like to talk about it, Tommy says. Neither do I.

I'm only saying, Linda says.

From the backyard: Thwack!

Linda, Tommy says. Leave him be.

Just so nice that Danny's home, Linda says. That's all.

From the backyard: Thwack!

He volumes up. She volumes down.

That's it, Tommy says. The moment you fall asleep, I'm taking your batteries.

Oh, honey, Linda says. As if I don't hide extra.

In the backyard, Lou long-snaps a pile of footballs into a distant archery target. Twack! Dead center. He grabs another. Twack! The dents show he's both accurate and precise.

The back door opens. Linda pops her head outside. Lou stands to catch his breath.

Honey, we're going out to eat in a minute, Linda says. You want to come with?

No thanks, Lou says. I'm going to do this for a while and

get some sleep.

Should we bring you something back, she asks.

That's fine, Lou says. I have half a sandwich from lunch in there. I should finish that.

Going to Mariucchi's, she says.

There's a long pause. Lou picks up a football.

Then maybe just a chop salad, he says.

Oh, now, she says. You do need your strength.

Lou thinks this over.

True, he says. Maybe only a couple of those little raviolis. But the appetizer, though. And I guess a calzone for later. But the veggie one. With ham and sausage. But that'll do it.

I'm getting the chocolate lava cheesecake, she says. I'll need you to split it with me.

Nah, he says. That's alright.

Otherwise, it'll go to waste, Lou, she says.

Yeah, Lou says. Alright.

Lou thwacks another ball into the target.

Thanks, honey, she says. Sure nice Danny's back, huh?

Yeah, Lou says. Sure is.

Reggie's skincare regimen involves a table stacked with creams and potions. He wears a brightly colored mud mask and studies his ponytail in a long mirror.

In the corner are piled Reggie's real estate yard signs and boxes of brochures from the self-help seminars he teaches. All featuring his same grinning glamour shots.

A timer bell dings on a fancy plastic gadget.

Kakorrhaphiophobia, the electronic Vocabulary Builder says. *The overwhelming and paralyzing fear of failure. In a sentence: Due to my constant study and self-improvement, I no longer suffer from Kakorrhaphiophobia.*

He does ten quick pushups while reciting the vocabulary word.

Kakorrhaphiophobia, Reggie says. The overwhelming and paralyzing fear of failure . . . With constant study and improvement, I no longer suffer from Kakorrhaphiophobia.

Correct, the Vocabulary Builder says. *Now in French.*

Reggie groans and does ten more.

Uh, he says. Kakorrhaphiophobia. L'écrasante et une . . .
Paralysante de défaillance . . . Raison de mon étude . . .
Kakorrhaphiophobia!

His walls are covered in motivational posters and yellow
Post-its with inspirational reminders. A full-size banner
reads *Believe In YOU!*

Correct, the Vocabulary Builder says. *Now in Portuguese.*

Reggie groans and walks over to a large to-do list on the
wall. He finds a pen and begins to write: *Google Portuguese.*

That's a new one, Reggie says. Now how the hell do you
spell Portuguese?

He gets about halfway through the word. A stack of mail
distracts him. He opens an envelope and finds a letter. *Ding.*

Too slow, the Vocabulary Builder says. *Now in Thai . . .*

Oh, come on, Reggie says. No longer require a personal
trainer as part of my personal staff? That's what you think,
lady. Ah, final check enclosed.

Reggie searches the envelope. No check. *Ding.*

Too slow, Vocabulary Builder says. *Now in Bengali . . .*

Of course not, Reggie says. That cheap . . . Crooked . . .

A different timer dings, this one from the bathroom.

Reggie carefully scrubs his face in the bathroom mirror.
From the other room, the Vocabulary Builder *dings* again.

Too slow, it says. *Now in Urdu.*

Reggie sighs in a moment of self-doubt. He opens his
medicine cabinet mirror to reveal a signed photo of Richard
Simmons, with the words: Reggie, you CAN do it!

No Richard, Reggie says. WE can do it.

Reggie returns to scrubbing. That was the lift he needed.

Dan stands under the shower in his tiny childhood
bathroom. After years sitting at a desk, the afternoon left him
stiff and sore. He slowly crumples with a long, painful

moan.

Later in the kitchen, wearing an old concert t-shirt and sweatpants. He finds his phone where he left it on the counter, battery dead.

Dan leaves and returns with a charger. He plugs it into the wall. Then the phone. The phone slowly returns to life. Dan stands for a moment, watching the screen load.

But then Dan unplugs the phone, sweeping everything into an empty drawer. He shuts off the light and walks out.

Yeah, he says. That feels a lot better.

The next night at the park, Tommy hands out equipment to a larger group of College Kids surrounding his van. The field is lit by the bright lights of the parking lot and a huge moon.

Dan stands at midfield with the football. Lou and Reggie arrive with their new players. They're all in plain uniforms with the matching, primer-blue helmets.

Alright, you guys, this here is the Lopamauas, Lou says. They're cousins. We served together for five years and kept getting put in the same detail. They're from Samoa and, believe me, they pack a wallop.

Both are muscular bowling balls with big hands, huge arms and very quick feet.

Lagi, says Lagi.

Loto, says Loto.

Fellas, Dan says.

And this is Lance and Janice, Reggie says. Friends of mine from the gym. Lance is a rugby champion and only speaks German. But he LOVES football. Janice is transitioning.

Lance and Janice are both wiry and tall.

That's right, Janice says. I was a cornerback at USC, but these days I feel much more like a free safety.

Then let's play some ball, Dan says.

Ja, Lance says. Football! Let's go!

The teams meet at midfield, where Tommy waits with his whistle and a large, shiny coin. The College Kids wear dark jerseys and primer green helmets.

Seven on seven, Tommy says. Four and out. Take the ball from midfield. First to three scores wins. Questions?

Who do you think you are, College Kid #1 asks. The ref?

Yes, Tommy says. Because I have a whistle. Once I blow it, though, I'm going over to my van to drink and watch you get your ass kicked. So, call it.

Call what, College Kid #1 says.

The coin flip, Tommy says, patiently.

Oh, yeah, right, College Kid #1 says. Heads.

Tommy's coin tumbles through the air and lands on heads.

Good luck, moron, Tommy says.

Tommy hands College Kid #1 the ball and blows his whistle.

The teams line up around midfield with College Kid #1 at QB. A quick dump pass falls incomplete.

Dan's team looks to each other with confidence. So far, so good. Maybe they can do this. They line up again.

The second play is a pitch and sweep to the sideline. The Green team meets the Lopamauas head-on for no gain.

The Blue Team lines up a third time, feeling good.

But the next play is a QB sneak. College Kid #1 drops back a step, then takes off as his receivers block and form a neat, open lane. He then simply outruns everybody.

Well, shit, Dan says.

Spectators from the nearby bike paths and basketball courts wander over to watch, drawn by the sound of colliding equipment. Soon they're all furiously posting and texting about the spontaneous game.

Tommy and Linda look around, confused by the growing crowd staring into their phones.

Excuse me, Linda says. Silly question, but what are you doing?

355

A High School Girl is watching a live stream from someone else in the parking lot filming the game.

Uhm, the High School Girl says. Watching the game?

But they're not playing in your phone, Tommy says.

Tommy points to the players on the field.

She holds out her phone, streaming the game.

I don't know what you mean, she says.

The Blue Team breaks their huddle and finds the Green Team waiting at the line, grinning like idiots.

Something funny, you guys, Dan asks.

Naw, just talking about where we'll go celebrate after we win, College Kid #3 says. In about ten minutes.

Hey, College Kid #1 says. Can we keep these helmets, like as a souvenir?

No, Lou says.

Lou snaps the ball and pulls left. It's a handoff to Logi. Lato lead blocks. Together they are a freight train. It takes fifteen yards and the entire Green Team to bring them down.

Now it's the Green Team's turn to share a worried look.

The next play is a hook pass to Reggie, with a devastating downfield block from Janice. As Reggie trots into the end zone, Janice helps up the College Kid she flattened.

Listen, now, keep your eyes open or you're going to get hurt out here, Janice says.

Screw you, lady, College Kid #4 says.

Why, thank you, young man, Janice says.

The Green team lines up for an obvious running play. The Blue Team members all spot this and blitz, descending on College Kid #1, who tucks the ball and takes a beating. Lou leans over him.

These helmets are for sale, though, Lou says. Tell you what, I'll knock ten bucks off yours, since we're getting your blood all over it and all.

In a closet-sized office at the nearest police station, a burly, angry Police Sergeant spills coffee across a stack of reports as his speaker phone squawks.

Crap bucket, the Sergeant says.

Dispatch on one, his phone speaker barks. *Noise complaint.*

He grabs the receiver.

What, the Sergeant says. So? How many? Why tell me? Have a unit send them home. I'm busy. What? Like, tackle? No, yeah. Huh. No, you're right. Good looking out. Tell you what, let me go ahead and take this one myself. I'll let you know. Yeah, no. Thanks.

The Sergeant slams the phone down as an Officer pokes his head around the corner.

What's happening, boss, he asks.

Clean this up before I get back, the Sergeant says and rushes out the door.

At the park, the Green Team scores again, celebrating with the crowd.

The Blue Team takes the ball, looking tired. Reggie lines up across from College Kid #2.

That's two, College Kid #2 says. One more, we win.

Hey, a numbers major, Reggie says. Tell you what, I'll tie it up here. Then we'll talk again. Alright? Alright.

Once I get ahold of that lame ponytail, you won't be talking so smart, dude, College Kid #2 says.

I genuinely hope you try, Reggie says.

Lou snaps Dan the ball and Reggie explodes downfield.

A timed pass is already waiting for Reggie as he puts out his hands. College Kid #2 is a step quicker and knows it. But rather than aiming for his body, he reaches out for Reggie's bouncing ponytail.

Gotcha, College Kid #2 says.

As he yanks the ponytail, which Reggie cut off and tucked into the back of his helmet, it falls free in his hand. College Kid #2 tumbles to the ground as Reggie crosses into the end zone.

The Green Team stands angrily over College Kid #2.

What was that, College Kid #1 asks. What happened?

College Kid #2 looks down at the ponytail in his hand, bound at one end by rubber bands, with a note written on one of Reggie's yellow Post-its: *Nice try, dummy.*

What a prick, College Kid #2 says.

Alright, College Kid #1 says. That's it. Line up.

The College Kids rush to midfield before the Blue Team can catch its breath.

Let's finish this right now, College Kid #3 says.

College Kid #1 snaps the ball before the Blue Team can get back into position. But most of the Green Team isn't ready either.

Confusion and a botched handoff send the ball bouncing across the grass, which begins a mad scramble with both teams wrestling for the ball as it keeps popping free.

At the last moment, Lance swoops in to recover. As the players part, he thrusts the ball into the air.

Fumble, Lance yells. *Ja!*

Tommy blows his whistle and trots onto the field with water bottles under his arm, noticing the police sirens in the distance.

Alright, Tommy says. Catch your breath. Make it quick.

Cool, College Kid #3 says. Can we get one of those?

Sure, right after you fuck off, Tommy says.

The Blue Team huddles up. They look around at the growing crowd and the angry College Kids across from them.

If we ever do this again, no kids, Dan says.

And no crowds, Reggie says.

And for goodness sake, no crying, Janice says.

Tears stand out in Lou's eyes and roll down his cheeks.

I can't help it, he sniffles. I just love this game so much.

Tommy arrives at the huddle with his best Vince Lombardi voice.

Alright, you guys, Tommy says. I'll make this fast. Hell of a show you're putting on out there. Hell of a show. But we're not done yet. This's our shot. Time to bring it home. Lucky for you, you got something those little shits don't even know about yet.

They pass the water bottles around.

No idea what you're talking about, Lou says.

Old Man Strength, Tommy says.

He's lost them.

What, Reggie says.

When you're a kid, you've got all the energy in the world, Tommy says. You can piddle around all day trying to get a window unstuck. But us, we don't have time for that crap. We take one big shot at it. And we make it count. All at once. Bang. Pow. Window closed. Or broken. Whichever. But not stuck, that's for sure. It's what you call Old Man Strength. And it's real.

Yeah, Dan says. But . . .

Hey, Tommy says. Any of you guys ever try to fight your Dad?

They all nod

How'd it go, he asks.

They all agree: Poorly.

Alright, Tommy says, trotting for the sidelines. So, what'll it be?

Deep slant left, Dan says.

No, Reggie says.

Yes, Dan says.

So, Janice asks. What about it?

That's the last play we ever ran in high school, Lou says.

You're sure, Reggie says.

You know I am, Dan says.

Then I am too, Reggie says.

The Green Team breaks huddle and strides to the line like the Spartans at Thermopylae. The Blue Team catches their vibe and counters with an angry energy all of their own.

Lou sets his hand on the the ball as Dan drops back into the shotgun formation. Muscles tense up and down the line.

Here we go, Dan says. And . . .

Blurp. Red and blue lights flash in the parking lot. Cops fan out to disperse the impromptu crowd.

Step away from the football and get flat on the ground, the Police Sergeant says through a bullhorn.

Aw, come on, guys, we got time for one more, Lou says.

Somewhere in the distance, a shotgun shell snaps into place.

Seems unwise to ask me to repeat myself, says the Sergeant through the bullhorn.

Both teams hit the ground.

Beneath a wash of flickering lights in the police station interrogation room, Dan, Lou and Reggie are shackled side by side. The menacing Sergeant looms over them.

So, I suppose we've identified you three super geniuses as the ringleaders here, the Sergeant says.

I have repeatedly asked for my attorney, Reggie says.

And I've repeatedly informed you that you are not under arrest, the Sergeant says. Though public nuisance calls like this are something we do take seriously. Very seriously.

Lou rattles his chains.

So then, what's this, he asks.

Don't worry about that, the Sergeant says. Minor mix up with the keys. The right ones will be along in a moment or two. Or three. Does serve to focus your attention, though, doesn't it?

You can't keep people from playing football together, Dan says.

Football, the Sergeant asks. You mean like a secret, tackle football fight club, operating in the middle of the night, less than a mile from my station? Maybe, maybe not. Though, I do have one question.

Yeah, Dan asks.

Those helmets of yours come in black and white, the Sergeant asks.

The Sergeant's in.
I'll make some calls, Lou says.

BONUS: THE TROP

Kitchenettes and monthly rates for characters on the down and out

Grand Opening shout balloons and banners covering a luxury car lot wedged onto a corner in aging East Hollywood.

Inside, at the complimentary coffee bar, Ralph L. Bitters, Certified Public Accountant, gruff by nature, unfriendly for sport, in cheap hair dye and a secondhand suit, is frustrated by a Cheerful Customer reaching for everything he's reaching for.

By all means, Ralph says and doesn't mean it. After you.

The Cheerful Customer fumbles under his glare.

Buying a car, he asks.

No, Ralph says.

Half-off oil change he asks.

What, Ralph barks.

Cool place, he says.

It's new, Ralph says.

Oh, you from this neighborhood, he asks.

Yes, I am, Ralph says. I came here when most of these palm trees were children. Built my various businesses. Watched the world change from these sidewalks. Then one day I couldn't find a way to leave. The streets bring me right back. The bus only stops on my corner. Did try to accept it, for a while, at least. But if it's all turning into this, I'm driving away as fast and as far as a half-price oil change will take me. And I am not coming back.

That got dark quick and the Cheerful Customer, still juggling sugar packets and lids, spills half his coffee.

Here, you go ahead, he says. I'll just, uhm, yeah, you go first.

Why, thank you, Ralph says.

Outside in the service pickup lane, coffee in hand, Ralph waves a twenty at a disinterested Dealership Employee.

THE TROP

The Employee is climbing out of a large and very
expensive grey sedan.
Here you are, my good man, Ralph says. Leave it
running.
Ralph hops in with a wave. The car takes off.
At the same moment, the Cheerful Customer emerges
from inside the dealership, coffee in one hand, service
receipt in the other.
Hi, he says. Grey sedan?
As the puzzled Employee blinks at him, the now empty
luxury car buries itself into a light post at the far end of the
parking lot. Airbags deploy for no one, horn blaring.
Ralph now sips his coffee beside them, only irritated.
Well, that didn't work, Ralph says.
Whoa, the Dealership Employee says. Are you alright?
Sure, Ralph says. I've been dead for years.
Wait, the no longer cheerful Customer says. Is that my
car?

Every day, sunset leaves a technicolor glow above the
classic, aging, and very cheap Tropically Motor Lodge. The
local landmark enjoys one constant season, except in June,
when it's cloudy.
Ralph stomps through the door of the motel office,
already muttering and frustrated, then finds the
complimentary coffee pot empty.
Oh, for all holy hell, Lloyd, he says. You need to always
have hot coffee here for the customers. Get in the game, boy.
Behind the counter, Lloyd, Ralph's sweet and dim-witted
nephew, is concerned.
You shouldn't drink so much coffee, Uncle Ralph, he
says.
So that what, Ralph asks. I don't get another kidney
stone?
Didn't work again this time, Lloyd asks.
I'm still standing here, Ralph says. Aren't I?

363

A chipper Nerd-Hipster Zombie, boyishly handsome
except for his drooping skin and bones poking out here and
there, drags a dead foot through the office door. He hauls a
loose stack of library books under his arm.

Hi, he says. I heard that you are, you know, cool about
the people who stay here and stuff?

At least the advertising still works, Ralph says.

That's us, Lloyd says.

The exhausted Zombie is relieved. He sets his stack of
books on the counter.

Great, the Nerd-Hipster Zombie says. Room for one,
please.

Books, huh, Lloyd says. Cool. Books.

Yeah, the Nerd-Hipster Zombie says. City College starts
Tuesday, so I thought I'd get started.

Lloyd doesn't see the connection.

Say, kid, Ralph says. You want hot coffee when you walk
in here, right?

No thanks, the Nerd-Hipster Zombie says. It's kind of
rough on my tummy.

Outside the office window, at an umbrella table beside
the pool, Masked Lucha Libre Sisters play cards along with
an authentic eye-patch-wearing Sea Pirate and huge-haired
Lost Time Traveler in a silver jumpsuit.

Gin, me-maties, the Pirate says.

In my time it's called Blarnx, the Time Traveler says.
Much more fun sounding, if you ask me. Blarnx! Yes. No
comparison.

My doubloons either way, the Pirate says.

The Pirate gathers his loot. They are playing with
buttons.

Nearby, an old pickup overflowing with chickens
bounces its way into the parking lot. A pigtailed Farmer's
Daughter climbs out with a suitcase.

. . . no, no, she says. This is it, I guess. Thanks for the lift.
Sorry about Pa. That squirrel shot usually works itself out in

a day or two . . .

The clucking truck squeals off, feathers flying, passing the glowing sign for a tiny, built-in diner that serves *Breakfast Around The Clock.*

Inside the mostly empty, grungy, ancient diner, an ageless waitress with the name tag Carol hovers a hot pot of coffee from table to table.

That nice Princess lady is, she says.

A Building Developer and Banker in expensive suits look up from a stack of legal papers and balance sheets. Mid-conversation, they are crammed into a cramped booth.

Excuse me, the Banker asks.

She tops off their cups.

She's really from Los Angeles, Carol says. You said nobody's from here. That everybody worth a damn is actually from someplace else.

You heard that just now, the Developer asks. But you were the whole way back in the kitchen.

That nice lady was on a TV show, Carol says. Met a real Prince. And then, don't you know, she became a genuine, real-life-thing, Princess of England! Plus, then she got to tell them all where to stick it!

The Banker and Developer exchange shrugs.

So, the Developers says.

So, she says. See? There's folks worth a damn from every place!

Point made, Carol grins as she walks away.

You were right, Banker says, this time a lot softer. This place is weird. And it'll sure make a great parking garage. Pedestrian malls do need plenty of parking.

You buy it, I'll build it, the Developer says.

They enthusiastically shake hands, drop cash on the table and hustle out the diner door.

By now Carol's behind the counter, pouring coffee into half-empty cups, whether the customers are still there or not.

Well, now, those were a couple of odd birds, she says. But

you know what you don't do? Judge. Still . . . I'm sorry, but I do find that guys in those fancy suits make my skin crawl.

At the end of the counter, in a threadbare costume and scary makeup, Creeps The Clown enjoys a large stack of pancakes. His voice is disturbingly friendly and calm.

You got that right, Carol, he says.

In broad daylight, the motel is an affordable dump with charm, snoozing beneath eighty years of touch-up paint and sordid history, on a dusty side street devoted to pawnshops, barbers, dive bars and palm trees.

The sparkling blue pool forms a parking lot oasis. The person floating on a inflatable raft looks dead, but it's just the Nerd-Hipster Zombie.

A minivan with Missouri plates parks near the office door. Proud parent stickers across the back window, include: *Don't Blame Us, Our Kids Are In College.*

The concerned Empty-Nester Mom squints at the motel while the Empty-Nester Dad happily jots trip mileage in a little book.

Father, is this the right place, she asks.

You bet, he says. See there, Mother, you've got yourself a pool and everything. I asked the internet just like you said. Plenty of rooms available. Quite the bargain, too. Must be the off-season.

The faded motel sign agrees with him: *Bargain Rates. Kitchenettes. Color TV. Pool. Vacancy! Daily-Weekly-Monthly. No questions asked. Health department and fumigation certificates are current and posted in office.*

Yes, she says. But did you only go by the price or also by the stars?

Well, now, I drove, so you'll have to find the movie stars all on your own, he laughs.

No, she says. The yellow stars. The ones they put next to the name of the place.

Oh, he says. I'm pretty sure this had one of those. Why?

Inside the motel diner, Carol sorts silverware and chatters endlessly from behind the counter to anybody listening.

... Aunt Joanie, you know, she stood right up and she said, gentlemen, everybody looks good in a cowboy hat, and left, Carol says. Didn't even put her pants back on. Bless her sweet heart.

The Empty Nesters shuffle wide-eyed through the door. They find themselves face to face with a wall of smiling black and white headshots covered in looping, illegible signatures.

See, here's your stars right here, the Empty-Nester Dad says.

Joseph Cotton, the Empty-Nester Mom reads. Cary Grant. Jack Klugman. They all ate here? My.

Suddenly, Carol is standing between them, holding menus.

Aw, honey, Carol says. We got these when the dry cleaner burned down up the street. A little charred around the edges, but still nice to look at.

So, then, the Empty-Nester Mom says, disappointed. Celebrities don't come in here?

Don't you worry, Carol says. This place is full of characters.

But no famous actors or performers, she asks.

Soupy Sales did stay here for a short, short while in the 1970s, Carol says. Such a gentle, tender man.

Carol wanders off with the menus, wistful and heartbroken by the memory.

Sprawled on his raft in the parking lot pool, fully clothed, sunglasses on, the Nerd-Hipster Zombie hears a room door open and pretends not to eavesdrop.

On the second floor of the motel, just above the pool, a Traveling Salesman pulls back on a rumpled suit, an oversized and jangling samples case in tow, as he's shoved out the door by the impatient Farmer's Daughter.

. . . alright, then, anyway, the Traveling Salesman says. As I was saying, uhm, earlier, our platinum juicer-plus-blender is simply . . .

She's all pigtails, freckles, cut-off jeans . . .

Yes, the Farmer's Daughter says. I heard you the first time.

. . . and a sudden, irritated look that sends him scurrying.

No offense, lady, but you sure run hot and cold, the Traveling Salesman says.

Tell it walking, pal, she says.

Fine, he says. Swell! Well, for that, you can just keep my card anyway, in case you or any of your friends have any further questions! Goodbye and remember our group discount!

The Traveling Salesman straightens his tie and storms off.

Her mood shifts when she notices the Nerd-Hipster Zombie floating in the pool.

Hey there, the Farmer's Daughter says.

He lifts his shades.

Hi, the Nerd-Hipster Zombie says, surprised. Wait, you mean me?

What're you doing, she asks.

I felt like I should get some sun, he says.

With all your clothes on, she asks.

I have boney knees, he says. And elbows.

Lots of people do, she says.

Yeah, he says. But I mean just the bones.

There is a mournful cry from one of the rooms.

Curses, cries The Great Figueroa. Curses! Curses!

With a splash in the distance, the Farmer's Daughter and the soaking wet Nerd-Hipster Zombie rush to Figueroa's open door.

They find The Great Figueroa in a decades-old, velvet-lined tuxedo with matching top hat and cape, his face in his hands, sobbing melodramatically.

THE TROP

And furthermore, curse it all, The Great Figueroa cries.
Hey, mister, the Nerd-Hipster Zombie says. You alright?
Figueroa gathers himself into a thoughtful pose. The
classically trained magician lost a few steps over the years,
but he's kind of a silver fox and knows it.

Ah, hello, Figueroa says. It's nothing. Thank you. I may
have misplaced something quite dear to me.

What did you lose, the Farmer's Daughter asks.

A coin of some value, Figueroa says. Curse my doddering
mind.

Tell you what, you ease up on the cursing, we'll help you
find your coin, the Farmer's Daughter says.

We, the Nerd-Hipster Zombie wonders to himself out
load. Yeah, sure we will. Us. The two of us. Here. Both.

I'm afraid you don't understand, Figueroa says.

Come on, the Farmer's Daughter says. Where'd you see it
last?

The room is packed to the ceiling with the props from
Figueroa's magic act. He raises his palm and eyebrows
dramatically.

Right here in the palm of my hand, he says with a quick
flourish.

They all look. No coin.

Darn, I thought that might do it, Figueroa says.

Alright, the Farmer's Daughter says. Take us to the
beginning.

Figueroa lifts a giant, dusty book from an end table,
opening it carefully to a specific page.

I will confess, Figueroa says. I was attempting a new
trick.

That's an old book for a new trick, the Farmer's Daughter
says.

I'm only up to 1835 at the library, Figueroa says.

What happened, she asks.

I sneezed, Figueroa says. At the very moment I was to
focus on the person in whose pocket my coin will appear. Yet

369

I must have seen a face for the coin to disappear. Someone from around the motel, I assume. Sadly, I do not recall who. It was a very big sneeze. The trouble is, I must speak a very special and specific phrase to whomever it is for the coin to rematerialize.

Ooh, Nerd-Hipster Zombie says. Try me.

Yeah, try us, the Farmer's Daughter says.

Right, us, the Nerd-Hipster Zombie says. Try us.

Figueroa seems concerned.

Are you certain, he asks.

Not if you keep stalling, the Farmer's Daughter says.

With a flourish, Figueroa flutters his hands and quickly wraps his long fingers around the sides of her skull. His eyes close dramatically as he concentrates.

Quickly, Figueroa says. Whisper in my ear . . . What was the name of . . . Your first . . . Pet?

Thank you for saying pet, the Farmer's Daughter says.

She whispers in his ear.

Alika-bippity-stinkotheferret-karramm-kazzam, Figueroa says.

What now, she asks.

The coin should be somewhere on your person, Figueroa says.

She checks her pockets.

Maybe behind your ear, the Nerd-Hipster Zombie says.

That's a myth, Figueroa says.

The Farmer's Daughter stops. There's something in her bra. She digs around a moment and finds . . . A three of clubs.

Is this your card, she asks.

Sadly, no, Figueroa says.

Then whose is it, she asks.

Haven't the faintest, Figueroa says.

Do me, the Nerd-Hipster Zombie says. Do me!

With a flourish, Figueroa flutters his hands and wraps his long fingers around the sides of the Nerd-Hipster Zombie's skull.

Quickly, now, Figueroa says. The middle name of the very first person you . . .

Figueroa pauses sheepishly.

Hey, the Nerd-Hipster Zombie says. I what? Oh. Hey!

My apologies, Figueroa says. I do not get to choose the necessary details.

The Farmer's Daughter grins.

Yeah, she says. Don't question the trick!

The Nerd-Hipster Zombie whispers in Figueroa's ear.

Very well then, he says. Shimballa-pocus-mocus-heylike-becoolman-Imaworkingonit-ok!

A small, white egg slowly emerges from the Zombie's mouth. Figueroa cracks the egg. A tiny bird pops out and circles the room before disappearing out the door.

Maybe that bird took your coin, the Farmer's Daughter says.

This may be worse than I imagined, Figueroa says.

In the diner, Carol sets large breakfast plates between the Empty Nesters' coffee cups, talking constantly to no one in particular.

. . . though I will be traveling soon, so I really should check the weather, Carol says. What's it like where they grow those really nice cantaloupes? Maybe I'll go there.

The confused Empty Nesters aren't sure if she's asking them.

Mother, the Empty-Nester Dad says. Do you know about cantaloupes?

No, the Empty-Nester Mom says. Not a thing.

That's so sweet, traveling with your Mother, Carol says.

Figueroa sits on his bed and sobs woefully. The Farmer's Daughter flips through his dusty book of magic.

None of this makes any sense, the Farmer's Daughter says.

You're telling me, Figueroa says.

Meanwhile, the Nerd-Hipster Zombie fails to look cool, leaning on a hunk of velvet stage dressing which begins to tumble. He tries to steady it, but weighs almost nothing himself, and together they slide slowly to the floor. He pops up, pretending it didn't happen.

I'll just put that right there.

Well, the Farmer's Daughter says. Sounds like we are definitely going to need to figure out whose pocket you were aiming at in the first place.

Pocket, he cries. Yes! Of course!

Figueroa rushes out. The Farmer's Daughter and the Nerd-Hipster Zombie follow him to the end of the floor and down the steps. Figueroa knocks at an open door.

A proper English Butler steps into the sunlight and raises an eyebrow, holding a silver teapot in one hand and a scouring pad in the other, wearing only a kitchen smock, dark socks, hard shoes and white gloves,.

My goodness, the English Butler says. Must this go on all day?

Last time, I promise, Figueroa says.

Very well, then, the English Butler says.

Figueroa flutters his hands and quickly wraps his long fingers around the sides of the Butler's skull.

Ready, he asks.

Yes, yes, the English Butler says.

Hold on, the Nerd-Hipster Zombie says. Don't you have to ask him like a question or something?

No, this one's always the same, Figueroa says. Fi-la-sha-da-pip-pip-twolumps-butnodairy!

The English Butler holds out his hands. Figueroa reaches into the Butler's apron pocket to find . . . A silver teaspoon.

Thank you, the English Butler says. I was looking for that. And, again, I never say pip pip.

My pleasure, Figueroa says, coldly. And I've heard you.

They are best friends with only their mutual disdain in

common.

Fine, but then, the Nerd-Hipster-Zombie says. Who's next?

No one, Figueroa says.

No one, the Nerd-Hipster Zombie says. Why?

Thank you all for your concern, Figueroa says. There's been a terrible mistake.

So, the Farmer's Daughter says. You didn't lose your coin?

Figueroa mournfully removes his hat. A rabbit pops its head out and looks around.

Oh yes, my coin is gone, Figueroa says. But what I've really lost is everything else. Time is undefeated, my friends. So perhaps the time has finally come to take off this hat for good. My mistake was leaving the protective arms of the Society Of Actual Magicians for the performance world. I was too brash. Why must I always speak my mind? Why must I crave the spotlight? Damn my pride! Yet! I ask you! If real magic is not to be enjoyed, what good is it anyway? Not now, Renaldo.

The rabbit shrugs and disappears back into the hat.

That's enough of that, says a gravelly voice nearby.

They turn to find a classic Cowboy, from his check shirt to his boots and kerchief, though no hat, twirling a lasso beneath a palm tree. His voice is rough, gravelly and low.

Thank you, Figueroa says. But unless you're looking to purchase some fairly used capes and wands . . .

The Cowboy silences him with a raised hand and a nod.

Now, he says, voice rolling slowly toward them. I couldn't help but hear you talking, and I can only hold my tongue for so long. Crossing the desert, you learn a few things. Sure, I've felt that desperate urge to plunk yourself down in the dirt for good. Give up. Surrender to the elements. That's all on you and I don't judge. But somebody starts talking about turning their back on a fine hat such as that one. Well, friend, then you do got trouble with me.

Understand?

The Cowboy lassos a soda can off the sidewalk, hauls it in and drops it in a trash can nearby.

Yes, Figueroa says. That is very good advice.

Figueroa returns his hat to his head.

And if any of you happen to see Aunt Joanie, the Cowboy says. Tell her fun is fun, but I would like mine back.

Lloyd sits behind the motel's front desk, staring blankly at an angry portrait of his late Uncle Ralph.

Figueroa leads the entire group through the doors. Lloyd stares on, not noticing any of them until the Farmer's Daughter rings the bell.

Hey there, Lloyd, the Farmer's Daughter says.

Lloyd grins like it's his own surprise party.

Hi, everybody, he says.

Hi, Lloyd, everyone says.

How can I help you, Lloyd asks.

We're looking for everybody that's checked in right now, the Nerd-Hipster Zombie says.

Lloyd's listening, but he also digs around on the desk for a handful of crayons and a torn piece of paper.

Cool, he says.

Absentmindedly, Lloyd begins to color.

It's urgent that I find and speak with everyone before the sun sets, Figueroa says.

Lloyd nods, coloring.

Why, the Nerd-Hipster Zombie asks. What happens then?

Nothing at all, Figueroa says. The coin will most likely not suddenly appear, burn red hot and then explode.

That's a relief, the Farmer's Daughter says.

Lloyd nods, coloring. He glances up and stops.

Hi, everybody, Lloyd says. How can I help?

All the stuff they just said, the Farmer's Daughter says.

Lloyd sets the paper between them on the counter. It's a

colorful, perfectly legible, to-scale map of the surrounding neighborhood, complete with landmarks, color key, compass directions and bus routes.

Right, right, Lloyd says. Well, this is where we are now. These symbols mark who works where. The individual color signifies their lunch hour. See?

Awesome, the Nerd-Hipster Zombie says. Now we just need to find a way to get there.

This is the route for the one-thirty bus, which passes by in about two minutes, according to the big clock on the wall, Lloyd says.

A huge clock hangs next to Ralph's portrait. Below the clock, an angry looking sign says: *Watch It!*

Aw, now, Lloyd, the Farmer's Daughter says. That sounds like a whole lot of bus tokens.

Lloyd winks and slides some coupons across the counter.

The city transit density office gives us these free vouchers for folks new to the area, but I won't tell if you won't, Lloyd says. No one asks for them.

Wouldn't think of it, the Farmer's Daughter says.

We'd better hurry, the Nerd-Hipster Zombie says.

If you do find a moment, I suggest the burrito truck here, the fresh fruit vendor here, but not here, and fabulous Thai carry out here, here, here, and here, Lloyd says.

Lloyd circles several spots. Figueroa takes the map.

Thank you, young man, such an enormous help as always, Figueroa says.

The group grab their vouchers and hurry for the bus stop. Lloyd sends them off with a giant and enthusiastic grin.

The Farmer's Daughter likes his positivity.

That all you got, she asks.

Well, Lloyd says. If you're in the mood for both dinner and a show, Jumbo's Clown Room is . . .

The Nerd-Hipster Zombie waits for her at the door.

Thanks Lloyd, he says.

No problem at all, Lloyd says. If any of you guys need tattoos or weed, I have coupons. Lots and lots of coupons.

Maybe next time, the Farmer's Daughter says.

We're always open, Lloyd says.

The door shuts behind the group. Ralph snorts mockingly from his home inside the portrait.

Well, gee, Ralph smirks. So we're just giving away the free vouchers now, are we?

Inside the motel diner, clearing dishes after another rotation of customers, Carol chatters to the Empty Nester couple from across the room.

Kardashians, Carol says. Sure, we see them around here all the time.

Oh, the Empty-Nester Mom says. You do?

Oh, yes, Carol says. Couple times a day. Zipping up and down the street.

Really, the Empty-Nester Mom asks, excited.

Yesterday I saw a beautiful, bright green one at a stoplight, Carol says.

Green, the Empty-Nester Mom asks.

Oh, yes, Carol says. Very pretty. Electronic cars aren't my style, though.

Meanwhile, Figueroa, the Farmer's Daughter, Nerd-Hipster Zombie, English Butler and Cowboy, bounce along on a crowded cross-town bus.

You didn't ask Lloyd any of your magical questions, the Nerd-Hipster Zombie says.

He's still a little self-conscious about his earlier answer.

Lloyd's a nice boy, Figueroa says. But some pools are simply too deep to swim in. Even my coin knows that.

At a nearby packing and shipping store, the masked Lucha Libre Twins process duplication orders with elaborate physical precision. Blocks of paper fly through the air as they manage seven whirring copiers at once.

The Twins rarely speak, but every step in the process is completed with a hand clap and muscle pose. An Impatient Customer checks her watch at the counter.

The Farmer's Daughter, Nerd-Hipster Zombie, English Butler, Cowboy and Figueroa burst through the door.

Quickly, ladies, Figueroa says. I need your help!

The Twins perform synchronous dives across the counter, landing attentively beside Figueroa.

Hey, says the Impatient Customer. What about my copies?

Figueroa grasps the Twins' skulls from either side and concentrates.

Now, I want each of you to whisper to me the name of the greatest wrestler of all time, Figueroa says.

The Twins whisper in either ear and their eyes grow wide. They look to each other to find the ends of colorful handkerchiefs suddenly poking from the mouths of their masks.

They each pull. And pull. And pull, as yards of colorful kerchiefs flow through their hands.

If that's a no-go, the bus's still at the corner, the Farmer's Daughter says. If we hurry, we can make it. Let's move!

The group hurries out. Figueroa dawdles a moment, touched.

It's just so adorable, Figueroa says. They both said each other.

Fantastic, let's move, the Farmer's Daughter says.

Figueroa leaves. The Twins begin to follow.

Wait, the Impatient Customer says. What about me?

In a set of fluid motions, the Twins dive back and forth across the counter, piling her with stacks of paper.

Bye, the Lucha Twins chime.

They flash her a thumbs-up as they leave.

Fine, but I'm stealing this pen, the Impatient Customer says to no one.

Ralph pops his head out from the store's back room.
Hold on, ma'am, he says. Those pens are a dollar-fifty.

A few blocks away, competing pay parking lots are across
the street from each other.

Star-Crossed Lovers wear vests with the parking lot
names on the back. They meet in the street on the yellow
center lines.

These terrible asphalt lanes between us are unbearable,
the Guy Star-Crossed Lover says.

Curbs as high as towering cliffs keep me from the arms of
my love, the Girl Star-Crossed Lover says.

Good one, the Guy Star-Crossed Lover says.

Felt like a good one, the Girl Star-Crossed Lover says. Go
again.

If the sky could only hear, the Guy Star-Crossed Lover
begins.

Ah, you did that one this morning, the Girl Star-Crossed
Lover says.

Right, right, the Guy Star-Crossed Lover says. Let me
think.

Yell when you're ready, she says, heading back over to
her lot.

The cross-town bus stops at the corner. The Farmer's
Daughter, Nerd-Hipster Zombie, English Butler, Cowboy,
Lucha Libre Twins and The Great Figueroa tumble off when
the doors open.

Hey, ladies, the Farmers Daughter calls. Mind holding
the bus?

The Twins nod enthusiastically. Before the bus can
continue on, they step in front, launching into an impressive
demonstration of wrestling holds, reverses and throws.

Through the bus's front window, both the Bus Driver and
Passengers are clearly very entertained.

They can't hold them there forever, the Nerd-Hipster
Zombie says.

Figueroa leads the group to the Girl Star-Crossed Lover in her parking lot booth.

Hi, the Girl Star-Crossed Lover says. I mean, hello.

She swoons a bit for effect.

Hi, the Farmer's Daughter says. How much to park our bus?

This genuinely catches the Girl Star-Crossed Lover off guard.

Uhm, she says. The whole bus?

She's kidding, the Nerd-Hipster Zombie says. She does that.

Thank goodness, the Girl Star-Crossed Lover says. What's up?

Mister magic man here has to grab your skull and ask you something, The Farmer's Daughter says.

The Girl Star-Crossed Lover now makes eyes at Figueroa, looking him over like a cut of meat.

Sure, I'm game, the Girl Star-Crossed Lover says.

Figueroa pauses at this shift in her affections, but shrugs. He grasps her skull and concentrates.

Quickly, please, Figueroa says. Whisper in my ear your favorite sandwich.

Let me think for a second, Girl Star-Crossed Lover says.

Finally, she whispers in his ear. Figueroa is struck momentarily speechless. His face is flush.

Shabba-Diba-Bang-Imalittlebusybut-thanksfortheoffer-younglady-Iguess, Figueroa says.

From inside her parking vest, a puppy emerges.

I always wanted a puppy, the Girl Star-Crossed Lover says.

Congratulations, Figueroa says.

Not to be deterred, Figueroa takes a deep breath and leads the group across the street, where the Guy Star-Crossed Lover leans against a fence post.

Oh, wow, the Guy Star-Crossed Lover says. What did she say? Doesn't she smell wonderful? Did she mention anything about grabbing some lunch? I'm starved and she has her Dad's credit card.

No, Figueroa says.

Yeah, that sounds like her, the Guy Star-Crossed Lover says.

Would you mind, Figueroa smiles, holding up his hands.

No worries, the Guy Star-Crossed Lover says. Go for it.

Figueroa grasps his skull and concentrates.

Quickly, now, Figueroa says. Whisper in my ear the city where you were born.

The Guy Star-Crossed Lover takes a deep, overly serious breath, then pauses again with another deep breath –

Oh, for goodness sake, the Cowboy says. Will you please pull it together, man!

– and whispers in Figueroa's ear. Figueroa sighs.

Seriously, Figueroa asks.

That's what I feel, the Guy Star-Crossed Lover says.

Izzy-wiz-habbity-bing-heartbreak-U-S-A-isnot-aplace, Figueroa says.

A giant groan from the group.

It most certainly is, the Guy Star-Crossed Lover says. And we're all living there!

As he sobs, a kitten emerges from his vest.

Strike ten, the Farmer's Daughter says.

Oooh, the Guy Star-Crossed Lover says. A kitty!

Figueroa clearly feels defeated.

You're not going to give up this easily, the English Butler says coldly. Are you?

No, Figueroa says, equally cold. Of course not. Let's go!

Figueroa pretends to gather his courage. The group rushes him back to the bus, still being stalled by the Twins. They leave the Star-Crossed Lovers behind.

The two Lovers meet again in the middle of the street, new pets in hand.

Look, the Girl Star-Crossed Lover says. Isn't it wonderful? We finally have a . . . Is that a cat?

Yes, the Guy Star-Crossed Lover says. Finally, a . . . Is that a dog?

Neither likes the other's pet. Their moods swing.

I need to work late tonight, the Girl Star-Crossed Lover says.

Me too, the Guy Star-Crossed Lover says.

A door opens to a tiny kiosk next to one of the parking lots. Ralph emerges, consulting a scribbled-over clipboard and counting cars.

Oh, for Pete's sake, Ralph says. What did I say about all the chit-chat?

The Star-Crossed Lovers turn their backs and stomp off to their respective parking lots.

At a nearby SmartPhone/Fixit/Vape/Bong shop, one of those multi-function junk stores that sells everything from vape pens to workout vitamins, the Pirate grumbles as he stocks a cooler with energy drinks.

Every Pirate loves the Stones, he says. That's a given. I'm just saying we all don't stumble around all day like Keith Richards. Though, I'd love to, believe me.

Behind the counter, the Lost Time Traveler fixes a broken screen on a tablet.

You know, in my time, many centuries from now, we don't have to replace the screen on these things every six months, he says.

Yes, yes. Technology is king, the Pirate says.

Of course, The Time Traveler says. With proper GPS data, you wouldn't have to stand around here all day complaining about never finding your gold.

I told you, I buried that treasure three hundred years ago, the Pirate says. There weren't any GPS then!

And as I told you, the Time Traveler says. You are purposefully missing my point!

These two have this conversation a lot.

A bell rings when the door opens. The Cowboy is the first

through the door. The Farmer's Daughter, Nerd-Hipster Zombie, English Butler, Lucha Libre Twins and The Great Figueroa are close behind.

No time to explain, The Great Figueroa needs your help, the Cowboy says.

They help Figueroa through the door. He's lost his spirit.

Come on, the Nerd-Hipster Zombie says. We can't stop now!

Figueroa wraps his fingers around the Pirate's skull.

Your parrot, Figueroa says. It's name was . . .

His name was Lawrence, the Pirate says.

Of course, forgive me . . . Paarry-barrey-pinkey-laaaarrrrry.

The group waits. From beneath his eye patch, the Pirate finds a rumpled corner of his lost treasure map.

Ay, the Pirate says. This is the piece with the compass on it! Thank you, Figueroa! Only hundreds and hundreds of tiny map pieces to go and I'll have me treasure again at last!

Working through this realization deflates his joy.

Next, the Farmer's Daughter says.

The group drags Figueroa over to the Time Traveler, who backpedals, wide-eyed and suspicious.

What are you doing, he asks.

Don't worry, the Nerd-Hipster Zombie says. It doesn't hurt.

What doesn't hurt, he asks.

They clamp Figueroa's hands on the Time Traveler's skull. The Time Traveler protects a big red button tattooed on his neck.

Fine, he says. But don't push my button!

Mate, the Pirate says. I told you. Nobody wants to push your button.

That's not true and you know it, the Time Traveler says.

Exhausted, Figueroa mumbles something under his breath.

He's saying, quickly, quickly, tell him something, the

Hipster-Zombie says. I think.

Fine, the Time Traveler says. What do I tell him?

I don't know, the Nerd-Hipster Zombie says.

You're not making this any easier, the Time Traveler says.

Sorry, the Nerd-Hipster Zombie says.

The sky, Figueroa says.

What about it, the Time Traveler asks.

In your time, Figueroa says. The sky. What color is the sky?

The Time Traveler thinks about this.

Bright clear, the Time Traveler says.

Argh, the Pirate says. That's not a thing.

As far as you know, the Time Traveler says.

Shimberlah . . . Shimberlee, Figueroa says.

Figueroa is fading.

You old fool, the English Butler says. You can do this!

Yes, yes, Figueroa musters. Whatever this guy said . . . Boomlamba-boom.

The last part particularly drips with sadness. The Time Traveler opens his hand. In his palm is a small, glowing cube. Figueroa slumps to the floor.

Ooh, the Time Traveler says. Anybody else want this? I am starving for some nice, squared metagluten.

He pops the cube in his mouth and chews happily.

Oh, it's food, the Nerd-Hipster Zombie says. What's it taste like?

Like total deliciousness, the Time Traveler says. A real treat in my time. Most comparable to . . . That stuff your elderly all put in the bathroom. On the back of your toilets. What do you call it?

Potpourri, the Farmer's Daughter asks.

What a treat, the Pirate says. When I find a time machine, I'm only going backwards.

I'm sure you would, the Time Traveler says.

I don't understand, the Nerd-Hipster Zombie says. What is potpourri?

Dried lavender and roses, the English Butler says. Though I do add a bit of apple cider or dried carob.

That's it, I'm going to lunch, the Time Traveler says.

That's it, Figueroa says. Lavender and roses!

Invigorated, Figueroa sprints for the door.

And now where are we going, the Farmer's Daughter asks.

To get my coin, shouts The Great Figueroa.

Everyone follows him out. At the far end of the counter, Ralph is at a workbench wearing jewelers' glasses, fixing a smart phone with a tiny screwdriver.

No problem, he yells. I'll lock up. What's a complete lack of work ethic between friends?

At the motel diner, Carol drops their check on the Empty Nesters' table.

. . . and, sure, the tar pits are nice if you don't mind repeating yourself in two languages, she says.

Sorry, the Empty-Nester Mom says. I don't follow.

In Spanish, La Brea means the tar, the Empty-Nester Dad says. Right? So that means when you say the La Brea tar pits, you're really saying . . .

The the tar tar pits, Carol and the Empty-Nester Dad say together, both grinning triumphantly.

I like you, honey, Carol says. You're fun.

Carol wanders off. The Empty-Nester Mom didn't like that last exchange. The Dad did, though, grabbing the check and reaching for his wallet.

The Empty Nesters shuffle out of the diner, into the parking lot.

I don't think this's the place for us, Father, the Empty -Nester Mom says. We should head home.

Home, the Empty-Nester Dad asks. Oh, poo. We only just got here. Plus the clerk in the office didn't even charge me. Just handed me the key, smiled big and went back to staring at the wall. This's my kind of place!

As they talk, the cross-town bus pulls up. The Farmer's Daughter, Nerd-Hipster Zombie, English Butler, Cowboy, Time Traveler, Pirate, and Lucha Libre Twins follow The Great Figueroa through the doors.

Figueroa and the Empty-Nester Mom's eyes meet. This isn't the first time. He sweeps toward her.

Well, hello, Figueroa says.

Why, hello, the Empty-Nester Mom says.

If I may ask, Figueroa says. Didn't I see you here, in this very spot, earlier this morning?

Why, yes you did, she says, blushing.

Excuse me, the Empty-Nester Dad says. When was this now?

Earlier, the Empty Nesters climb out of their minivan right after they first arrive at the motel.

Wait here, the Empty-Nester Dad says. I'll check us in.

Alright, she says, still very concerned about the looks of the motel.

As her husband disappears into the motel office, Figueroa emerges from the diner with a steaming travel mug.

Good morning, he says.

Good morning to you, she says.

Figueroa tips his hat as he passes and they share a definite moment of flirtation.

She tracks him slyly as Figueroa sails up the stairs toward his room, aware she's watching him. He tips his hat again at the motel room door. Caught, she blushes.

All set, the Empty-Nester Dad says as he emerges from the motel office. Let's get some grub.

Now in the parking lot, with everyone gathered around, Figueroa takes the Empty-Nester Mom gently by each hand.

Allow me to guess, he says. Lavender? And maybe just a little rose water.

My, what talented nostrils, the Empty-Nester Mom says.
She's nervous and this came out all wrong.

If you only knew, Figueroa says. Klando-Lavorosie-
Neeto-Mantar . . . Lovely.

The crowd waits impatiently. The Empty-Nester Dad's
face is growing brighter and brighter red.

Now, madam, Figueroa says. Would mind opening your
purse?

The Empty-Nester Mom does, clicking open a little brass
latch. She reaches in to find a shiny commemorative coin.

Summer, Coney Island, nineteen fifty-two, she reads,
placing the coin in Figueroa's open palm. How interesting!

This coin is a memento from the very day I first
discovered that real magic is meant to be shared, not hidden
away in some musty library and mumbled about over tea,
Figueroa says. Blah, blah, blah, I knew King Arthur, and so
on, and so on. I certainly do thank you, young lady.

Figueroa tucks the coin safely into his top pocket. The
relieved group pats him on the back as they disperse.

My pleasure, the Empty-Nester Mom says. Have a nice
afternoon.

Indeed, indeed, he says, turning toward his room. A
lovely day.

The Empty Nesters now find themselves stunned and
alone beside their minivan. She's elated. He's not.

Get the bags, Father, she says. We're staying!

Get in the van, Mother, he says. We're going home!

Lloyd and Ralph watch from the motel office door.

That was neat, Lloyd says.

Neat, Ralph says. Top grades at the finest business
schools and customers chasing off customers sounds neat.
That's my boy.

Gee, Lloyd says. Thanks, Uncle Ralph!

Thanks For Reading!
More Info:
AdamFike.com
Goodreads.com